MW01233253

MARY CRAWFORD

So THE Heart CAN Dance

HIDDEN BEAUTY NOVEL 2

Hidden Beauty Series

HIDDEN HEARTS SERIES

Identity of the Heart

Sheltered Hearts

Hearts of Jade

Port in the Storm (novella)

Love is More Than Skin Deep

Tough

Rectify

Pieces (a crossover novel)

Hearts Set Free

Freedom (a crossover novel)

The Long Road to Love (novella)

Love and Injustice (Protection Unit)

Out of Thin Air (Protection Unit)

Soul Scars (Protection Unit)

OTHER WORKS:
The Power of Dictation
Use Your Voice
Vision of the Heart

COPYRIGHT

DEDICATION

This book is dedicated to everyone who has a story and is afraid to share it.

May you find the strength to tell someone—

You could change someone's life with your words.

A special thank you to all those who take the time to listen.

CHAPTER ONE

TARA

MINDY, THE NEARLY SEVEN-year-old foster daughter of my best friend Kiera, is making it her mission to cheer me up. She refuses to allow me to be a wallflower — the role in which I'm most comfortable. "Are you sure you don't want to dance? It's really fun. I bet Mr. Jeff will dance with you. He's a really great dancer."

I freeze as her words lance my heart, yet my soul yearns to dance as the bass thumps through the speakers and I feel the rhythm deep in my bones. I study the crowd of people pressed together on the dance floor and I shudder. "I'm sorry, Mindy, I don't know how to dance. I guess I'll have to sit this one out," I shrug nonchalantly, but I can't quite square my gaze with hers.

Mindy scowls and narrows her gaze as she examines me from the top of my head to the tips of my freshly painted toenails. "Miss Tara?"

"Mm-hmm?" I try not to squirm under her perusal.

"Um … you know I can pretty much tell if a grown up is trying to trick me?"

I nod, primarily because my ability to speak seems to have taken an intermission.

"So, why are you fibbing? I think you're a dancer because your feet look funny, just like the dancers who came to my school from the Portland Ballet Company. Plus, you kicked your tae-kwon-do teacher in the teeth when he said, 'You punch like a girl and should wear a tutu.' I don't get why you'd lie about dancing, but whatever," Mindy shakes her head and shrugs.

I feel like she punched me in the stomach. I never meant to hurt Mouse in a million years. I feel lower than a caterpillar.

I glance back at the dance floor. Donda is dancing with the bartender she's been flirting with all night as she takes a break from being the DJ. By all appearances, her efforts have paid off. They are dancing so close together that you'd be hard pressed to fit a single sheet of paper between them. I pale as I watch the handsome bartender grab Donda's waist and grind his hips into her backside. I draw in a harsh, startled breath while I try to find my voice to call for help. Suddenly, Donda looks over her shoulder, gives him a wink, and kisses the underside of his jaw.

See, Tara? Donda wants him. Not all contact is bad. Pull it together, I mentally command myself.

"Are you okay, Miss Tara?" Mindy eyes me anxiously. "You're shaking. Should I go get Miss Kiera?"

"No, I'm fine. Maybe I just need to eat something."

"Can we dance after we eat?"

I slowly look around at the amazing reception

unfolding around me. I want this level of perfect for me and maybe, someday, I'll be able to believe in perfect again. Sadly, today is not that day.

I grasp Mindy's hands and squeeze them lightly as I whisper hoarsely, "I'm sorry, Mindy Mouse. I'd love to dance, but I just can't."

Movement at the edge at of the dance floor catches my eye, I look up to see a look of sadness cross the face of the man walking up to the piano. Astonishingly, he winks and signs, "Bull Crap!" before he sits down at the piano and plays.

Bull Crap? Who is this guy and what does he mean by that? As I watch him play, I try to figure out if I know him. I'm pretty sure I don't, but there is something oddly familiar about those moss-green eyes.

Suddenly, I feel the urge to be anywhere but here. "Mindy, do you want to go get some more cake?" I ask, a little too brightly.

"Sure thing! I want more of Miss Heather's food, too. She cooks too good to make food on a truck. It's silly. She should have a restaurant with fancy tablecloths and napkins."

As Mindy chatters on about her favorite foods and what kind of restaurant she would own if she were a grown-up, I can't help but think about what that piano player said. How could he possibly know about my dancing ability? It's a weird thing for a stranger to comment on. He acts like he knows me. There's something oddly disconcerting yet thrilling about that.

Mindy scampers off to play with her cousin, leaving me alone with my thoughts. I'm fighting a primal urge to simply escape out the back door. Weddings never get any easier for me. I was hoping this one might not be as hard. Kiera is one of my very best friends. Heather, my co-maid of honor, is equally close. Together, we've formed the Girlfriend Posse. Once you're in, you're in forever. We've got each other's backs at all times. This explains why I'm wearing a shiny new dress when I'd rather run naked in the snow. Admittedly, it's a nice dress and Kiera and Mindy tried very hard to choose one which minimizes my discomfort. There are some things that go beyond the cut of a dress.

There are precisely two people on the planet who can persuade me to wear a dress. Now that Mindy is in my life, there are three people who have that honor. Since Kiera and Jeff expanded their family, mine has grown exponentially as well. I consider Mindy, or as I affectionately call her 'Mouse' to be my kindred spirit and honorary niece. Mindy is an exceptionally bright kid who has an ancient soul. Someday, I'm certain I'll be wearing a dress for her special day too.

Kiera's husband, Jeff, has become the brother everyone wishes they could claim. We click well because we share a tendency to be reserved and shy around strangers. Much to his credit, he hasn't monopolized Kiera's time to the exclusion of her friends. Instead, he has assimilated himself into our world, as bizarre as the shenanigans of the Girlfriend Posse can become. Even Jeff's mom, Gwendolyn, and his sister, Donda, have become honorary members of our ever-growing group. It's no surprise Jeff and Kiera's circle of friends intersected to throw them this amazing wedding.

As I look around Kiera and Jeff's wedding

reception, I see reminders of her fairytale love story. Every personal touch, no matter how innocuous, speaks to the incredible depth of their relationship. Every person involved in the wedding has contributed their own special touches that make this wedding incredibly personal to Kiera and Jeff. You would never guess that this wedding didn't take a couple of years to plan.

It seems everyone is intent on honoring as many small but meaningful traditions as possible. Even Mindy got in on the act by making hand drawn invitations to the wedding. Jeff's mom, Gwendolyn, who is a florist, made bouquets based on words that Kiera and Jeff used to describe each other. Denny, Kiera's father, gave the couple a set of engagement rings which were family heirlooms.

Heather also seems to have missed nothing; she paid tribute to her best friend's love story with a beautiful lace and pearl encrusted wedding cake she made herself. She even made edible flowers out of sugar mirroring the first bouquet Jeff gave Kiera.

As a chef, Heather is meticulous when it comes to food. Each glass of ice tea is graced with small peach slices and a dash of freshly grated cinnamon, and the hors d'oeuvres must be served at exactly the right temperature. Heather's fabulous culinary skills are on full display; everything I've tasted so far is amazing.

Since cooking is not my thing, I made gift bags for all the guests. Although I don't have much experience in the craft department, they didn't turn out half bad.

As I survey everyone's hard work and hear Jeff and Kiera's effusive praise, a profound sense of melancholy and loss settles over me like a thick fog on a rainy morning. Yes, this is all pretty much perfect. I step back into the shadows under the eaves and wrap my arms around myself as I try to remember the last time I believed in perfect. Even though it's all around me, begging me to lap it up like a thirsty kitten licking cream, I can't let myself believe.

A sense of utter isolation overtakes me as I watch Jeff cradle Kiera gently against his chest in an agonizingly sensual first dance to Bryan Adams' *Heaven*. Couples seem to have broken out like a virus. Even Heather, who usually keeps men at a very polite distance with her good humor, is tucked neatly under Tyler's chin, with her cheek resting on his broad chest. She seems oblivious to his large hand splayed across her lower back and hip, but then I notice Heather flush as Tyler murmurs something in her ear and gives her hip a squeeze. Perhaps she's not as oblivious as I first thought.

Denny and Gwendolyn are dancing a very traditional waltz. In fact, I'd be willing to bet Denny has seen the inside of an Arthur Murray dance studio a day or two in his life. He is holding his own with the socialite. Amazingly, he's showing more than just a polite interest in the soon-to-be-former Mrs. Buckhold, who appears to be thriving under his attentive care.

Jeff's sister, Donda, is twirling a very contented, squealing Becca in her arms. Apparently, the key to keeping Princess Peanut happy is to have brightly colored hair and dangly earrings. Even Mindy has found herself a dance partner in Jeff's nephew. As I study Gabriel's body language, I am surprised to find that although he seems nervous, he is not an unwilling participant. He has the stiff, gangly movements of a preteen, but the affable, confident, yet shy charm of his uncle. It is clear by the way Mindy hangs on his every word, she is drawn to him like a hummingbird to nectar.

As the newlywed's first dance ends, they transition into the father-daughter dance. Denny walks behind Kiera and puts his arms around her shoulders. When Heartland's *I Loved Her First* plays, they sway in time to the music, in their own adaptive dance. Jeff walks over to the sidelines and collects Mindy. He grins down at her and places her feet on the top of his as he carefully navigates her through her first ever father-daughter dance.

The sight is too much for me as vivid visions come clattering back into my consciousness of a time, a lifetime ago, where perfect once lived. The sudden assault on my system is overpowering and I end up pulling some weirdly complex yoga/dance hybrid move to plop my butt onto the deck, as quickly as I can, before I pass out. Memories play in my mind like a psychedelic slide show. My heart clutches as I remember standing on my daddy's feet as we danced, me in my pink tights and purple tutu with silver sparkles, in the living room of our walk-up apartment. I still remember my mom putting up my long black hair in a small bun and securing them with my Hello Kitty barrettes. Those vignettes are my last memories of perfect. Shortly after that, perfect vanished from my life to be replaced by waves of unending pain that shredded my soul.

I draw my knees up to my chest, fold my arms over my knees and bury my head with a heavy sigh, as tears slide down my cheeks. As I try to repair my wall of silence and polite distance from the world, I feel a butterfly-light touch on the top of my head. I jerk my head up, alarmed to be caught off guard.

"It's okay, Miss Tara," assures Mindy as she meets my startled expression with a somber look. "I just came over to see what broked your heart today. You look really bummed again. I still think you should dance with Mr. Jeff."

Her uncannily accurate reading of my current mood gives me a taste of what people always say after they've had an encounter with me. It makes me wonder if Mindy and I share more than just a tragic past. "Thanks for checking on me, Mouse," I reply, wiping my face carefully with a cocktail napkin, trying not to lay waste to any more of my artfully applied makeup. "I'm sure your daddy's a great dancer, but I'm fine. Weddings just make me sad."

I glance across the dance floor on the patio and I notice the piano player studying me with great interest. *Hmm, maybe there is a bright spot, after all.*

CHAPTER TWO

AIDAN

I WATCH THE EXPRESSIONS flit across her face as she tries to put what I've just signed to her into some kind of context. I'm disappointed when I see no sign of recognition. I mentally kick myself for my own arrogance. I'm not sure why I thought she would remember me. It has probably been more than a decade since she's seen me. Just because I once thought the sun rose and set at the command of this ethereal creature, it doesn't mean she knows me from Adam.

Once again, I am reminded that it really sucks to be the marginally gifted little brother of a super-star. I bet she remembers Rory. Most likely, she probably carries a torch for him. Almost every woman I've ever met, young or old, seems to — much to the amusement and occasional chagrin of his wife, Renee.

I guess my expectations were a bit lofty. I was hoping for something closer to a cheesy music video. The kind where the girl finds out the hunk at the class reunion is really the skinny nerd with acne who used to offer to carry her books in junior high. I was that kid. I had glasses, braces, and acne. I was the trifecta of nerdiness. If you add the fact that I had the build of a dancer without the grace — paired with a fondness for Broadway musicals and big band music — I was pretty much a lost cause. It didn't help that my brother was everything I wasn't. In a family of dark, suave Irishmen with jet-black hair and bright blue eyes, my red hair is so light that most people consider it blond and my eyes are a nondescript murky green. As I grew up, the playing fields leveled out some. At six-foot-two and one hundred and ninety pounds, I'm bigger than Rory now, and my rock-climbing keeps me in great shape. It's a blow to my ego that she doesn't recognize me, but hardly surprising since nearly everything about me — both inside and out—has changed in the last decade.

I scrutinize Tara while she talks to the little flower girl. She has undergone some changes in the last dozen years or so as well. The Tara I remember attacked life with irrepressible energy and optimism — with a work ethic that would make a Navy Seal scream for mercy. Whatever happened seems to not only have dimmed her inner light and taken the wind out of her sails, but also made her jumpy around any male attention. I don't even want to contemplate the blows she has suffered to bring her to this point. She seems like a fragile shell of her former self. It's so sad because when she occupied Rory's world, Tara was a masterful sight to behold. She was beauty and light, emotion and pain. Most of all, she was poetry and art in motion. I fell for her hard when I was about six. I remember telling my mom when I grew big and strong, I would marry her. Of course, that was before my life was knocked off course by a series of blows. I'm a far different person than I was as an idealistic six-year-old.

The first blow started innocently enough. I was a few weeks shy of my eleventh birthday and I had just returned from music camp when I woke up covered in an itchy rash. At first my parents didn't think much of it, figuring I had been exposed to poison oak during camp. However, the next day, I got a splitting headache. I became extremely lethargic, and my neck and joints became stiff. My life became a big, scary blur filled with doctors, nurses, needles, medicines, tests, and machines. It all seemed never-ending.

After a very painful lumbar puncture, they determined I had meningitis. I was too young to understand the ramifications and too sick to care. A couple days before, I had been busy playing my piano, riding my bike, and pestering my big brother, and the next thing I knew, I was in the hospital hooked up to half a dozen different machines. As my body fought off the bacteria, it became increasingly more difficult for me to remain conscious, and I floated in a strange dreamland between life and death. Just when I thought it couldn't get worse, it did.

As I recall that day, in an instant, I become my eleven-year-old self. Everything comes back as vividly as the day it happened. I can still smell the strange musky smell of hospital food and feel the scratchiness of the odd blankets with the basket-weave pattern. On my ninth day in the hospital, I discovered my world is completely silent. At first, I thought maybe Rory was playing a practical joke on me. I searched for earplugs, cotton balls, or Q-tips. I was desperate for any explanation of why I couldn't hear. When I didn't find one, I started to cry. Yet that made matters infinitely worse because I could longer hear the sound of my own sobs. I panicked and choked on my own tears.

Finally, a nurse came to check in on me. She began talking to me, presumably to ask what's wrong. To my horror, I understood nothing. I was all by myself in a world where nothing made sense. Even my parents were gone. Rory had an important audition he couldn't miss. So, family emergency or no, they were at his side. The nurse became extremely agitated when I failed to respond to her. Another nurse came in and had the idea to write me a note. She took out an old yellow legal pad and wrote something down. I looked at it and reluctantly admitted, "I'm not very good at reading cursive."

The nurse took the tablet and scratched out the cursive and printed in a nice neat print, "Hello, my name is Delores. What's wrong?"

I looked up at her and threw up my hands in a helpless gesture as I screeched, "I can't hear anything!"

The "mean" nurse just rolls her eyes as she grabbed the pad and scribbled angrily, "That's not funny young man. Where are your hearing aids?"

My eyes widened as I read the words. There was a kid in our school who uses hearing aids. They attach to a box and his mom has to sew special pockets in his clothes. The bigger kids are always using the cord to pull them out of his ears. I am tall and skinny with glasses; I don't need one more reason for the kids to pick on me. I frantically argued, "I don't have hearing aids! I could hear yesterday."

Delores steps up and places her hand on my shoulder, and she begins calmly and methodically taking my vitals, examining my head and neck carefully. After she finishes, she sits down on the edge of my bed and started with a fresh sheet of paper as she composes a long note. I wait impatiently for her to finish. "Aidan, you have been very, very sick. Your body has been so busy fighting the meningitis that you were in a coma for about three days. Sometimes deafness is a side effect of meningitis, but they'll need to run a few tests to make sure. Don't panic yet. Sometimes, the side effects of meningitis are temporary."

I took the note from her. I read it several times. I kept stumbling over the big word. I pointed to it and asked, "What's this?"

She wrote an explanation. "Men-in-gi-tis: it's an infection that attacks the lining of your brain and spinal cord. It's pretty rare, but it can be caught through coughing or sneezing."

Alarm coursed through my body. Oh no! If Rory got it, he wouldn't be able to dance. I tried to form a question, dreading the answer. If I've been out of it for so many days, Mom and Dad should have been back from Rory's audition by now. He must've been sick too. My parents would kill me. Rory was planning to be part of the American Ballet Company in New York. That's why we moved all the time to follow his teachers. I tugged on Delores's lab coat to get her attention as I asked, "Did I make my brother sick? Is that why no one is here?"

Delores hugged my shoulders and smiled. I breathed a sigh of relief. She wouldn't have been smiling if he's sick, right? She picked up the tablet and wrote, careful to print even though I could tell she wanted to write in cursive, "No, everyone is fine. The doctor gave everyone medicine when you first got sick, Rory just got a call back and then there was a freak snow storm in Boston and your family couldn't leave."

Boston? I thought I'd get a vote this time and we would be able stay on the West coast. I liked my piano teacher and I was learning lots. Icicles surrounded my heart. Was. I *was* learning a lot. I couldn't learn piano anymore. I was good. Not Rory good. I mean, people didn't go around whispering words like prodigy, genius, and phenomenon around me like they did with him. I heard words like musically inclined, very talented, and inspired—or at least I used to. Now, I could hear nothing. How would I live in a world of silence when music feeds my soul and makes me who I am? I wondered where I am going to fit in my extraordinarily talented family, now that I don't have talent. Tears streamed down my face as I tried to bury my head in my pillow.

When I woke up, I found a big gift bag of art supplies Delores left by my bedside. It contained a book like my mom's diary, except it had a treasure map on the front and blank pages inside. There was also a nice pen. It's like the one my Pa had in his office. I saw a tiny note on the gift bag. As I pulled it off to read it, I was shocked when I read the familiar print. "Aidan, just because you can't hear the music doesn't mean it's not inside you. Every piece of music needs a good lyricist." By understanding my secret fear and helping me overcome it that day, Delores and I forged a friendship that remains strong to this day.

She was by my side helping me find treatment options when my parents were too tied up with Rory to notice or care what was happening with me. My mom really tried for a while. When you grew up being a concert violinist, receiving the adoration of crowds, the drudgery of speech therapy, audiology appointments, and special education gets old quick. As Rory grew more famous, so did the chasm between my family and me. They seemed willing — even eager — to leave me behind. Finally, the summer I turned fifteen, they gave up any pretense of filling the parental role and let Delores take me in.

By that time, I had lived in a virtually silent world for four years in near total isolation. My mom refused to learn sign language because she was from a good Irish-Catholic family and she was convinced a miracle would be coming soon. My dad didn't even try. He was sure if I would "man up" and put mind over matter, I wouldn't really be deaf anymore. He was convinced if I only tried harder to hear, I would no longer be totally oblivious to sound. Ironically, the only person who accepted the new me was Rory.

When I turned sixteen, I became eligible to take part in a medical trial of cochlear implants. Even though cochlear implants are considered controversial in the deaf community, I jumped at the chance. Hearing aids were doing me no good and I was tired of the isolation. My world had shrunk to just Rory, Delores, and a few special education kids; I needed more. Once again, Delores was by my side when everything in my world changed.

I remember the day I was "plugged in" as clearly as if it were yesterday. I lost my hearing at such a late age that I had a clear memory of what sounds should be like. I had spent five long years dreaming of what it would be like to leave this silent prison I'd been living in. I could hear music in my head as surely as I could feel my own heartbeat, and I couldn't wait to hear it again.

When no one was looking, I would go to an old abandoned church and play the piano, just so I wouldn't forget how. I always left my private practice sessions in a twisted emotional state. On the one hand, my body had phenomenal muscle memory which allowed me to fall into the rhythm of playing, as if it were a well-loved dance partner I never left.

As therapeutic and calming as it was to play, every press of a note was like a nick to my soul with a rusty razor blade. No single cut was fatal, but collectively the effect was the slow and excruciatingly painful death of the person I had been. Despite the best efforts of Delores, I became a sullen, angry shadow of the person I once was. I struggled to maintain my optimism about an experimental procedure to treat my type of deafness. The risk was great. Choosing the procedure meant destroying the four percent of hearing I had left. If the activation didn't go well, it would amount to nothing and I would actually emerge worse.

When my receiver was turned on, I immediately wanted them to turn it off again. Nothing made sense! My brain felt like scrambled eggs in an earthquake. The sound was loud and screeching like a radio station tuned to two stations that were receiving only static and feedback. I was devastated. This was not how I had imagined it would be. I knew some deaf people had trouble processing sound after an implant; I just never figured it would be me. I was so sure my brain would just remember how to process sound and I would be normal again. It was a steep learning process for me. Eventually, as the audiologists tuned my implants and my brain started to develop nerve pathways to better interpret the feedback from the cochlear device, I coped much better and adjust to my new perception of sound.

When I turned eighteen, I had a second implant placed in my other ear that helped me hear music even better. My implants will never restore my normal hearing, I'll always be deaf and sadly, music will never be quite the same. If I were to describe it to a hearing person, I would suppose it's like sound filtered through a highly distorted synthesizer.

When I first got my CI, I had a hard time even recognizing music, let alone individual notes. Gradually, with more practice, I could recognize songs I knew before I became sick. I played along to recordings of them, so I could get accustomed to the altered sound of the notes. I practiced piano like a novice, relearning all my scales and chords. I worked like a fiend until I could associate the memory of music I had in my head and heart with the new version of music I heard coming through my implants. By the time I was done, I had developed thick calluses on the pads of my fingers, but some of the ones that had formed around my heart and soul began to fall away. After almost a half a decade, I was finally a musician again.

I shake my head to bring myself back into the present as I slide back behind the piano, place my lemonade on the coaster, and play *Piano Man* by Billy Joel. I slip in one of my original songs and no one seems to object. In fact, the Judge guy gives me a thumbs up sign. I am pleasantly surprised. Usually, when I play these gigs, I'm invisible and no one gives a tiddlywink what I do.

As I continue to play a mix of cover songs, I see an older man burst in, although perhaps it's more accurate to say I smell him first. It appears he's been bathing in Kentucky Bourbon. His face is a mask of fury and he appears to be yelling obscenities. As near as I can tell, his anger appears aimed at the groom's mother. However, there is a lot of chaotic background noise, and even with my cochlear implants, it is nearly impossible to hear accurately. In these situations, I depend on lip reading to clarify things. He swings around, wildly looking for the bridal party. This causes his disheveled shirt to gape, revealing the distinct silhouette of a handgun. *Crap! Where's Tara?*

I vault over the top of the baby grand and nearly run over a very startled Judge as I remember to utter, "Gun. Saturday night special. Older guy. Reeks. Probably drunk. Looking for the groom's mom."

The Judge starts to ask me a question, but I push past him as I search for Tara. Finally, I spot her and the rest of the bridal party in the gazebo in the flower garden. My heart racing, I take off in a dead sprint until I am a couple of yards away from the back of the gazebo. I flatten my body against the side of a small potting shed and glance over to the bridal party. The big cowboy and the blond pin-up gal are juggling peaches in some sort of friendly competition, and the wedding photographer is busy snapping pictures as the bride and groom watch with bemused grins on their faces. My movement seems have caught Tara's attention at the same time the armed and angry guy charges toward the front of the gazebo yelling physically impossible profanities. I quickly sign, "Gun! Careful!"

Tara's eyes widen as she processes what I've just said. Her body language changes ever so slightly as her spine stiffens, her stance widens, and her muscles tense in a manner I recognize from the martial arts classes I took as a teenager. A look of grim determination settles over her face as she studies the ugly situation unfolding in front of her. I can feel the tension roll off of her like heat waves off of asphalt in August. I move closer, but Tara cuts me off with an imperceptible shake of her head and a small "no" sign.

I hear more yelling, but the anger in the man's voice is distorting the sound and I am not in a position to read lips to help me. I'm not catching every word, but what I am catching is nasty and vile. The groom looks like he'd give everything he owns or could ever hope to own to lock his lovely bride in an ivory tower right about now. Before Tara could warn anyone about the gun, the guy points it at the groom. The whole confrontation is over in a blink of an eye. I'm still not sure what happened. One moment, the asshat seemed to hold all the cards. The next, the groom has the drunk guy hog-tied in what seems like a nanosecond.

I have to shake my head and blink my eyes when I suddenly realize the delicately shaped foot planted firmly across the guy's neck is Tara's and she has a can of what looks like bear repellent aimed at his face. If looks could kill, this creep would be vaporized into the atmosphere by now. He looks like he's about to pee his pants even though he's continuing to spew profanities like an overheating radiator. Finally, the police department gets here to cart the perp away, and I notice he did indeed piss his pants. I smirk until I glance back up at Tara and notice her sway as she sees the front of his pants. I run to catch her before she crumples to the ground. Just then, the bride warns urgently, "Don't touch her! You'll only make it worse."

Even if I were inclined to follow that advice, it came about three beats too late as Tara collapses in my arms, in a cloud of blue lace and wispy stuff. Reflexively, I gather her up to my chest and stride out of the gazebo in one fluid motion. I anxiously study her limp form in my arms as I see her pulse quiver in a strong, regular cadence at the hollow of her neck.

After a tense discussion with the groom about her well-being, I walk over to the porch swing on the side porch, being careful not to jostle her too much. I take off my jacket, roll it up and place it under her head. I search in vain for something to place under her feet to elevate them. Finally, I decide to just use myself as a prop. I sit down and place her legs on my lap. During all the ruckus, her beautiful hair has come out of the fancy bun she had it in for the wedding. Remembering what a stickler she was for a perfectly straight bun even as a child, I reach over to brush a stray hair out of her face.

Her lashes flutter a few times before she opens her eyes. I can't even begin to describe her amazing eyes; I've never seen anything close to them on another person. Even when she was little, people would accuse her of wearing weird contact lenses. I know her eyes are natural. I saw her deal with the very real repercussions after my brother went out and partied with his friends the night before an important dance competition and nearly blinded her when he skipped warm-ups and missed a lift, scratching her cornea. Slowly she opens her eyes, squinting against the sun. I hold my hand above her forehead to provide some shade and meet her eyes with a steady gaze.

I've forgotten how strikingly beautiful she is. Her eyes are light gray, with a band of brown around the outside, and a naturally occurring tear in one pupil. As she examines me, she is clearly confused, but then she chuckles under her breath and signs as she speaks, "AJ?"

I nod as I confirm, "Yeah, it's me, but I go by Aidan now."

CHAPTER THREE

TARA

AJ? THAT FINE SPECIMEN of manliness is little AJ? He can't be the same gangly, knock-kneed kid who followed me around trying to persuade me to solve his Rubik's cube or babysit his DigiPet. His hair, which once was an unfortunate study in frizziness, is now a hairstylist's dream of glorious tousled curls, gold blond shot through with highlights of red, brushing his shoulders as he plays the piano. I've been trying to carefully ignore him all night. "Your hair is a lot longer," I blurt.

Really, Tara? You haven't seen the man in over a decade and that's the best you can come up with? I suppose it could've been worse. I could have been a little truer to my natural tendency to be spectacularly blunt at inappropriate times. I could have just told him I suck at relationships, but I find him drool-worthy. Since he's a really talented musician, I wouldn't mind borrowing a few of his sperm so I can become a mom. He wouldn't have to stick around for the tricky parts — like a relationship and parenting. He could enjoy the fun part and leave. This isn't a fully formed strategy in my head. It's just an idea that's been rolling around in my brain for a few weeks, since Kiera and Jeff announced they were planning to adopt the girls.

I am glad life has taken this turn for Kiera — I can't think of anyone who deserves it more. Sadly, my life isn't quite so perfect. First, I'm chronically unemployed, unless you count my shifts at the Shell station as a career, and I still have a little more than a year to go before I finish school. Second, I wouldn't fare as well during the criminal background check as Kiera did. I once took a stand to help someone, and my background check shows the evidence in black and white. I'm not the ideal choice as an adoptive mom and guys like Jeff don't grow on trees. I'm kind of sorry-out-of-luck. I can't believe my thoughts are even going there. I'm so not in the same stable place in my life as Kiera and Jeff.

"Yeah, I'm a musician now," Aidan interrupts my train of thought. "My hair has to look the part." He gives me the same self-deprecating smile I remember so well from childhood, but the grown-up version is devastatingly sexy. If I had known the awkward kid with a mouthful of metal braces and glasses, which could never quite perch squarely on his nose, would turn into such a knockout, I might have paid more attention all those years ago. Instead, I had an embarrassingly obvious crush on his older brother.

I scramble to get off his lap and sit up with some degree of decorum, I study him carefully as he holds out a hand to steady me. I love to look at the lines in a person's body as they move. I haven't danced in years, but the way a person moves still speaks to me. Aidan's body whispers like a familiar lover. His fingers are long and graceful, and his forearms are well developed with strong natural muscle that only come with hard work and discipline. His hair defies description. It isn't really red like Kiera's, but it's too vibrant to be called blond. I wonder if he still hates it. It used to irritate him to no end when Rory would needle him and call him "Berry" as a pejorative offshoot of strawberry blond. His tousled mane of curls is wildly rugged now. "It's a look that suits you." I look down at my feet and watch a ladybug crawling across my big toe. When I was little, my dad used to tell me, if a ladybug landed on my hand, I would soon marry. I wonder what it means if it lands on my toe. I chuckle at the random memory.

Aidan regards me with a look of alarm as he asks, "I'm sorry, did I miss something? It's kinda loud in here and I lost my focus for a minute."

I draw in a quick breath as the puzzle pieces abruptly start to fall into place in my head. I recall his rapid signing and his laser-like focus on my face. Why hadn't I noticed he's been repositioning himself all night to get a clearer view? It's my job to notice such things and respond. What kind of professional will I make if I miss something so obvious?

I immediately take off the sparkly tennis bracelet Kiera gave us for being bridesmaids and tuck it in my pocket so it's not distracting. "It's fine, you missed nothing," I assure him, speaking and signing at the same time. I point to the ladybug that just made its way to my anklebone. "I was remembering an old wives' tale my dad used to tell me about ladybugs and it made me smile."

Aidan grins. "Hey, I'm Irish and I was raised by a lady who grew up in Louisiana. There isn't much in the way of a limerick, folklore, or superstition I don't have at least a passing knowledge of. I know at least two versions of the story and in either superstition I come out a winner. It's only a matter of how you define luck."

"AJ, there is no possible way you could know! We haven't even seen each other in a dozen years. I'm a completely different person now," I argue, signing emphatically.

"You're great at signing, but I don't really need you to. I have bilateral implants," he explains, pulling his hair to the side to expose the two devices attached to his skull.

I cringe slightly because it looks like it must've hurt to have them put in. "Do they bother you? I think I'd feel a bit like a robot," I inquire, studying it closely. I slap my hand over my mouth. I wish I had some magical power to teleport right now because I'd rather be anywhere else in the galaxy.

When Aidan looks at my expression, he throws his head back and laughs. I breathe a sigh of relief. At least he doesn't seem terribly upset over my idiotic remark. "Sometimes I do feel like a robot, especially when they have me hooked up to a computer to calibrate my units," he answers. "The implants rarely bother me much, unless I'm working out or I get them wet. I ruined a pair of receivers when a groom and his buddies got rowdy at a reception and threw me in the pool. Lucky for me, they stepped up and got me new ones. I suspect they had great homeowners insurance."

"I am glad they are not a lot of hassle," I'm

mortified by my lack of sensitivity. "Still, I am a professional — well, close enough — and I should know better."

"A professional dancer?" he asks, confusion wrinkling his brow. "No surprise there. So was Rory until he blew out his Achilles one too many times. You were as good as he was."

I flush at his compliment. No one ever puts me in the same league as his brother. I always felt lucky to even breathe the same air as my former dance partner. Even as I soak in his praise, the pain of what I've lost washes over me. I fight to stay composed as I struggle to find the words to explain my life. "I am a sign language interpreter—or I guess, more accurately, I am learning to be one. I'm in the ASL Interpreting program at Western Oregon University. I have about a year to go. I don't dance anymore."

Aidan's jaw goes slack for a moment before he shutters his expression. "Congratulations on your interpreting gig. I've heard it's tough, and they only take the best. But I must have misheard you. This is the second time tonight I thought I heard you say you don't dance." He shakes his head and rakes his hand through his hair as he continues, "That can't be right. You're the best dancer I've ever seen. Sure, Rory danced with technical precision and was a master at his craft, but you were still a million times better. You danced with the very essence of your being. Your love of the art flowed through you, spilling from every pore of your body. I have never seen someone so compelling to watch. I know what I'm talking about, because there were some phenomenal dancers surrounding Rory's life. I don't understand how someone like you can just stop dancing."

Tears well up in my eyes as I watch him search my face for answers. His tender, concerned expression was the last chink my armor could stand. "I don't understand either. I can't dance anymore. It's like my inner music is gone. I can't hear it. He took it from me; just like he took everything else."

Emotions fly across Aidan's face like clouds in a spring thunderstorm as he processes my words. "What did Rory do? I always told him he needed to be more careful. If he hurt you that much, I'll kill him myself. I don't care if he's my brother." Aidan bunches his fists at his side. He drags his hand through his hair with such agitation he practically tears it out at the roots. "He was a self-absorbed prick back in the day, but I never thought he would stoop that low —"

I hold up my hand to stop him. "Aidan, you're completely misunderstanding the whole situation. I wasn't hurt dancing. It was much more personal, and it wasn't Rory's fault. Your brother would've actually had to notice I existed for that to happen. It was one of his so-called-friends who hurt me. As far as I know, Rory didn't even know." As memories assault me, I tuck my feet under me and curl into the corner of the porch swing and rock gently. I begin to violently tremble. Although it's been almost a decade and a half since the incident, the horrifying memories playing in a loop in my head never fade. Unfortunately, I remember the attack like it was yesterday.

Aidan picks up his jacket, which I've been using as a pillow, and drapes it over me. He gingerly tucks it around me, being careful not to be offensive. He's so gentle that tears spring to my eyes.

When a lock of my hair falls across my eyes again, he tucks it behind my ear and regards me quietly. Finally, he gruffly asks, "Gracie, will you be okay here until I get back? I'll just be a minute."

Memories of an entirely different sort wash over me and I grin. "I can't believe you even remember that, AJ. It's been forever since anybody called me that."

"Well, I always thought your name was uncommonly beautiful, Ms. Tara Grace Windsong Isamu," he responds with an easy smile and a slight blush. "Some of my fondest childhood memories revolve around that George Burns and Gracie Allen vaudeville bit we did for the talent show. I've never forgotten the time we spent together, Tara. I always hoped our paths would cross again."

"Things were just so mixed up for me back then, I've forgotten the fun times. I think I'll be fine. Go do what you need to do."

"I'll be right back," he assures me as he tucks the jacket more securely around my shoulders. I watch as he disappears into the crowd on the dance floor.

I rest my head against the swing rail and try to remember the last time someone tucked me in with such care. It used to be a daily occurrence before the Chinese government mistook my daddy for a dissident and assassinated him on an anniversary of the uprising in Tiananmen Square. My dad was merely doing his job as a translator, and they killed him for it. The bullet didn't strike my mom, but it might as well have. She started dying of a broken heart the day he lost his life. I miss them both so much I ache. A tear slides down my face. I jump when I feel tapping on my knee.

"What's wrong, Miss Tara?" Mindy squints up at me as she fiddles with the ribbons in her hair. "Did the policeman put you in time out because you stepped on the bad guy's neck? That's no fair because you helped save Dad's life."

I laugh out loud at her logic. "No, I'm not in time out. I just got a little queasy from all the excitement. My friend brought me over here to lie down so the grass wouldn't get my dress all dirty."

"Friend? *What* friend?" Mindy eyes narrow with suspicion. "All of your friends are waiting for you so we can take more pictures. They have to throw something at you before they'll let me take my dress off so I can shoot hoops with Gabriel. He is going to teach me to play basketball like a big kid. He says I'm already one of the jumpingly-ist people he knows, so I should be a natural."

"Aidan, the piano player, and I went to school together a long time ago. He saw that I was having trouble, so he brought me over here just to be safe," I explain.

Mindy's eyes grow big as she exclaims, "You're friends with a musician? The man that looks like Prince Harry, only way cuter?" Mindy covers her mouth and giggles. "His hair is so long Daddy could braid it. It's like Shaun White's 'cept it's not quite so red. I wonder if he can skateboard. Do you think he would sign my recorder? Oh wait ... I had to leave that at my old school. Do you think I'll get a new one? My friend Laura had a cool one that was pink and purple. Can I get one like that? I promise not to be bad anymore."

"Whoa, Mouse. It's clear we need to cut back on your cake consumption. From the sound of things, you've been skipping the cake part and just licking off the frosting," I comment with a laugh. "First, AJ and I met when we were about your age, but we haven't seen each other in a really long time. Yeah, I guess he looks a little like both Prince Harry and Shaun White, but I'd lean more toward the Harry side if I was comparing them. I have no idea if he knows how to skateboard, but it wouldn't surprise me if he does. He always wanted to learn as a kid. I do love the long hair. Mine is so straight and boring, I always envy people like you, Aidan, and Kiera with your amazing hair. Mine just hangs there, and it's plain old black," I answer, blowing an errant lock out of my face.

"Miss Tara!" Mindy puts her hands on her hips. "Do you even look in the mirror? You could be a Disney princess. I can't decide if you look more like Pocahontas or Mulan because you kind of look like both. You are so pretty. Your hair looks like the sky at night with lots of tiny stars."

I blush when she says all of that. I've downplayed my looks for so long, I don't even notice how I look. I do a basic teeth brush and booger search and consider it good. "Thank you, Mindy Mouse. That's sweet of you to say. I know nothing about Aidan's career, so I don't know if he can help you with your recorder. You really should ask him though. I'm sure he wouldn't mind."

"Okay," she replies with enthusiasm and hope. "By

the way, my mom says you need to meet everyone in the gazebo in fifteen minutes with your smile on." Mindy skips off toward the gazebo pretending to play hopscotch. The kid's got phenomenal rhythm and balance. It's too bad I don't dance anymore, or I could definitely teach her a few things.

Just then, Aidan reappears on my other side. His hands are full. I take a loaded plate from him. It looks delicious, and I suddenly feel ravenous. It's piled high with fruits, vegetables, cheeses, and cold cuts. He sets a steaming cup of coffee on the table. "AJ, this looks amazing, but you didn't have to go to all of this trouble for me."

"Don't be silly. It was nothing. I was hungry too. I just grabbed an extra plate for you. As I recall, you like meat and cheese. You look cold, so I brewed coffee up for you too. I hope you like cream and sugar since I added a touch of each. I was afraid to leave it black because it looks strong enough to strip wallpaper. I even got you strawberries for dessert."

"Thank you so much, Aidan," I muse. "This is the nicest thing to happen to me in a really long time."

"Gracie, if that's your bar for the nicest, we need to raise your bar a bit."

Chapter Four

Aidan

It doesn't take a rocket scientist to figure out Tara was raped. I guess I didn't do a very good job of protecting her like I always promised. Rory's friends are so much older than me, I don't know any of them. The whole situation makes me furious. Where was Rory? Why didn't he step up? Maybe he could have stopped the devastation if he had just paid attention to her for once.

The assault clearly has changed her whole life. I expected Tara would be the principal dancer in a major company by now, or happily settled into retirement and teaching another generation her infectious love of dance. Her inability to dance is a tragedy of epic proportions in the world of the arts. Most people might not consider it much of a loss. For people like me, though, a life without music, art, dancing, or photography would make our souls wither and die. It was during a preschool class trip to see the musical *Oklahoma!* I learned music and words could be combined to make a story fascinating. What if some little kid somewhere is missing their moment of inspiration because some scumbag decided to take what wasn't his?

What kind of sick freak does that to an innocent girl the size of Tara? She may be a buck-oh-five on a rainy day. She is tall for a dancer, but she's fine-boned. I can circle both her wrists with just my fingers. Her muscles are sleek and toned, but no match for a man intent on assaulting her. I'd like to string up the jerk over a ravine somewhere and let him swing by his balls. I wonder if he knows that he changed who Tara turned out to be because he couldn't keep it in his pants. It makes me sick.

I hate to leave her alone, but I need some distance to get myself together. Seeing her nearly go into shock, just talking about it, sends daggers into my soul. I hope seeing me isn't painful for her. I'd be crushed if I made matters worse.

Waiting for her coffee to brew, I watch her talk to the little flower girl. If anyone can cheer her up, it's this little sprite. She is a character for sure. I look more closely. Are they talking about my hair? Seriously? Sometimes, the ability to read lips has its drawbacks. I learn things I'm just better off not knowing. Did Tara really just call her hair boring? She has no idea how stunning she is. Her hair reminds me of a raven's wing — dark, shiny, and ever changing. A man could and should get lost in all that hair. I shake my head in disbelief when I see that she considers herself plain. Tara Grace Windsong is many, many things, but plain is not one of them.

I wait for the little girl to leave before I carefully approach, balancing coffee and plates of food. She jumps a little at my presence, but she recovers quickly. She takes the plate from me and mumbles something about me not needing to go out of my way for her. I assure her it was no problem. Yet she calls it the nicest thing anyone has done for her in a while. Really? It's just a plate of food. It's not like I helped her move or babysat her cat or anything — either of which I'd do for her in a heartbeat. "Wow, Gracie. If that's your bar for the nicest, we need to raise your bar a bit."

Tara flushes as she blows on her coffee. "You're probably right. I don't get out much these days," she replies with a wry chuckle.

"So, you go to school. Anything else interesting?" I ask as we eat our snacks.

"Well, I work evenings and weekends at the Shell station." She pops a piece of cheese into her mouth.

"Is that safe?" I ask, alarmed.

"Well, yes, I think my coworkers feel much safer with me around. I'm a black belt in tae-kwon-do," Tara responds with a raised eyebrow.

"Point taken. I'm not usually such a male chauvinist pig, but you are pretty small and Monmouth is right off the highway."

"So, you've been to my charming little town?" Tara asks with a mischievous grin. "If so, you know it's not a hotbed of activity after about seven at night."

"That may be true, but creeps can crop up anywhere. You wouldn't believe the stuff I see."

"Aidan, don't you think I know that better than anybody?" Her voice drops to a husky whisper, "I've worked really hard to be better prepared if there's a next time."

"There's the Gracie I remember." I brush some stray hair from her eyes. "You were always prepared for every contingency."

"You might want to rethink your nickname for me, AJ. I am not feeling very graceful these days."

"Somehow, I find that hard to believe. I bet you even snore gracefully," I reply, with a grin.

"Aidan Jarith O'Brien! I'll have you know — I don't snore, thank you very much," she insists, her tone slightly indignant.

I smirk. "I'm just wondering how a person figures that out. I mean, we all sleep through our own snoring and the people we date have every motive in the world to spare our feelings. It's quite possible we all snore like freight trains, but no one wants to fess up. You never need to worry about that problem with me. I take my receivers off at night to clean them. I am as deaf as a fence post. You could snore loud enough to remove roof tiles and I wouldn't even know it."

"Geez, AJ! Presumptuous much?" she asks, incredulous. "I think I was in the eighth grade the last time I saw you and now you have us sharing a bed. It's quite a leap, even for you."

"True. At this point, it's just wishful thinking. Still, I can't deny I've always had a crush on you, Tara Grace."

Tara stabs the grapes on her plate with a decorative toothpick from an hors d'oeuvre. "Umm, I don't even know what to say, except I'm not the girl you remember," she states softly.

"Perhaps not. But, I'm not the snot-nosed kid you recall either. Trust me, the world is a better place because of that. I was pretty obnoxious as a kid," I retort.

Tara nods thoughtfully. "I hate to break up this truly surreal reunion, but I'm supposed to go avoid a bouquet, before Mouse collapses from sheer anticipation."

Tara stands up and I help her balance as she slides her slim foot into impossibly high shoes. When one sticks a bit and I reach down to help her adjust the thin strap around her ankle, I feel like Prince Charming helping his Cinderella. The only difference is that I knew I had found my princess over two decades ago. The hard part will be convincing her.

"Donda looks intent on capturing the bartender. I'd better get back to the piano, so she can have a shot at the bouquet," I tease.

Tara smirks. "Well, more power to her. She's more than welcome to it. I don't want it — not now, not ever."

I'm surprisingly bummed by Tara's sarcastic answer. I work lots of weddings and I don't think I've ever wished I was a close personal friend to the bride or groom more than tonight. I could really use someone to toss a bouquet in Tara's direction.

———————◆ ◆———————

I smother a grin as I watch the little flower girl weave her way through the guests, arranging them like chess pieces on the dance floor. "Miss Tara! Stop hidin'. I tol' you; you and Miss Heather are 'upposed to stand in the front row. Put your listenin' ears on," she insists in a loud whisper, tugging on Tara's dress while Tara is frantically trying to escape the deck.

"I know you're trying to be nice, Mindy Mouse, but I don't need to get married. Someone else can catch the bouquet," Tara explains.

Mindy studies Tara for a couple of moments, tilts her head to the side, and says philosophically, "If you say so Miss Tara. But, sometimes, the stuff that scares us the mostest is 'xactly what we hafta do."

"Oh, Mouse, you don't know what you're asking," Tara responds, exhaling shakily.

"Actually, Miss Tara, I kinda do, 'member?" Mindy interrupts impatiently. "I runned away from home with my baby sister, a yucky man kissed me, then I was in the hop-spital and my family didn't care enough to come get us." Mindy shrugs sadly.

Tara hugs the little girl close and re-pins a braid which fell from her elaborate hairdo. "Mindy, as usual, you're right. I need to put my big girl panties on and get over it," Tara concedes.

"You're not wearing any underwears!" Mindy shrieks. "That's gross, Miss Tara." The whole dance floor seems to stop to look at Tara and listen to the odd interaction.

At first, Tara is frozen with embarrassment, but then she notices Mindy's mouth trembling with laughter. She quirks a raised eyebrow. "Has anybody told you that you're downright diabolical, Mouse?"

"Does that mean I'm funny?" counters Mindy, "'cause it should. I tol' a really funny joke. I heard some peoples laughin'.'"

"No, you silly goose, it means you're too smart and clever for your own good," Tara responds, gently tweaking Mindy's nose.

Mindy nods slowly as she processes what Tara just said. She suddenly grins. "Yeah, I am really smart, huh? So you need to listen to me, even if I'm only a kid. Follow me. I'll even hold your hand if you're a'scared."

Tara is shaking her head with such vigor, I am surprised she's not dizzy from arguing with that pint-sized force of nature. "Mouse, are you sure about this? There are lots of women here who want to catch this thing. Shouldn't I give them a chance?"

"Miss Tara, didn't I tell you I just know stuff?" she insists impatiently tugging at Tara's hand. "Come on, please, we're gonna be late."

"Okay, Mindy Mouse, if it's that important to you, I'll come," Tara answers reluctantly, attempting to smile politely.

Mindy looks over at me and I'm embarrassed to be caught openly gawking at them. Yet, Mindy doesn't seem to think there's anything odd about the fact the piano player and alleged professional entertainment for the evening has been rubbernecking the whole conversation like a twenty-car pile up on the interstate.

"Hey Mr. Music Man, can you play a drum roll thingie?" she shouts across the dance floor.

"I'm sure I can come up with something, Princess," I assure her chuckling. "By the way, my name is Aidan."

Her eyes grow wide. "For reals? Were you ever in a

band? Can you play the recorder? What about the flute?" she peppers me with questions at a mile a minute.

I laugh out loud at her rabid curiosity. "Whoa, Mindy a musician can talk forever about their work. How about I give you the short answers for now and we'll talk more later? Yes, I've played in several bands, but nobody was very famous. I can play the recorder. Although, I prefer the alto sax. I'd be happy to show you," I answer solemnly.

Mindy nails me with a sharp glance. "Are you sure? No trickin'?"

I shake my head no and hold up my pinky. "Pinky swear," I offer.

Mindy gives me a lopsided grin and tugs on Tara's hand to get her attention as she announces. "I am going to call Mr. Aidan, Band-Aidan, because he's Miss Tara's friend, and he helped saved Mr. Jeff from the bad guy. He needs an epic nickname." She runs across the dance floor to give me a hug.

I can see Tara is fighting to hold back tears. So I turn back to the piano and begin to play *You Are My Sunshine*. "Mindy, after this song is over, I'll play you a drum roll. Sound like a plan?"

"Roger Dodger!" Mindy exclaims as she drags Tara to the assembled guests and awaiting bride. "Miss Kiera, everybody's here now. We're ready!" she announces as she arranges Tara next to the other bridesmaids.

I quickly press the drumroll button I have programmed into my soundboard. I prefer to play the piano, but for times like this, the synthesizer and MP3 player come in handy. I wink at Mindy as she gives me a thumbs up. I watch as Tara swallows hard and looks as if she's about to face a firing squad. She grabs her friend's hand. "Heather, aren't you obligated as my best friend to stop them?" she pleads.

Heather throws her head back and laughs. "Sorry, Tar. Girlfriend Posse or not, you're on your own. This baby is mine. I've been a bridesmaid way too many times."

"You don't understand!" Tara sputters, "I don't want to catch it."

Heather raises an eyebrow at her. "Well, I suppose you could try ducking. Still, aren't you the one who's always telling us we can't avoid fate, and all that?"

I try to smother a grin when I see Tara practically stomp her foot as she rolls her eyes. "You guys know I hate it, when you make me take my own advice."

Just then the bride wheels to the center of the dance floor and spins her wheelchair around. She grabs the bouquet off her lap and counts to three. She heaves it over her head with such force she almost topples her chair over backward. The groom swoops in to catch her before she falls. He purposefully tilts her chair back and kisses her deeply. I feel a twinge of envy. The love between these two shines like the sun on a hot summer day.

I hear shrieks of laughter as Heather wrestles the bouquet away from a teenage girl who isn't trying very hard to keep it. Heather raises the bouquet in triumph and gives Tara a high five. Tara smiles at the appropriate time, but her eyes are blank and the dimple in her cheek is non-existent. Before I can study the situation further, the groom lets out a wolf whistle and performs a complicated dance maneuver with the bride. He kneels in front of her, reaches up under her wedding gown, and fishes out a delicate garter belt as she leans over and murmurs in his ear. Whatever she said, it must have been racy because he loosens his tie and the tips of his ears turn red as she teases, "Oh trust me guys, you are all going to want to catch this, because I have a feeling married life will be more fun than he can handle."

I start my sound effect shtick for the garter-throwing routine and I hear Mindy yell across the dance floor, "Hey Band-Aidan? You ain't married, right?"

"Uh, nope. I'm not married," I answer carefully.

"Then get your tuckus over here! What is it with you grown-ups and directions?" she asks with frustration.

"Sorry, I didn't think you meant me. I have to work."

"Of course we meant you. You can take a little break. After all, you can't mess with fate," Mindy announces.

Almost before I can turn around with all the other single guys, the groom sends the garter flying directly into my hands as if there was an invisible force drawing it there. The guy in the cowboy hat scowls at me as he says, "Dude! For a little guy, you have fast reflexes. Do me a favor and keep those quick mitts off my Gidget." I look up to see a wide grin on the blonde bridesmaid and a look of stark devastation on Tara's face.

Oh man, this is bad. It's just a lame tradition. It wasn't supposed to make her sad.

I'm rarely called little at six-two, but sure enough, I have to look up at him. "Gidget? I thought Mindy said her name is Heather," I ask as I try to follow the strange conversation in this loud atmosphere.

The cowboy chuckles and sticks out his hand. "I'm Ty, by the way. I forgot you don't know the story. I called dibs on the blond a couple of weeks ago. I call her Gidget so she remembers I'm around."

I return his handshake with a grin. "Whatever, Ty, she's all yours. I have my eye on the other one."

He pats me on the back as he lets out a low whistle of admiration. "Wow! Nothing like choosing the biggest challenge in the room. Tara is a knockout and a talented artist, but she is more skittish than a new cutting horse."

"How well do you know Tara?" I ask in what I hope is a casual tone.

"Well enough to know she shouldn't be selling Red Bull and Doritos at three o'clock in the morning. That girl could be working in some art gallery in Seattle or New York," Ty responds.

"Art gallery? Don't you mean dance company?"

Ty's eyebrows shoot up in surprise. "Dance? Huh. I guess the little filly has been holding out on us."

Immediately, I regret sharing Tara's story if she didn't trust people here enough to share on her own. Ty catches my expression and addresses me soberly. "Relax, Aidan. I won't say anything to her. My best friend is married to her best friend, and she still jumps when I walk into a room. It's obvious Tara has some real ghosts in her past, yet I've seen her stand up to a guy meaner than the devil himself twice now. She has real grit." He takes off his leather jacket and digs out his phone. "Want to see what Tara painted?"

I try not to look like a kid waiting for Santa Claus as Ty wipes the fingerprints off of the screen with the edge of the tablecloth. He hands the phone to me and explains, "Jeff's sister, Donda, did the teddy bear room, and Tara did Mindy's."

To my surprise, instead of a few little snapshots, there is a fully produced slide show. I raise an eyebrow in question.

Ty shrugs. "Jeff's nephew, Gabriel, is a computer genius. He could make a music video or infomercial better than most adults."

Suddenly a portrait of Mindy comes into frame; it is so realistic that it's spooky. The next frame is a much younger version of Mindy. Both are dressed as fairies. As slide after slide appears, it is clear Tara has created a phenomenal fantasyland for one very lucky little girl.

"Wow, was it Mindy's birthday?"

"After all they went through before, I think of their rescue as a birthday of sorts, Especially if the adoption goes through, like Jeff and Kiera hope."

"I was wondering why Mindy calls them by their first names," I remark, curious about the unusual situation.

"I know. Isn't it wild?" Ty replies. "Jeff took one look at Kiera and knew she was the one for him. They only went out for about four months before today. When Kiera decided she needed to step up and rescue the girls,

Jeff was right beside her. At first, I thought he had a few screws loose. But then I met Mindy, and I totally got it. That kid is irresistible, and Becca is as cute as a button. It's a good thing I've never met those girls' parents and grandmother while I was on duty. I'd lose my badge for sure if I had to spend any time alone with them."

"That bad, huh?" I ask, grimacing as I remember the scars on her hand.

"Just think of your worst nightmare and multiply it times a hundred, and it might come close to explaining what those little angels have endured." Ty runs his hand through his hair in frustration.

"Are they going to be okay?"

Ty sighs. "I expect so. Jeff and Kiera have made it their mission to love these girls and get them the help they need. I don't know Kiera all that well yet, but Jeff is my best friend, and he's always been an overachiever. I don't think it will change. Besides, Jeff and Kiera have awesome friends to help out." He grin and tips his cowboy hat.

I return his grin. "I can't argue with you there. I happen to think at least one of Kiera's friends is totally amazing. But I'd better get back to the piano."

Getting ready for my set, I hook my cell phone up to the auxiliary jack of the soundboard and turn on the "Do not disturb" setting. I pull up a special playlist and watch for Tara's reaction. She is across the dance floor talking with Kiera and Heather when the opening notes of Lee Ann Womack's classic *I Hope You Dance* break through the chatter in the room.

As soon as she recognizes the song, she shoots me

a startled glance, narrows her eyes and frowns slightly as she signs abruptly, "You know I can't."

I quickly respond in sign, "Tara, listen to the rest of the lyrics before you get ticked off, please."

Tara's jaw sets and she rolls her eyes at me. Her spine is stiff and her muscles tense as she listens to the artist sing about chasing dreams and being brave. When the lyrics refer to giving heaven more than just a passing glance, a single tear rolls down her face. It takes all of my willpower to keep myself planted behind the piano. She looks like she could shatter at any moment. Yet, as the song progresses and the music and lyrics wash over her, Tara kicks off her strappy sandals, flexes up on the balls of her feet, and sways to the music.

I breathe a sigh of relief. I know I'm taking a huge gamble pushing her buttons in public. There is no guarantee that any of this is going to even help. She could think I rank right up there with a huge pile of dog poop before the night is over, but I have to at least try. I can only imagine that to her, a world without dance is as crushing as a completely silent world was to my musician's soul. Even if she hates me just a little, if I can help bring dance back to her life — it might just be worth it. She bobs her head to the music and a huge hunk of her hair comes out of her up do. Tara calls out to Jeff, "Hey, can you ask your other half if she has enough pictures? I am falling apart here, and I don't think there's enough hairspray in the world to put me back together. I just want to get comfortable."

Kiera laughs. "Well, I was going to tell you to take your shoes off and make yourself comfortable, but you're already two steps ahead of me as usual. I already told Mindy she could change, so knock yourself out."

At lightning speed, Tara grabs a plastic cup and sets it on the table next to where she is standing. She bends at the waist and runs her fingers through her hair, flinging bobby pins and rubber bands into the cup as if they're on fire. After she removes the last one, she stands up, runs her fingers through her long main of hair, and shakes it out. Her hair is magnificent. It's the kind of hair that inspires song lyrics. It forms a dark inky curtain nearly to her waist. Usually, it's straight, but today it has soft waves from being restrained in a complicated hairstyle all day. My fingers itch to touch it. I decide that I'd better give my fingers something to do. So, I play the '80s classic *True Colors* by Cyndi Lauper. Tara instantly recognizes the song. She swings around to glare at me. I merely shrug and wink.

Tara sighs and signs, "Okay, you win. I love this song too."

Chapter Five

Tara

WHAT IS IT ABOUT Aidan that makes me feel different? Maybe it's because I knew him from before the day everything in my life changed. There's a sense of comfort around him that I haven't felt in a really long time. It's as if I am finally free to take a breath, after holding it for years. Aidan certainly looks different, but I can tell the quirky, quick-witted sense of humor he had as a kid has changed little. He always seemed fully aware of my moods, even back then. If I was stressed out over a big performance, he would always "coincidentally" be learning the same music on the piano so I could break the dance down count by count. It's funny, it took me awhile to notice he always needed to start his piece over whenever I needed a reset on my choreography. When he was satisfied that I had the dance memorized and was obsessing over trivial stuff, he would launch a campaign to distract me. He had a seemingly endless supply of horrifically bad knock-knock jokes and could sing more Broadway tunes than anybody I'd ever heard.

At one point, Aidan even tried ventriloquism to keep me smiling. He was so terrible at it; I couldn't help but laugh at his efforts. It was also the first time I remember him and his brother, Rory, almost coming to blows over me. Aidan couldn't get the jaw mechanism of the dummy to work, and I was trying to help him. Rory walked in on us and said, "You should get this one to sit on your lap. She's as flat as a board and dances like Pinocchio. She'd make a good dummy."

I was wounded to the core of my being. I had decided Rory was my White Knight — my one and only. If he would only wait for me to grow up, I knew I would be his perfect match. Hearing he thought I was childish and a bad dancer was just too much for my rather fragile twelve-year-old ego, and I burst into tears.

At that point, even though Aidan was only ten and a half (for some reason he always made a huge deal of telling me about the half), he made a move to sock Rory in the midsection—or lower. He got right up in Rory's face and yelled, "Rory Silas O'Brien! You apologize right now or I'll tell Ma. That's no way to talk to a lady, and you know it."

I was so stunned I stopped crying. Rory is a lot older than Aidan and he was freakishly strong. He could lift me in overhead lifts as if I weighed less than a feather. Rory was the golden child. His parents did not like hearing bad news about him. Even the dance instructors wouldn't call Rory on bad behavior for fear of upsetting Mr. and Mrs. O'Brien. Aidan was risking a lot by standing up for me. Aidan O'Brien called me a lady. How weird was that? This is the boy who just put a stink bomb in my locker and pop rocks in my Gatorade. I smile at the memory.

Aidan sure grew up fine. I may have been crushing on the wrong brother all along. Who knew that tangle of gangly limbs, shiny orthodontia and coke-bottle glasses would sort itself out into this poster boy for hotness? He looks like he could easily model for Columbia Sportswear or Nike. I can tell he spends some time outdoors. Maybe he runs or cycles. It seems like two out of three guys I meet say they do one or the other. I suspect, in most cases, it's just a pick up line, and they really hibernate in their dorm rooms playing video games. Still, I caught a glimpse of those forearms earlier, it is clear Aidan has to be doing something sweat-inducing in his free time. Since Aidan looks so good, I randomly speculate whether "hunkiness" evolution works in reverse. I wonder if Rory, who once looked like he could walk off the pages of any teen idol magazine, now needs hair transplants and a tummy tuck. That would be funny since I've never met anyone more in love with his own reflection than Rory.

I hear Mindy's irrepressible giggle in the distance, so I look over to see what she's up to now. She has changed clothes and is wearing overall shorts and a gingham top. She must have had her dad re-braid her hair, because she is wearing it in pigtails now. She has her tongue pushed out between the gap in her teeth in total concentration as Gabriel is teaching her to dribble; he is patiently working through drills, making sure she can dribble with both hands and catch the ball. I creep closer to take pictures. I watch Mindy blow her bangs out of her eyes and sigh.

"Gabriel, you said you were gonna teach me to play basketball. This ain't really basketball because the hoop thingie is all the way up there," she complains pointing at the basket.

Gabriel laughs and ruffles her hair. "You gotta learn it all, if you want to be a decent ball player. You can't just have all the glory shots."

Mindy's brow wrinkles in confusion. "Why not? I like to shoot baskets. You think girls can't play?"

Gabriel's eyes widen and he awkwardly bounces the ball off his foot. "What? I didn't say that! My mom plays way better than Uncle Jeff. I just meant you can't hog the ball if you want people to pick you to play."

Mindy looks a little shell shocked. "You mean we get to do this again with your friends and everythin'?"

Gabriel looks at her with a puzzled expression as he shrugs. "Duh!" He tosses the ball at her. "You're kinda like my cousin now. What did you think was gonna happen? You gonna take a shot or just hold that thing like it's a doll?"

Mindy narrows her eyes and launches the ball toward the basket. It arcs and brushes the bottom of the net.

Gabriel smiles and claps. "Whoa! That was super close. Just bend your knees a little and spread your fingers apart on the ball like this." He holds up the ball to demonstrate how to hold it and then tosses it back to her. "Here, try again. I know you'll get it this time."

I snap some pictures as Mindy dribbles the ball, her tongue pressed between the gap in her teeth. She squints as she bends her knees and lets the ball fly. The ball hits the rim and balances for a split second. I hold my breath as I watch it slowly spin around the perimeter before finally swishing through the net in what seems like frame-by-frame animation.

Mindy gasps as she sees the outcome. She lets out a whoop of celebration and chatters happily, "Didya see what I jus' did? I can't beleibe I jus' did it! I'm pretty awesome, huh?"

Gabriel gives her a high five and agrees amicably, "Yeah, Little Bit, you're pretty awesome. You can play on my team any time."

I smile at the tenderness in his voice. It reminds me of all the times Aidan brought a smile to my face when we were kids. Mindy too reminds me of the way I was as a kid— always trying to be grown up and not cause any waves. Although Mindy's circumstances are far more traumatic than mine ever were, in our own way we both lost parents. After my dad was killed, my mom slowly died from grief. Every second my mom was away from my dad, she lost a little more of her will to live, until she had none left.

Aidan could always sense when I was having a rough time of it at home. Sometimes his tactics were silly. He once had us wear clown noses all day, claiming we needed to do it to get in character for the Vaudeville act we were doing. When he discovered I have a ridiculously long name that reflects both my Native American heritage and my Caucasian grandmother from Kansas, he insisted on calling me Gracie for the rest of the school year. If I got too studious when we did our homework, he would wink at me and murmur under his breath, "Well, there goes Windy again." All of this went over the tutor's head because, at the time, AJ was the only person in the world besides my mom who knew my whole name. Of course, I also had leverage; back then, there was nothing Aidan hated worse than his name, other than broccoli. He once told me he would be a famous concert pianist just so he could go by his initials, A.O.

The flip side of Aidan was extraordinarily tender and generous. I vividly remember when I was ten, I was breaking in new toe shoes and had blisters so bad I could barely walk. My mom was lost in her own fog of sadness and couldn't get out of bed, and my dance teacher told me that a little pain would make me tough. I was afraid to tell anyone my feet were getting worse because I didn't want to lose my spot in the recital. I was sure, if anything would get my mom out of bed, it would be the chance to make a pretty costume and do my hair and makeup like she used to before Daddy died. Aidan was the only one to notice something was amiss. He made me take my tape off and show him. I'll never forget the look of anguish that crossed his face as he saw the raw, oozing sores on my feet. Even now, I recall the incident like it was yesterday.

I remember sitting on the wobbly wood step-stool with a fuzzy-haired Aidan kneeling in front of me, the smell of talc and sweat heavy in the air.

"Tara," he hissed, "you know those are infected, right? You could get real sick. My uncle is a soldier and he's told me stories 'bout people's feet rotting off."

I grimaced. "I know. But, if I tell anybody, they won't let me dance and my mom will be even sadder. I don't know what to do. My daddy did all this stuff before, but he's dead now."

Aidan looked at me for a really long time before he answered me. I was sure he is going to tell his parents. Part of me wasn't sure I didn't want him to, because as intimidating as they were, everything they wanted to happen seems to magically occur. I needed a little magic in my life. I was getting tired of peanut butter sandwiches and dry cereal.

The muscle in Aidan's jaw flexed and his eyes shut as he shook his head sharply as if to clear an image. When he opened his eyes, he held my gaze, pushed up his glasses and whispered, "I'll take care of you."

I felt better for having shared my secret, but how in the world could Aidan help? He was even younger than me. I was so very confused. When we got back to our tutoring session, I'm afraid I had made Aidan mad, because he barely even looked at me. Instead of eating lunch with me in our spot under the big Douglas fir, he announced that he was going to go to the store with Rory to buy Pokémon cards. I was in the corner eating my stupid sandwich alone and wishing I had some of the rice crispy treats I used to make with my dad. My dad and I used to speak only Japanese on those late night kitchen raids. I was bummed because I couldn't remember as many words as I used to because I had no one to practice with. I've tried with Aidan, but his accent was terrible and I couldn't make him say the words in the right order. He thinks it's like English, and it's just not.

I pulled a Nancy Drew book from my backpack and tried to tune out the world around me and disappear. Suddenly, Aidan squatted in front of me and dropped a bag on the ground. I was familiar with this routine. I waited for him to pull out the Starburst candies and sort them. Strawberry and cherry for me and the rest for him. It's what he always does. I never, ever had to ask. One day when the teacher handed out lollipops, he noticed that those were the flavors I preferred and every day since— it doesn't matter if he has Skittles, Starbursts or Dum Dums — I always get first pick of the strawberry and cherry. I know he likes them too because Rory about fell out of his chair in disbelief the first few times he saw Aidan do it.

"Tara, take your shoes off," Aidan directed.

"Why?" I asked, confused. "Rory and I have to meet with the choreographer after lunch."

"We need to hurry, lunch is gonna be over soon." He dumps the bag out on the floor. My jaw drops open in shock. This isn't Pokémon cards and candy. It's an assortment of first-aid stuff, mole skin, and even cotton balls.

"Where'd you get this stuff?" I asked in disbelief.

"I bought it, silly," he answered as he crossed his eyes to make me laugh like he always does.

"How?" I pressed, still not quite understanding.

He shrugged casually. "I've been saving my allowance for my Pokémon collection, and Rory was too busy flirting with girls to notice what I was doing."

I quickly took off my shoes and the athletic tape I tried to apply to protect my poor feet. Aidan picked up my foot and began applying hydrogen peroxide and blowing on it to take away the sting. The fierce scowl on his face was in direct contrast to his gentle treatment of my feet. He swiftly finished applying ointment, then moleskin, and wraps my feet like a professional trainer.

"Holy cow! How do you even know how to do that? You play the piano!"

"Who do you think patches up my knuckle-head brother when he gets in fights 'n doesn't want to get busted by Ma?" he explained with a grin.

"Thanks for taking care of me." I tucked my bloody socks into my backpack and slipped my shoes on.

He blushed. "It's no big deal. I said I would."

"It was still really nice of you," I mumbled. For the first time in my life, I felt shy around AJ.

I'm still lost in my memories, the magic of a late summer day and a childhood yet to be lived, when I feel a jacket being draped over my shoulders. I am so startled that I immediately send an elbow flying in a self-defense move.

Aidan counters with an evasive move of his own, and I barely miss his rib cage. "Whoa, I'm friendly. I thought you might be getting cold. It's getting a little breezy out here, and the mosquitoes are going to eat you alive in a few minutes."

I bury my head in my hands. This makes about three times tonight I have done something stupid in front of Aidan. "I'm so sorry. I was woolgathering. You scared me. Usually, that doesn't happen." I let my explanation trail off as I realize it's not making any sense. I pull the jacket tighter around myself. It's comically large on me, even as tall as I am, and it smells warm and spicy. I resist the urge to sniff it like a bloodhound.

A look of open curiosity crosses his face. It's so similar to one I remember from our childhood back when he wanted to know my every thought; I'm not at all shocked when his next question is, "What were you thinking about?"

I burst out laughing, unable to contain myself any longer. When I finally regain my composure, I manage to reply, "I see being a responsible grown-up hasn't taught you any boundaries."

I swear he blushes a bit, but it's hard to tell in the subdued hues of dusk. "Come on now, this is us we're talking about. Cut me some slack. I've seen you with the chicken pox, remember?"

I smile. "I do remember. You couldn't stay in your own space then either, so you ended up just as itchy as me."

Aidan's expression sobers as he continues to study me. "Tara, were you thinking about me? About us?"

I sigh. I've never been able to hide a single thing from Aidan. There's really no use in trying now. I nod. "It's been a really long time since I remembered what life was like before I entered my own private hell." I let out a wry chuckle as I will my body to stop shaking and continue my explanation. "It's ironic, really. I thought the times I went through after Dad died, and my mom just faded away, were awful. Turns out they were just the warm up act. In retrospect, they were the best years of my childhood. After my dad died, you were the only person who was there for me until I met Kiera."

Aidan looks like I gave him a roundhouse kick to

the face. "Tara, if those were the best days of your childhood, I swear I'll send that creep through a wood chipper and no one will ever see him again. There were days you were so worn out from taking care of your mom, it's a wonder you didn't fall asleep in the middle of dance lifts. I remember one month your mom forgot to pay the power bill one too many times, and they cut your power off and you accidentally let it slip you were eating soup cold from a can. After that, I brought two of everything. Ma thought I had an eating disorder. I had to blackmail Rory not to tell. Fortunately for me, he had some *Playboy* magazines under his mattress, and I used it to my advantage," he recounts.

I'm embarrassed that he remembers all the humiliating stuff. "Aidan, don't waste your energy on the jerk who attacked me. He isn't worth it. There was nothing you could have done. What's done is done. I've learned from it. I'm prepared for the next bad guy," I assure him.

"But that's just it —"

"*What's* it?" I interrupt, thoroughly confused.

"If I hadn't been so wrapped up in my own personal drama, I could have been there for you. If I had been there, your life might not have descended into hell," Aidan clarifies.

"Or not," I reply bluntly. "I was pretty naïve and blinded by flash and muscles back then. I might have just shaken you off as Rory's pesky little brother. You had your own serious crap to deal with. Don't downplay your struggles because you feel bad for me. To borrow your line, 'This is *me* you're talking to'."

"Touché," he concedes. "What can I do to make your life better, Tara?"

"Honestly, I don't have an answer for you. Some days are great, and other days, if a newscaster uses the wrong phrase I'm puking in my kitchen sink. I can't make any guarantees. What do you want me to do?"

Aidan stands in front of me just like he used to as a child. His green eyes are intense even under the paper lanterns. As I contemplate what might come out of those lips, he slowly reaches out and links his left index finger with mine. The wave of nostalgia is staggering as I remember the gesture which became our 'secret pact'. We made it up during a rare trip to the library, when we discovered a book on the mysterious world of sign language and took a pledge, at seven, to be friends for life. Linked index fingers were our secret handshake based on the sign for friend. It's odd how comforting I find that simple gesture, even now.

"Tara, I want to keep the promise I made way back then. I want to take care of you. I want you to take care of me too. I miss you," Aidan confesses in a low whisper against my temple.

"What if I can't do that?" Panic starts to make my voice tremble. I sway a little and cross my arm over my stomach as a wave of nausea threatens to overtake me.

Our single point of contact remains our left index fingers, yet somehow he manages to channel calming energy into me. He looks at me and crosses his eyes. I laugh just like I've done every other time he's pulled that trick.

"See, that's the Gracie I know and love. Breathe. I'm

not scared off by a little puke. You used to be like a cat with hairballs before every performance or test," he teases gently.

"Don't be feeling too smug there, Mr. O'Brien. I've cleaned up a fair amount of your puke in my day. Remember the day you decided you needed to perform in your recital with a one hundred and two degree fever?" I ask, counting the infractions down on my free hand. "Or what about the time you thought it was a great idea to eat three chili dogs and a funnel cake before you went on the Tilt-a-Whirl? Maybe you remember the time Rory dared you to eat earth worms and you took him up on it because you thought it might make him hurl?"

He holds his hand over his mouth and makes an exaggerated gagging sound. "You win! I am definitely the grossest person in this relationship. Clearly, you have nothing to worry about."

"That's a pretty low standard of acceptable dating behavior. Are we seriously going to build our relationship around who pukes less?" I ask, my voice laden with skepticism.

Aidan shrugs nonchalantly. "Just think of it as a starting point, while we see how much we've still got in common." He reaches his hands behind his neck and rolls his shoulders in a stretch I've seen him do a million times. I don't ever remember being enticed by the play of the muscles under his clothing before, but we were kids then — and now we're not. I am so mesmerized by the artistic play of muscle and tone, I completely miss the fact that he has resumed speaking. I'm sure he'll get that Bambi caught in the headlights feeling when he realizes the messy situation he's backed himself into. Instead of freaking out, he gives me a gentle smile and nervously asks, "I've got a late gig on Thursday in Salem. Can we grab lunch somewhere?"

I pull my schedule up on my cell phone. I have a rare day off on Thursday. I take it as a sign. I nod cautiously. He can't possibly know what a huge leap I've just taken with that simple nod. I remind myself that this is Aidan. He probably knew before he even asked and had four creative ways planned to defeat any objection I might have thrown his way.

"Great, I'll text you," he answers with a crooked grin. "I better get back to the reception, but seriously … running into you is the best thing that's happened in ages."

Thoughts are swirling in my head as I watch him turn to leave with an easy long-limbed stride across the dance floor. Suddenly, a thought occurs to me. "Wait, Aidan!" I call out, shrugging his jacket off of my shoulders and holding it out in front of me. "You forgot this, and you don't have my number."

Returning to me, he takes the jacket from my fingertips and drapes it back around my shoulders. "Tara, do you really think I'd take it from you? I can see your goose-bumps from here," he chides gently. "I'll just get it back when I see you on Thursday."

Standing in front of me, Aidan gives my arms a light squeeze as he winks at me and confesses, "It seems I've already passed inspection with your friends, so I'm covered with your number. I'll be in touch, Gracie."

The heat of his hands is radiating through the soft

wool of his jacket where Aidan is lightly grasping my upper arms. Reflexively, I sway toward him. It's an odd sensation to enjoy being touched. Aside from grappling sessions in my self-defense classes, I haven't let anyone outside of Kiera, Heather and Mindy touch me in years. Shaking hands is an arcane social convention I engage in only if I can't find a polite way to evade it. I've developed quite a reputation as a klutz and severe allergy sufferer. I'm actually neither, but no one outside of the Girlfriend Posse knows.

I never planned for my rapist to commandeer such a big chunk of my life. Initially, I just felt stupid for being so gullible. What did I expect? I was fourteen, about to enter high school. I wanted to be cool and hang out with Rory and his friends. Rory was on his way to Juilliard and I thought if I could act grown up, I might catch Rory's eye and it might be like some romantic reenactment of the scene from *The Thornbirds*. In that book, a much older guy falls for a younger girl. My mom loved the mini series so much. She watched it over and over until her VHS tape broke. She didn't live long enough for me to get it for her on DVD. She died two weeks after I was raped.

The doctor told me she might have hung on for eight years after my dad died, but she really started dying the day he was killed. It just took her body a while to catch up to her brain. I'll never know if she even knew about the rape. She was probably too far gone in her own world of grief to notice.

After my mom was gone, I no longer had to keep up a pretense of being social. I retreated into a world of stillness. I didn't trust myself anymore. My body, which was supposed to be an elite specimen of athletic strength and prowess, had completely frozen when it counted. I felt like a failure for putting myself in the situation. I felt guilt over not being able to get away without getting hurt. I added even more shame to the growing pile because I felt I should be able to just stop thinking about it. The fact that I couldn't made me feel weak.

I didn't seek help until my *sensei* refused to work with me until I'd worked with a domestic violence counselor. I saw her for six months before I could admit out loud what was done to me was rape. It didn't matter that I'd worn a mini skirt, that I had agreed to go out with him, that I was in the car with him, that I had kissed him, or even that I failed to get away. Warren Jones didn't have the right to have sex with me. I said no. No *means* no. Period. It never was my fault. Yet, somehow, I still feel like I should have done something. To this day, I wish I'd had the guts to prosecute him right away. I worry about who else he harmed, while I got it together. I feel bad about that too. An involuntary shudder passes through me. I turn my face away from Aidan.

Gently he reaches up to cup my chin so I have to raise it to look at him. I flinch when he touches me. He draws his fingers back as if he's been burned by a flame. "Shh, Tara, it's just me. I'd rip off both of my arms and beat myself stupid with them before I'd harm a single hair on your head," he murmurs softly.

I hang my head in frustration as tears start to fall. Finally, I gather the strength to look at him and whisper, pointing to my head, "AJ. I know that here, and I'm pretty sure I even know that here," pointing to my heart. "It's the rest of me that can't make heads or tails of it."

Aidan gingerly places his hand back on my upper arm and gives a slight squeeze. He tilts his head to the side, silently seeking my permission. I slowly close my eyes and draw in a steadying breath. Blinking away tears I nod, almost imperceptibly.

A look of relief crosses over his expressive face and I watch in fascination when his Adam's apple bobs up and down as he tries to cover his emotion. He looks like he'd like nothing better than what he used to call a "spider monkey" hug when we were kids. If I was feeling down, he would ambush me with a hug and not let go until I smiled. One day he threatened to stay attached through the whole math test. I finally caved to avoid detention.

He stares at me with a disturbingly haunted look on his face. "If I make you uncomfortable, you need to tell me. I can't see the scars on your soul. You have to tell me what hurts."

His words shatter me further. "Scars on my soul? I've had years of therapy and seen half a dozen rape counselors, yet I don't think anyone has understood so completely."

Aidan links his index finger with mine in our familiar gesture of friendship. He doesn't even seem to be aware that he's doing it. "I think you have been adding layers to that scar tissue since your dad died. Every blow life has dealt you has been like one more string in a silk cocoon, trapping you in a life of pain. You need someone you can lean on to set you free."

"Some days, I want someone like that in my life, Aidan. But, then I remember loving someone that deeply, flat out killed my mom," I respond sadly.

A pained look crosses Aidan's face. "Gracie, you trust me to always tell you the truth — even if it stings a little, right?"

I squint my eyes as I scrunch up my nose and study him carefully. Still, the Aidan I know isn't cruel for sport. I shrug as I concede, "I guess so."

Aidan takes a deep breath, then sighs before going on. "Please think about this before you decide to hate me, okay? Remember, I knew the little girl who could tap dance like a tornado and could bring an audience to tears as a swan." He pauses to study me for a few more seconds and swallows hard before he asks with a voice so tightly strung with emotion, it almost cracks, "Are you *living* now, Tara? Or are you simply surviving each day, just digging in your fingernails and hanging on for dear life?" Aidan's shoulders slump as he delivers the verbal dagger.

My body physically recoils from his words and I almost drop to my knees.

Aidan grabs my waist to keep me from falling and murmurs in my ear, "Easy, Tara, I've got you."

"Holy crap, Aidan," I hiss, steadying myself and pulling his hands away. "You don't pull any punches, do you? What could you possibly know about what I'm going through?"

Aidan rakes his hand through his mop of curls. For a moment he says nothing, then he steps back explaining his movements as he proceeds, "Gracie, I'm going to show you something, but I have to take off my shirt. I won't touch you, all right?"

Before I can analyze the ramifications of my decision, sheer curiosity compels me to nod. I'm

64

disconcerted when I feel a flutter of excitement in my stomach as he loosens his tie and shrugs out of one side of his shirt. I can't stop the gasp which escapes my lips as I study his sculpted body.

He is an artist's dream. As my eyes travel up his body, I notice an intricate tattoo covering the left side of his pec and down his arm. I step closer to get a better look. When I examine it closely, I see that it's made up of hundreds of musical notes. The ones nearest to his heart are completely clear. As they travel up his shoulder and down his arm, they are gradually shaded in with vibrant colors. Eventually, the conventions of sheet music are lightly spiraled down his arm as the notes float free again.

Without conscious thought, my fingers reach up to follow that remarkable storyline as if just taking it in visually isn't enough. When my fingers come in contact with his rock solid chest muscles, his nostrils flare and he stands as still as I have ever seen him.

Alarmed, I draw my hand back. "Did I hurt you?" I ask, embarrassed, fearing I've screwed up yet again.

"No, Gracie, your touch is not painful. Explore all you like," Aidan replies with a tight grin. Yet, I get the feeling he's leaving a lot unsaid. Sometimes, no matter how brilliant the canvas, pictures are not enough.

CHAPTER SIX

AIDAN

MY MUSCLES SCREAM WITH the need to move. I breathe in deeply through my nose, in an effort to distract myself. In half a heartbeat, it becomes clear that I've made a grave miscalculation in strategy as I catch the scent of coconuts and ginger coming from Tara's wrist as her cool fingers trace over my tattoo. I will my body to settle down, using techniques learned from many years of rock climbing. The parallels with climbing run deep. If I move too fast without knowing my limits, someone may get hurt. Yet, if I don't trust my instincts, I get nowhere. The first thing I need to do is earn back her trust. If that means posing like a store mannequin, then that's what I'll do.

Just then, Mindy comes barreling across the yard and practically pushes me over in her excitement. "How's come you're takin' your shirt off? Are we going to go swimmin' in the ocean? I didn' bring no swimsuit, can I swim in my underwears?" she peppers me with questions at a frightening rate.

Tara gently untangles Mindy from my thigh as she says, "Mouse, slow down and take a breath. We can only answer one question at a time."

Mindy backs up and stands beside Tara. She dramatically draws in a breath and blows it out. Looking up at me, she places her hands on her hips and demands, "Well?"

I chuckle at her body posture. Tara used to throw me that same kind of attitude whenever she was annoyed at me. "No, Mindy, it's too cold to swim in the ocean here without wet suits, and I didn't bring one today. Maybe we can come back another day," I explain, trying not to ruin her day.

At first Mindy's shoulders slump, but then her eyes brighten. "For reals? You ain't trickin'?"

I catch Tara's gaze. She smiles and nods. I turn back to Mindy and hold my hand out for her to shake as I say, "I'm a man of my word, Mindy. I promise. I think I've got some of my niece's old gear around too."

Mindy grabs my hand to shake it vigorously practically shouting in her excitement. "Deal! I've never been in the ocean before. Do you think the fishes will bite me?"

Tara laughs and drapes an arm over Mindy's shoulders. "Mindy, you're too sweet to be fish food, so I think you'll be safe."

Abruptly she turns toward Tara. "I forgot to tell you. Miss Donda tol' me to say since you were both preoppufied, she would be happy to play dance music from her iPod."

A dusky hue tints Tara's lovely skin as her eyes lower.

I chuckle softly.

"Mr. Band-Aidan, what was Miss Donda talkin' about?" Mindy asks as she fiddles with the ends of her pigtails.

I cough back a laugh. "I'm sure she just meant we lost track of time catching up. I guess I should let Tara get back to her job as a bridesmaid."

Mindy shakes her head no. "Nuh-uh, I heard Miss Kiera tell Miss Heather she was dismissed and could just have fun at the party. Miss Heather is dancin'," Mindy explains.

"Oh, I see —" I start to say.

"Will you dance with me Mr. Aidan? Mr. Jeff is kinda busy right now and Papa says he's tired," Mindy looks crestfallen and waits anxiously for my answer. Seriously, how could anyone ever hurt this child? But the scars on her hand are a sobering reminder someone has inflicted hell on her.

I wink at Mindy. "Let me see if I have a spot on my dance card," I reply as I turn to Tara. "Tara, do you mind if I dance with Princess Mindy?"

Tara curtsies and gives her approval. "I think that's a fabulous idea."

"How'd you know one of my nicknames is Princess Mindy?" she queries.

"Because I saw you dancing earlier and you looked prettier than Cinderella at the ball." I take Mindy's hand and lead her to the dance floor. Tara is standing along the edge watching us. We catch the end of a Black Eyed Peas Song. Mindy is an enthusiastic dancer, but underneath all that zeal I can see she has an innate sense of musicality.

The music fades into the cult classic *YMCA* by The Village People. I turn to Tara with a delighted grin. "Come on Gracie, this is more like an aerobics class than dancing. We haven't done this since I sprained my fingers playing football with Rory and had to come up with something to do for the talent show with less than two hours until curtain. You totally bailed me out that day and saved my grade in Performance class."

Mindy joins the plea, "Yeah, Miss Tara, it'll be way more fun with more people. Pretty please —"

Tara looks uncertain for a moment, then straightens her spine. She runs her hands through her hair in a jerky motion. But then she gathers it in a ponytail and ties her hair in a knot at her neck. She lines up next to me and addresses Mindy, "Have you ever danced to this one, Mouse?"

Mindy nods, "My P.E. teacher taughted us this one and the *Macarena*."

"Aidan, you might be sorry you asked me to do this. I don't even dance for my cat anymore. I'm more than just a little rusty."

"Well, there's no time like the present to knock off a little rust. Come on, it'll be fun," I coax.

The song is faster than I remember, and Mindy's pantomiming skills are impressive. Keeping up with Tara is no easy feat — you would never know Tara spent one month away from the dance studio, let alone years. She looks spectacular. When we finish the dance, we all collapse in a fit of giggles in the middle of the dance floor.

I lean over and whisper in her ear, "Welcome back, Tara. The world has missed you."

———◆●◆———

I sit on the edge of the bed in another dingy hotel room. Judge Gardner paid me well for my services, and I'd be more comfortable if I upgraded, but I'm saving up to buy studio time so I can cut a decent demo of my own songs. I'd like to get some work as a session musician on a major label, but I've got to get my name out there first. It's dark, dank motels for me, for the foreseeable future. I just wish the beds were longer. I can tell by looking that my feet are going to hang off the end. This short bed is going to make for a very long night.

My phone plays *The Saints Go Marching In*. I glance at my watch and a feeling of dread washes over me. Delores is a retired nurse and takes her insulin like clockwork. But it's past midnight and abnormally late for her to call. I answer the call with some trepidation, "Hello?"

I hear crying, rhythmic tapping and the sound of Delores's Cajun accented speech, "*Mon P'tit Boug*, how did your wedding go? Did you get to play lots of your beautiful music?"

I smile at her nickname for me. I've never really been her little boy, considering I was already taller than her on the day we met. Still, the fact that she has a term of endearment for me, just as she does for her own kids, always made me feel more welcome. Of course, that worked two ways; when I screwed up, she still grounded me and took my car keys.

"*Mon Cha*, it was phenomenal. Like an answer to a prayer. But, why're you calling so late? Is everything okay?" I ask, concern coloring my voice.

"Oh you worry too much about me. The only thing keeping me up tonight is a grand-baby with colic," Delores replies with a soft chuckle.

"You want me to play something for her?" I offer, reaching for my acoustic guitar I left propped against the wall. It's a well-loved graduation present from my mom.

I start to play a piece that's been floating around my head since earlier tonight. It's not finished, but the notes flooded my brain as soon as I saw Tara coming down the aisle in her bridesmaid dress. I play it softly like a lullaby, but in my head I hear the notes as loud and confident. As I play the bridge, the quality of the notes changes to reflect Tara as I saw her tonight, a whisper of her former self trying to find her inner song. Slowly, I add more complicated notes, chords and rhythms as I envision who Tara could be, if she had someone to share her burdens with.

I don't have an ending yet, so I let it fade out with a few hushed notes. I hear rustling on the other end of the phone. Eventually, Delores comes back on the phone and says in hushed tones, "I don't know why I'm always so surprised, but she's out like a light. Thank you. That's a new piece, isn't it? What inspired that?"

I chuckle. "I'm not sure it's a good thing if my music puts the ladies in the room to sleep. Anyway, it's not really about *what* inspired me. This song is all about the *who*."

Delores clicks her tongue at me in mock disapproval as she quips, "Really Aidan, you meet a *joli faire* at a wedding and you write a song about her? Got any other clichés you'd like to trip over while you're at it?"

Laughing out loud, I remember Delores's critiques of my early song writing efforts, which were strongly influenced by whatever I watched on television or based on my memory of music in the old days, before I lost my hearing. They were pretty bad back then. Hopefully, I've gotten better with time.

"Oh, I've got a doozy for you. Not only is she a pretty girl, I've been in love with her since I was about six." My voice trails off as I wait for her response. It's important to me that Delores understand my relationship with Tara. I am not sure how to explain it to her when I don't quite get it myself. Tara and I both have changed a lot over the years, and everything might be different now.

Delores gasps as she responds in a hushed tone, "You found your Gracie after all these years? Was she performing her ballet at the wedding, or was she the bride?"

My heart sinks to my stomach when I consider that I could easily have been playing for Tara's wedding today. So, as challenging as our next steps may be, my timing really could have been worse.

I sigh in frustration as I try to explain the avalanche of changes in Tara's life, "No, *Cha*, she doesn't dance anymore. She says she can't feel the music."

"Well, you know a little something about that, don't you?" Delores replies.

"Yes, but my situation was different. I don't know how to help her. She lost her music because some lowlife attacked her and raped her."

Delores is silent for a minute. I can almost hear her gather her thoughts. Finally, I hear her take a deep breath as she answers in a resigned voice, "You know there are no easy answers to this? She'll never be the same as before. The best you can do is give her new memories to chase away the evil handprints on her body and in her mind. If you plan to wimp out in the middle when times get tough, don't you dare start. She needs to believe you'll love her no matter how ugly her shame or pain."

"I won't abandon her!" I practically shout into the phone, my voice rough with indignation. "What kind of guy do you think I am? I was raised better than that. *You* raised me better than that."

"Aidan, hush now. I didn't mean to say you would ever plan to hurt this girl. But this will be harder than you imagine. In many ways, it may be harder than your own recovery. You'll hear things you can't un-hear. You will unearth pain in her that you can't rebury. She may remember that she hates men and forget you're one of the good guys. What you need to work through has no start and stop date. It's just there, like a case of asthma, living under the surface and waiting to attack when you least expect it — even when you think it's under control."

"You're saying I should just ditch her like every other person, including me, has ever done in her life?" I demand.

"Aidan Jarith, now you're being obtuse just to be a jerk," she scolds. "I'm just saying; unless you plan to be around until the end of the game, there's no point in throwing your hat in the ring. You need to decide what your plans are with this *fille*."

"*Cha*, it's been a long time since I've seen Tara, but I don't suppose my feelings for her have changed a lot since I was six. I know it's all going to be harder than ever, now. But my Tara is in there somewhere, under all that pain. I know we can't figure out if there is anything to save between the two of us, until she finds her way back."

"I just don't want you to expect that everything is going to be the way you remember it," Delores cautions, worry tingeing her voice.

I sigh, suddenly feeling very exhausted. "I know that *Mon Cha*. But I can't give up. This is Gracie we're talking about. I've got to believe that tonight was no accident. There's some reason our worlds collided again."

"I hope it works out for you, Aidan. You had your heart broken so much already. I don't want to see it happen again. I worry about you," she observes quietly. "Good night. I need to get these old bones to bed."

"I know, Delores. I'll be careful. I love you. Good night."

As I set my guitar down. I think about the odds of running across Tara again after all these years. I've lived like a nomad for more than ten years. At first, it was because I had a feeling I didn't belong anywhere. Don't get me wrong, Delores is amazing and her family did the best they could to make me feel welcome. Yet, I had a sense of restlessness I couldn't describe or tame. I don't know if it's intrinsic to my deafness or completely coincidental. I spent so many years completely isolated from the world of sound and music that when I got it back, it was difficult for me to adjust. Everything felt jarring. I almost couldn't decide if I was running away from sound or toward it. I split my time between loud, garish nightclubs and bars, and the silence of climbing rocks.

After I got my second cochlear implant and could more fully integrate music into my life, the restless feeling dissipated. Soon, I ran for an entirely different reason. I tried to chase all of those years that got away from me. I wanted to be something in my own right, not just Rory's defective little brother. The one who couldn't do it; the not famous one.

At first, people thought it was ridiculously funny to hire a deaf piano player. I was treated like some twisted sideshow at a roadside circus. I played many of my first gigs for the cost of my drinks and a couple of appetizers, but gradually I built a reputation, and bar owners requested me. After a couple of years, my Tuesday night bookings turned into Friday and Saturday nights and I got a portion of the cover charges. These days I'm booked out about eight months in advance. The only reason I was available to perform at Kiera's wedding was because the bat mitzvah last week was canceled due to an outbreak of mono.

It's an okay life, for now, but it's not a life I'm hoping to build. I've been messing around with something new. I haven't even told Delores or Rory about it because I don't know what their reaction will be. The only person who knows is my speech therapist. He says I sound great. I think he's probably full of it. After all, isn't he paid to say stuff like that? I think I'll keep it under wraps for a while longer, until I get better. I've been writing a bunch of new songs I would like to get on demo tape, though. This one I'm writing for Tara might be the most powerful song I've ever written.

———————•●———————

I struggle through levels of consciousness, not really wanting to wake up. My dream was so realistic. I could've sworn that I would roll over and find myself entangled in Tara's long mane of hair. My hands tingle from the imagined sensation of running my hands through her hair. I almost lost it last night at the wedding when she took it down at the reception, and that was in a public place. If we were alone, all bets would be off.

The crazy thing is, Tara seems oblivious to the fact that her mere presence in a room renders most men speechless. She was always a complete puzzle, even as a kid. She was ferociously competitive and often bested my older brother in both technique and artistic interpretation, even though he was older and had more dance experience. Yet, she was always shy and self-deprecating about her talent. Gracie always seemed incredibly sensitive to the emotions of the people around her. If she thought someone might be unhappy with her performance, her level of stress went through the roof. Yet, in those high-pressure situations, Tara always performed flawlessly because she put in ten times more effort than my brother ever dreamed of applying.

In my dream, strangely enough, I was her dance partner. Although I feel music in every pore of my body, I don't have highly refined reflexes like Rory, so dancing has never really been my thing. But this fantasy dance was unlike any other. Tara and I were dancing a slow, sensual rumba. She turned in my arms and I placed kisses along the delicate arch of her spine, ending at the tender pulse behind her ear. Her pulse was beating like a humming bird. She leaned her head back into my shoulder and stood on her tiptoes to kissed the underside of my chin. The unexpected touch caused me to draw in a deep breath. She giggled at my discomfort and spins dramatically in my arms. "Was there something you need, Aidan?" she asked with a smirk.

"You. I need you, Tara," I replied as I leaned down to softly kiss her on the lips.

"Well, that's pretty blunt," she retorted as she backed away slightly.

"Yes, but when have you ever known me not to say exactly what I mean?" I responded, arching my eyebrow.

"But you haven't asked me what I want." She pointed out, looking at me somberly.

Her comment just about stopped my heart for a second. My mouth turned dry as I waited for her answer. I thought of a million things I want her to want. I have no idea if she's on the same wavelength as me, so I tried not to jump the gun.

I looked down at her as she blew her hair out of her eyes and smiled up at me. "I don't know if I want to hear this, Gracie." My voice was gruff with more emotion than I want to reveal.

She glanced up at me with a flirtatious grin as she teased, "Oh, I think you will want to hear this, Aidan."

I breathed a sigh of relief as I quipped, "In that

case, by all means, please go ahead. Don't let me stand in the way of a good confession."

"I've been watching you all day at the wedding, and I've decided I want to kiss you," she confessed, looking down at where my hand is resting lightly at her hip.

I took a slow breath and tried not to crowd her. Her scent fills the air with hints of coconut and ginger. I reached out to tilt her chin up with my finger. "I'm on board with your plan," I murmured, as I leaned down to kiss her.

As is typical of any epically good dream, my stupid brain chose that precise moment to wake up. It always happens right before I get to the great part. *Just fabulous!* I grouse to myself. Well, from the looks of the plumbing in this place it isn't likely I'm going to get a warm shower this morning anyway.

Luckily, I don't need to be anywhere in a hurry today, so I'll have time to enjoy the Oregon coast. The weather can be dicey this time of year, but they really lucked out with this wedding. It's a cool crisp morning, but the weather is gorgeous. It's perfect for a run on the beach. Since I'm up anyway, I'm going to grab some pictures of Haystack Rock. Like a true Oregonian, I dress in a couple of layers of Under Armor, grab my running shoes and head out the door toward the beach with my iPhone tucked into an armband.

As I reach my favorite vantage point for taking pictures, I'm not surprised to see Tara in her bare feet standing *en pointe* in the sand in perfect silhouette against a gorgeous sunrise. She is the picture of grace and poise. The time away from dancing hasn't diminished her skills one bit and yet, as I quietly study her movements, it soon becomes clear that she isn't really dancing at all—at least, not in the traditional sense. Instead, she appears to be performing some elaborate martial arts kata. It's intricate and precise, but also a sensual and flowing expression of Tara's command of her body. The same movements could be lethal, too, if given more force. If Tara has to face a bad guy in battle, my money's on her.

Suddenly, a gust of wind catches the colorful scarf Tara is wearing in her hair and blows it down the beach, but Tara's discipline doesn't waver, even though her hair is now wildly whipping around her face. The sight is entrancing. The energy and chaos of her unrestrained hair, juxtaposed against those utterly calm and contained movements, is a sight to behold. I start to take a photo. Finally, she reaches the end of her kata and raises her head to look directly at me. She stares at me intently for a couple of seconds, then glances at the camera in my hand. She scowls and puts her hands on her hips. She signs sharply, "Happy, not!"

I grin to myself. I've learned two things this morning. First, she's got a good handle on the idiosyncrasies of American Sign Language. Second, not much has changed in all these years; she still hates to have her picture taken.

I raise my hand to wave. "Good morning, gorgeous Gracie. How are you this morning?"

With apparent caution, Tara waves back and replies, "I'm fine, now that the wedding is over. I'm thrilled for Kiera and Jeff, but weddings aren't really my thing. Why are you here? Why are you taking pictures of me? It's a little creepy, don't you think?"

I chuckle under my breath. "No, and if you could see how stunning you look against the sunrise, you wouldn't think it was creepy either. Not every woman can look drop-dead gorgeous at 6 A.M. and trust me, Gracie, you do."

"Aidan Jarith O'Brien! You're cute, but you lie like a rug. I'm far from drop-dead gorgeous material. At this moment, my eyes are all bloodshot, my cheeks are wind burned and I have sand up my nose. Go tell your fibs to some girl who's more gullible than me, because I'm not buying them. I know you well enough to know when I need to get out the BS shovel."

"Ah, *Mon Cher*, you are so wrong," I argue, brushing the hair out of her face and retying the bandanna around the loose strands. Tara startles at my touch, so I slowly remove my hands. She scoffs at my lopsided ponytail, so she threads the bandanna under her bra strap.

I raise an eyebrow. "Need another set of hands?" I ask, not so innocently.

"AJ! You're just incorrigible," she declares as she scoops her hair up into a perfectly balanced and arrow straight ponytail. "I'm fine, thank you for offering to help. By the way, Rory and I competed internationally, so those fancy French words won't work on me."

"I was raised by a woman with Cajun roots. I assure you, my French is not just a phony come on. I say a lot of stupid stuff and I seem to lack part of the filter most of polite society has which tells them this would be a really good time just to sit down with a bowl of popcorn and be a spectator." I explain. "But the one thing I don't do is lie just to give a person an inflated sense of themselves. If I tell you that you're the most beautiful thing on this beach, I mean it whether I tell you in English, French, Creole, or ASL. Did I spell that out clearly enough, or would you like me to show you the pictures on my camera to prove it to you?"

Tara groans. "Can't you just delete those?" she pleads. "I'm pretty sure I have snot dripping from my nose."

"So what if you do? We'll just call it morning dew and you're good to go. Seriously, after I finish my run, I'll be in the same boat. I'll even let you take pictures of me. Do you want to come along? Loser buys breakfast."

"How far are you planning to run?" Tara asks, biting her lip in indecision.

"A couple of miles. I can take it slow if you need me to," I reply.

"I don't think that'll be a problem," she assures me.

"Okay, I want you to be sure. I run pretty fast," I tease. I remember very well that if Ms. Isamu puts her mind to it, she can leave me in the dust. When she was dancing with Rory, her training regimen rivaled any Olympic athlete. As she does some preliminary stretches in her yoga pants and oversized sweatshirt from Western Oregon University, I can tell she hasn't changed her workout routine much over the years.

I take a long drink from my water bottle, then offer it to her. She pulls her sleeve over her palm and wipes off the spout. She looks up at me and shrugs as she takes a large swig. She cringes and chokes when she tastes the sweet liquid.

"What in the *heck* did I just drink, AJ?" She sputters for air.

I pat her back, between her shoulder blades. I can't help but laugh at her expression. "Relax, it's just cherry PowerAde."

Tara wrinkles her nose in distaste. "Geez, Aidan! Are you still twelve? This stuff is like fancy Kool-Aid. Whatever happened to good, old-fashioned water?"

I shrug and wink. "Maybe I need the sugar to make me sweeter."

"You need something, that's for sure," Tara mutters under her breath.

"Yeah, I need breakfast. So, are we going to run this morning, or what? Being the gentleman I am, I'll even give you a head start," I offer magnanimously.

Tara stands up from her hamstring stretch and places her hands on her hips. She looks me square in the face and says bluntly, "Trust me, Aidan, that's a really terrible idea. As gallant as it is, would you care to reconsider that offer?"

That's the Tara I remember. Fair to a fault, but competitive as hell. If she's going to beat you, she wants it to be fair and square.

I acquiesce, "All right, Gracie. I'll leave the starting order up to you. But hurry up, whatever you do, because I'm hungry."

"Okay, because of my superior running skills, I'm going to give you a ten-second head start," she replies with triumph in her voice.

I laugh out loud at her tactic. "Ooh, smooth move,

Gracie. You look so innocent and demure. I forgot how crafty you are. Okay, gorgeous — you want ten seconds? You got 'em. Count me down — nice and loud."

I take my finger and draw a line in the sand. I assume a runner's starting stance and wait for her command to go.

Waiting expectantly at the start line, I hear nothing but crashing waves, the clamor of seagulls, and the howl of the brisk morning winds. I wait for one beat, then two. As five seconds stretches to seven, I sneak a glance behind me. To my shock, Tara seems to be frozen mid-stride. It feels like she is dissecting my body with her eyes. I wasn't expecting to run into her today, so I'm just wearing my casual running gear. When I'm running in cooler weather, I like to wear Under Armor running leggings with a long-sleeved shirt that wicks away the sweat and a pair of running shorts. The ones I'm wearing today happen to be the University of Oregon colors. If you're from Eugene, it's almost a mandatory uniform. Sure, I look like a geek, but I doubt that's what's going on in her head.

Crap, I don't know what to do. Should I stay here and let her work through it on her own? Should I pretend that nothing is going on, or should I say something funny to break the tension?

In the middle of my very awkward mental conversation with myself, Mother Nature comes to the rescue. A very noisy seagull lands at Tara's feet and pecks the sand in front of her. I start laughing at the bird's antics, but Tara's body language shows that she doesn't find it quite as amusing. She's adopted the "ready" pose I remember from my martial arts training.

I grab my jacket I'd laid aside before stepping to the start line and shoo the bird away. "Now that the pregame entertainment has concluded, shall we proceed?" I ask with a smirk.

"Aidan, you're such a jerk!" Tara screams at me. "You know I'm afraid of birds. Did you bury something in the sand to make the stupid bird do that?"

I hold my hands up in front of me in protest as I declare, "No practical joke this time, Gracie. I wouldn't do that to you. Okay, maybe I would've as a kid, but not now. Are you ready to race?"

Tara throws her hands up in frustration and growls, "Okay, fine. I need to run off some of my tension."

Although it's totally against my nature to let a good line like that go unanswered, in the interest of keeping peace and not ticking Tara off any more, I let it slide.

"I'm ready anytime you are, Gracie." I crouch down into my runner's stance once more.

From behind me, I hear Tara shout, "Go!"

I take off at a dead sprint. I know from our childhood Tara does not appreciate being pandered to. If she challenges you to a contest, she expects you to give 110%. The quickest way to lose her respect is to expect less of her because she looks fragile. Underneath that fragile façade beats the heart of a warrior. I'm mentally counting off the seconds in my head. She padded my lead by far more than ten seconds.

The sound of her footsteps behind me is absorbed by the sand and wind. Her timekeeping puts me at a distinct advantage — or it would if I stood a chance of winning this race. In this particular athletic endeavor, Tara has a slight advantage over me. Although I run to keep in shape, it's never been my passion. When I get her on my playground, the odds will even up. I can't wait to introduce her to my sport.

Soon, I see a blur over my left shoulder as she flies by. Running is an awkward sport for most people. Runner's eyes squint, their cheeks puff out and their mouths are often distorted. Yet, somehow Tara looks like she's merely pausing between shots of a high-fashion photo-shoot. The only sign Tara is expending any effort are the small puffs of air that appear as mist around her mouth as she runs. She reaches the large log at the end of the small beach area. She sits down triumphantly and digs out a cell phone from her pocket. She points it in my direction and clicks a series of pictures as I eventually reach her perch.

I'm trying not to show how winded I am, but it's been a while since I've run at a full sprint, and even longer since I've run on sand.

Tara looks up at me with a wide grin on her face as she asks, "What took you so long, slowpoke?"

"Who says my view wasn't better from back here? That may have been my strategy all along. You're not the only one that's sneaky," I reply with a teasing grin.

"Aidan Jarith O'Brien, did your mother teach you that the way to a girl's heart is to talk about her backside?" she scolds, tongue-in-cheek.

I squirm a little and blush a lot. "No, ma'am. In fact, if you told her, or Delores, they would take away my card for chivalry. I spent too many hours with Delores and her 'unofficial finishing school for gentlemen' to lose that honor. I deeply apologize for any offense."

Tara puts her finger up to her lip. I remember how hard she fought to break her habit of biting her nails. "Do you really think I have a nice butt?" she asks curiously. "I always thought I was too skinny for that."

"Men are visual creatures. We're just wired that way. We mean no offense, but it's natural for us to look at women. I appreciate women of all sizes. I'm probably breaking the man code by telling you this—but, when I see a woman, the first things I check out are her eyes and her smile. Then, my eyes naturally travel down her body to her breasts and her butt. Tara, I can honestly tell you that you are lacking in none of those areas."

Tara blushes a dusky red. "I can't believe I'm having this conversation with you. You used to make underarm farting noises at me, and you're the little brother of my dance partner."

"First of all, I'm taller than my 'big' brother now. Secondly, we decided *you* were the underarm fart champ, so that's bogus too." I argue. "Do you have any other reasons I can't think you're sexy?"

A look of profound sadness crosses Tara's face and she wrings her hands in front off her as she tries to explain, "Aidan, I don't think you get it. I'm screwed up. I'm not normal now —"

I sign for her to stop, "No."

She looks startled. "No?" she asks.

"*You* are perfectly normal, Tara. What was done to

you was sick and screwed up. There's a difference. If I ever find that sick bum, he'll know what screwed up means," I answer, anger toward her attacker coloring my voice.

Tara, turns away sighing. "I wish it could be that simple, but it isn't. Warren Jones changed me that day, and nothing will ever undo that."

"What if I helped build some positive memories with you? Can we pack your brain so full of great stuff so it crowds out the bad stuff?" I ask, intent on finding an answer.

"I honestly don't know if that could ever work, Aidan. I haven't had many positive experiences to plug into my life." She digs her toe into the sand.

I mentally kick myself. I knew she was barefoot. I had no business challenging her to a race. When am I ever going to learn to engage my brain before I shoot off my mouth?

I place my hands on her shoulders and she visibly flinches. I want to kill that slimeball. There used to be a time when, if I did that, she would've given me a hug. This time, I don't immediately drop my hands; instead I turn her gently in my arms and give her a crooked smile from a few inches away. "Well, Gracie … I'm thinking we probably don't have to plan it all right up front. If we build one memory at a time, soon we'll have a group. Then, that group will become a collection," I suggest.

She sniffles as a tear rolls down her face. She wipes it with her sleeve. Instinctively, I reach up to brush away the tear with my thumb. It's a small victory when she doesn't pull away.

"You make it all sound so easy," she replies in a hoarse whisper. For a brief moment, she leans her face into my hand before pulling away.

"Gracie, it's always been easy between us. Don't let him take that too. How about we start small? I lost fair and square, so I owe you breakfast. If I remember correctly, coffee and a strawberry filled donut are your speed, right?" I try to sound casual. I don't think I've ever had so much riding on a single coffee date.

There's a lull in the howling winds and the seagulls scatter. The sound of my heartbeat seems thunderously loud even in contrast to the waves as I wait for her to reply.

Abruptly, Tara sits down on the large piece of driftwood and buries her hands in her pockets. She peers up at me through her long eyelashes. "I guess it's a good thing I worked up such an appetite."

Chapter Seven

Tara

IT'S ODD TO BE hanging out with Aidan again. It's almost as if my body and mind have some form of muscle memory when it comes to him. We've fallen into our old patterns of friendship in a way I never thought possible. I'm more at ease with him than I've been with anyone in years. It's weird, even after all of this time, I find it easier to open up with Aidan than the Girlfriend Posse.

We decide to walk to one of the little restaurants in the touristy part of town. As we prepare to sit in the booth, Aidan helps me take off my jacket. It's such a courtly thing to do that it makes me smile.

"What are you laughing at, Gracie? I haven't even spilled any food yet," Aidan looks around the restaurant to see if he's missed something.

"Nothing, really." I'm embarrassed to be caught openly gawking at him. "I was just wondering when you went from leaving earthworms in my shoes to being such a gentleman."

As we settle into the booth and the waitress leaves

menus, Aidan responds, "I will never live my past down, will I? I was pretty mean to you sometimes. I'm so sorry for that." Aidan glances away with a look of shame on his face.

I nudge him with my knee under the table, to get his attention. "It might surprise you to hear this, but I don't really remember anything all that terrible. I wasn't a really big fan of the stink bombs and the hidden pop rocks, but other than that, you were pretty benign."

Aidan shakes his head at the memory. "You must've thought I was a holy terror," he observes with a grimace.

"Are you sure we're remembering the same childhood? Because I remember you helping me learn all my dance numbers and taking care of me when I didn't feel well. The thing that stands out the most in my mind is that you were my friend. You often stood up for me when no one else did."

At that moment, the waitress comes back to take our order. Not much has changed. Aidan still eats enough for three people. I'm losing track of his gargantuan order. I hope the waitress is having an easier time than I am. Taking pity on the poor waitress, I keep it simple and order just a jelly filled donut and a cup of black coffee.

After the waitress leaves, Aidan picks up the conversation as if she'd never been there. "If I remember correctly, you did your fair share of sticking up for me too — or at least covering for my mistakes," Aidan counters, a rosy hue flushing his cheeks.

"Well, we were like two peas in a pod. I don't think that teachers ever saw us apart unless we had to be for class. Who looks out for you these days? Do you have a girlfriend?"

The look of shock on Aidan's face is priceless. "Do you really think I would be working so hard to get you to go out with me if I had a girlfriend?" he sputters indignantly.

I shrug indifferently. "Some guys do."

Aidan sits straighter in his chair and looks me directly in the eyes. "Well, not this one."

I study him for signs of deception. Although I don't see any obvious tells, I really wish my 'gift' worked better in my own life. I'd like to have a sense of the outcome of the game before I play. Sadly, my intuitive senses don't seem to work for my personal life.

I can't stop the feeling of relief that goes through me after I receive his reassurances. Since this is Aidan we're talking about, I go ahead and ask the question that's been bothering me since last night when he tried to ask me out, "Why?"

Aidan looks perplexed at my question. "Why what?" he inquires.

"Why are you still single? Have you developed some other strange habits besides underarm fart contests?" I ask.

Aidan pretends to remove a sword from his chest. "Geez, that's a little harsh Gracie; especially since you were part of those."

"You're dodging the question," I narrow my eyes and glare at him.

"No, I'm not. I don't really have a good answer. I've been living from place to place and working in temporary jobs. Women don't find that trait particularly attractive once you're over eighteen," he responds candidly. "I guess I never really felt the need to push the issue because I've been so focused on getting my music career going."

"What does your mom think about that?" I ask. "I'm surprised she doesn't have you and Rory in some sort of competition to produce grandchildren."

Aidan chuckles. "Well, it's not for lack of trying. She's been dropping hints for a long time."

"So what do you do about that? As I recall, your parents are pretty persuasive and not easily dissuaded."

Aidan grins at me and confesses, "I beg Rory and Renée to have another baby to take the pressure off of me."

I arch my eyebrow at him in a look of mock outrage. "Tell me, exactly how long do you expect this strategy to last? There's a finite limit to the number of kids Renée can have."

"So far, I've been lucky because she likes to have kids. Much to my surprise, Rory makes a really decent dad too."

"Well, eventually your luck will run out. Then what are you going to do?" I ask, curious about how he feels about kids.

Aidan hitches his shoulder up into a half shrug as he replies, "I don't know, I guess I'll deal with it all then. What about you? Do you have any suitors I need to worry about?" he inquires.

"Very funny Aidan," I retort, dryly. "What part of I don't date and have to virtually be dragged out of my apartment to have any fun, didn't you understand?"

Aidan blinks about three times before he says anything, "You never know, you could have someone out there who has always had a colossal crush on you and just isn't brave enough to say anything," Aidan proposes.

"I could, but it's unlikely. I'm not very crush-worthy. I'm more like 'crazy cat lady' than 'girl you take home to mom'," I say with a small self-deprecating smile.

"I don't know about that," Aidan argues. "My mom likes you just fine. But, even if my parents didn't like you, it wouldn't matter to me. I'm on 'Team Tara', remember?"

The warm fuzzy feeling I get from Aidan's words is a little frightening, but so nice. I'm trying to stay in the moment and just enjoy these moments for what they are. I realize Aidan was right. Maybe I will be able to push back the bad memories by surrounding them with good ones.

I look down shyly before I meet his gaze, "I like that you are on Team Tara," I admit, feeling awkward.

Aidan gives me a crooked smile. "I'm glad I'm on Team Tara too because now you can help me eat all this food. I don't know what I was thinking."

"I don't know either. But, our waitress thinks you have a tapeworm," I tease.

"What? How do you know that?"

I blush. "Well, I might have eavesdropped while she was chatting with her coworker."

"Why was she even talking about me?"

I roll my eyes. "You're a cute guy Aidan. Girls talk

about you all the time."

"Do *you* talk about me?" Aidan leans forward, putting me on the spot.

"No, you haven't made the agenda yet, but I have a feeling the next time my friends get together you will be the number one topic of discussion." I inform him, not entirely in jest.

"Just be kind please, I won't be there to defend myself," Aidan jokes.

"I take no responsibility for what gets said or not said in the Girlfriend Posse; it's confidential," I remark with a grin as the restaurant staff starts to clean a ceiling fan a couple of feet from me.

I look at Aidan and grab my purse as I whisper hoarsely, "I'm sorry I can't stay. I've got bad allergies and I'll get really sick if I stay here."

"Tara, wait just a minute and let me take care of the bill," Aidan replies.

"I'm sorry," I say as gracefully as I can. "I really need to go, but I'll touch base with you later." I'm trying hard to hold it together in such a public place. I feel my heart racing and sweat running down my back. I don't know who I was fooling when I thought that maybe I could lead a normal life.

As I'm fleeing, I see Aidan throw a $50 bill on the table and scribble on a napkin, "Keep the change," he yells at the waitress, "I left you money on your top in your section. You may want to collect it."

I can hear Aidan run up behind me as I'm jogging away from the restaurant like a deranged person.

"Tara, are you okay?" Aidan asks when he catches up to my side. "You're looking a little shaky. What happened? I thought we were having a good time."

I sigh in defeat. "We were until I smelled the dusting spray they were using at the restaurant. When Warren Jones raped me, he smashed my face down into the seat of his car and held it there until I couldn't breathe. Whatever he used to clean his leather seats on his fancy car smelled almost the same as what they were using in there. I told you, none of this makes sense and it's irrational — but my body can't seem to forget. I just had to get out of there. I'm sorry I ruined breakfast."

"Tara, you ruined nothing," he insists. "I had a great time. I was going to leave soon anyway, I need to get on the road. I have to work my day job tonight. I'd like to get home in time to take a nap since my bed was about a foot too short for me and my tips suck when I wait tables tired."

"Are you sure?" I press anxiously.

"Gracie, it's all good. Let's celebrate today. We had a great run and a delicious breakfast. That's a victory over the scum ball because today you reclaimed your freedom."

A tear runs down my face as I realize what Aidan says is true. Aidan leans in and sweetly kisses my forehead.

"Still, I wanted to make *more* progress," I protest wistfully. "You know this isn't about you, right? I trust you. I just have to convince my body to listen to logic instead of panic."

Aidan pulls me in for a hug and whispers in my ear,

"This isn't a race, Tara. I'm here for you until you tell me to go. There will be other breakfasts."

I nod mutely because I have too many emotions welling up to speak. "I'd like that," I sign in ASL.

Aidan signs back, "Thanks for being a bright spot in my life today. I'll call you."

━━━━◆◗━━━━

As Heather's 1957 Bel Air convertible speeds down Highway 101, I'm trying to corral my scattered thoughts. I've lost track of whatever Heather is trying to tell me about the happy couple. I'm hoping she doesn't notice my inattention. Unfortunately, true to form, she nails me with a sharp glance. "What's with you this morning? I know you're not usually as chatty as I am, but you're making Tibetan monks look like Oprah Winfrey over there."

I shrug noncommittally. "Nothing, I've just got a lot on my mind."

Heather grins knowingly. "Uh huh, and I bet that lotta something is about six-foot-two with hair that would make any woman jealous and hands that make you wish you were an instrument that could be played," she teases.

I can't help myself from blushing. Heather's remarks are always so outrageous, yet so spot on. "I'm not going to confirm or deny your statement," I answer stiffly, but I can't keep the mirth out of my eyes.

Heather laughs. "I figured as much when you missed our celebratory mimosas this morning. What I can't figure out is how it all ties into the big blob of strawberry jam you have on the front of your shirt. You

96

hardly ever eat sweets. What's up with that? I have to practically hogtie you to get you to try any of the pastries or cakes I make."

I slump down in my seat. I don't even know how to begin to explain to her all that's happened in the last twenty-four hours. Heather and Kiera know about the rape in the general sense of the word. They understand something bad happened to me, and they know some days are better than others. They know I don't date. Even though I consider them my best friends after Aidan, I haven't told them all the horrific details of my ordeal. At first, I didn't tell them because I was ashamed about what happened. After I worked through the shame with my rape counselor, I elected not to tell them because I didn't want them living with the mental pictures and the psychic dirt they leave behind. I've done my best to encourage Heather and Kiera to take self-defense classes and have top-notch security without having to completely erode their sense of personal safety. To this day, I'm still not sure I've done enough to protect them. I guess I wanted to shelter them from it all. As hard as things are for me now, I've actually made real progress. It took me months to share my story publicly and far longer to take back my identity by calling my rapist by his name. I still wonder if I should have been more insistent and told my whole story in gory detail, not pulling any punches.

I weigh my options carefully. I know Heather deserves my trust. I'm just afraid her perception of me will change once she knows the whole story. I swallow hard and pivot in my seat so I'm facing Heather as I speak, my voice heavy with trepidation, "I'm not really sure you'll want to hear my answer. It's long, complicated, and really ugly."

Heather swings her head around so fast I'm afraid she's going to crash her car. "What did that rat-bleep do to you? My family is Italian, they have connections you don't want to know about," she threatens.

"What did *who* do? AJ? Oh geez, no! He'd never hurt me. I've known him since elementary school." Even as I explain that to Heather, I realize the starkly simple truth of that statement. Aidan is many things. He is loud, funny, effervescent, irreverent, and sometimes totally inappropriate. Still, the one thing Aidan could never be is intentionally cruel. Now, if I can only get my irrational, panicky side to remember that.

Heather looks confused. "AJ? I thought his name was Aidan."

I chuckle as I clarify, "Oh it is. But I sometimes call him AJ, and he sometimes calls me Gracie. It's a thing from our childhood."

Heather shakes her head in dismay. "What is it with you lovebirds and all these nicknames?" she teases.

I snicker. "Gee, I don't know, Gidget, why don't you ask the Cowboy, the next time you see him?"

Heather turns bright red as she insists, "For the record, I did not ask that oversize G.I. Joe to call me Gidget. He came up with it all on his own. In fact, I told him to knock it off. The big old oaf refuses to address me by my name." Her eyes are flashing with outrage.

I grin at her as I remark, "Uh huh … and the reason you call him Cowboy instead of Ty or Tyler is what exactly?"

Heather sticks her tongue out at me. "Now you hush. We're supposed to be discussing your love life, not mine. Now, where were we?"

"Heather, I'm serious. Are you sure you want to talk about this? It's not going to be fun and it might change the way you think about me forever —"

Heather holds up her hand to stop me from speaking. "This might be a good time to remind you I only look like a ditzy blonde. Do you think Kiera and I have been your friends for as many years as we have without knowing there's some deep, ugly pain buried deep inside you? We figured you'd tell us when you felt the time was right."

I swallow hard as I look out the front window, taking in the Oregon coastline as it goes flying by.

"Pain is pain," Heather continues. Her words catch my attention. I turn my gaze toward her. "The precise details aren't really our business unless you choose to tell us. Nothing you share with me will make me stop being your friend, so you can just stop worrying about that right now. After all, once you're in the Girlfriend Posse, you're in for life."

I blink in shock as I process the passion in her voice. I guess I've been so busy monitoring what I think everyone else needs. It failed to occur to me that someone might be doing the same for me.

"It's just that you and Kiera both have a bunch of family drama and I don't want to pile anything else on," I confess cringing at the words even as they leave my mouth.

Heather studies the highway for a while then

glances back at me, the pain clearly evident in her eyes as she asks, "Do you really believe Kiera and I think our problems are more important than yours?"

"No! It's not like that at all. I was just trying to protect you guys from my nightmare. You don't need to know the garbage that goes on in my head! Trust me; I'm just trying to protect your happy."

Heather sighs and shakes her head in disbelief. "Oh honey, I really wish you hadn't tried so hard to be tough. I know a lot more about what you're going through than you think I do," she responds.

My stomach clinches with fear at her words, "Oh no, not you too —" I whisper in horror.

Heather places her hand lightly on my arm as she replies, "No, I didn't mean to scare you. It feels almost as devastating though. It happened to my sister after somebody slipped her a roofie at a party during her first week of college. She's never been the same."

Even though I'm well aware that in America someone is sexually assaulted every two seconds, I still flinch at the idea of someone attacking Madison. I've only met her a couple of times, but I would've never guessed that the cool and sophisticated journalist is a part of the same unwilling survivors club as me.

"Heather, I'm so sorry. I didn't know. Still, she seems to be doing well —" I start to say, but quickly change my mind. "I know better than to say crap like that. People can put up all sorts of fronts which have nothing to do with reality." I'm uncharacteristically at a loss for words.

She interrupts me, her hands gesturing wildly in

frustration, "That's just it! I can't tell how she's doing. We don't talk about real things any more. It's all surface talk. I don't know how she really feels about anything. I'm so worried about her."

I reach up and squeeze her hand as I carefully formulate my comments. It feels so strange to be talking about all of this. I haven't spoken out loud about it since I was in my support group a few years ago, and now I've had three conversations in three days. "Well, I can't speak for Madison, but I have many more days that seem normal than days which aren't," I respond, in an effort to cheer her up. Heather is usually unfailingly upbeat and optimistic. Seeing her so distressed is disconcerting.

Heather arches an eyebrow at me. "Let's say for argument's sake, I believe you. What kind of day are you having today?"

I glance out the car window and start chewing on my thumbnail as I try to evade the answer, "Umm —"

"No, wait," Heather interrupts "I can tell it's not a good day. You're usually so calm you make a yoga instructor look like they need to take Ritalin, but today you're so antsy, you can barely stand to ride in this car and you probably trashed the manicure we just got yesterday. I can tell that things are not right in your world. You might as well tell me what's going on."

"Okay, but you need to understand that I had a lot of stuff going on before my rape even occurred. So, my reaction was really extreme and Madison is probably coping much better than I ever did."

Heather nods. "Oh, I know everybody's story is different."

I give Heather a wry grin. "Unfortunately, my life story reads like a badly written soap opera script. My parents had a really epic love story. It was the kind that really good movies are written about. But, my dad was labeled as a dissident by the Chinese government and killed right before I turned six. I remember being so angry that he missed my birthday party. After he died, my mom forgot how to live. Unfortunately, it took her body eight years to catch up with her brain. My only salvation during that time was my dancing. I was a competitive a dancer."

Heather shoots me a confused look, as she asks, "Dancing, not art?"

I shrug. It's weird bringing these two parts of my life together. To me, they're intertwined. However, Heather and Kiera didn't know about the dancing and Aidan didn't know about the art. I guess I really am two very broken halves of a whole. "I didn't start the art stuff until I stopped dancing. It's like I have a very bright line which divides my life into before and after."

"Anyway, you met Aidan at the wedding last night," I continue. "He was the little brother of my dance partner. But, he was so much more to me back then. He doesn't know this, but some days he was the only reason I bothered to get out of bed when the sadness of my dad's death threatened to overtake me. None of the grown ups in my life ever wanted to talk about Daniel Isamu. People seemed to think if they stopped talking about him, I'd suddenly forget he ever existed. It doesn't work that way. I was a daddy's little girl. Nothing would change that."

Heather nods. "People tried to do the same thing when my cousin died."

"Aidan didn't care what people thought was 'appropriate' for me to talk about. We spoke about everything and nothing. He let me talk, laugh and cry. He tried so hard to make sure most of it was laughter. I used to try to match his level of intensity. I soon realized it was an exercise in futility. So, I just went with it. He became my personal entertainer and I, his biggest fan," I explain, finding comfort in the memory. "When I got back from dance camp, Aidan was gone without a word. I didn't see him again until last night."

Heather gasps and her eyes tear up. "That's so sad. You must have been devastated. Did you ever figure out what happened? Why did he leave? Did you ever try to find him? How did he react when he saw you?" she ambushes me with questions.

Suddenly, a peculiar expression crosses her face. "Oh ... wait! Now I understand what happened when he screwed up the wedding march at Kiera's wedding! That's the moment he recognized you. How romantic is that?" she exclaims excitedly. "So, what's the problem? It's clear from the way he treated you at the reception that he still cares about you. The man was ready to slay dragons if anyone so much as touched you. He was so worried when you passed out. I thought he was going to call the ambulance. It was all Jeff could do to convince him he's a trained EMT and that you were fine. I thought Jeff was going to have to produce his credentials on the spot."

"Oh man," I let out a sigh of frustration before I haltingly continue my explanation, "if you thought I was weird before, this is going to take it to a whole other level." I pick at loose strings on the bottom of my sweatshirt.

Heather clicks her tongue at me as she chides me, "You do realize that we're driving down the coast in a vintage cherry red Bel Air and I'm dressed like Rosie the Riveter, right? It's not as if you're cornering the market on being odd. So, stop worrying about what I'm going to think and just tell me."

I take a deep breath and decide to tell the unvarnished truth. "So, you know how Aidan picked me up and held me last night?"

Heather shrugs and nods.

"Well, aside from a few martial art competitions, that's the first time I've been touched by a guy since I was sixteen. I was raped when I was fourteen. I went through a stage where I thought if I had enough 'normal' sex, I could somehow undo what had happened to me and erase the past. When it didn't work, I stopped letting people into my personal space."

"Oh Tara, I'm sorry," she whispers.

"My mom died right after I was raped. People who hadn't been around during the eight years that it took her to die, suddenly pretended to care. It literally made me sick. At first, I was so angry. I stopped hugging people. Then, I stopped shaking their hands. After a while, it got difficult to look them in the eye. It wasn't long before it became a struggle for me to even leave the house. Since I had been taking care of myself for so long, it wasn't difficult for me to prove to the court that I had the right to be emancipated."

Tears are gathering at the corners of Heather's eyes as she starts to make a comment. I shake my head to stop her. I need to finish before I lose my nerve.

Taking a deep breath, I continue my sad monologue, "Eventually, I had to earn a living and I joined the carnival circuit. Initially, they played on my exotic looks and used me as a fortuneteller. I was never very comfortable in that role. My mom was part Native American and as you know, I have certain sensitivities when it comes to people's emotions. I felt like playing a psychic was taking advantage of those gifts. So, I worked hard on my artistic skills and became a face painter so that people could pay me for something legitimate."

Heather chuckles. "I've seen your spooky self in action. I can understand how you would feel that way. Your ability to read people is definitely a God-given talent. The rest of it sucks though. But, what does all of that have to do with that Aidan guy. He doesn't seem like he'd be the type of guy to care."

"He probably isn't," I reluctantly admit. "The problem is with me. I don't know if I'll ever be able to handle a relationship. The sad thing is, up until yesterday. I wasn't even sure I wanted one. Seeing, Kiera and Jeff fall in love has been hard because I know I'll probably never have that in my life. Being around Mindy and Becca has convinced me I really want to be a mom even if I can't have a guy around. I'm not sure how I'm going to make all that work yet. I'm still figuring it out."

Heather glances over at me with an incredulous look on her face. "So, let me get this straight — you like this guy and he obviously likes you, but you're not going to give the relationship a chance. Why the heck not?"

"Why should he have to deal with all my emotional baggage?" I shoot back, in frustration. "I couldn't even make it through a simple breakfast this morning!"

"I understand where you're coming from Tara. Still, shouldn't that be Aidan's choice?"

"You don't know all the stuff he's been through. I argue.

"Do I need to?" Heather asks, confused.

"As a child he got sick and went deaf!" I explain, emphatically.

"Seriously? He's a deaf piano player?

How cool is that? You're a sign language interpreter, so what's the problem? It seems like fate to me. Aren't you always preaching we can't fight our ultimate destiny?"

"The problem is that his life is already complicated enough without adding my issues to the top of his pile," I insist, feeling agitated.

"Well, it seems to me that anyone who's been through all that and can still be the phenomenal musician he is, would have the emotional integrity to deal with whatever life throws at you guys. Are you sure you're not throwing this one back a little too soon?"

"Yes. No. I don't know!" I respond in rapid succession.

Heather chortles. "Well, that's about as clear as a set of aviator glasses at a mudboggin' contest," she remarks.

I look at her helplessly and throw my hands up in the air. "I don't know what to do. This isn't just any guy.

This is Aidan. Then again, I don't know if he's the same guy I knew as a kid. What if he's completely changed?"

"What if he hasn't?" Heather asks softly.

"What if he hasn't," I repeat to myself. My hands start to shake.

"Honey, what do you want to do?" Heather asks after a minute.

I sit up straight in my seat and grab her hand for support as I answer, my voice steady and forceful, "I want to take my life back from Warren Jones. I want to be a typical, average, and boring woman. I want to go to lunch with Aidan O'Brien. I want to try again — I'm not ready to give up."

Heather examines me from top to bottom and smirks. "Well, many people consider me a gifted make up artist, but even *I* could never make you typical, average or boring. You'll have to settle for stunning."

"Oh shut up!" I retort. "Are you going to help me get ready for my date, or not? I haven't done this in more than a decade. I need all the help I can get."

"Don't worry, the Girlfriend Posse has got you covered," she answers.

———— ⬤ ————

Kiera studies my outfit carefully. "What did Aidan's text message say again?"

"He was very cryptic. His instructions were: "Rest well. Dress in layers. Comfortable shoes. Extra socks. Come hungry. Bring imagination and camera. Be ready at 6:30 AM. The road to happiness can be long and windy.

PS: Thanks for spending the day with me.

— AO"

I recite the text message back to her verbatim. I've parsed it out countless times trying to find some hidden meaning.

Kiera's eyebrows go flying toward her hairline as she asks in surprise, "Extra socks? He doesn't have a weird foot fetish, does he?"

I giggle in response to her outlandish suggestion. "No, at least not that I know of. Maybe we're going roller-skating. I always wanted to do that as a kid, but my coaches thought it was too dangerous."

"Take lots of pictures for us. Now that Jeff and I have the girls, we don't have very many mystery dates. We have to live vicariously through yours," Kiera teases.

I nod. "I don't know Kiera, I might be too nervous to take any pictures." I dry the palms of my hands on my jeans. "Are you guys sure these look okay?" I ask as I look in the mirror and try to examine my backside to see if they're too tight.

Heather gives me a hug and slips an extra hair-band in my pocket. "Relax honey. You look gorgeous. The poor man is going to have to roll up his tongue and stick it back in his mouth when he sees you. You've got Ty's phone number in your phone, right? He'll be right there if you need him. All you need to do is call."

After Kiera got home from her honeymoon, I finally sat down with Kiera and Heather and told them the whole story in painful, excruciating detail. I knew Kiera wouldn't be judgmental because of the nature of her job as a social worker. Perhaps that's why I waited so long to tell her. I didn't want to become one more statistic for her or another person to add to her caseload. Yet, I should've known better. I know Kiera takes sexual assault very personally as she had issues with abuse and her own family.

True to form, the Girlfriend Posse has been amazing. However, I've also received phenomenal support from Kiera's husband, Jeff and his best friend, Ty, who is an officer with the sheriff's department.

"I really think I'll be fine." I assert. "The Aidan I know is a nice guy. Given all the threats he's recently received as a former Supreme Court Justice, Justice Gardner wouldn't have hired him to play at Kiera's wedding if he hadn't done a thorough background check. Besides, I already went to breakfast with Aidan and he was a perfect gentleman."

Just then, the doorbell rings. I rush to answer the door before the others can get there. Who knows how long their inquisition could take? As I open the door, the sight of Aidan casually dressed in well worn Levi's and a thermal Henley shirt is enough to take my breath away.

I hear Heather's voice behind me, "Oh Lordy, is this not too cute for words? They match. You two go on and have fun now. We won't stay up for you."

Aidan tips an imaginary hat at them as he drawls, "It was a pleasure meeting you both ma'am. I can't guarantee I'll have her back by a decent hour. I'm going to just play it by ear. I'll have her call and let you know." With that pronouncement, he whisks me out the front door.

As we walk down the driveway toward the street, I hiss at Aidan, "Why did you tell them that? You made it sound like we're going to spend the night together or something."

Aidan chuckles at my outrage, "Relax, Gracie I was kidding ... mostly. You know me; I'm a spur of the moment type of guy. I don't like to set my plans in cement or anything," he explains.

"Well, thanks a lot. I may know that about you, but my friends don't. Now, they think you have a night of debauchery planned."

"Hmm, if that's one of my options, I might just change my approach to this, 'no planning ahead' idea," he teases.

"Aidan Jarith! What would your mother think of your depraved mind?" I say with mock outrage.

"My deprived mind? The debauchery was all your idea, gorgeous Gracie," he quips.

The early morning dawn hides my bright red blush. We stop in front of a Volkswagen bus that looks like the sixties chewed it up and spit it out. When he pulls out a set of keys with a peace symbol and unlocks the van, I burst out laughing.

When I'm finally able to catch my breath, I wheeze. "Are you serious Aidan? Do you really drive a Scooby-Doo van that looks like a Grateful Dead T-shirt threw up on it?"

Aidan shrugs. "I'm a musician and I haul gear around all the time. Besides, it suits me. Why? Does it offend you?"

I shoot him a conspiratorial grin. "Do we have a second?"

He nods and by force of habit, I link my first finger with his and drag him around the side of my house to reveal what's under my carport. Together we pull back the layers of blue tarp.

When Aidan sees my baby, he lets out a low wolf-whistle. "'73?"

I shake my head. I'm impressed by his knowledge of vintage Volkswagens. "It's a '72."

"Wow! I've seen these in magazines and on television, but I've never known anybody who actually had one. I can't believe you have a 1972 Super Baja. Did you do the airbrushing? It's amazing," Aidan gushes.

I flush a dusky red at his compliment. "I did. After my mom died, I traveled the carnival circuit for a while. This was one of the few things I cherish that belonged to both of my parents. I made a deal with the owner of the troupe. He said if I could make it look like a clown car, he'd allow me to bring it with us. So, I made the base coat, a sparkly lime green color and added daisies and colorful butterflies to it."

Aidan runs his fingers over each flower and butterfly, tracing the intricate outline of each figure. He mutters half to himself, "Tara, you would've made a hell of a tattoo artist. Your eye for detail is amazing and your perspective is right on. So, why aren't you driving this work of art?" he asks with open curiosity, his head in the trunk of the car.

"There's a couple of reasons. First, there is some sort of issue with the exhaust and I need to find a part.

Second, my hours just got cut at work, so even if it were running, I can't afford the insurance on it right now."

Technically, I guess I could afford to get it fixed now. Though for so many reasons, I don't want to think about that right now. I try to bring my mind back to the present.

Aidan takes one last look before he covers it up. "That's a shame, because a car like this deserves to be driven. Thanks for showing it to me. Are you ready to get this show on the road?"

"Sure." As we walk back to his van, much to my mortification, I blurt out a random observation. "Hey Aidan ... I'm so glad you haven't turned into some shallow pop star like Justin Bieber and started driving a gas guzzling Humvee or school bus yellow Ferrari."

"Me too, Gracie. Me too," he responds as he helps me into his van.

Chapter Eight

Aidan

I TRY TO WIPE my hands surreptitiously on a rag next to the seat in the van. I don't think I've ever been so anxious for a date to go well. I feel like I'm balancing on the edge of one of the massive arches in the Moab Desert in Utah, and I'm about to drop over the side without knowing if my rope will reach the bottom.

Speaking of rock climbing, I know today's choice of date is unconventional at best. When we were kids, Tara tended to worry herself sick over small details. I figure the date will go better for us if her mind is kept so busy she has no time to sweat the small stuff. Of course, this could all be one giant miscalculation and it may all blow up in my face.

For today to work, she has to trust me. I'm not sure she trusts anyone. She may trust herself even less than she trusts me. I don't want to screw this up. It's a huge gamble. I hope I'm doing the right thing. I'm still thinking about today's plans when she pokes me in the ribs with her elbow.

I let out a startled bark of laughter. I can't help it. I am insanely ticklish. It's freakin' embarrassing to be a grown man and nearly pee yourself when someone touches your ribs.

"What?" I snap, more sharply than I intend, mortified that one of my Achilles heels has been revealed so early.

"Geez, AJ!" she says in response to my surly reply. "I was just going to ask you if I could have a hint about where we're going yet. It sounds like you could use an infusion of coffee first."

"That's a great idea," I concede, feeling like a world-class jerk. "I saw a little coffee place as you head out of town. Are they any good?"

"They make great coffee and their hot chocolate is even better. They serve a decent bagel too."

"So what do you want this morning?"

"Well, since you got me up at the rooster's butt crack of dawn, I'd like a large black coffee, please. Can you ask them to put an extra shot of espresso in it for me?"

"While it's enlightening to find out that roosters have butt cracks, I'm afraid I can't do that," I answer, regretfully.

She does a double take worthy of a Saturday morning cartoon as she questions me about my answer. "I'm sorry? You can't what?"

"Have the barista put extra caffeine in your drink — it might mess with our plans for the rest of the day."

Tara groans. "I changed my mind. I don't think I

want to know what we're going to do. I don't suppose it's something as simple as dinner and a movie?"

I chuckle at her perceptive guess. "When have you ever known me to do simple? Did you really think I was going to start on our first date?" I tease.

Tara grabs the red baseball cap from the seat beside her, threads her long braid through it, and pulls it down over her eyes. "I'm afraid to see where we're going. I think I'll just take a nap since you refuse to do the humane thing and give me a decent dose of caffeine. Besides, technically, this is our second date. You would've been safe picking something mundane. There's no need to show off," she argues.

I reach over and flip the bill of the baseball cap up as we pull up into the coffee line. I look at her beautiful face and arresting eyes. "Gracie, if you were mine for sixty minutes or sixty years, I'd never want to stop showing off for you."

I sound like a huge sap, but it's true. All those years, I watched her pine after my brother, I could never figure out what the attraction was. My brother is a decent guy, now that he's found Renee. But back in the day, to call him a narcissistic butt-head was putting it nicely. He barely knew Tara existed, and when he did notice her, he was a jerk. I may have been a kid, but I could recognize what an amazing gift she was. I can't imagine someone not treasuring her.

"You're sweet," Tara replies with a small smile. "Although, you might find out that I'm not the cute, innocent girl you remember. I have lots of hard edges now. I've also got some holes that may never be filled."

I smile at her analogy. "So, basically you're telling me you're a thunder egg? Quiet and unassuming on the surface, but stunningly beautiful with a heart of gold in the middle."

Tara rolls her eyes. "I'm not sure which would be more challenging — arguing with Jeff, who's the lawyer, or you who crafts words into lyrics. Something tells me I should put my money on you. Jeff has to make his words follow the rules, whereas yours can go as far as your creativity takes you."

"It depends. Are you going to argue every time I call you gorgeous?" I raise an eyebrow.

I can see a faint flush on Tara's cheeks as I hand her the coffee and bagel with strawberry cream cheese.

Tara chews on her thumbnail as she mutters, "Well, maybe not *every* time."

"In that case, I suppose the amount of arguing is up for negotiation." I tease.

I somehow manage to get more of the cream cheese on my hands than on the napkin. By force of habit, I lick the excess off my thumb. I look over to see if Tara has caught my lapse in manners. Sure enough, she is watching my hands with fascination. At first, I'm completely mortified. Then, I take a closer look and I notice there is heat in her eyes. I try not to move a muscle, but inside, I'm doing cartwheels. This is the first sign I've seen to indicate that she sees me as anything other than the little kid she remembers. Already, this day is looking up.

I look out the window as I pull on to Highway 99 and head toward Corvallis. "It's going to be a perfect day out there. Are you ready?"

"How can I possibly know if I'm ready when I don't know what we're doing?"

"Patience and faith, Gracie. Patience and faith. All will be revealed soon."

"I guess I'll just have to take your word for it. It's just too early to argue about it." She settles back in the van seat, tucking her feet up under her, criss-cross style. "So, do you do the musician gig full time now?"

I let out a wry laugh. "I guess it depends on who you ask. In my heart, I'm a full-time musician. If you consult my tax return, it still lists my occupation as a waiter. Depending on the venue, I sometimes even work as a bouncer. My bookings are pretty steady these days, but the venues don't always pay well."

"Still, I'm very proud of you. It takes a lot of guts to live your dream."

"You may not be so proud when you find out my definition of fine dining is Top Raman with Pop Tarts for dessert."

"Really? You sounded so great at the wedding; I figured you'd have tons of fans. We'll have to get Kiera's nephew to set up a You Tube channel. He set one up for his fantasy basketball league, and he has tons of subscribers. It's pretty snazzy."

Touched by her concern, I tell her more. "That's great, Tara. I'll be sure to ask him about it. But I'm doing okay. Things are slim around my house by choice right now. I'm trying to save up for rehearsal and studio time. I want to hire a decent sound engineer to help with a demo tape since it's hard for me to pick up the little stuff."

"Oh I see." She twirls the string from her jacket between her fingers. "How will a demo tape help you? People are pretty familiar with how the piano sounds, right?"

Her answer strikes me as funny. "I suppose Gregory Hines and Paula Abdul are the same because they were both dancers?"

She snorts and chokes on her coffee. "Not hardly!"

"Well, I'm not the same as every other piano player either. I've been writing songs since I could hold a pencil."

"I didn't mean it that way, Aidan," she clarifies. "I just meant to ask if folks going to be able to tell the difference? Are your songs any good?"

"That remains to be seen, I guess. Remember those songs I played at the wedding which weren't covers?" I ask, hoping she does. It'd be humiliating if she doesn't. "I wrote those."

"Those were beautiful," she remarks. "When did you write them? Each one sounded so different."

"It depends on the song. Some of them took years to write, others only hours. One of them, I started before I lost my hearing. It took a while to finish those, obviously."

"What was it like for you to lose your music?" Tara asks, with sympathy.

"Lonely. I felt hollow. Like the part of me which explained my very existence was gone. The loss of hearing sucked in general, but life without music was soul crushing. I was lost for a while."

"But you're back now?" Tara studies me.

"It's hard to explain. I have music now. It won't ever be what it was before. My music and I are both changed by my deafness. I straddle two worlds. I don't really fit in either one. I'm a deaf guy born with hearing and a musician who can't entirely hear. It's an odd place to be."

Tara nods. "Do you ever wonder what could have been if only you hadn't gotten sick?"

"At first, I obsessed about it all the time. Rory was getting more famous. I guess you were probably traveling with them, at that point, doing the European competitions —"

"I remember those years," Tara interrupts. "We practically lived out of our luggage. I was in costume so much, I was growing sequins as a second skin."

The visual made me laugh out loud. Tara was never one for dressing up. "I bet," I say, chuckling. "I happen to know you can rock a sequin just fine, Gracie. With very little prompting, I'm sure my mom would be happy to haul out her photo albums and videotapes as proof."

"Wait a minute!" Tara exclaims as a thought occurs to her. "Speaking of your parents, they traveled with us during that time. So what happened to you?"

"There was a nurse on the pediatric unit who took me in. Her name is Delores. She invited me to join her family."

"Well, it's a good thing someone did. I can't believe your parents did that. Parenting isn't like 'The Book of the Month Club'. You don't get to just cancel your subscription to your kid because you find it overwhelming or you prefer one kid over the other. That's insane," Tara blurts, with a ferocious expression and fire in her eyes.

I'm touched by her instantaneous defense of me. It must be hard for her to understand my parent's choice, when she lost both parents under such tragic circumstances.

"Tara, it's okay really. I made peace with it several years ago, and I have started rebuilding a friendship with my parents If it were not for their choices, I wouldn't have Delores in my life. She has been my guardian angel and life mentor. I cannot imagine my life without her."

Tara sighs. "You're more forgiving than I am. I know it's not fair, but on my toughest days, I am still mad at my parents for dying. I feel like such a whiny witch for even saying it out loud. But I wonder, if my dad hadn't died, if he would have been around to protect me from Warren. Maybe, if my mom hadn't been so checked out of her life, she could've warned me of the dangers."

"Tara, I don't think there is a person alive who has been through loss that doesn't have those same thoughts. When I first became deaf, I would yell at God, then scream in horror because I couldn't hear my own cries. I think it's okay to be angry at your circumstances, it's what you do with the anger that matters."

Tara slumps in her seat, eyes full of regret. "I've done stuff I'm not proud of."

"Join the club, Tara," I reply. "Still, I think you are far too hard on yourself. The way I see it, you kept your mom alive for years after she threw in the towel. You were basically running the household by the time you were about eight. I remember the dance instructors talking about it when they thought no kids were around. You had to bury your mom as a teenager, which is something that just shouldn't happen. Yet, you somehow managed to graduate from high school and you're attending college with no family support, in an age when it's common for kids to live in their parent's basement."

"But, I live life scared. I'm years behind where all my friends are. I still have more than a year to go on my undergraduate degree. Jeff and Kiera both graduated from grad school. Even Heather has finished culinary school."

"If academic chops are your only measure of success, I may be in some serious trouble here. I made it through high school, but college was never in the cards for me."

"Oh no, Aidan! I didn't mean it as a slam. That's not what I'm saying at all. I'm just disappointed with how Warren Jones changed my life. My dad was a translator who could speak four languages. Daddy would want me to be out exploring the world, not looking at it through peep holes and chains in my front door. My parents loved to dance. I used to put on little recitals for them. My dad was so proud, he'd call all the neighbors over and have me give them an encore. He would be so devastated if he knew I don't dance." Tara finishes in a rough whisper.

I wish I could reach across my van and give her a hug. I settle for linking my finger through hers. I stroke the inside of her wrist with my thumb.

"Tara, you have to know that your parents are so

proud of the woman you've become. You are beautiful and so amazingly talented. Your friends adore you and little Mindy thinks you are a Disney princess."

Tara smiles. "It's true, Mouse is pretty special."

"So are you, Gracie. I guess my question to you is, would you like some help to find the lost music in your soul? You know, I've got personal experience with tracking it down. I'd be honored to be your first real dance for fun." I try to keep my tone light, but light and breezy is not how I would characterize the pit of my stomach as I wait for her answer.

Tara draws a deep breath. For a minute, I'm sure her answer will be no. She gives me a tumultuous smile and mutters, "I only hope you're not as terrible as Rory made you out to be, and if I so much as see a whoopee cushion, I'm gone. Understood?"

"Yes, dear. No junior high school pranks while dancing. I've got it. Are they fair game otherwise?"

She buries her head in her hands as she mutters, "Oh Geez, what have I gotten myself into?"

The three-hour drive to Crater Lake passes in the blink of an eye as we talk like the old friends we are. I pull into the turn lane and look over at Tara. "It's time to shut your eyes."

"Seriously, we've been driving forever and now you're telling me to close my eyes?" she questions. "What's next? Counting to one hundred?"

I ponder the question a moment. "Nope, not this time, but it might make things more fun the next time we do this."

"Aidan! You better not be planning anything dirty over there!" she cautions.

I smile and give her a wink as I walk around the van to open her door. "Planning? No. Hoping? Well, yes. Any guy is flat out lying if he tells you he doesn't have designs on mussing up the polished exterior of his girl just a little. A little mutual sweat is fun."

"Well, that's a tad gross, Aidan," Tara protests, crossing her arms in front of her.

I chuckle. "What? I am just saying a little smeared lipstick may be one of the many reasons relationships can get messy."

Tara sighs dramatically as she closes her eyes and grumbles to herself, "You do realize you're like an overgrown ten-year-old, right? Some women may not find that attractive."

"I'm not interested in what most women find attractive. I want to know what you think." I watch her response carefully.

"I don't know, Aidan. The jury's still out on that one."

She's teasing, but I'm sure there is a kernel of truth in her words. "You never told me why I have to have my eyes closed," she protests.

"Actually, I did," I clarify. "Remember we talked about patience and faith? This is an exercise in both."

A look of frustration and confusion crosses Tara's face as she challenges, "Are we actually going to have any fun on this date? I read somewhere that dating is supposed to be fun."

I quirk my lips into a lopsided smile at her offbeat sense of humor.

"It's all about perspective, I guess. I know *I* plan to have a great time on this date," I respond. "What about you, Gracie? Are you ready to check out your new perspective?"

"Heck yeah, let's get this show on the road. I've been dying of curiosity ever since you sent me the text message," she replies, dancing around to get her feet warm.

"Okay, Tara, open your eyes," I whisper. I'm eager to see what she thinks of what I consider to be my definition of paradise.

She immediately opens her eyes and gasps as she takes in the giant Douglas fir trees and crystal blue skies. She slowly spins in a circle as she glances around. "This is amazing," she declares. "Just so you know, it's not even remotely close to where I thought we were going."

I raise an eyebrow in question. "What were you expecting?"

Tara blushes slightly. "I thought we might be going roller-skating." She looks down at her feet and scrapes the pine-needles with her toe. "Never mind. It was a silly idea. I just thought —"

"You thought what, Tara? You thought I'd remember you never got to go to the class party and decide to take you skating on our first date?" I suggest.

"Well, I didn't expect the idea to sound so dumb when you said it out loud," she admits with a self-deprecating laugh.

"It's not so dumb. In fact, I was thinking about doing just that — but the two closest to us are closed for renovation. It turns out great minds do think alike."

The smile on her face is so huge, I feel like I've won the lottery. I can only imagine how happy she would've been if I'd been able to pull off the skating.

"I thought maybe I was the only one who remembered."

I walk her to the back of the van and start to remove our gear. "I think you'll find that I find everything about you memorable," I admit.

"Very funny, AJ. What are we doing here — building a commune?" Tara asks, pointing to the ever-growing pile.

"No, Gracie, I thought I'd take it old school and go on a picnic. It'll be like old times. There is one catch though, it will be a bit of a stroll."

"How much of a stroll?" she asks skeptically.

I try to sound nonchalant as I say in my best announcer voice, "Watchman Peak Trail is a 1.6 mile trail located near Crater Lake, Oregon that features a lake and is rated as moderates of moderate climb with many scenic outcroppings with historical markers to provide rest areas."

"Oh, okay — just so long as you don't think I'll break a sweat or anything," Tara teases.

"I didn't say we wouldn't work up a sweat. I just don't care. I think sweaty, hardworking girls are hot!"

"Is there anything you don't find hot?" she demands.

"Oh, trust me, I have quite a list. Though, I doubt any of them apply to you."

Tara rolls her eyes. "You're such a guy," she mutters under her breath.

"Why Gracie, I'm flattered you noticed," I quip. Working my shoulders into my backpack and clipping the strap around my waist, I carefully tighten the straps to make sure my load is balanced. I put on my emergency locater beacon.

"You're scaring me, Aidan. Just how far are we going? It looks like you're planning more than a small hike," Tara comments anxiously.

"No, I like to be prepared. I know it's a hike, but sometimes I like to go off trail and do some climbing. So, a little extra safety doesn't hurt." I respond, buckling her climbing helmet at her chin and snapping the locater beacon to her belt loop. I put on my own climbing helmet. To my surprise, Tara reaches up to help me latch it. I can easily do it myself, but I'm more than happy to accept her help. Her delicate hands brush the bottom of my chin as she buckles the latch. I'm amazed at how strongly I respond to her unintentional touch. I hold my hand out to her. "Speaking of prepared, did you bring your camera? It's beautiful up here."

Tara sticks her hand in her pocket and pulls out her cell phone. It's hanging from a lanyard which she places around her neck. "I've gotten good at taking pictures with this, since I never seem to remember my camera anymore," she comments, reaching to take my hand. Fortunately, the trail is wide enough for us to walk side-by-side, yet not so wide that there's much distance between us.

At first we walk in silent appreciation of the sunrise filtering through towering evergreen trees, our path lit by patches of early morning sun. I carefully lead her around the overgrowth of wild fern and Oregon grape creeping across the trail. Finally, curiosity gets the best of me.

"I hope you don't think I'm too nosy, but I have to ask. How in the world did you go from professional dancing to being an interpreter for the deaf?" I ask, searching for a place for the conversation to begin.

Tara giggles. "Since when do you ever worry about being nosy?"

I blush a little. "Okay, you might have a point. Still, maybe I'm trying to change."

"I'm just teasing, Aidan. Compared to your normal conversational skills, that question pretty much counts as coloring inside the lines," Tara responds.

I nearly choke on the swig of water I just drank as I snicker. Tara was always sneaky that way. She looks sweet and fragile, but under all that refinement, she's as sharp as a stand-up comedian.

"Clever!"

"Thank you. I try," she retorts. "Anyway, I don't know if there's an easy answer to your question. You know that my dad was a translator, so learning languages came pretty naturally for me. But studying Japanese made me too sad. I remembered learning about sign language when we were little. It was so empowering to have a language only the two of us could understand. I guess it left an impression on me."

"For a few years after the rape, I went into a sort of self seclusion where I didn't interact with anyone unless I absolutely had to for my job, or in order to survive. I even learned to do face painting with an airbrush, so I didn't have to actually touch anyone any more than necessary, and I've got at least six ways to dodge a handshake."

"Didn't you get lonely living that way?" I ask, curious.

"Yes, I suppose I was lonely. But I was too busy surviving to notice. I had a class in self-defense taught by an instructor who had lost his hearing in the field. So, gradually I used sign language and martial arts to integrate myself back into regular society."

"You sign like you dance," I remark, without thinking. "It's like poetry in motion. You're very good. But don't you miss the dancing?"

My direct question catches Tara off guard and she trips on some underbrush. I reach out to catch her before she falls. With my left hand, I grab the back of her jacket; my right hand cups her waist and my fingers splay over her hip. The momentum of her fall has spun her around so she's facing me and she is mere inches from my face. It would be so easy to lean in and kiss her right now. The temptation is almost too much. The only thing that's stopping me is the fact that Tara hasn't moved a fraction of an inch or taken a breath since I first touched her. So I decide humor is the best approach.

"Easy there, Gracie. I can't carry both you and the picnic lunch. I'd hate to have to choose which one to leave behind."

Tara blushes as she takes a deep breath. That doesn't keep her from retorting, "Knowing how much you like food, I'm sure you'd leave me here in a heartbeat."

"I wouldn't be so sure. I've come a long way since I was ten. I'm much more of a gentleman now."

"I don't know — stink bombs and whoopee cushions aside — you were not too shabby in that department, even then," Tara says with a grin.

"I notice you're still really good at changing the subject when you don't want to talk about something. Why do your best friends not even know you used to dance? Not to mention that you were given an invitation to try out for The American Ballet Company."

Tara sighs. "If I didn't talk about it, it was easier to pretend my life before Warren Jones didn't exist. I didn't want to confront what I'd lost. They couldn't ask me about what they didn't know."

"Doesn't your soul cry out for the music?" I ask in a whisper, my body aching from the pain I feel rolling off of her.

"*Every freakin' day*, Aidan. There, I said it. Are you happy? You got me to admit that I miss dancing about as much as a SCUBA diver misses air when her tanks run dry. So what?" Her shout echoes on the empty trail.

Tara starts to tremble like a leaf. Personal boundaries be dammed; I reach out and gather her into a hug. Resting my chin on the top of her head, I murmur, "Gracie, I promise I'll help you find your music again. I know I can. Do you trust me?"

For a moment I feel her muscles tense, but they gradually relax. She takes a shuddering breath as tears form on her lashes. "I've always trusted you, Aidan. I don't see any reason that would change," she quietly answers.

Palpable relief courses through my body when I hear her halting reply. I lightly kiss the top of her head. I have to take a moment to collect myself. For once, I'm at a loss for words. I know this is a decision she hasn't come to lightly. Trust isn't something she gives away freely. I will do everything in my power to earn her trust. My mission today is to just make sure she has fun and forgets the world is such a serious place. Reluctantly, I drop my arms and back away, but not before I take my thumbs and wipe the tears from her eyes. "Let's not spoil the day with tears. We've got a picnic to get to." I link my fingers with hers. To my relief, she does not pull away.

Tara pulls me along the path, letting our hands swing freely between us like we did as kids. I am relieved the lighthearted mood of the day hasn't been completely shattered by my clumsy attempts at conversation. "What about you?" Tara's quiet voice breaks into the atmosphere.

"What about me what?" I respond, wondering if I had missed a crucial part of the conversation while lost in my thoughts.

"Well, you were wondering what part of my life I've put on hold; I'll ask you the same question. Are you happy being a waiter-slash-bouncer and putting your music career on the back burner?" she prods.

Whoa, I guess she isn't throwing any softballs

either. It's a fair question. I can't expect her to be raw and exposed to me if I am unwilling to do the same. "The short answer is, 'Not in a million years.' A slightly more complicated answer is I'm not exactly sure how long I'm expected to pay my dues before I catch my big break. I wish there was a formula where you knew that you had to put in X amount of years in a menial job before you got Y amount of notice and publicity."

"So what's stopping you?" Tara's brow wrinkles in confusion. "You're phenomenally good. You were great when you were eleven and you're even better now. So what you waiting for? An engraved invitation from Elton John, Billy Joel or maybe Juilliard?"

I look down and kick the pine cones at my feet. I can't even look at Tara. "Actually, they already invited me to play as part of the application process at Juilliard."

"And?" she prompts.

"And nothing," I admit, still kicking myself over my stupid decision. "I was still adjusting to my cochlear implants and I was spectacularly angry at the world. I looked at their offer like it was the equivalent of a pity screw. I wanted to prove I could make it without affirmative action and all that diversity crap. I still hoped the cochlear implants would take away my deafness."

"I was pretty naïve, going into the process. I mean, the doctors and audiologists told me all the risks and limitations. But somehow, I guess I thought it would be different for me, because it hadn't been all that long ago I could hear. I guess I figured it would be like plugging in a telephone to a house which already had service installed. When it wasn't like that for me, I went through a period of rage and despair. Initially, I regretted having the surgery at all, but I gradually adjusted to my implants and things got markedly better. Turning down the opportunity to apply to Juilliard is one of my biggest regrets. I always tell people college is just not my thing. But what if it was, and I totally missed my chance?"

Tara reaches up and brushes my hair out of my eyes. The simple gesture makes me catch my breath because it's so rare for her to touch me, or anyone. The sun is bathing her in a beautiful morning glow, and the teardrop shape of her iris is amplified in the intense light. As she gazes at me intently, she says, "It's taken me many difficult counseling sessions to come up with this theory, but what if it takes all the difficult, sucky times in our lives to bring us to the spot where we are right now? What if we're exactly where we are supposed to be?"

I can't help but smile. "Well, that's one way to look at it."

"Do you have a better explanation for the soap opera that disguises itself as my life?"

"Actually, I like your theory just fine," I concede.

The path narrows abruptly, and I step ahead of Tara to help her up the steep incline. I'm able to navigate the muddy obstacle with relative ease, so I turn to help Tara up the treacherous grade.

I grab her hand to pull her up. As I lean back to provide leverage, the small boulder I am wedging my weight against dislodges itself and rolls down the hill, and I slide with it. One second I'm on my feet, and the next, I'm flat on my butt. But of more interest to me is exactly where Tara lands. When we start to fall, I instinctively reach out to protect her. So we're now lying face-to-face. Her lithe, supple body is plastered against my front like a cozy snowsuit. Don't get me wrong, I am not complaining. I just want to lie here and hold her. I wonder how long she'll let me do that?

I look up to study Tara's expression and I notice her lip is bleeding. Shoot! I must have caught it with my elbow or something on the way down. Reflexively, I reach my hand out and draw my thumb across her bottom lip to wipe away the small drop of blood. "Are you okay?" I question softly, regretting my clumsiness and recalling too late why I'm not the dancer in the family.

As we scramble to our feet, Tara looks thoroughly confused. "Of course I'm okay. It's not like I'm made of glass or anything. We're not even doing anything tough yet. That barely counts as a fall."

I hold up my thumb for her to see the blood that's quickly drying. "See, you're bleeding. I didn't mean to hurt you." I pull pine needles out of her hair.

"Aidan, I don't even think this counts as being hurt. I've done worse damage by sneezing. Will you please relax so we can have some fun? I'm beginning to miss the whoopee cushions. Despite what it looks like, I am a big girl and I can take care of myself."

I hook my fingers in her belt loops. Honestly, I would like to let them roam elsewhere. From our impromptu getting-to-know-you session.

I know she's hiding some very nice curves on her tall, athletic frame. I would love to confirm my findings with more research. So I pull her a few inches closer and murmur in her ear, "I know you can do it by yourself, but what if you didn't have to? I'd like to be on Team Tara."

Chapter Nine

Tara

What if I don't have to do it all on my own? I can't even wrap my brain around that concept. I've been by myself for so long. I am not sure I can process what that would mean. After my dad died, my mom was there physically, but her heart and mind were already gone in search of my dad. What would it mean if I could lean on someone else for a change?

My heart hammers as I think about the implications. The grown-up version of Aidan is incredibly hot and much to my surprise, when I was in his arms, fear was not my first response. I felt comfort, security, and the thrill of desire. Only after that came the usual dose of apprehension. I'm used to my heart pounding and my hands sweating in the presence of men, but with Aidan, I feel like a flock of wild butterflies has taken up residence in my stomach. These feelings are new and different, and terrifying on a whole new level.

Suddenly, he pulls me closer and reminds me he's already on "Team Tara". I didn't even know I had a team, but the fact that he is willing to back me speaks volumes.

"I think I'd like that very much," I whisper. "I'm new to the world of teammates. The last one I had was your brother."

A slow smile crosses Aidan's face as he processes what I told him. "I'll be happy to show you the ropes," Aidan promises as he winks.

"Do I start with something like this?" I stand on my tiptoes to place a light kiss on Aidan's cheek.

Aidan looks stunned for a second. After he recovers his power of speech, he answers, "Very nice, Gracie. But we may need to work on your aim a little."

I shake my head in mock dismay. "Perhaps my aim was just fine, AJ, and the problem is your need for instant gratification" I tease as I stick my tongue out at him.

I watch, intrigued, as Aidan's affable countenance gets intense. His eyes darken as he watches my mouth. I nervously lick my lips, and the simple movement elicits a groan from Aidan.

"Tara, if I told you how long I've been hoping you would kiss me, it would scare the living daylights out of you," Aidan confesses softly as he tucks some stray hair behind my ear.

He turns bright red, as only a red-head truly can, and it cracks me up. It doesn't fit how brash and inappropriate he can be at other times.

"I'm not sure why you're embarrassed Aidan, I figured out you had a crush on me a long time ago," I reply matter-of-factly.

Aidan sighs. "Yeah, I guess I was never hard to read,

was I?"

"Don't worry about it. I think it's very sweet and it earns you extra brownie points. Don't try to deny it now," I chide gently.

Aidan's eyes light up with laughter. "So it's not instant gratification at all. I've been waiting a really long time to kiss you, and patience like that should be richly rewarded."

I chortle. *Who knew I could still chortle?* "I have to admit, somewhere in there is a logical argument. I'm not quite sure where, but I'll give you extra points for creativity and good use of nostalgia."

Aidan's eyes widen. "Just to be clear, Tara, are you saying what I think you're saying? May I kiss you on the lips?" he asks solemnly.

I nod. Suddenly, I'm too nervous to speak and my hands are as cold as ice. Finally I whisper, "Please be gentle. I'm so scared. What if I freak out and turn into a basket case?"

Aidan walks me over to a tree stump. He sets down all of our belongings and lifts me up to sit on top of the sun-warmed surface. He climbs up and sits beside me.

Aidan leans in and says, "Whatever happens, we'll work through it together. I promise. Don't let that creep take your happiness for one more day."

"Okay," I agree with a touch of false bravado.

"Okay? I'll take that as my license to do this—" With little warning, Aidan, places a whisper soft kiss on my lips.

This is not how I remember kissing. This is so much

better. A moan escapes the back of my throat. Weirdly, I need him to kiss me harder. I never expected to feel this way. I'm so confused.

"Wow," I breathe. My heart is still racing, but my responses are no longer driven entirely by fear.

"Wow good, or wow bad?"

"Would you be upset if I told you I don't really know the answer yet?" I ask, befuddled by my body's responses.

"Gracie, why do you think I would be upset? Under the best of circumstances, a relationship is like a dance. Couples need to feel each other out and figure out how to work as a team. It's going to be especially true in our case. Contrary to every Disney movie ever written, it won't be perfect from the word go. There are going to be some ups and downs and bumpy spots."

"I just don't want you to be frustrated with me. My emotions are so chaotic, I don't always make myself clear. Sometimes I know what I want, but I don't know how to get there," I trail off, feeling a little crazy with my rambling explanation.

"Tara, relax." Aidan drops a kiss on my forehead. "We don't have to figure out all of this today, tomorrow, or even next month. Besides, we've got a leg up on everyone else. We already know we make great friends. Everything else is just a bonus."

Reflexively, I fold my legs up to my chest as I try to compose myself and calm my wildly beating heart.

"Stop thinking so hard. I can practically hear the gears in your head turning," Aidan gently chides. "Hikes are for communing with nature –- and kissing — not for thinking so much."

Even the kiss he meant to be comforting makes my skin tingle. I draw in a deep breath and change the subject. "When are we stopping for lunch? I'm starving." My stomach lets out a loud growl.

Aidan grins at me. "I forgot that you have the metabolism of a hummingbird. Don't worry, though. I've got you covered," he says as we resume walking.

Just then we round a corner and encounter a small meadow with an outcropping of trees. Aidan gives me a small bow and winks. "Will today's facilities meet your dining expectations?"

Dropping into a deep dancers' curtsy, I practically touch my toes with my nose. "Why yes, I do believe I would like to sit over by the large shade tree." Aidan sticks his elbow out like an old-fashioned gentleman from a Rodgers and Hammerstein musical and holds my hand on his forearm so he can function as my escort. When we reach a shady spot, he pulls a survival blanket out of his backpack and lays it on the ground. He motions for me to sit. When I have, he removes bowls of food from his backpack and arrange them on the blanket.

He is whistling a song I remember him singing in a talent show when we were kids. I had completely forgotten about his total adoration of Broadway tunes. He knew them all forward and backwards. He was always a great singer. I suppose it would be rude to ask if he can still sing. It's so weird, knowing so much about him as he was, yet realizing I may not know the man he's become at all.

I look up and notice Aidan studying me with a bemused expression on his face. "You were not paying attention, were you? I asked you if you wanted regular chicken salad or something spicy like Indian curry or Thai." I look around and see that Aidan has laid out a mind-boggling amount of food.

"How in the world did you fit all that in your backpack? I'll never be able to eat all of it!"

Aidan throws his head back and laughs. "I never intended you to. Am I supposed to starve? You have to leave me some crumbs at least."

He holds up a bite of an exotic looking chicken salad for me to try. I try to delicately take a bite, but unfortunately, my stomach decides to loudly announce my hunger with a plaintive growl. Whatever it is, the bite of food is fantastic. "Was it the Thai or the Indian?" I ask. "How did you even know I like Thai food? It's a weird thing to guess about somebody."

Aidan raises his eyebrow at me. "Oh, I don't know. You always had a thing for spicy food. You were the only kid who knew what kimchi was and actually ate it. Remember the time Rory dared me to eat those extra hot Slim Jim jerky sticks? He couldn't even eat them. You ate two and wanted to know what the fuss was about. I figured you probably still like spicy food, but I also anticipated your palate may have matured some. Thai and Indian curry seemed like a good bet. In case that didn't work out, I brought cherries and fresh strawberries dipped in chocolate."

For a moment, I'm stunned into silence. I can't believe how much thought and preparation he put into a single lunch. This wasn't something he threw together at the last minute; he took the time to really think about my likes and dislikes. I don't think I've had anybody care so much about what I think or want in a really long time. It's disconcerting. I'm used to observing other people and giving my opinion only when absolutely necessary. One of my favorite things about being an interpreter is fading into the background, like a piece of furniture.

"I'm not sure you should've gone to all this trouble just for me."

"Why wouldn't I, Tara Grace Windsong Isamu? For a long time, you were my best friend. Now we've reconnected and the person I see in front of me is still my best friend. Why would I treat you differently today?"

When he puts it so starkly, it's hard to justify my fears. From his perspective, nothing much has changed. I'd like that to be true for me as well. I want to pick up where we left off, if possible, and pretend nothing has changed. The best way to start, I suppose, is with baby steps. "You're right. I'm just rusty at this dating thing. Let me try again. Aidan, the Thai chicken was delicious. I can't wait to see what else you brought. Better?"

Aidan grins approvingly. "Much better! Now, do you prefer a nice and orderly approach to lunch or are you a rebel at heart, with a yearning to start with dessert?"

I pause to think for a moment before answering, "I do love strawberries, but I'm more of a delayed gratification kind of gal."

Aidan looks like I told him Santa Claus has died. His shoulders slump. "I was afraid you would say that. We'll play it your way this time. But first, I have to do one little thing." He removes my baseball cap and sets it on the blanket beside me. He cups my face in his hands, and kisses me. At first I'm startled. But there's no aggression or anger, just pleasure. Lots of pleasure. Soon, I hear myself mewing for more.

Aidan breaks the kiss and murmurs in my ear, "I am not a delayed gratification kind of guy, but that was certainly my kind of appetizer."

The combination of his sexy words and his kiss send a wave of heat to my core. It's been so long since I've had the unadulterated pleasure of a good old-fashioned flirting session, I've forgotten how much fun it is.

"Good things happen when you feed me, Aidan." I flip my ponytail to the other side of my head for reasons which totally escape me.

"Just how good, Gracie?" he responds with an exaggerated leer.

"Well, you never know —" I trail off, blushing hotly as I realize what a double entendre I've just left hanging there.

"Hmm … I guess it's a lucky thing for me you have such fast metabolism," Aidan winks.

I really wish the rest of the Girlfriend Posse were here. Kiera would know how to get herself out of this situation. She'd be one of the guys with her girl-next-door charm, while Heather performs verbal gymnastics better than anyone I've ever met. Without a doubt, she would find the perfect thing to say to relieve the tension and have everyone in stitches. Me? Not so much. All of this feels awkward. My brain has gone on vacation and I can't think of anything funny to say. In fact, I can't think of anything to say, at all. I feel as useless as the dried pine needles I'm absentmindedly weaving together.

Aidan notices my impromptu craft project and remarks, "Hey, that's really cool. How did you learn to do that?"

I give him a surprised look. "Did you forget about my heritage? Learning to weave baskets is mandatory cultural education among Native Americans."

"You are a woman of many talents, Tara Grace Windsong."

We spend the next few minutes talking about his friend Delores and her obsession with Pinterest and all things arts and crafts. While we eat lunch, Aidan mentions he sometimes uses pictures to illustrate his song ideas. When he lost his hearing, Dolores encouraged him to use drawing as a way to capture his thoughts so he could write lyrics.

An odd thought occurred to me. "I wonder how she knew how important music would be to your life, even though you were deaf. A lot of people would've tried to keep you away from the world of music. I imagine it was painful to continue to be involved with music."

"I don't know how she knew music was like food for me. I couldn't live without it. Yet, for a while there, I couldn't live with it, either. Music and I eventually had to reach some sort of truce. When I started researching cochlear implants and realized they were a viable option for me, I started practicing the motions of playing the piano before I could even hear it. Talk about a leap of faith," Aidan explains with a chuckle.

"Still, it's amazing she was so supportive of all that."

Aidan gets a faraway look in his eyes. I can tell he's remembering a painful time from the distant past he'd probably rather forget.

"I didn't leave her much choice. I didn't tell her what I was planning to do, but I did all the research on my own and contacted the National Institutes of Health and every implant manufacturer I could find, trying to be included in a study."

I'm almost afraid to ask, but curiosity gets the best of me. "What did she say?"

Aidan smiles. "Oh, she was very typically Delores. As a pediatric nurse, she had a million and one questions about its safety and effectiveness. However, what I didn't know at the time was she was doing all the same research so she could bring music back into my life."

"What did your parents think of all this?"

"Are you kidding?" he asks with an edge of sarcasm. "My parents jumped all over the opportunity to turn me back into the magical normal boy they once had."

"Well, that's just ridiculous!" I seethe. "You are their son. They should love you regardless of whether you can hear. It shouldn't matter if you're some famous concert pianist or not."

Aidan kisses the back of my hand. "That's what I've always loved about you, Gracie; you've always been my biggest fan."

I look around the old restaurant with its dilapidated seventies decor and stir my coffee to cool it down. Squirming in my seat, I try to avoid the scrutiny of my friends by changing the subject. "Why are we even talking about me? We should be talking about Kiera. She just came back from her honeymoon. Her stories are probably more interesting than mine."

Heather arches an eyebrow to indicate she's on to me. "Oh, don't worry, I plan to get to Mrs. Newlywed over here, but first I want to hear your story. Don't even try to change the subject." She narrows her eyes.

Kiera grabs my hand with the stirring stick to make me stop. She simply holds on to my hands with both of hers. "Tara, I know you thought I wasn't paying attention at the wedding — but my head wasn't so far in the clouds I couldn't tell you like this guy. Didn't you send a text during your date to say it was going well? So what happened? Why do you look like someone kicked your puppy?"

I'm not even sure I can explain this in a way they can understand. So I take a moment to sort through my thoughts. "The date was everything I ever hoped a first date would be — even if it was really our second date. He was sweet, charming, and attentive. He was funny and irreverent. He remembered I like spicy food and strawberry-flavored Crush. How obscure is that?"

"That sounds great," Heather interjects. "What's the problem?"

I've been analyzing the situation for several days.

145

Running it over and over in my head, I can only reach one conclusion. I sigh in frustration as I reply, "*Me.* I'm the problem. We had a great lunch. He fed me chocolate covered strawberries and black cherries — which is amazingly sexy, by the way. Then he took me on a great hiking and climbing adventure. As crazy as it sounds, even when we were hanging off the side of a cliff on a skinny little rope, I felt completely safe because he was with me. He had to have his hands all over my body to help me and keep me safe, but he was very discreet and never lewd or disrespectful."

At this point, Kiera pipes up, "Well, I should hope so. Because if he hurts you, he'll have to deal with Jeff, Ty and probably William. I'm sure they all gave him all sorts of warnings at the wedding. Aidan strikes me as a smart guy. I'm pretty certain he doesn't want to tick off a former Oregon Supreme Court Justice and a police officer."

My jaw drops in shock. "Do you really think they all said something? They haven't known me long."

Kiera and Heather both nod. "Of course they did, you're one of us, and we protect our own. You'd do the same for me. You helped protect me from my crazy would-be stepfather-in-law," Kiera explains with a teary smile.

Heather clicks her tongue. "This is all very sweet and will make a neat scrapbook page, but it doesn't explain what happened on your date. Why do you think it's so disastrous that you're heaping blame on yourself by the truckload?"

"It was like a nightmare. It came out of nowhere

and snuck up on me when I wasn't expecting it. We'd been laughing, having a great time reminiscing about our childhood and we were talking about our dreams for the future."

Kiera reaches over and pats me on the knee in support as I wipe away a tear.

"We were having a wonderful day. He was kissing me throughout the day. Did I mention that he's an amazing kisser?" I sigh as I remember the sensations. "I never expected to like kissing again because my last experience was such a nightmare. I didn't just like it — I loved it. In a weird way, it felt like I've finally found my way home. Aidan is scorching hot, but not overwhelming. He touched me; but it didn't feel like he was trying to break or possess me."

Heather gives a small gasp of glee as she nods her head in encouragement.

"It's so hard to explain…" I exclaim as I throw my hands up in the air. "He was in my space challenging me to expand myself, yet totally respectful. I can't even describe how wonderful he smelled. I mean, is that even possible? We were hiking. Any reasonable person would have been sweaty and gross. I don't even want to think what a fragrant bouquet I was, but he didn't seem to mind."

Heather grins. "I'm so happy for you. If things aren't going to work out for me, I'm happy to live through the romantic exploits of the Girlfriend Posse. Proceed —"

I take a deep breath and continue with the darker side of my tale, "Anyway, the weather turned warm and I was wearing a tank top under my clothes — the one that says, 'Sign Language Interpreters Do It With Their Hands!'. When Aidan saw it, he chuckled, and then he said, 'Why, Tara, I didn't know you were such a little tease…'"

Heather cringes as she puts her hand over her mouth.

"I know he meant nothing by it. In fact, he probably meant it as a joke, but it was so similar to the words Jones said to me the night of the rape, it put me into a state of shock. I pushed Aidan away and I haven't been able to say another word to him since. I feel so stupid that Warren Jones can have this much power over me all these years later. They were just words and Aidan didn't mean anything by them. When I got home, I showered for an hour until I ran out of hot water. It's like I couldn't help myself, and I haven't made any progress since I was fourteen. How can I ever hope to have a normal relationship if I can't even go on a date without freaking out?"

I start to tremble. I hate this about myself. I wasn't always like this. I used to have excellent muscle control. I could hold a pose for hours—even *en pointe*. I was solid as a rock.

Kiera reaches over to gather me into an embrace. I'm sure it looks funny to anyone else because I'm so much taller than her wheelchair. Still, it works for us because Kiera gives the best hugs in the whole world. "I'm sorry for all that Warren Jones took from you. He had no right. I hope someone in prison is doing exactly to him what he did to you."

I choke out a startled laugh. Leave it to Kiera to say exactly what I think every night. But then again, she is the daughter of a trucker. "I hope so too. You know what they say about karma —"

"How did Aidan react to all of this?" Heather asks. "Please tell me the boy did not turn his tail and run."

I trace the pitted surface of the table with my fingernail. I'm embarrassed to meet Heather's questioning eyes. "I'm not sure," I admit. "Like I said, I was practically comatose with shock. I remember getting cold, even though it was about eighty degrees outside. He put his jacket around my shoulders and the picnic blanket around my legs after we got in his van. He tried to hold me and comfort me, but I totally freaked out, so he backed away. After he walked me to the door, he checked all my locks to make sure they were sound. He's been texting a couple times a day to check in on me. I'm so embarrassed by my meltdown, I haven't even read them and if all of that wasn't crazy enough, I swear I heard him singing to calm me down. Isn't that bizarre?" I say, shaking my head, as I remember the soft, rich, gravelly baritone voice serenading me that night.

Heather gives me a look of sympathy as she says, "Well, I've seen your powers of telling the future and divining deeper meaning of things at work and I'm definitely a believer. But in this case, I think it would be easier to just read his text messages."

"Very funny, Heather. You know good and well, my powers don't extend to my own life. I wish they did. I could've avoided a whole lot of heartache if I'd known not to go on that stupid date when I was fourteen," I mutter.

"Seriously, Tara, what do you have to lose? If you don't read his text messages, you'll never be able to gauge his reaction to the situation," advises Kiera.

"Honestly? I'm afraid if he catches a glimpse of how devastated I truly am, he won't want to stick around to deal with the aftermath. He still remembers an unsullied little girl, not the basket case I've become," I admit with a raw openness I've never exposed to anyone before.

"Tara, if he's the kind of man who would think less of you because your rape caused a post-traumatic stress reaction, then he doesn't deserve you," Kiera states emphatically.

Heather nods her head. "Preach it, sister!"

"I know you're right. I just don't know what to do about it now. I should have responded right away when he texted me. He's going to think I'm a royal witch."

Heather throws her head back and laughs, practically choking on her cherry 7-Up. "Well, that's just stupid. Anybody who has even just met you knows better. Stop stalling and read the messages."

I pull out my phone and read. At first, they're just what I would've expected from Aidan. Light and perky messages affirming he had a great time. Gradually, as there was no response from me. I can sense the tone of his texts change and the worry creep in as he leaves a series of messages inquiring about my well-being.

He left a final, heartbreaking message, "I said I'd be here for you. I mean it. If you're done puking — literally or metaphorically — let me know. Or better yet, let me be there for you so I can hold your beautiful hair so it doesn't drag in the toilet. I thought we already decided life is messy and I'm not scared of a little bit of puke. Seriously, Gracie, please stop hiding. I don't know exactly what I did to upset you. But, I won't know unless you talk to me. I'll try to do better next time."

Wordlessly, I hand my phone to Kiera. Tears are streaming down my face. Heather is straining to look over Kiera's shoulder. "Man! Where do you guys keep finding these perfect guys? If you decide you don't want this one, I'll take him. How sweet is he?"

"No way! I saw him first. Besides, the way I hear it, there is a pretty amazing cowboy who already called dibs on you."

"I'm not even going to think about that man because a.) He annoys me and b.) We're talking about you right now," Heather answers, dismissing my words with a wave of her hand as if they were just annoying gnats.

"Hey, wait a minute! You didn't let me use that logic when you changed the subject from Kiera's honeymoon to my dating life."

Kiera laughs. "Well, that's because everybody knows Ty and Heather are a foregone conclusion. The man is just biding his time until she comes to her senses. So, for now, they are old news."

Heather sputters in outrage and practically hisses, "*Foregone conclusion?* You have actually met him, right? He's overbearing and opinionated. He doesn't have any sense of personal space. He says any old thought that comes into his head. It's just weird."

It's amazing to observe a blush overtake Heather and travel clear up to her hairline, which is covered in Shirley Temple corkscrew curls today. "That may all be true, but he also has the manners of a southern gentleman, is an above-average dancer, is dashingly handsome and is a kick-butt law-enforcement officer. Is it possible you set the bar a tad too high?"

Heather nods and concedes, "It's not only possible, it's probable. Can we not talk about my love life, or lack thereof right now? It's just too depressing. The question is, what are you going to do about yours?"

I pick at a snag in my sweater and the yarn starts to come unwound. Kiera grabs my hand before I completely destroy the entire thing. She carefully scrutinizes me. "Tara, he left the ball in your court. Do you want to pick it up and play?"

Without hesitation, I blurt, "Oh, *heck* yes. I'm not sure I know how. What if it's too much to ask him to wait for me to learn?"

Heather gets up from the worn booth, walks over, and envelops me in a huge hug. "Honey, I think the man has already made it clear that he'll do whatever needs to be done. You just have to take the first step. And the next. And the next. Baby steps, honey!"

I slump down in the booth in defeat as I wrap my arms around my body. "I'm so frightened. What if I can't do this?"

"What if you can?" counters Kiera. "What if it's the best thing that's ever happened to you? You'll never know unless you take the first step."

"All right, I'll text him. I wouldn't be surprised if

he's moved on to greener pastures by now. It's been almost two weeks since we went on our hike." The ache in the pit in my stomach grows larger by the second.

I fumble nervously with my phone for a couple of minutes because my fingers don't seem to want to cooperate. Finally, Heather takes my phone away from me, in frustration. "Consider me your temporary social secretary and Internet guru. Tell me what you want to say and I'll type it. This way, we might get an answer some time before the end of this millennium. Are you his friend on Facebook?" she says, as she's scrolling through applications on my phone.

I roll my eyes. "I was his best friend when we were kids. What do you think? Of course I'm his Facebook friend. I also liked his fan page and left him a review on Yelp. What does that have to do with anything? He sent me a text message — or twenty-five, remember? Aren't you going to reply to those?"

Heather smirks at me, "Well, I suppose I could if you want to be simple and straightforward about it," she replies, trying to keep a straight face. In the end, she's unsuccessful and breaks out in a huge grin.

"Funny," I reply with a long-suffering sigh. "Can't you tell I'm about to jump out of my skin here? Can we please just get this over with before I lose my nerve? I want to say:"

'I'm sorry for listening to my brain when I should've been listening to my heart. Can we pretend the last half hour of the date and the drive home never happened? I'd like a do over, please. I promise to take you bowling and spot you twenty pins.

Love, Gracie'

"Would you like me to repeat that?" I ask.

Heather grins and finishes in a flurry. "Nope, I've got it. Although, I still can't say I understand why he calls you Gracie."

I smile to myself as I respond, "It's one of my middle names and the topic of an inside joke."

Heather perks up at the prospect of getting an inside scoop, but I quickly derail her plans. "That's a topic for another day."

Heather sticks her bottom lip out in a mock pout. "Every time we get to the good stuff, something more important interrupts us."

"Speaking of the good stuff, we never got to talk about Kiera's honeymoon. But unfortunately, I have to go study. My signing skills have gotten rusty over the summer. I've got to keep my grades up to keep any hope of a scholarship."

Kiera pats me on the shoulder. "No worries. We'll get together soon and you can have some of the juicy details then. Note — I did say *some*. There are some things even the Girlfriend Posse don't need to know. Though, trust me, there are many, many, many upsides to being married. That's about all I'm going to say about that for now because I don't want to distract you from your homework."

Heather sticks her tongue out at Kiera. "Well, it sucks to have to wait. But maybe by then you'll have your own stories to tell," she says, pointing her finger at me.

"Don't get your hopes up, it's been fifteen minutes and he still hasn't returned my text."

Just then, my phone rings with the ring tone of *Oklahoma* in honor of Aidan's love for Broadway musicals. I answer cautiously, "Hello?"

"So, gorgeous Gracie wants to go bowling? I'm good with that. I bet you look hot in polyester and rented bowling shoes. I'm all in. What does your schedule look like?"

I consult the schedule on my phone before I answer, "It looks like I could spare a couple of hours on Sunday, but I would need to get back early because I have a test on Monday."

"Works for me. I'm playing a wedding in Corvallis on Saturday. But what's with this spotting me points business? Don't you think I can beat you fair and square, just because I'm not a fancy-schmancy dancer? I'll have you know I have moves you've never seen, Ms. Gracie. Consider yourself warned. I'll pick you up at about eleven o'clock, okay?"

"Okay, I'll talk to you later. Thanks for calling," I say as I prepare to hang up the phone. When I pull the phone away from my ear, I hear him say one last thing.

"Oh, Tara, just so you know — you just made my whole week. I can't wait to see you on Sunday," he confesses as he hangs up.

As I grip my phone tightly in my hands, the full impact of what I've just done hits me. Did I just ask a real live guy on a real live date and did he really just accept? *Holy crap!* I think he just did. Before I can chronically over think it, Heather high-fives Kiera. "I take it from this look of stark terror on your face that the conversation went spectacularly well," she deadpans.

I grin. Trust Heather to put it all in perspective. "Well, yes. Actually, the conversation went spectacularly well and I have a date. I'm even thrilled about it, but it doesn't keep me from being scared spit-less."

Kiera reaches out and squeezes my hand. "Perhaps this is a good time to remind you — one of the first things you told us about Aidan is that he would never hurt you. Relationships are scary, but they can also be amazing. You can do this. You've known Aidan for a long time and you might not trust yourself, but you have the best ability to read people I've ever seen. You just need to believe in yourself. If you can't do that, believe in him."

I think back to the day we spent together, hiking and climbing rock structures. Aidan was so careful with me. He was attentive, observant, supportive, and encouraging. Until I destroyed the atmosphere of the day, it had been picture-perfect, figuratively and literally. Logically, I have no reason to believe anything will be different about future dates. But the problem is getting my heart and soul to listen to my brain. I can't seem to turn off my fight-or-flight reflex even though I know that Aidan is one of the good guys. "I hope I can, Kiera. I really do. I like this guy so much, it's a little frightening."

Kiera smiles a small secret smile as she pats my hand in a comforting gesture. "Don't worry, Tara. That's exactly how it's supposed to feel. If it didn't terrify you at least a little, I'd be worried. You're doing just fine."

CHAPTER TEN

AIDAN

I'D PRETTY MUCH GIVEN up all hope that Tara would contact me again. I want to kick my own impatient butt. Things were going so well, I forgot my plan to go slowly and cautiously. It could've cost me any chance with her. After her text message arrived, I read it several times, hoping it means what I think it means.

Finally, I sucked it up and called her. If I misread the situation, it certainly isn't the first time I've made a fool of myself in front of her. It seems to be my full-time occupation when I'm in her presence. I don't know if it's her waif-like appearance or her sad eyes, but even when I was a little kid, I felt it was my duty to bring a measure of joy to her life. My sense of responsibility for the talented girl with steely determination was well on its way to puppy love when fate rudely intruded in the form of meningitis.

When the call ends, I can't seem to wipe the silly grin off of my face. Bowling it is. It's not the most romantic date on the planet, but I can deal with that. I need to stay flexible to make this work, if that's even possible. I'm still not sure what happened last time. Things were going fine until I made a seemingly harmless joke. It wasn't the cleverest thing I've ever said, but I didn't think it was awful. Tara had an extreme, visceral reaction to it. She lost so much color in her face, I thought she would pass out again. She went almost catatonic and remained that way the whole trip home. It scared the crap out of me. Tara's not a big talker, but this was scary silent, even for her. I offered to spend the night on her couch so she wouldn't be alone. She refused my offer, saying she had to shower. After an awkward air hug at the door, I heard nothing until today. Regardless of why it happened, I don't want to stick my foot in my mouth again.

Scrolling absently through my email, I click on one which catches my attention. ATTENTION! Are you a Singer/Songwriter? Five Star Creative Industries and Arts Needs You.

I'm working on the singing part, but I'm definitely a songwriter. I guess, in many ways, I was lucky. Delores always felt it was important for me to stay as oral as possible even though in the days before my implants, I could hear nothing. She insisted I speak while I used sign language, even though I couldn't hear the outcome. As a result, I avoided atrophy of my vocal cords and surrounding structures. The therapist and vocal coach are very pleased with my progress. I hated every second of my speech therapy sessions while I was growing up, but Delores's hardline attitude might just save my singing career now. That's a huge leap of faith for me, because I literally cannot hear my voice as other people hear it. I can't tell how much it's been changed by my deafness, let alone how it measures up to other singers. I have to trust in the opinions of those around me. I know from hanging around Rory and Tara — when people think they can get something from your career they'll tell you anything you want to hear, whether it's the truth or not. I saw it happen all the time with Rory. By the end of his career, he could barely burp without fourteen people having some sort of say in what happened. I'm worried that the people telling me my voice is progressing well are the same people I'm paying to improve my skills.

I'm tempted to put it all out in the open and sing for Tara just to gauge her opinion. Technically, I guess I've already done it. She was in such a state of shock that night; I doubt she noticed though. I trust Tara to be totally honest. She wouldn't sugarcoat things to make me feel better. I guess I'm avoiding it because it would be crushing if she hates the way I sound now. In all honesty, I'm struggling with the direction I should take my career. I'm passionate about the piano and songwriting. However, in this day and age of YouTube videos and reality TV shows, you have to be media savvy on all fronts. It's not enough to be exceptionally good at one skill anymore. You need to be a triple or quadruple threat. This push to be everything for everybody puts an artist like me at disadvantage.

I open the email from Five Star Creative Industries and Arts. It claims I've been chosen to be part of a reality show featuring up-and-coming singer/songwriters. They want to do a casting call in Los Angeles this weekend.

A wave of emotion overtakes me. This exactly what I've been working toward for so long; I can't even remember wanting to do anything else. I wonder if it's way too soon. I haven't been working with my vocal coach long. I'm not one hundred percent confident in my singing skills. I haven't even debuted them in public yet. I did lay down some tracks on my computer while doing some songwriting and, for kicks and giggles, I sent them to a former band-mate to see what he thought. He thought I sounded decent but needed to enunciate better. I didn't disagree. I've been practicing, but I have no way to know how much I've improved over time. Eventually, I just let the matter drop. My bandmate never mentioned passing my tape on to anyone else — but he must have, since I don't know how else the casting agency would know I exist.

Besides Tara, the only other person on the planet who will provide a brutally honest assessment is Rory. His evaluation will be so blunt, I'll probably feel like he's peeling my skin off layer by layer. If I had other options, Rory and my parents would be among the last people I would ever tell that I was pursuing a career in the entertainment field, because I know I'll never measure up to the success Rory has already accomplished. But the timing of this contest has taken the decision out of my hands. If I'm serious about doing this, I need to be all in — including telling people about my plans to sing.

"Rory O'Brien! You quit being mean to your little brother or I'll make you sleep on the couch tonight," Renée plops a bowl of popcorn in my brother's lap and settles in beside him, tucking her feet under her as only girls can do. "I think it's cool you're going to sing for us. I thought you only played piano."

"How come you can say that, but I can't? All I said was, I hope he's gotten better. The last time I heard him sing, he was prepubescent and his voice cracked."

Renée whacks Rory on the knee with a decorative couch pillow. "You are so bad. Apologize to your brother."

Rory looks over at me, eyebrow raised. "What? It's totally true, isn't it?"

I chuckle at the look of total outrage on Renée's face. "I appreciate your support, dear sister-in-law, but Rory's probably right on this one. I was, in fact, a preteen the last time he heard me sing. One can only hope I'm better by now."

Rory crosses his arms and taps his toe impatiently in typical big brother fashion. "Aidan, it's time to put up or shut up."

I take my guitar out of its case and adjust a few strings and the strap. Raising an eyebrow to show him that I'm not intimidated, I ask him, "Any requests from the peanut gallery?"

Rory's eyes light up at the prospect of a challenge. I may be older, but we're still brothers and he never misses an opportunity to best me in a contest, no matter how trivial. "How about *Fields of Gold*?" I smile at his tactic. He's banking I won't know the Sting ballad. Well, score one for me, big brother. I may know every Rogers and Hammerstein song ever written, but that doesn't mean I can't cover an astonishing variety of other songs. You can't be a touring musician without a huge library of songs in your head.

After a little last minute tuning — yes, I'm stalling, I start to sing. I try to lose myself in the melody and forget this is really my first mini-audition. If Rory gives me a thumbs down, I'm not sure what it will mean for my career. I trust his opinion. Sure, he can be an pain, but he doesn't pull any punches and since he's met Renee and had kids, he rarely does it just for entertainment anymore. The music flows through me as I strum the guitar and relax into the song. I open my eyes to peek at their reactions. Renee has tears in her eyes and Rory has an unreadable look of concentration as he watches me perform. As the last notes float away, my heart is in my throat as I wait for their verdict. Renee is the first to react as she quickly dabs away her tears and begins clapping wildly. "Oh, Aidan!" she exclaims, "That was beautiful. I had no idea you were this talented."

"Me either," agrees Rory. "It seems you've been holding out on us. Why didn't you say something? This is totally cool. Ma and Pa will be over the moon."

I can't stop myself from flinching at his words. "Maybe I was hoping just plain deaf Aidan, part time waiter, would be enough for them," I retort sarcastically.

Rory sighs and scrubs his hand over his face. "I can't defend their behavior, AJ. We both know it sucks. I think they've started to change and value us for who we are, instead of the spotlight we can draw. Strangely enough, since our girls arrived, they seem almost normal."

I grimace and carefully choose my next words. It's been a hard road back for Rory since his career-ending injury and I don't want to screw things up between him and my parents. I've come to grips a long time ago with knowing my relationship with them will probably never be fully repaired, but we have come a long ways There was a time in my life, shortly after they turned me over to Dolores, I envisioned never speaking to them again. If I had to characterize it, I'd say we've reached the point of warm civility. My next career move could change that in either direction. "I hope you're right, because things could be changing for me —" I start to explain before Rory interrupts me.

"I knew you didn't come over just to sing for us. That's not your style. So what's the rest of the story?" Rory leans forward, rests his elbows on his knees and braces for bad news.

I set my guitar down and lean forward to match his body language. "As bizarre as it sounds, I've been invited to compete in a reality show which focuses on singing and songwriting. There's a casting call in Los Angeles this weekend. I'm debating whether I should go for it. I have concerns. For one thing, I'm worried it could turn Ma and Pa into competitive monsters like they were during your dance career. More importantly, I'm not sure I'm good enough to compete as a singer. This little demonstration I gave… well, it's the first time I've sung for an audience since before I became deaf. I do pretty well with my cochlear implants, but the mechanics of hearing is different through CIs. Things like pitch and tone are different. I've been working hard on those issues with my voice coach, and I've been working on pronunciation and enunciation with my speech therapist. They both assure me I've made amazing progress, but they have a financial stake in telling me what I want to hear. I wanted to hear from someone who wouldn't give me any bull." I shrug my shoulders.

Rory studies me for a second. "I can't predict what our parents will do. I think you need to make your decision independent of them anyway. As far as your talent goes, I think they're going to love you. Your voice is strong, your piano playing is phenomenal, and you play more than a passable guitar."

"Great. That's what I needed to hear."

Rory holds up his hand to stop me, "Wait, I wasn't done yet," he continues. "Is your voice perfect? Probably not. But your back-story will more than make up for it. No one can resist the story of a handsome deaf guy who can play music, write a beautiful ballad, and also sing it to them."

Frustration overtakes me in a giant wave and I struggle to keep my voice even as I practically hiss at Rory, "That's just it, Ror. I don't want to be The Deaf Guy on that show. I want to be a talented guy from Oregon with a shot at winning just like anyone else."

Renée gets up, walks behind me and starts to massage my shoulders. "I'm sorry to break it to you, Aidan, but I don't think you get to choose how the public perceives you. Lord knows, if I had a choice, I'd rather people think I look like Cindy Crawford, not the little girl who played on the Wonder Years. But I'm five foot nothing. I get mistaken for a child, even though I have three children of my own," she offers in support.

I grin as I remember the last time we went out for pizza and she was offered the kids menu. "But you make such a cute munchkin," I tease. "Look on the bright side, you'll be carded until you're seventy."

"Not that you asked for my opinion, but I'll give it to you anyway," Renée says. "The only way you're going to prove the stereotype wrong is to go on the show and act like a regular contestant. That includes talking about your background, just like every other participant. It doesn't mean you have to make a big deal of it. Regardless, your talent will speak for itself. Once the novelty wears off, they'll forget you're even deaf. I do all the time. The only time it seems to be an issue for you is when you're in a noisy environment or you're terribly nervous."

"I hate to be the cruel voice of reality here," Rory interjects, "but aren't those the exact conditions he'll be facing during the audition process? Aidan, are you sure you want to put yourself out there for this? The odds of winning can't be very high — for anyone."

"I usually have a problem only if I am ambushed by a situation I don't expect. In this case, I'm aware of the dynamics ahead of time, so I should be okay." But even as I say those words out loud, doubts are creeping in. This will be the highest stress situation I've been under in a long time, maybe ever, and my voice is untested in public.

Rory looks unconvinced by my bravado. "Whatever you say, Aidan. I want to make sure you know what you're signing up for. I can tell you from personal experience, the competition circuit is grueling."

I nod in agreement. "I remember what you and Tara went through, but I think I need to try this or I'll always wonder what could've been, and I'm not a woulda-coulda-shoulda kind of guy."

After I get home from Rory's, I reflect on how the visit went. It actually went far better than I expected. I wonder what Tara would think about Rory and Renée. *Oh crap!* The auditions are this weekend. I'll have to postpone my bowling date with Tara. I don't want to disappoint her and break her trust. It's a sucky way to start a relationship.

I grab a can of Strawberry Crush from the refrigerator and pull out my phone. She answers on the third ring.

"Hi, gorgeous Gracie, what are you doing on this fine day?" I ask, cringing at the overly perky tone in my voice.

"Um, I'm working at the gas station. Have you looked outside in the last couple of days, Aidan? It hasn't stopped raining. I'm may have to turn my Beetle into a boat," she answers with amusement in her voice.

"As a matter of fact, I just came in from outside," I reply. "You're right, it's downright awful out there. But, my day became perfect the minute you said hello."

Tara lets loose an uncharacteristic peal of laughter. "Aidan Jarith O'Brien, has anyone ever told you the amount of malarkey you spout could be dangerous to your health? You're very sweet, but a little over-the-top. Do women actually buy the lines that come flying out of your mouth?"

I bite back a snort of laughter at her candidness, "Well, I don't need all womankind to buy it, just you."

"Well, here's a tip, AJ. If you want me to believe a single word you say, you might want to tone it down a little."

"Hmm, good to know, I'll keep it in mind. Just for the record, talking to you really is the highlight of my day. There is no a trace of malarkey," I respond with total sincerity.

"Thanks, I guess," Tara stammers awkwardly. "I'm sure you didn't call to embarrass me at work. Was there something else you needed? It's quiet here tonight, but I really shouldn't be on my phone."

I should know better than to distract her while she's at work. "I'm sorry. I should call at a better time," I concede.

Tara laughs lightly. "Relax, Aidan. It's fine. I'm night manager tonight and I need to be a role model for the newbies. Eric is with me on pumps tonight, so we'll be fine. What's up?"

I stop to take a couple of deep breaths before I continue. I'm not sure why this is so difficult. I've rescheduled dates before and sometimes even broken them. In high-school, I even stood someone up for a school dance. I only did that once because Delores made me go to the beauty shop with her and have every woman in the place from fourteen to eighty-three tell me about every experience they'd ever had with being stood up. I learned three things that day. First, women put a lot of trust in men to treat them right. Second, being stood up hurts no matter who you are or what your station in life. Third, women have *really* long memories, so try your best not to screw up.

I learned a fourth thing too. A woman's capacity to forgive is great too. I'll never forget the story one of the ladies told. Her husband stood her up on their wedding day because he got wrapped up in playing the ponies and lost track of time. Eventually they did marry, though, they were married 67 years, and had two sons and a daughter. I hope Tara has the same forgiving spirit. I finally go for broke and jump right in.

"I'm sorry Tara, something has come up and I need to reschedule our bowling date."

"I knew my meltdown was going to come back to haunt me," she mutters under her breath on the other end of the phone.

"No!" I practically shout. "Tara, that's not it at all! It's a work related thing."

"I thought you said you have a wedding on Saturday. How does that impact Sunday?" Tara asks, confused.

"Crap! You're right. I was so focused on Sunday, I forgot about my Saturday plans. I have to find someone to cover the gig for me. My friend, Stetson Stillwell, had a big gig cancel on him Maybe he can cover for me."

"So, what does this have to do with me?" she prods.

"Tara, I got offered a reality show based on a singing and songwriting competition. The casting call is this weekend."

I'm not sure what I expected, but total silence was not among the options I considered. After about a minute, I finally ask, "Gracie … are you still there? You didn't hang up on me because I have to postpone our date, right?" I laugh, trying to cover-up my nerves.

"I'm sorry, Aidan," Tara responds haltingly. "I was

trying to gather my thoughts before I said anything because quite honestly, they're scattered everywhere. At first, I thought you were calling to cancel because I acted like such a basket case at the end of our last date. Then, when I heard your news, I was totally thrilled for you. As I thought about it, I realized you're so good, you'll be gone for a long time. I'm not so cool with that part of it. I just found you, and it kind of sucks you will be going away again. Saying this all out loud makes me sound like a weird, stalker-ish girlfriend. Officially, we haven't even been out on two dates yet. Forget I said anything but 'congratulations', okay?" Tara's speech trails off into silence.

"Actually, we have," I answer.

"We have what?" she asks, confused by my reply.

"We've gone on two official dates," I clarify. "I took you out to coffee and I took you on a picnic. This would've been our third date. It still will be — I just need to reschedule it. By the way, what you said to me was the nicest thing I've heard in a while. It feels good to know you believe in me and that you'll miss me."

"Of course I believe in you. You're insanely talented. Have you ever been to one of these casting calls? It's a total zoo. They're usually held in large conference halls or sound-stages and the acoustics are terrible. There's a reason they call them cattle calls. Will that be difficult for you?"

It shouldn't surprise me Tara immediately hones in on my unspoken fear. She has always been able to read me like a dime-store novel. I almost growl in frustration as I explain my dilemma. "I don't know what to do. Since

I got the cochlear implants, I hardly ever use sign language interpreters anymore. I don't want to draw any unnecessary attention to my deafness. I want to be treated just like every other contestant. The audition is exactly the kind of environment where I probably need an interpreter."

"It's your right to have an interpreter. If you need one, you should ask for one," Tara argues.

"I know it's my right to have one, but I'm afraid if I ask for one, I'll be singled out and treated differently and I want to be like everyone else. Do you know what I mean?" I ask, not knowing if I'm making any sense at all.

"Maybe. When I was a kid, if someone found out my parents died, all of a sudden any normal conversation we were having suddenly stopped. They would immediately start praying for me or speaking in psychobabble. It was so annoying. Finally I stopped talking to people. For many years, you were my only friend because you were the only person who treated me like a normal person instead of a tragic soap opera character."

"See, you totally understand what I'm talking about. Some days, I want things to go back to the way they were before I got sick. I mean, not every day, but I think the struggles I've gone through with deafness, and meeting Delores and her family wouldn't have happened without it. The meningitis has taught me a lot and made me a better musician. Sometimes being different is a pain. This is one of those situations, and I don't know the best way to deal with it. I don't think I'll need an interpreter after the competition is underway, though. In most situations,

I don't need one, even when I'm working in a bar."

Tara says abruptly, "Aidan, can I call you right back?"

Startled by the sudden shift, I stammer, "Sure, you can call any time. I'll talk to you later."

Tara responds with a light laugh. "I'll call you right back. I promise. Bye."

I hang up the phone, unsure what happened. On the surface, I failed on every level. I didn't get to reschedule the date, and she hung up on me. She doesn't seem angry and she did say she would call me back. I'm in a holding pattern until I can figure this out.

I message the wedding party and Stetson to see if I can arrange a last-minute substitution for my gig. They respond to my text message immediately and thanks to YouTube, the bride is familiar with Stetson's work, so she has no trouble with the switch.

Now I need to choose songs for the audition. The rules say I need to choose songs from four different decades. I want to do *Piano Man* by Billy Joel and *Candle in the Wind* by Elton John, but sadly, they were released around the same time in the *70s. Dock of the Bay* would be cool and I think it was the late 60s. For my current song, I think I'll go with Sam Smith's *Stay with Me*. I might give the 90s a nod and show I have crossover potential with *Standing Outside the Fire* by Garth Brooks. My most surprising song choice might be Michael Jackson's 1987 hit, *Man In the Mirror*.

I like to sing songs that matter to me. I think it'll be important to follow this strategy in the competition setting. Eventually, as I progress through the competition. I will also have to write a song. I have most of the melody down for the song I'm writing for Tara, but I haven't worked much on the lyrics. I haven't sung in public since before I lost my hearing, so writing lyrics has not been a high priority. That's about to change. I'm sure Delores will be thrilled to hear it, because she was disappointed when I put my lyric notebook away under some old books from high school. She probably still has them in my old room. She often threatens to take my stuff to the dump, but I doubt she ever will — at least, not without checking with me first.

Just as I finish verifying the copyright dates on all the songs, my phone rings with the special ring tone I have reserved for Tara. Even though I'm expecting the call, my heart still races when I see her phone number come up on the caller ID.

"Well, howdy, gorgeous Gracie — that didn't take long."

"Didn't I warn you about the empty puffery?" Tara asks, pointedly.

"Well, I'm pretty sure it's neither empty, nor puffery, when it's simply true. You are gorgeous, so I'm innocent on all counts."

"You sound lawyerly enough to give Jeff a run for his money. I called to tell you I've made arrangements so I can be at your beck and call this weekend, if you need me. Consider me your interpreter," Tara declares.

I shake my head to clear it. I must have misheard. I'm pretty sure Tara didn't just say what I thought she said. "Excuse me?" I sputter.

Tara giggles. "You heard me, AJ. I may not be a full-fledged interpreter yet, but I can more than hold my own. I've cleared my schedule and I'm all yours for the weekend. I just need to know your flight info," she explains.

I did in fact hear what I thought I heard. It's just as stunning the second time, if not more so. The generosity of her offer is simply mind-boggling. The new school year recently started for her, and she's juggling two part-time jobs. I also know crowds are not her thing. This is more than just getting away for the weekend. She's making a huge sacrifice to help me.

"Tara, I appreciate the offer more than you can imagine," I reply. "But I can't let you do that. The cost to book a flight this late is beyond outrageous. It's way too much to ask of you."

"Why don't you let me decide what's too much? I wouldn't offer if I couldn't do it. It just so happens I'm one of those rare people who was grandfathered into my frequent flyer miles program. I still have a kazillion miles left over from when Rory and I used to travel all over the world when we competed internationally. Quite frankly, they get annoyed that I never use my benefits, since it means they have to pay a cash bonus on my credit card instead. They'll probably throw down some cartwheels if I fly somewhere."

I'm not often at a loss for words, considering I write songs for a living. An amusing thought crosses my mind. That's probably the longest explanation I've ever heard from Tara on any subject.

I go with a starkly honest answer, "Gracie, it would mean the world to me if you were there. Whether or not you end up interpreting for me, I think I'll perform better, just because you're in the room. On the other hand, you'll also be a hell of a distraction."

"Uh oh, maybe I shouldn't go, then."

"Now wait a second … I never said what you were a distraction from. Maybe I need you to distract me from all the nerves and craziness. Make no mistake, Tara, I want you by my side for this adventure. If my best friend isn't there, what fun will it be?"

I can hear Tara's sharp intake of breath as she utters, "Wow, Aidan, you're good. My heart kind of skipped a beat, there."

I smile into my phone, not even caring that she can't see it. I'll take any sign of progress and celebrate it, no matter how small. Tara Grace Windsong accepting a compliment with grace and good humor is a victory indeed. There is a road trip in my future. Things are definitely looking up.

Chapter Eleven

Tara

"I'm certifiably insane, right?" I ask Heather as I throw my dingy workout clothes into a suitcase. "I don't know what came over me. It seemed like a good idea at the time. Somehow in the excitement of the moment, I forgot that some days, I can't even eat at a restaurant without freaking out."

"I'm not just saying this because you can kick my butt in fifteen very painful ways. You are my favorite Warrior Chick and to people who don't know you extremely well, you look like you have totally together all the time. You rarely ever have a lock of gorgeous hair out of place." Heather examines a faded tie-dyed T-shirt. "Now, just because *you* scream confidence doesn't mean your wardrobe is speaking the same language." She shakes her head in dismay.

I laugh out loud at her expression. The woman does have a point. There are trolls living under bridges who dress with better class than I do. If it's big, bulky, ugly and old, it's in my closet. "It's safe to say I don't invest a lot of money in clothes." I smirk and pick up a pair of sweatpants with the left knee completely blown out.

Heather rolls her eyes at me. "Dare I ask what you did with the five hundred dollar gift certificate my mom got you from Nordstrom's for Christmas? Because, clearly, you have *not* used it for wardrobe enhancement."

"I'm a college student. What am I going to do with clothes from Nordstrom?" I shrug. "It's not like I go anywhere. I work at a gas station. It would be fashion sacrilege to wear clothes from Nordstrom there. The gift certificate is still in the bottom of my purse."

"Well, how fortuitous for you that my mother's taste is completely ostentatious and over-the-top. Because to put it bluntly, you, my warrior friend, are having a fashion emergency."

This time, there is no hope of holding it in. I let loose a loud guffaw of laughter. "Well, duh! Tell me something I don't know. I think I have bigger problems than what to wear. The whole point was to be helpful. Do you think he's serious about me being a huge distraction?" I ask, trying to resist an urge to chew my fingernails.

Heather shakes her head at me. She grabs me by the shoulders and walks me over to my closet door. I try to avoid this area of my room whenever possible because there's a huge floor-to-ceiling seventies-style sliding glass mirrored door. It's a bit pitted and warped with age, but it clearly shows our reflection. "Honey, take a good, long hard look at yourself. This is why he'll be distracted. Because even in ratty yoga pants and a T-shirt four sizes too big which should've been recycled a couple decades ago, you look absolutely stunning. Unlike the rest of us, it doesn't even matter you haven't bothered to comb your hair or put on any makeup, you still look adorably sexy. If you weren't my best friend, it would be easy to hate you."

"Oh, I'd be crushed if you hated me —"

Heather holds up her hand to stop me. "As your best friend, I know you hate the idea that you're attractive. Unfortunately, there isn't anything you could do to make yourself not be a distraction to Aidan. He finds the fact that you breathe distracting. That's true whether you're in Los Angeles with him or not. You might as well go with him and be helpful."

"It's too weird to me that he thinks I'm sexy. We were kids the last time we were together."

Heather snickers at me. "Isn't that a tad hypocritical since you think he's hotter than the sun? Weren't you just telling me how awesomely sexy he is? Yes, I think you were. In fact, I remember a rather detailed discussion about his kissing prowess. It didn't seem at all childlike to me."

"Oh wow! For all your Miss Manners charm, you don't sugarcoat things, do you?"

"Face it, Tara. The two of you have grown up and are on the verge of a mature relationship, with all it implies. It sounds like Aidan is willing to work through whatever it takes. I'd say that boy has been in love with you since before he could shave. It doesn't seem like the decades away have changed his mind at all," Heather observes as she grabs my hairbrush and works through the tangles in my hair.

"That's almost what I'm afraid of most, Heather," I admit. "I don't think he can possibly understand how much I've changed from the girl he once knew. I don't even think I know. What if he doesn't like the person I've become?"

"What if he likes this version better?" Heather counters. "Tara, I know this is not a situation you ever expected to find yourself in, but you can't sell yourself short. You are an amazing survivor. You went through more things in the first fifteen years of your life than most people face in a lifetime. Not only that, you didn't curl up into a little ball and quit. You are a phenomenally talented person who is genuinely nice to other people."

I blush and look away.

"If you hadn't decided to share your story, I wouldn't have known any of this occurred. I mean, I knew you were skittish around guys. But I know a lot of women who have bad experiences with exes and are a little gun shy, so I didn't think anything of it. All I'm saying is this dysfunctional picture of yourself you have in your head may be slightly exaggerated. The rest of the world doesn't see you like that, including Aidan. In fact, it's probably especially true of Aidan, because he sees you in the best light possible."

I shrug. "You're probably right. Even as kids, Aidan said I was way too hard on myself. His world has been turned completely upside down since then. I wonder how much it's changed him."

"I think you guys should look at this LA trip as a chance to get to know each other as the people you are now, as opposed to the kids you used to be. You may find you like each other on a whole different level."

I look at the chaos around me and swallow hard. "Do you think I'm ready?" I ask, a note of panic entering my voice.

"Well, we have a few days and we might have to call in reinforcements from the Girlfriend Posse — but we'll get you there," Heather assures me.

———————•◦•———————

As I watch Aidan gawk around the first-class cabin, it reminds me of the times I used to fly with my dad. I was really young when he died, but I remember occasionally traveling with him when he went on informal translating jobs for diplomats. There was this one time, shortly before he passed away, when he did some translating for a high-level official. I don't remember if it was a congressman or a wealthy CEO, but we traveled with the man's family on his private plane. His little girl and I played with Barbies together on the floor of his multimillion-dollar aircraft as if it were a totally normal thing to do. It was also the last time I remember my mom being truly happy. She and the client's wife were exchanging recipes and talking about their days in college. Of course, I had no way of knowing that this impromptu family vacation was going to be the last one our family would ever go on.

Aidan runs his fingers along the soft leather of the seats and studies the upgraded headsets. He lets out a soft wolf-whistle in my ear. "I've always wondered how the other half lives, but at the risk of sounding like a totally geeked out teenager, 'This is dope.'"

I laugh. "Well, that's one way to put it. They'll even serve you more than peanuts, if you ask them to."

"You know what I don't get?" Aidan says, as he flips through the airline evacuation instructions.

"What?" I ask, raising an eyebrow.

"If you can fly like this all the time, why don't you? If it were me, I'd be going on … I don't know … four or five vacations a year," he concludes thoughtfully.

Honestly, the question stumps me. I don't really have a good excuse. As of four and a half years ago, technically I'm not even poor anymore. The court found Warren Jones criminally and civilly liable for my rape. So, for the event which shattered my life, I was awarded a very large chunk of his very sizable trust fund. It should have made me happy to be filthy rich. Instead, it just makes me feel filthy. I no longer feel like I caused myself to be a victim, but I wonder if there were other victims because I was too much of a mess to make him stop sooner. That question haunts me more nights than I care to admit. I try to shake off my dark thoughts. I can't dwell on this. I need to focus on Aidan.

"I don't know. I guess it's because travel was such a family thing growing up, and it seems wrong to enjoy it without them. Besides, it's not fun to do stuff by myself. Have you ever gone out to eat alone? The looks of pity can be unbearable."

"Yeah, I suppose they would be. I guess I was thinking how much fun it would be to go places with your friends," Aidan says as he gestures around the plane.

"If it makes you feel any better, I'm taking Mindy and the family to Disney next summer. She's even planning to dine with the princesses."

"Well, that sounds like the only way to truly do Disney. Are you going to go to Universal Studios to learn how movies are made? It wouldn't surprise me if Mindy turns out to be the next Angelina Jolie," he offers with an easy smile.

"Oh, I wouldn't doubt that for a second," I concede. "But for now, she has her sights set on being a trucker like Kiera's dad. We'll have to wait and see. Although, with her level of curiosity, I'm leaning toward doctor or scientist."

"You're so good with Mindy. Do you have any plans to have your own passel of rug-rats?"

Something about the way he asks the question strikes me as funny and I develop an uncontrollable case of the giggles, not at all befitting a person sitting in first class. Even Aidan, who usually takes great glee in cracking me up, is looking at me strangely as tears leak out of the corners of my eyes.

He reaches into the pocket of his leather jacket and pulls out a neatly folded Kleenex and hands it to me. "Geez, Gracie, are you okay? I thought it was a pretty straightforward question."

"Yeah, it could have been if we had been on more than two dates." I manage to answer between my fits of giggles. "You seem bound and determined to have our relationship go at warp speed."

"I can't deny there's some truth in that statement." Aidan admits, blushing slightly. "I swear, this time I'm innocent! I was only making conversation, but I clearly lack basic social skills. I was genuinely trying to give you a compliment about your relationship with Mindy. I'm sorry if it sounded presumptuous."

I try to keep a straight face, but I can't even almost get there. "AJ, you haven't had enough coffee this morning, if you can't tell that I'm just yanking your chain. You are trying way too hard to be perfect." His hair has fallen into his face and I can't see his expression. I reach up to tuck it behind his ear.

Aidan captures my hand and holds it there with my fingers threaded through his thick curly locks. The expression in his eyes is intense, as he studies me. It is so mesmerizing, it's difficult to look away. Finally, he murmurs, "I hope you decide to have kids one day, Tara. That'd be an amazing thing to see."

I can't stop the flush that spreads through my body under his scrutiny. I wonder what he would think if he knew I was thinking about borrowing him for his studly services. That idea seemed fine in theory, but when I'm face to face with the reality of Aidan and I'm reminded what a sweet, funny guy he is, I know I could never do the deed and run.

"Thanks, I think," I reply shyly, uncomfortable with his intense focus. "I don't know what kind of mom I'd make. It's not like I had a bunch of parental guidance growing up." I shrug and duck my head.

He runs his finger down the side of my cheek and under my jaw. He uses it to gently tilt up my chin until my eyes are again meeting his. "Tara, listen. That's how I know you'll be a phenomenal mom; you had none of the advantages — yet you're one of the most beautiful people I know, both inside and out. You are amazing."

I do what any reasonable girl in my shoes would do at this point — I melt right there in Seat 3B. There's no point in pretending otherwise. The man is good. For all intents and purposes, despite my plans to be all objective and rational, you might as well put a fork in me and say done.

Now what am I going to do? This is going to be way more complicated than a bowling date. Darn. I can't call the Girlfriend Posse for advice from thirty-thousand feet in the air. I sure wish I knew why my gift of insight and perfect timing seems to work on everyone else's life but mine.

"Earth to Tara," Aidan whispers as he kisses me softly on the lips. "Why is it, when I give you a compliment, it seems to stun you into complete silence?"

"What?" I answer, befuddled by both his statement and the random kiss. As my brain unscrambles what he said, I hurry to set the record straight. "No, I'm just thinking. You caught me off guard. Your unabashed support of me is sometimes overwhelming. So, what about you? Do you see the pitter-pat of little feet in your future?"

Aidan seems amused by my question. Yet, he seems thoughtful. "I'm not sure. Rory's girls are super cool and they've really mellowed him. I've always wanted to have kids, but I'm not in the greatest position to support a family right now. It'd hardly be fair to bring kids into the picture if I'll be on the road all the time."

"Wow, you've given this more thought than I expected."

"What? You expected me to be shallow and vapid

because I'm a musician?" he teases.

I blush hotly. "No! Well ... maybe," I stammer. "You have to admit most guys are not all that concerned with the repercussions of their choices."

"Not the guys you know — maybe, but I was raised better. Ms. Delores would have my hide if I ever disrespected a woman that way. Dealing with the consequences of your choices was a mandatory part of sex education in our household. We got those lessons right along with our condoms. I suppose it's one reason my adopted brother, Jarrod has custody of his daughter after his wife decided manicures and designer jeans were more important than her own kid. He's doing a great job, but I don't want to be like him. This is a job I want to do with my wife. Seeing as how I don't have one of those at the moment, the daddy part will have to wait awhile."

"You're right. My carnie friends and coworkers at the gas station aren't the best role models for stable, long term relationships, I suppose. I'm often too quick to lump all guys together. I'm sorry."

"Don't be too quick to apologize," Aidan cautions. "Some stereotypes exist for a reason. If your gut is telling you something is off, you have to trust that."

"Um, okay. Thanks for the warning, I guess. Don't take this the wrong way, Aidan, but I can't shake the feeling maybe you're trying a little too hard. Maybe I'm being paranoid, but you seem to say and do all the right things all the time. Aren't you a jerk every once in a while?" I ask with some trepidation.

When I see the look of total shock on his face, I wonder if I pushed the boundary a little too far. Slowly, a grin crosses his face and the corners of his eyes crinkle up with laughter. "Oh boy! You and Delores are going to get along like two peas in a pod. She'll love you. She's always telling me I'm such a cool customer butter wouldn't melt in my mouth. She said she couldn't wait until I met the one person who would look past all my blarney and see the real me."

"You actually want me to meet Delores?" My eyebrows raise in surprise.

It was Aidan's turn to give me a comical expression of surprise. "Of course I do, I'm closer to Dolores and her family than I am to my own. Why wouldn't I want you to meet them?"

"I'd love to. I just didn't think we were there yet in our relationship. The whole 'meet the family thing' seems like a big step. I don't know what the rules and boundaries are for us. We've been friends for such a long time, but we haven't seen each other in forever, so we're also strangers."

Aidan turns in his seat and takes my hands in his. "Why do we have to figure it all out and put labels on it? Why can't we just be 'us'—whatever that turns out to be? We've never been good at following rules anyway. We were best friends at an age when boys and girls are supposed to be mortal enemies. You were a dancer and I was a piano player. Heck, I was the little brother of the guy you had a crush on. If we could make all that work when we were just kids, we can work through our obstacles now. We'll take one day at a time, okay?" He squeezes my hands and leans in and kisses me softly on the forehead.

The stark sweetness of that simple act is my final undoing. I have no more defenses left. I crumble slightly in the seat and a tear rolls down my face as a realization hits me. I can voluntarily set down my armor. Aidan isn't the enemy. I can stop fighting. For the first time in almost half my life, I can stop being afraid.

It's such an earth shattering paradigm shift I don't know how to process it. Bizarrely, even though this is a good thing, my body seems to be going into shock. I start to shiver uncontrollably.

Aidan immediately flags down a flight attendant and asks for a blanket and pillow as he peels off his jacket and tucks it around my shoulders. His voice is gruff with concern as he peppers me with questions, "Are you okay? Why didn't you tell me you were a nervous flyer? We could've done some meditation or something —"

I sign for him to please stop. When he sees me resort to sign language, he stops mid-sentence.

"AJ, stop, please." I plead. "I usually sleep like a rock when I fly; that's not the problem."

"Oh crap, I've pushed you too hard to work overtime so you could go on this trip and now you're sick. I knew helping me would overload you," he mutters.

I sign, "No." He looks at me with concern creasing his brow, but at that moment the flight attendant returns with the bedding. "Is everything all right here or do I need to find some medical assistance?" When she reminds Aidan of our precarious position in the wide blue sky, he visibly pales.

I grip his hand after he drapes the blanket over my lap and tucks it around my feet. "Aidan, I'm fine. I got lost in my thoughts for a bit and let my nerves get away from me." I hold my hand out in front of me to demonstrate I'm no longer shaking like a leaf. "See, I'm feeling better already."

Aidan kisses my hand like an old-fashioned gentleman. Our flight attendant winks at me as she says in a conspiratorial whisper, "Clearly, I'm not needed here, so I'm going to skedaddle. Y'all let me know if you need anything, okay?"

I nod wordlessly, but Aidan pulls some bills from his pocket. "May we have some Champagne please?"

"Of course sir, but there's no fee. It's covered in your fare," the flight attendant graciously explains.

Aidan gives her a wide grin. "No wonder the passengers up here always look like they are having so much fun."

The flight attendant sticks her bottom lip out in a pretty little pout. "I always thought it was my stellar customer service skills. But, you're probably right; free booze and food never hurts the cause. Y'all have a good flight now."

After she leaves, Aidan brushes the hair from my eyes as he examines me carefully. "Oh man, Gracie," he murmurs in a rough whisper. "I haven't been this scared since Rory practically blinded you with his elbow. What happened? It seemed like you were okay one moment and destroyed the next. I'm wracking my brain trying to figure out what I did."

A tear rolls down my face, but I manage a wry smile as I try to explain my existence. "Welcome to the wonderful wacky world of post traumatic stress disorder

— where your body thinks good news is as catastrophic as bad. I was thinking being with you would mean I wouldn't have to be frightened all the time. Even though it makes me ecstatic beyond words, the idea of being truly free shook me up and sent me into a bit of shock."

"Maybe it's more like the metamorphosis a butterfly goes through when shedding its cocoon. During the process, her strength is sapped, but the payoff is awe-inspiring. There may be hiccups along the way, but in the end, it's going to be so worth it for both of us," he declares with conviction.

I laugh lightly. "Aidan, only you can make a panic attack seem like a relationship affirming event."

Working around the armrest, Aidan gathers me into a tight hug. "I know you can't help it, but I'd like it if you didn't make a hobby of doing that again. I'd like to make it past my fortieth birthday, and episodes like that are hard on a man's heart."

As always, there is a lightness to his words. Yet he can't quite hide the pain. Without even thinking about it, my fingers travel to his brow as I try to wipe away the slight frown on his face. He leans into my touch. I pull his head closer to mine as I return the kiss he gave me a few minutes earlier. I tenderly kiss him on the forehead. I move to the bridge of his nose, then to the tip of his chin. I find the angle there to be fascinating. It's strong and sharp, yet it has a charming dimple he never seemed to outgrow. The freckles which seemed so prominent when he was a child have faded and are barely noticeable on the bridge of his nose. Anyone else might focus on Aidan's hair as his most outstanding feature. Don't get me wrong, it's gorgeous. I'm tempted to run my fingers through it and play with those incredible curls. Even so, Aidan's eyes get me every time. To describe them as green would be like saying the world's ecosystem is made of water and dirt. His eyes convey a seemingly infinite spectrum of colors and moods. Aidan's are the only eyes I've ever seen that truly twinkle with laughter—although right now it's not laughter. What I see in those eyes is blatant desire. It's completely unnerving for me.

I feel a tingle of excitement travel through my body. It's what I used to feel like when I nailed a complicated lift for the first time or could surpass a choreographer's expectations. Still, there is a little voice in the back of my head that asks if I can handle what happens next.

Aidan shifts slightly in his seat and cups the back of my head as he angles for the perfect kiss. As his firm lips touch mine, my breath catches. Pleasure sweeps through my body like fire. I am embarrassed by the intensity of my reaction. It's a normal kiss in a public place; it's not like he's stripping me naked or anything.

I'm not sure my racing pulse is the way I expected to react to Aidan. This is a brand new experience for me. I've never wanted anyone before. Sure, I thought I wanted Rory when I was a teenager, but that wasn't anything like this. I feel like a plant that has long existed, half-alive in the desert, and Aidan's touch is the first rain in years, just in time to mean the difference between life and death.

As I'm relaxing into the simple joy of being expertly kissed by my very own rock star, I hear a delicate cough behind me. "I'm so sorry, y'all, but the captain has turned on the fasten seatbelt sign because we're expecting turbulence. I hate to interrupt, but the Captain is asking all passengers to face forward and fasten your seat belts," the flight attendant says with an apologetic grimace.

I smile at her, thinking how awful it must be to deal with folks who resent your presence every day. I'd probably get a little cranky with people who wouldn't turn off their electronic devices. "That's okay," I assure her. "I don't want anything to happen to this handsome face. He's going to be a big star."

Aidan whips his head around to look at me as he asks, "Really, Gracie? You believe that?"

I squeeze his hand and lace my fingers through his. With my other hand, I sign as I speak to underscore my message, "Yes, Aidan. I believe that with my whole heart."

Aidan draws in a rough breath. "Umm, I guess it's my turn to be at a loss for words."

CHAPTER TWELVE

AIDAN

IT'S BEEN A REALLY long day. While we were waiting for our luggage to arrive in baggage claim, Tara seemed to lose steam. Now, riding in the taxi to the hotel, she's curled up next to me like a kitten, dead to the world. My arm is falling asleep, but I don't want to wake her after the day she's had. She's doing a good job considering how hard this is for her, but I can see the stress on her face when she thinks no one is watching. I still can't believe she wants to do all this for me to help me succeed. Though, I shouldn't be surprised; she has always been exceptional.

If the episode today is an example of the terror she's been living with since that creep attacked her, it's a wonder she managed to stay sane, let alone practically raise herself, graduate from high school, go to college, and learn self-defense skills. Today was a wake up call. Being a good guy may not be enough. I was so sure that if I was the anti-Warren Jones, it would be some kind of magic elixir which could bring her long nightmare to an end. This must be what Delores was warning me about.

I need to take my own advice and not try to define, label, or script our relationship. Whatever 'us' is, it will happen minute by minute, moment by moment, until we've built a definition which works for us. This may be the single easiest and also hardest thing I've ever done.

Tara and I have fallen into our old friendship as if nothing has changed. In some ways, she's still the wickedly smart confidant and companion who 'gets' me like none other but is not afraid to call me on my bull. Still, incidents like the one today remind me things are not the way they used to be. Underneath all the normalcy, there is the shadow of a monster named Warren Jones. I don't know if it's within my power to slay the monster for her, or even if it's my right to do so. Maybe she has to slay him all by herself. It may take everything I have within me to stand on the sidelines and watch her do it. If that's what I have to do to make us stronger, I'll have to put my protective instincts aside.

Honestly, the most difficult thing for me will be not hunting down the jerk and feeding him his balls on a skewer. Slow castration with a rusty nail would be far too kind. I wonder if he even realizes his five-minute power play, a dozen years ago, changed the person Tara became. I'm a true believer in karma and I hope his new prison buddies are taking care of any discrepancy in the sentence he got and the one he deserved.

It's an incredibly difficult challenge to feel this connected to Tara and yet keep arbitrary boundaries between us. She seems to be relaxing the invisible buffer between us and crossing it voluntarily more often. I wish we could go back to the way the things were before. We were so close that we almost didn't have to speak to communicate and there were no physical limitations between us. She would think nothing of jumping on my back for a piggyback ride, arguing her feet were insurable through Lloyd's of London and therefore too valuable to touch the floor. I think I carried her around for two weeks before we moved on to the next game. I believe she tried to teach me Jenga, next. It's a good game for her, because she has the patience and determination of a saint. Conversely, I royally suck at the game because I want to play all my big moves right up front. I'm not willing to take my time and let the game unfold.

I want to believe I've learned some lessons in life since I was eleven and have developed the patience needed to slow down and take this experience moment by moment. I certainly don't want to add more stress to Tara's life. Let's face it, the woman is incredibly sexy, and I am not a kid anymore. I don't know if I can always keep a lid on that. It will be an interesting weekend, to say the least.

As the hotel comes into sight and the taxi slows down, Tara wakes up with a start. Her head flies up, nearly striking me in the chin. For a second, her eyes are wide with terror. It's yet another disconcerting glimpse of what she's been living with for over a decade. It feels like punches to my gut.

Watching her eyes focus, I interlock my index finger with hers in our familiar gesture. "Hey, Gracie, are you ready to help me tackle L.A.?"

Tara nods, appearing grateful to have something

tangible to focus on. "Let's go tame this beast, Aidan — or are you still planning to go by A.O.?" Her eyebrow lifts in amusement.

I snicker over the idea, flattered she remembers my childish plans. "No, that's quite all right. Aidan O'Brien will do fine, thank you," I reply, still chuckling.

"Are you sure? The initial thing seems to work for k.d. lang, B.J. Thomas, Mr. T., and the artist formally known as Prince."

Tara's feisty sass and teasing manner fills me with relief. This is the Gracie I remember; it's like watching a butterfly emerge from its cocoon.

"Those are very good artists and they would be wonderful mentors, but for now I think I'll stick with my full name. If I ever make the big leagues, I might consider more exotic names. My name is as plain Jane as it gets, but at least it belongs to my family."

"If we're going to dream, we should dream big. You want to be known by your first name like Elton, Michael or Billy," she replies.

"Billy Jack?" I tease.

"Uh … no!"

I walk around the taxi and open the door to help her out. As I do, I lean over to kiss her behind the ear and murmur, "From your lips to God's ears."

We link fingers and walk up to the reservation desk. "Aidan O'Brien, I have a reservation under Five Star Creative Arts and Industries," I state, handing the reservation clerk a piece of paper with my confirmation number.

"Okay, Mr. O'Brien. Your room is 317 on the third floor. The ice machine is down the hall on the left. The pool is open from 11:00 AM to 8:00 PM," he explains as he hands me a map with the room number highlighted.

Studying the map, I notice a problem. "Excuse me, sir. Is this room ADA compliant?" I inquire, hating this part.

The reservation clerk looks at me skeptically as he replies, "Why? You don't look handicapped. Maybe you and your girlfriend should go play your kinky role-play games somewhere else. Those rooms are reserved for people who really need them."

Tara's jaw drops open in shock as her eyes widen and meet mine. She tilts her head slightly at me, then back at the clerk, and raises an inquisitive eyebrow. I nod tightly. Oh boy! This guy might wish he had stayed in bed this morning. Tara is usually as laid back as an arthritic basset hound until you give her a cause, but then she turns into a Jack Russell terrier. I figure this guy has about two-seconds of 'nice' Tara left.

My best friend winks at me and digs in her purse for a minute. With a gleam in her eyes, she shows me a hair band. Almost before I can blink, she has her long hair in a slick high ponytail. She winks at me and starts to sign as she addresses the clerk, "My client here may or may not have heard you since he is deaf. However, I can hear you just fine. The stuff flying out of your mouth could keep your boss tied up in court for years." Tara turns to me to confirm. "Years? Right?" she signs for me and voices the question to the clerk.

"Absolutely," I agree, trying hard not to grin ear to

ear with pride.

She turns back to the clerk, but continues to sign. "Perhaps you've not heard of invisible disabilities? My friend Kiera is in a wheelchair, but she needs the room even less than Mr. O'Brien does."

"He doesn't look like he needs anything," the clerk argues. "If he's so deaf how come he can talk? Why isn't he doing all that weird stuff with his hands?"

I roll my eyes. "I can hear you, you know," I say dryly.

"Oh, can I have this one?" Tara asks, turning to me.

I shrug. "Sure, you're on a roll."

"Thanks. You're so good to me," she responds with a small grin.

Tara looks over at him and studies his name tag. "Well, Eddie K. If you took the time to figure out a little about the world around you, you'd understand not everyone's disability is the same. Mr. O'Brien here wasn't born deaf, so his speech is not as impaired as someone who was. Also, he's one of the lucky ones who has benefited from cochlear implants. In most situations, he can function pretty well. However, at night he has to take them out to clean and recharge them. Despite his amazingly handsome and debonair appearance, which I'm sure intimidates the heck out of you, he remains deaf. Without his implants in, Aidan cannot hear the smoke alarm, the phone, the alarm clock, or a knock at the door. That, Eddie, is why Mr. O'Brien asked for an accessible room. That is not to say there won't be some kinky stuff going on in those oversize bathrooms. But I'll leave that to your under-sized brain and over-sized imagination."

Poor Eddie K. looks like he's been punched in the chin by Evander Holyfield. I kind of feel bad for him. He had no way of knowing Tornado Tara was coming. She is so magnificent. She looks like a strong wind would knock her over, but when her mind is set on something, you'd best get on board or get out of her way.

It's all I can do not to laugh out loud at his expression. I look back at Tara. She's suddenly very interested in the nail polish beginning to flake off of her thumbnail. I catch her eye and sign, "Impressive. Scary, but impressive."

Tara gives me a micro smirk and shrugs one shoulder as she signs back, "Really? I was going for educational. But scary works. He's a Neanderthal."

I almost choke on my tongue trying not to laugh. "You're so bad," I sign, trying to be discreet.

Eddie notices, though. He turns to Tara and practically shouts, "I thought you said he didn't have to do that weird stuff with his hands."

Okay, that's it. I'm done. I don't know why this guy feels like he has to be an asshat. The only one he's embarrassing is himself. Does he think he's the only person who thinks talking louder is somehow going to make me less deaf?

"Eddie, I'm sorry, you're absolutely right. That was probably rude of me. I shouldn't have had a conversation in front of you in a language you don't understand without translating for you." I admit. "But, since it was a private conversation and all, I figured it was none of your business. Speaking of rude, you never answered my original question. Is the room equipped with what I need?"

Eddie K turns to his computer and begins banging on the keyboard. I hope his employer has insurance on it, because after tonight I suspect it's going to be toast. He turns back to me and says, "No, I'm sorry. That room is not equipped. The only room we have available that's equipped is a single, smoking room."

Tara meets his gaze with fire in her eyes. "I want to make sure I understand this correctly. Even though we called and made arrangements days ago for specific accommodations and made it clear why they were necessary, you're telling me no such room exists in your huge hotel? Tell me, Eddie, if we ask your supervisor the same question, will we get the same answer?"

Tara points to our confirmation printout which clearly spells out the fact that we asked for a non-smoking, ADA compliant room. We even had a specific room assignment given to us by the person making reservations. Eddie rips the paper out of her hand and resumes pounding on his keyboard. After a few minutes, he snarls, "My mistake. One of the executive suites just opened up. I'll be happy to change your reservation, sir." The last syllable was dripping with sarcasm.

Two can play this game. I don my most engaging smile and reply, "Why, thank you Eddie. We appreciate your exemplary customer service skills."

I take the new key and paperwork from him and hand it to Tara and I grab our suitcases. As we're walking away, I hear Eddie mutter, "Stupid retards. They think they run the world."

I grab Tara's hand to stop her from using her

considerable repertoire of martial arts training to tear this guy apart limb-by-limb.

"Let it go, Gracie." I direct softly. "We can't change people like him. It doesn't matter what we say or do, his opinion is always going to be the same."

A tremble passes through Tara's body as if she's shaking off a bad dream and she pops her neck as she rolls her shoulders. She sounds anguished as she hisses, "AJ, did you hear what he called you? You want me to walk away from that?"

I drop the luggage and gather her up in a hug right there in the middle of the lobby. I really don't care who's watching. "Yeah, baby, I do. He can't damage me, and he can't hurt us. If he chooses to remain ignorant and intolerant — that's on him. It's not our responsibility." I kiss the top of her head.

Just then a luggage attendant comes by and offers to take our bags to our rooms. I wasn't planning to use these extra services because I don't have a lot of money for tips. She must have read the look of panic on my face because she says, "No worries, this one's on me."

As the attendant, a tall woman, steps on the elevator with us and maneuvers the cart around, she waits until the door closes before saying, "Look, Eddie doesn't represent all of us, or even most of us. He's a really big jerk. My son has autism. Everybody has something that makes 'em unique. Normal is boring. I apologize for him. I'm going to have my friend Sarah send you something down from the kitchen. She is an amazing pastry chef."

I reach out to shake the lady's hand, but Tara has beaten me to it and has her wrapped in a hug. When she's done, I shake her hand and say, "Thank you, ma'am. Your words mean a lot."

She blushes slightly. "You all have a great stay. It was nice meeting you. Please call #211 if you need anything."

"Thank you so much, you have a great day too," Tara says as she slips her a five dollar bill.

"You don't have to do that," the attendant insists.

Tara nodded. "I know. I want to. You made a crappy situation better. Besides, a trucker gave me that last night on a ninety-nine cent cup of coffee. It would be creepy karma to keep it," she explains with a cheeky grin.

The attendant shrugs. "If you insist. It doesn't matter to me. Money's money. Thank you. I appreciate it. Good night, folks."

After I lock the door, Tara walks up behind me, places her arms around my waist, and hugs me. "Thank you, Aidan. That was a pretty epic save back there," she mumbles into my shirt.

"Really? Because, from where I was standing, you didn't need much saving. In fact, you were the one slaying *my* dragons."

"No, Aidan. I'm serious," Tara argues. "If you hadn't stopped me, I might have ruined the whole trip. I was about to go ballistic on that guy, I might've gotten arrested and you'd have to visit me in prison … a bad scene all around."

I grin. "Yeah?"

"Seriously, I got in trouble once because this perverted old man was trying to jerk off in the presence of a young girl on the city bus, and I was trying to divert his attention so she could get away. It worked, but somehow, I ended up with a criminal record over it. I'm not even sure he was ever caught and punished."

I turn around so her face is buried in my chest. I feel her tears through both layers of cloth. "Now they might not let me in the schools or adopt a little girl like Mindy, because I was so stupid," Tara hiccups as she sobs the words.

"You did the right thing. Don't give up yet. There are things which can be done to clean up your record. I'm sure you remember my dad is a sort of big-shot in the business community. He's got a stable of lawyers at his beck and call. I'm sure one of them can do something to fix the whole mess, because that's just wrong."

Tara walks over to the nightstand and grabs a Kleenex to blow her nose. "I hope so. I'd hate for this to ruin my chance of working with kids. I was trying to help her and it was a long time ago. I would probably handle things differently now. I saw the potential danger and reacted without thinking it through. I wonder if I've made a lot of progress since then." "Come on Gracie, it's been an epically long day, and since the hotel has been so gracious as to provide this awesome room with a sunken tub, you should totally take advantage of it."

"Oh, sounds heavenly! I wish I had some of Heather's homemade bubble bath. It smells phenomenal."

"Does Heather make your perfume too?" I inquire. "Because you always smell spectacular."

Tara grins at me and answers with excitement in her

voice, "Yes! She makes it for all of us, and it always suits our personality. I keep telling her she needs to go into business professionally. But she's so talented, she can't decide which business she wants to get into. She is also a spectacular chef and needs to open a restaurant. Unfortunately, her family has undermined her confidence and she's too scared to take the leap. I'm working on her, though. She has an old dilapidated food truck she's working out of now."

"From what I've read, it's not easy to run one of those trucks either," I respond. "I'll let you take a bath while I get things unpacked and work on the stuff I need for the audition. I need to be ready for the meeting tonight at seven o'clock."

<hr />

I'm trying to play it cool and act like this is not the most nerve-racking thing I've ever done. I'm glad Tara gave me the warning about the acoustic environment. We are in the middle of an old soundstage. Sound bounces off cement and metal everywhere. The line we're in snakes around the whole perimeter of the building and out into the parking lot. Fortunately, we got here early and I'm one of the first people in line.

Not to use a really bad pun or anything, but the noise in this place is deafening. It's an echo chamber. I'm grateful I can communicate with Tara without adding to the cacophony. Even so, processing all the input is giving me a huge headache. Tara notices my grimace when someone knocks over a rack of folding chairs. The sound ricochets through the building like a string of firecrackers. The insane level of the sound input reminds me of when I first got my cochlear implants, and my brain was first learning to interpret sound again.

She touches my arm drawing me back to the present. "Aidan, do you trust me to have your back?" She surveys the room.

"Of course." I answer without hesitation. I'm totally confused by the random question. Maybe I missed part of a conversation because of the extreme environment.

"Just turn your receivers off, then. Obviously, you're not getting any usable input, and they're about to scramble your brain. So let me be your ears. That's what I'm here for."

My whole body sags in relief. It is incredibly fatiguing to try to sort all this out in my head. Tara's idea is brilliant. On the other hand, I don't want to be treated any different as a "special needs" contestant. I run my hands through my hair in frustration. There's really no good answer. Either choice has a downside. But just then, a couple of teenage girls start to shriek in excitement. In a normal environment, this wouldn't be a big deal. But we're in a building with no carpet, with metal walls and hundreds of other people also making noise. It's the proverbial straw that breaks the camel's back. Wearily, I reach up and turn off my implants.

I watch as Tara swallows hard and her eyes mist over with tears. "Thanks for believing in me. I'll take care of you," she signs. Today, she's dressed like a traditional interpreter. Her clothes are solid black with very little embellishment or frills. Her long hair is caught in a single braid down her back. She looks buttoned-down and corporate. If someone were to meet her for the first time, they would never believe under all that cool perfectionism beats the heart of a passionate artist.

The silence feels like a cloud of marshmallows. For the first time, I can study the crowd around me. When I do, I begin to feel positively ancient. After doing some mental math, I decide it's mathematically possible some of these kids trying out alongside of me could be my own children. Now isn't that a happy little thought? I'm a tad late to this party.

Tara notices the glum look on my face and starts to interpret some of the conversations taking place around me. Up until now, I had only gotten glimpses of her interpreting skills. Some interpreters are so boring that it's the equivalent of listening to someone speaking in monotone. It's enough to put you to sleep. The other extreme is an interpreter whose facial expressions are so exaggerated their signing gets lost in the process. Tara has the perfect balance. When she's interpreting the conversation of a large group, she plays each speaker just slightly differently so it's easy to keep track of which person is talking. She is animated and entertaining, but not to the point where it's distracting.

Listening to conversations around me, via Tara, distracts me from my own nervous energy and provides me with some interesting information. For example, many of my fellow competitors have never actually sung for a crowd before. I find that approach to be absolutely stunning. I think back to my early days on the stage. I can't imagine what it would be like to make your singing debut for the whole world to see, on national TV. It's not lost on me that I'm doing virtually the same thing. Aside from Rory, Renée and Tara, I've kept my singing ability a big secret from the world. This is my debut as well.

Unconsciously, I start to gnaw the inside of my cheek. Tara notices what I'm doing and signs stop. "Aidan, relax. You got this. You've had this since you were five. It's just taken you a while to capitalize on your talent."

I give her a grateful smile as I sign, "I'm so glad you're here. Not only are you a phenomenal interpreter, you make a kickin' cheerleader, too."

Tara winks at me as she signs, "No problem. I'm glad I could help."

Finally we get to the check-in table and I hand over my paperwork and confirmation number, along with a headshot Renée was kind enough to take.

The event coordinator starts rattling off instructions at a million miles an hour. I have turned my receivers back on, but I still look at Tara so I can follow the conversation. *Geez, this lady needs to cut back on the Red Bull.* When she notices what I'm doing, she stops mid-sentence and screeches, "You're *deaf?* Deaf people can't sing!"

A mutinous expression crosses Tara's face, but she stays in the role of interpreter.

"With all due respect, ma'am, my audition tape says differently. You guys contacted me, remember?"

The stage manager or talent coordinator gets extremely flustered. She begins rapidly talking into her headset and making wild gestures with her hands. She has her back turned. Unfortunately, in this echoey environment, I can't figure out exactly what she's saying. Eventually, she turns around and begins talking to Tara, "Tell him that out of fairness to other contestants, we need to hear him sing before we can register him, to make sure he didn't doctor his audition tape."

Tara signs what the woman is telling her. But then she turns to the woman. "I'm sorry, I didn't catch your name."

The woman seems startled by the question as if we should know who she is. "Oh, it's Clover. Clover Branch." When she catches a glimpse of our expressions, she provides further explanation. "What can I say? My parents were TV stars in the seventies."

"I don't know if you know this Clover, but it is common courtesy to speak directly to a deaf person and not to the interpreter. I'll be happy to interpret for you," Tara offers.

I'm so proud of her because I know what effort it's taking for her to stay professional and detached from the conversation.

I sneak a wink at Tara as I reply to the concerned woman, "Certainly, I understand. I have nothing to hide. Would you like me to play the piano or my guitar?"

This question prompts another round of frenzied conversation over the headsets. Eventually, she looks up at me and inquires, "I'm sorry, Aidan. We don't have the piano available at the moment. Do you mind using your guitar?"

"Not at all," I answer. "Although, if possible, I would prefer to sing in a quieter environment."

After consulting with someone on the other end of her headset, Clover states, "That won't be a problem. Follow me, please."

She walks us briskly to a back room, all the while talking frantically on her headset. When we get there, she asks me to remove my leather jacket and to turn over any electronic devices including my cell phone. Clover looks at Tara, clearly expecting her to do the same. Tara shrugs and takes off her blazer.

"Is there a problem?" I ask, curious about her actions.

"Oh, we just want to make sure you two aren't cheating somehow. You know, like Mille Vanilli," she answers as she writes on her clipboard.

This is going to be fun. I love it when people have really low expectations and I can blow them out of the water. "Okay, you're going to be sitting two feet away from me so I don't even understand how that's possible. Whatever floats your boat is fine with me," I respond with an easy shrug.

I pull my guitar out of the case and give it a quick tune. I look up to see Tara has brought me some bottled water. I turn to the talent coordinator and ask her if she has any requests. Her eyebrows shoot to her hairline. Obviously, she was expecting me to choose something I had already prepared. I figured if she suspects I'm somehow cheating, why not put the ball in her court?

I've been a stereotypical wedding singer for almost a decade. I've worked with a few bands here and there, and I write a lot of my own material, but the way I put food on the table is by playing songs other people want me to play. So I can sing everything from Frank Sinatra to Pharrell Williams. I doubt she's going to throw anything out I haven't covered. It's a gamble I have to take. She takes out her cell phone and pulls up her playlist. She thumbs through it briefly and states, "I want to hear *Beautiful* by James Blunt."

A large smile crosses my face. I can't help myself. I have a legendarily bad poker face. I thought she was going to throw something challenging at me — not one of the biggest hits of 2005 I've performed literally thousands of times. I swear I've performed this song at nearly every wedding in the last nine years. I think Tara knows too because I see her draw in a sharp breath. When I look up again, though, Tara is the picture of professionalism. I nod at Tara and Clover. "Sure, I'd be happy to. *Beautiful* is one of my favorite songs too."

I've done this song so many times, I've had ample time to develop enough creative guitar licks to make the song my own. I play a few bars of an elaborate introduction and start to sing. I try to tune everyone out except Tara and pretend I'm sitting in my living room, playing just for her. The expression on her face is making that easy to do. She looks totally enchanted by my performance. Her eyes are wide open as she watches every strum of my fingers. Her cheeks are slightly flushed and her bottom lip is caught in her teeth as she concentrates on what I'm doing. When I get to the chorus, her eyes flutter shut and she starts to silently sing along. As I finish the song with all the emotion I want to convey to her, she opens her eyes and looks straight at me. Even though I'm a few feet away, I can see her breathing is fast. Almost imperceptibly, she signs,

"Wow!"

My pulse is beating faster. I understand now how intoxicating it is to have someone who matters in the audience. I've had a few transient relationships over the years, but nothing with staying power. Women always told me it seemed like my heart was somewhere else. Now that Tara's back, I wonder if they had a point.

Abruptly, I hear clapping from a few feet in front of me.

Oddly, it startles me. I completely forgot anyone else was in the room besides Tara. Clover has big tears running down her face and her mascara makes her look like a raccoon. "Oh my! That was just so beautiful. I can't believe you can actually sing. You did such a spectacular job, too. It's so courageous of you. You've overcome so much. Our viewers aren't going to believe this. You'll be raking in votes by the millions. Maybe we can even arrange a field visit to one of those deaf schools. You could be a mentor or something."

It's a good thing I have my guitar in my hand to ground me. I make a point of adjusting the strings on my guitar. At this point, I'm doing it randomly, I'm not even sure what key it's in and I don't care. I'm simply giving myself a chance to chill out before I say something stupid and ruin my chance at a career before it even starts.

This is exactly what I didn't want to happen. I want to be treated like every other contestant with no special heart stopping back-story with its own theme song. Yet if this lady has anything to say about it, it looks like that train has left the station. I look at Tara and quietly sign, "Help."

Tara looks at me. "Aidan, do you mind if I step out of the role of interpreter?"

I have no idea what she plans to do, but I trust her, so I roll with it. "No, feel free." I move back so Tara has a better view.

Tara steps forward and shakes the talent coordinator's hand, "Hi, I'm Tara Isamu. I'm Aidan's best friend and sign language interpreter. I don't sing, but I used to be a competitive dancer. I know a bit about how these shows work. I'm just curious if you're putting other competitors at a disadvantage if you make a big deal of Aidan's deafness. You might make him the target of bullying and bring negative publicity to the show. Wouldn't it be better if everyone started out completely equal, and it was only talent that distinguishes them?"

Clover is thoughtful for a moment. You can almost see the gears turning in her head as she rethinks her strategy. She studies me. "Well, it's not as if you don't have stud appeal all on your own. If you do well on this show, you'll probably have a ton of endorsement deals for hair products." She turns to Tara. "It's true, fans are remarkably fickle and the mob mentality can take over. There could be a fan riot if Aidan had a perceived advantage, and that might lead to voter backlash and cyber bullying. Forget what I said about the deaf identity stuff. People might not even notice. We won't hide it, but we won't mention it either. Is that okay?"

"That sounds like a great plan. I'm not ashamed of my deafness, but I don't want to advertise it for sympathy votes, either. Do you need anything else from me, Ms. Branch?"

She looks uncomfortable for a moment, then stretches her hand out for me to shake and admits, "Mr. O'Brien, I owe you an apology. I totally thought the deafness was a gimmick at best, and that you were trying to perpetuate a fraud on our show. I apologize for my ignorance. I'm not supposed to say this, but I think you've got what it takes to go far in this competition. Trust me, I've seen a lot of audition tapes and no one moved me like you did. I'm glad you held true to your principles and chose not to use your deafness as an excuse. It shows a lot about your character. Despite what you've heard about our town, character goes a long way. After you sign all the papers in the packet, I'm done with you for the day. You can come back tomorrow morning."

I nod.

"Officially, check-in is at eight o'clock, but those who are smart get here about 7:15. Bring your signed paperwork with you. You can save time tomorrow if you get it notarized tonight. The hotel has a notary on staff," she instructs.

Tara steps forward to shake her hand, but Clover ignores the gesture. Instead, she asks Tara, "You're not going to be like an overgrown stage mom are you?"

Out of habit, Tara interprets her words for me, but then she makes her own editorial comment on the side in the sign language equivalent of parentheses where she asks me, "Is she serious?"

"No, actually, I don't plan to be his stage mom. I came to be his interpreter. Does he *need* a stage mom?" Tara responds with a fair amount of sarcasm, but she's careful to keep her voice even and professional.

The lady looks at Tara blankly and went on as if Tara had not answered her question. "I don't know where everyone fits around here, so I don't want you helping him too much," the talent coordinator explains.

Tara raises an eyebrow at her. "You are aware sign language interpreters take college classes and are extensively trained, right? We don't get this job accidentally. We have professional standards we have to live up to."

This time, Clover has the grace to look slightly embarrassed. "I had no idea. There's a lady at my church who does it for her son, and she just learned it from a book."

This response seems to mollify Tara some and she softens her stance. "That's okay, it's a complicated field and there's a lot of things people don't know. There's a big difference between knowing some sign language and being a sign language interpreter. I know you probably didn't mean to offend us. So, it's not a big deal. I'm here to help Aidan in whatever way he needs. Primarily, my job is to be his interpreter. However, I've also known him for many years. I can't say honestly that I'm not also here to cheer him on. But I won't do anything to jeopardize the competition."

Clover looks down at her clipboard and declares in a no nonsense voice, "Well, good. I'm glad we got that cleared up."

Chapter Thirteen

Tara

"Well, that was a bigger adventure than I planned," declares Aidan as he flops back on the couch.

"I'm not sure whether my presence made it better or worse." I toss him some orange pop from the mini fridge. "I think you might have been better off if I hadn't been here."

"Are you kidding me? Did you forget I had to turn my implants off to avoid having a mini stroke from all the noise?"

"Exaggerate much, Aidan? Headache? Yes. Stroke? Not so likely," I tease.

"Anyway, the point is — I wasn't coping very well. If you hadn't been there, I probably wouldn't have been able to cope at all. You're more than my interpreter. You calmed me down and made it possible for me to do what I needed to do today. I needed you there for many reasons."

"Well, I'm glad I could help. I just hope I don't turn

out to be an issue for you. Aidan, I hate to be a downer, but has your dad looked into these people? Call me insane, but I have a bad feeling about this one."

"I didn't really fill him in on all the details," Aidan admits sheepishly. "Rory is the only one who knows what's going on. He's been around all of their craziness. We decided to wait to tell them for now. I can't guarantee you what he'll do if I do well in this thing."

I remember what he's talking about. His parents gave a whole new meaning to the phrase competitive. I often felt sorry for Rory. He had the opposite problem of me. I couldn't get my mom to be remotely interested in what was going on in my life and he couldn't get his parents to be uninterested. Somewhere in that equation, Aidan got lost.

I always felt like I was abandoned by my parents, which I know, is irrational since they both died. But, weird things happen in your brain when a parent passes away before you're old enough to understand what death is about. My dad was the center of my universe. One day he went to work and never came back and everything I knew about life changed that day.

I cannot imagine what it was like for Aidan to cope with the fact that his parents tossed him aside like a sweater which no longer fit when he became deaf. Every time I think about it, I become incensed all over again. The strange thing about it all for me is I was with the O'Brien family nearly every day for weeks at a time after Aidan almost died and no one bothered to say a word to me—even though we'd been best friends for several years. I had no idea his life had undergone as much of a catastrophic upheaval as mine.

I'm sitting cross-legged in the center of the bed surrounded by a copy of the paperwork the talent agency provided to Aidan. I stopped by the business center at the hotel to make a couple of copies before we fill them out. I read them while Aidan took a shower and I have some serious doubts about this operation. "Um, AJ, did you read this?" I study the documents more carefully. "This says they may edit your image and portray you any way they choose into perpetuity. If I remember correctly from taking my SAT exam, the term perpetuity means they can change any publicity materials they may have on you forever. That seems weird to me. I keep thinking about all the weird stuff they do with famous movie stars after they pass away — you know like holograms, tribute songs and advertisements — it's creepy. I'm not a lawyer like Jeff but I think a contract like this would allow them to do something like that." I shiver involuntary as a feeling of dread creeps up my spine.

"Don't they use a lot of boilerplate language in those contracts that nobody bothers to read? I'm sure it's probably no big deal. Why would they want to do that stuff anyway?" Aidan asks as he picks notes out on his guitar.

"I don't know, Aidan." I struggle to put a voice to my feelings without crushing his dreams. "Something about this feels off to me. Why would an independent company without the backing of a record label be trying to find songwriters? And why do they have to have exclusive rights to the songs you create for the show forever? Also, why is the talent pool so uneven if they allegedly recruited everyone based on their talent? I mean, you saw those kids. Some of those kids were barely old enough to change a Band-Aid by themselves, let alone write their own songs. How will a teenage girl who's never performed in front of anyone other than her cat going to compete against those of you who have been doing it for more than a decade? It's not fair to you or the other contestants."

Aidan shrugs. "I don't know, it seems to have worked out okay for Kelly Clarkson and Phillip Phillips."

"But, that brings me back to my original question, why would a giant corporation be interested in sponsoring what amounts to a fancy talent show?"

Aidan flinches at my words and I feel like I kicked a kitten in the face. "I didn't mean it as a slam against you, AJ. A lot of things don't add up. For example, they claim to be a show that promotes songwriting, yet not once during the audition process did they ask you for a sample of your songwriting skills. For a show that's supposed to support artists and songwriters, all the protection in this contract is geared toward the corporation."

"Isn't that typical of big companies?" Aidan counters. "Aren't they supposed to look after their own interests?"

"Well, yes. But, it's not usually this one-sided. This company wants to basically make you an indentured servant for the rest of your life. They own your likeness and any creative content you put on the show. They basically can be the puppet masters. You have no power in the situation."

"Of course, I have the power. If I don't like how they're treating me, I can just quit," Aidan reasons.

"That's a cute thought Aidan. Not realistic, but cute. I'm speaking from personal experience here. Your parent's got Rory and me booked on a children's show when we were younger. It was a joke. It turned out the whole thing was an elaborate pet project for this guy's trophy wife to provide cover for his non-family-friendly activities. Because he was a lawyer, he had the resources to push the project regardless of the cost. So, we were stuck in a country we didn't want to be, in a job we didn't want to do, speaking a language we didn't speak — all because no one thought to read the small print. It didn't matter if we didn't want to do it. They just edited around us. This meant they made us into the villains of the century."

"Yeah, I vaguely remember that. Ma and Pa were steamed for a whole month. I remember a lot of angry phone calls to the attorneys. I think Rory thought it was great to have his good-boy halo knocked a little askew."

I snort back laughter, which was a dangerous thing to do, because it made me inhale the crème soda I was drinking, Aidan comes over and pats me on the back until I stop coughing. "Are you going to survive over here?" he quips.

"Yep, I was just having a hard time with Rory and halo in the same sentence when it doesn't include video games. He doesn't seem the type. The only love he shared was self-love. It's a good thing we didn't have selfies back then. He would've never had time to learn to dance," I respond with my tongue firmly in my cheek.

"I can't give an unbiased opinion, so I think I should probably refrain from commenting." Aidan takes a drink of his pop.

Smirking, I toss the throw pillow at him. "Well, don't ever play poker because your body language tells the whole story."

Wearily, Aidan sticks the throw pillow behind his head and closes his eyes. "Tara, what am I supposed to do with all this? Do you expect me to walk away from the opportunity of a lifetime because they *might* make me look like a clown at some future date twenty years down the line? So, they will own the rights to one song I have yet to write — is that the end of the world? I write lots of songs. Some of them are fantastic and others are crap. What if this is my one and only chance to make it big? Can I afford to walk away from that?"

I knew I should've just kept my mouth shut. I didn't come here to be a dream killer. Now, I feel like I've made matters worse. Aidan was right, I've turned out to be the worst kind of distraction. He looks completely destroyed. Before I have a chance to second-guess myself, I go over to the couch where he's still sitting with his eyes closed and curl my body next to him. I lay my head on his shoulder. "I'm so sorry Aidan. I wish there were easy answers to this. I wish this was the straight out fairytale ending you were hoping for. I'm sorry I ruined it for you."

Aidan wraps his arms around me in a tight hug as he shakes his head against my temple. "Gracie, you ruined nothing. You didn't stick the crazy language in the contract —they did. You just had the smarts to point it out. Now, I have to decide what the heck I'm going to do about it."

"Well, you haven't signed anything yet. Do you have to sign the deal exactly as it's written? Can you modify it at all?"

Aidan scrubs his hand down his face in frustration as he answers, "I don't know. That Ms. Branch lady made it sound like everything needed to be notarized by eight o'clock in the morning for everything to go smoothly."

"That's true. She made it sound urgent. On the other hand, she absolutely loved your audition and they might be willing to make a few concessions to have you on the show. It might be worth it to ask. I'm not sure you want to take this deal lock, stock and barrel. There's not much upside for you as it's written."

"What if messing with the deal costs me the whole game?" Aidan asks, his green eyes intense with emotion.

Stuffing my hands in my pockets so I'm not tempted to bite my nails, I regard him carefully as I answer him somberly, "Aidan, only you know how much you have at stake with this and how much you're willing to risk. I can't make the call for you. I'll support your decision either way."

Suddenly, Aidan envelops me in a huge full-bodied hug reminiscent of our childhood days. "I never had a second of doubt that you would, Tara. You always were my biggest fan, whether I was a star or just the geeky kid who sat next to you in class telling awful knock-knock jokes."

"Hey, there's a lot to be said for the power of knock-knock jokes," I tease.

In an uncharacteristic move, Aidan doesn't follow my lead. Instead, he continues to hold me loosely in his arms and massage my neck with his thumbs. He pauses for a moment as he gathers his thoughts. "Gracie, I know I screwed up when I turned down the offer from Juilliard. I don't want to do that again. You don't know what it's been like to dink around the edges of success for all these years pretending to have an identity as a musician but still having to take somebody's mashed potatoes back to the kitchen because they're not hot enough or having to apologize to the customer because the fourth new chef in three months doesn't know how to cook a steak medium rare. It's demoralizing. What if this is supposed to be my big break and I pass it up because of some fussy language in a contract that might never apply to me?" He rests his forehead against mine.

"Aidan, you forgot I was at the audition today. I heard you sing. I know with my whole heart that even if it's not this venue, you will make it in the music business. You are a phenomenal musician — you always have been. What you showed out there today is only a small fraction of your talent. So, you're going to make it with or without this show. If they won't do it on your terms, maybe this isn't the right vehicle for you," I insist firmly.

Aidan's body is still filled with tension and his face is drawn tight with fatigue and indecision. Finally, I decide perhaps the best thing I can do is be the distraction he feared I might be. I thread my arms around his neck and press my body against his as I stand on my toes to plant a kiss on his very surprised lips.

I am not sure which of us is the most shocked. I have been fantasizing about doing this since the wedding, but I never imagined I'd actually have the nerve to follow through on my wild thoughts. My heart is beating a million miles an hour. I didn't expect such a benign, simple touch to seem so erotic.

My eyes drift shut involuntarily. I feel like I've suddenly stepped into sunshine after years of being frozen. I just want to sit there and bask in the warm touch and allow my icy layers to fall away. I give a little happy moan of pleasure.

Aidan's long fingers tighten around my waist as he answers with a groan of his own. "Gracie, are you still okay with what's happening here?" he murmurs in my ear.

Tears spring to my eyes as I think about the implications of his question. But, I'm determined not to allow Warren Jones to ruin every relationship I will ever have. It's time for me to take my power back. Still, it shows so much about Aidan's character that he would even bother to worry about how the simple act of kissing would impact me. I am incredibly touched by his concern. I open my eyes to study his handsome face and answer directly as I can. With as many unknowns as I have in my life right now.

"Aidan, I don't know if this will still be okay in two minutes, five minutes or in two hours. But for right now, it's amazing. Can we continue? I promise to tell you if I feel uncomfortable," I beg, desperate to stay in my cloud of desire.

The tension in Aidan's body seems to disappear for a moment as he gently cups my face and wipes away my tears with his thumbs. "There is no better way to celebrate today than kissing you. It's better than I imagined. Trust me, you and I have spent many hours kissing in my dreams."

I flush at his frank disclosure and try to hide my face.

"Tara, I didn't say those things to embarrass you. I said it to let you know this is important to me too. I've been waiting a long time for you to notice me."

I flash him a crooked smile. "I think you can check that off of your bucket list."

Aidan grins back and whispers, "With pleasure," as he leans in for a leisurely, but delightfully thorough kiss.

I lean back and study him for a few moments, not sure where to start.

"You still with me, Tara?" he teases. "Do you need some help?"

I'm sure I look like something straight out of a Looney Tunes cartoon as my jaw drops open. "Um, I don't think so. " I stammer, blushing hotly.

"Oh man, why can't I ever keep my big mouth shut?" Aidan mutters as he pulls me closer and kisses my forehead.

"Wait! I wasn't done with you," I protest. "I was just trying to come up with a plan."

Aidan chuckles lightly. "Gracie, I'm not sure you need to make a plan for this. I think you just pick a spot and do whatever makes you happy."

As my lips brush his chest, Aidan shudders and blows out his breath in a slow hiss. I instantly freeze, unsure what to do next.

His arms curl around my shoulders pulling me to his chest. "Shh, Tara. I just need a second. The impact of you is more than I expected," he murmurs in my ear.

I completely understand. I am overwhelmed by my senses. The heat radiating off his chest is like a roaring campfire. I have been so careful to avoid men for so many years, it has completely escaped my attention that they can actually smell good — so very good. Conveniently, my nose is a couple inches below his earlobe as I inhale deeply. I saw in some late night science show once our nose has more receptors for pheromones for people we like. I remember thinking they were making the whole thing up. Now, as I am shamelessly sniffing Aidan like a narcotics dog on a takedown, I think the theory actually might have merit.

I kiss the side of his neck and I smile a bit when the pulse beating there surges to a staccato beat. While it's empowering to realize my actions can inspire that kind of response, it's also a little reassuring to find out he is out of his element too.

"You are a little more than I expected too," I confess. "I never dreamed I would feel so good. It's a total surprise."

"We're quite the pair, aren't we?" Aidan remarks as he takes the lead. He captures my face in his hands and begins plundering my mouth with his tongue. It is very sensual and intimate. I did not expect to feel so transformed by a few kisses. But, Aidan has given me the gift of remembering the joy of being a sexy woman.

As our kisses deepen, my hips undulate against his. Aidan responds by arching his hips up into mine.

I have to leap off of him and run to the bathroom where I barely make it to the toilet before violently retching. When I can do no more, I collapse into a ball in front of the toilet and sob. Vaguely, I register the sound of water running in the sink. My brain is stuck in the past—I'm reliving flashbacks from my attack like a sick movie trailer stuck on play. I start to shiver uncontrollably and my world goes black.

The next thing I'm aware of is the rough texture of a warm wash cloth on my face. Aidan is sitting on the couch with me cuddled in his lap. He's holding me as if he's trying to keep the world at bay and protect me from everyone on the planet. Meticulously, he wipes my tears away.

"I'm so sorry," I whisper, my voice hoarse from crying.

"Sorry for what, Tara? *You* haven't done anything wrong." Aidan insists.

I hiccup and let out a small sob. "But, I screwed everything up. This is what I was afraid of. You don't want someone like me in your life because I will never be the girl you remember. I thought I could do it, but apparently I won't ever be that for you."

Instead of letting me go, Aidan places one arm over my thighs and rubs the back of my neck with his other hand. I'm conflicted because I shouldn't really stay here, but I don't want to leave either. I'll miss the feeling of safety in his arms.

"Tara, you don't know anything quite yet." Aidan argues. "We've just started. You can't give up so soon. It's going to take some time. I'm not going anywhere. You can't scare me off so easily."

"Aidan, I can't ask you to make that kind of sacrifice. It's not fair to you."

I feel Aidan's muscles tense around me. "I don't recall you asking. This is something I freely volunteered for because you're worth it."

"I wish that were true. It might even have been true before Warren Jones came into my life. But, now I'm not worth the risk," I insist, feeling defeated.

I try to change positions so I can read Aidan's eyes. Yet, he somehow is able to maneuver me without allowing any more distance between us.

"How about you let me decide what I think is risky?" Aidan asks. As he studies me intently from head to toe, he gingerly prompts me, "Can you tell me what I did wrong so I can avoid hurting you in the future?"

"That's just it, Aidan. I don't know if you can," I explain. "Everything was fine until you move your body in a certain way and it triggered a flashback. I never know when they'll hit me. It's like the other day with the cleaning spray. It can be entirely random."

"Was it because I was kissing you?" Aidan asks with concern in his voice.

I sigh and wipe away more tears with the back of my hands. "No, I was really enjoying your kisses. In fact, I felt like I could have done that all night."

"So what changed?" Aidan pushes.

"This is so embarrassing!" I mutter under my breath.

"Gracie, we have been friends forever. There aren't any secrets between us, remember? This is really important," Aidan cajoles.

I blush as I try to be as candid as possible, "I was

doing okay until you pressed up against me and started breathing heavily in my ear. I think it was too much like my attack. Warren tied my hands behind my back with his belt and pinned me down. The whole time he was doing this, he was spewing all sorts of vile words in my ear. At fourteen I didn't even understand."

"I told you what I want to do with that sorry son-of-a b —," Aidan seethes. "Mr. Jones is lucky he is in jail because if I ran into him on the street, he would wish he was dead."

I'm a little alarmed at the stone cold look in Aden's face. But, I have studied enough martial arts to know it's not personal. Aidan is just sizing up his opponent. But, in this case, his opponent happens to be a monster. "Aidan, don't do anything to get in trouble for me. Warren Jones has disrupted my life enough already."

"With that guy, I make no promises," Aidan declares. "Now that I know more about what happened, I can be more careful not to do things which would trigger a flashback."

"Do you realize how ridiculous that sounds?" I challenge. "It's almost as if you're asking to choreograph all of our interactions to keep me safe. We can't live this way in the long run."

"Tara, all the caution will only be necessary temporarily. Just think about how far you've come in a matter of a few weeks. When we first reconnected, you could barely tolerate having me in your personal space and I totally invaded your personal space tonight," Aidan says with a tight grin.

I can't help but smile back at his hopeless play on

words. "Yes, you were definitely in my personal space, not that I'm complaining or anything."

"For the record, you're invited to invade my personal space any time you like," Aidan continues the joke.

I look up at him through watery eyes, "What are we going to do, Aidan?" I ask somberly.

Aidan gives me an achingly tender kiss as he replies, "I think we live every day and try to deal with whatever issues come up. I told you the other day I'm on Team Tara and I meant it. You are not alone any more. Get used to it."

A part of me wants to believe Aidan will stick around. But, right now the scared little girl in me is winning out as I question him again, "Are you sure? It's going to be hard."

"Tara, I'm not afraid of hard work. That's what it takes to make any relationship successful. We will have to work a little harder. Haven't you ever heard the saying, 'work hard and dream big'? As far as I'm concerned, we're just paying in our dues and anything we get out of it will be part of the big dream."

Finally, Aidan reaches me through my layers of panic and I hear the sincerity in his voice. I nod against his chest. "I'm ready to take back my life from the monster. Are you ready too?"

Aidan flashes me a regretful grin. "I need to take a rain check. Tonight, I need to go to bed; I've got a big show tomorrow. I've got a few monsters of my own to take down. Care to join me?" he offers cheekily.

I smirk at his casual suggestion. "No, I think I'll take the hide-a-bed. I have a feeling that us in the same bed would not result in a good nights sleep," I quip.

Chapter Fourteen

Aidan

On the balcony, I struggle to focus my thoughts as I strum my guitar. I've been up since 5:30. Today could be the big break I've always wanted, or it could be a colossal mistake. The problem is, I don't know which outcome is more likely. Part of me wants to just brush aside Tara's concerns and sign the stupid contract, just to get it over with. Unfortunately, I can't un-hear the conversation and pretend everything is hunky-dory. On the other hand, I can't discount the very real risk that this might be one of my last chances to make a name for myself. Lord knows I've been trying for almost a decade. There's only so much publicity I can draw as a wedding singer.

The contract is burning a proverbial hole in my pocket.

The sliding door behind me opens and Tara steps out. She's carrying two cups of coffee. I can't contain my grin when I see her. Much to my relief, Tara returns the smile with a bright one of her own. Her distress of last night seems to have dissipated.

"I got you some coffee." Tara gingerly sets it on the small table next to me. "I figure today will be a long day, and you might need it."

"Thanks, Gracie," I respond as I pick it up and drink deeply from the large coffee. "You're a lifesaver."

"What are you doing out here?" Tara asks between sips of coffee.

"I'm trying to decide which song to start with," I explain. "We all need a song from each decade, but I think it's up to us which one we choose to perform first."

"I was going to ask you what songs you chose, but I changed my mind. I want to be surprised like everybody else. It doesn't matter what you sing anyway; whatever you sing, I know you'll knock it right out of the park."

"It's too bad you can't sit on the judging panel," I quip.

"It'd be nice, but you don't need that kind of help. You're going to do just fine," Tara says as she walks over and gives me a kiss. It catches me off guard. After last night, I expected her to be withdrawn and shy this morning. It doesn't take long before instincts override logic and I kiss her back. Her kisses taste like coffee and cream, and I struggle to keep my body calm. I don't want to trigger a setback again.

Reluctantly, I break the kiss and draw her into a hug. I rest my chin on the top of her head. I can't help but marvel how natural it feels. All the nerves and angst I was feeling melted away when she walked onto the balcony.

"I have to say, this is my favorite way to start the day, ever," I murmur against her hair.

Tara giggles. "It doesn't suck, that's for sure."

"Well, technically, it could," I quip, wagging my eyebrows at her.

Tara rolls her eyes. "You couldn't just leave it at sweet and romantic, could you? You just have to push those boundaries."

I grin, "You know me, I have a talent for sticking my foot in my mouth."

"It's going to be hard to sing around that!"

I laugh and tweak her nose. "You're so funny, I forgot to laugh."

She ducks and laughs, "You sound really mature there, AJ. Are you sure you're old enough to enter the singing competition?"

"Did you not see that nine-year-old yesterday?" I counter.

Tara arches her eyebrow. "Exactly!"

As I glance around at the warehouse-turned-sound-stage I notice there are far fewer people today, yet the sound level is just as extreme. Even Tara winces as a group of teenage girls shriek wildly. Tara winks and puts on her name tag. She signs, "You may as well take advantage of the silence. I don't think you'll miss anything right now."

I gratefully sign, "Thank you," and reach up to turn off my receivers. "I owe you big-time for thinking of this."

Tara shrugs and signs, "That's why I'm here, and there's nowhere I'd rather be."

I find a quiet deserted corner of the warehouse and pull out my guitar. I start with a dry run through the cords in the song I plan to do first. I'm on the third practice run when Tara alerts me that Clover Branch has arrived. I place my guitar on the chair next to me and stand up to shake her hand. "Good morning, Ms. Branch. How are you, this morning?"

"Oh, Aidan, I'm glad to see that you made it bright and early. Are you ready for this?" she asks as she fiddles with the clipboard she's carrying. She seems surprised to find me here. I don't know if it's because she expected me to chicken out or if she's merely distracted.

"I honestly don't know. Is anyone ready for all of this?"

"No, but it helps us sort out the people that aren't serious about this. I'm sure you will do just fine. Do you have the paperwork I gave you yesterday?"

I walk back over to where my stuff is and pull the paperwork out of my guitar case. Clover takes it from my hand and leafs through it. "You missed the signature page," she observes as she points out the empty page.

"Actually, that was intentional. I have some questions about the contract." I respond. I know this is a huge gamble, but there are things in the contract which bother me.

Clover looks surprised. "You actually read this whole thing?"

Now it's my turn to be perplexed. I ask Tara in sign language if I understood correctly. When she confirms I did, I ask Clover, "Doesn't everyone read the contract before they sign it?"

Clover grimaces. "You'd be surprised. Most people only check to see how much they're going to get paid. They never read the rest of the contract. The fact that you did impresses me."

"Wow, that shocks me. This contract basically means I'm signing my life over to you forever. I'm not sure I'm okay with that. Can we see about changing the language in the contract?"

Clover looks as if I've slapped her in the face. Her confident body language disappears; she definitely looks less than intimidating now. "I don't know the answer to that," she responds. "I've never had anybody ask about the language in the contract. I'll have to talk to my supervisor. I'll let you get back to practicing while I make a few phone calls," Clover instructs brusquely.

I glance at Tara to gauge her reaction, but she has her professional front up, she's in full interpreter mode. Her expression is completely placid and neutral.

"Well, I guess I'll go back to tuning my guitar. You know where to find me." There's not much else to say. I really can't believe people sign up for things as big as this, without reading what they're committing to.

I gather up my guitar and notes and leave the room with Tara following. As we return to our little corner of the holding pen, I turn to Tara and sign, "Can you believe that?"

Tara nods. "You'd be surprised what people agree to, when they think it might get them fame or fortune. More often than not, common sense is left at the door."

"I wonder what she'll say? I can't believe they've never had this issue come up before."

Tara shrugs. "I don't know, but almost any modification, if you can get one, would be an improvement."

A few minutes later, Clover returns to where Tara and I are sitting. She motions me over to a small office. "The show's producers want to know what you object to in the contract," she demands in an agitated tone.

"Well, I guess I don't understand why you would need my image in perpetuity. If I win this contest, I would be touring and doing publicity for the show for a couple of years — that should be enough."

Clover's eyebrows scrunch together as she writes my comments down on her legal pad. "Is there anything else?" she inquires, in a tone which conveys the message that she would really rather not hear any more of my concerns.

I'm not sure if I'm about to commit professional suicide, but I push ahead. I could be kissing my dreams goodbye. "Well, I would like the contract to be amended to reflect our discussions about not using my deafness to promote me over other contestants," I add.

The corners of Clover's mouth turn down in a full-fledged frown. "Well, I'll see what I can do. I can't make any promises." With that big declaration, Clover abruptly leaves the room.

Tara and I look at each other in shock. Suddenly, Tara giggles. "What's so funny?" I inquire.

"I don't think Ms. Branch is very happy with you. You just made her day exponentially harder. But, I'm so proud of you for standing up for yourself."

I lean over and give her a quick kiss on the forehead. "How can I not? How could I disregard what you have to say?"

Tara smiles. "I wondered how long it would take you to say that," she says with a wink.

"What do you think she plans to do?" I nervously pace the length of the small office.

"I have no idea. But your singing career is safe because you're just amazing. If your big break doesn't come on this show, it will be something even more promising. I don't know what it is about this show, but things may not be as they appear. So, I don't think it's a bad idea to let them know upfront you have boundaries."

"What if I pushed too hard? I know this seems like just a stupid reality show to you. Still, it's more visibility than I've ever had. I'm not sure I can afford to turn it down."

Tara shrugs. "Well, you've already put it out there. You can't take it back. These things have a way of working themselves out, in the end. I think this show needs you more than you need them. Maybe I'm biased, but most of the other talent just isn't even close to what they need."

"I hope you're right," I mutter. I pull my guitar out of the case. Since the environment is somewhat quiet, I turn on my receivers again.

Tara looks at me quizzically. "I totally forgot you had unplugged. How can you tune your guitar without hearing it?"

"It's easier with the cochlear implants, but before

the implants, I got used to playing a guitar with no hearing. Each note is a vibrating string, and I can feel it in my fingers. After all these years, I know what a note should feel like. My vocal coach was blown away when he compared my results to a tuning fork."

"Wow!" Tara exclaims. "That's so impressive."

I shrug as I brush off her praise. "It's not all that impressive, it's just what I do."

"It may be easy for you, but I'll bet nobody else in this building can do it. Eventually, news will leak that you're deaf, and people will be fascinated by what you can do. It's human nature."

I stop pacing to look at Tara. "Sure, but I don't want people thinking I'm milking the deafness card."

"I understand that, but whether you like it or not, people will see you as a role model. Think about what your example can mean for other deaf people. You're not the only one affected. You want to be self-reliant, and I admire that, but take it too far and you could be considered selfish."

"I have no choice, do I? It's not like I can get up in the morning and shave off all my deafness," I answer sarcastically. I feel like pond scum when Tara's smile disappears and she stiffens.

"Forget I said anything," Tara says tightly. I watch in dismay as a glacial mask falls over her expression and she retreats behind the wall of professional behavior.

"Sorry, Tara, I'm tired and cranky, but you make a valid point."

"Aidan, I know this stuff is crazy stressful, but you

can't let it all get in your head," Tara advises.

The door opens abruptly and Clover walks in followed by a serious guy wearing a suit. I look at Tara and my uneasy feelings must be written all over my face because her professional mask slips for just a moment. But as if she realizes her distress will only make things worse, she slams it back in place.

"Do you want me to interpret?" she signs small enough so only I can see.

"Yes, it looks like they brought in a legal eagle. I'd better make sure I understand every word."

"Okay, no problem," Tara signs. When everyone has their head down looking for paperwork, Tara gives me a reassuring smile and a wink. It's just the comic relief I need at this moment. I take a deep breath and blow it out.

"Mr. O'Brien," Clover begins after she clears her throat. "You've made some unprecedented requests. As you know, your requests could place Five Star Creative Industries and Arts in an awkward situation. Other contestants could view your requests for accommodation as unequal treatment," she explains patiently, as if she's talking to a three-year-old.

I can feel my muscles tense like I'm getting ready to get in a fight. I know this feeling well because Rory and I used to fight all the time when we were kids. I look Mr. Uptight in the eye and shake his hand. "I've had the pleasure of meeting Ms. Branch, but I don't think we've met," I say, letting my words trail off.

Startled, he extends his hand and responds, "I'm Theodore Nordson, legal counsel for Five Star."

Well, that didn't take long. I can probably kiss my chances in this competition goodbye. Maybe I should have brought Jeff with me. He told me at the wedding if I ever needed anything, to give them a call. I wonder if this was the sort of situation he meant?

"I didn't know I needed an attorney. You have me at a disadvantage." I withdraw my hand.

Mr. Nordson bristles. "Surely, Mr. O'Brien, you must realize your requests are quite unusual for us."

"I'm surprised you haven't heard from other singers about the contract. I find it hard to believe everyone else thinks it's fine to sign away their rights to their image forever."

A mutinous expression crosses his face as he answers in a clipped tone, "I'm not at liberty to discuss other people's contracts."

"Great!" I try to keep a smile off my face. "That means you won't have any trouble keeping the details of this conversation private."

Mr. Nordson clenches his jaw in frustration. "We are prepared to offer you a contract without the perpetuity provision," he states. "However, we can't change the marketing piece to guarantee that your deafness will not be discussed."

"That's not exactly what I was asking for —" I try to interrupt to clarify.

"Mr. O'Brien, we cannot change our marketing piece just to accommodate you," Mr. Nordson argues firmly. "We can try our best to not make it the focus of your contestant profile. Beyond that, we make no promises."

The pressure is immense. I glance at Tara, but she's busy trying to observe the conversation between Clover and Mr. Nordson. For a moment, I wish I could have her available now as my friend, rather than my interpreter. Their offer seems fair enough at this point. They seem to have taken out most of the provisions that Tara found objectionable. When I'm able to catch her eye, I sign, "Would you?"

She gives me an almost imperceptible smile and signs, "It's your dream; if it's worth the risk, go for it."

So, this is it. It's time to reach for the brass ring. Am I brave enough to be serious about this? As I think back over the last ten years, there's only one obvious answer.

"Mr. Nordson and Ms. Branch, with the changes you've agreed to make in the contract, I'd be thrilled to join your talent show."

When I see the expression on Mr. Nordson's face, I wonder if I should've pushed harder. He looks positively gleeful, like the Cheshire cat who just ate a canary. I don't know if it only means that they're happy I agreed, or if it means they're still trying to pull one over on me. Either way, it makes me nervous.

Clover looks me over. "I can't wait to get you into hair and makeup. We'll get you all cleaned up and give you a more modern look. It's a shame to cut all that hair, but I think it needs to be done."

"Clover, not to disrespect your advice, but my hair serves more than just one purpose. It's not there just to make me look like a rock star." I pull my hair away from my scalp and show her my cochlear implant receiver.

Clover and Mr. Nordson recoil at the sight. "Oh my! That is quite disturbing."

This is not the first time I've heard similar comments, but it is the first time I've heard it in a professional setting. I'm not sure how to respond, but humor is often my best weapon.

"Yes, I agree it's a bit freaky. My own mother just about fainted, the first time she saw this. She's the one who suggested growing my hair long so she wouldn't have to look at it."

Clover is chewing on the end of her pencil as she glances back and forth between Tara and me. "Maybe we should explain your hardware to the viewers. We wouldn't want them thinking you're using some type of device to cheat," she suggests with a thoughtful look.

Dolores insists that one of these days my mouth is going to get me into trouble. I still can't resist my impulse to set the record straight, "Now Clover, I thought we had resolved the question of whether I was cheating. Anyway, they're receivers — not speakers."

Clover's eyes light up as she announces, "That's a spectacular idea," she says, totally ignoring my point about what the devices do. "We can have all the contestants sing songs called out by the audience, the same as I did with you earlier."

"I have no problem with that, as you know from my demonstration yesterday, but some of the other contestants may be upset. If they are like me, they have planned ahead and come up with a set."

"Oh, I think they'll be fine. The rules state we can change the format of the show as we see fit. We'll try to announce the change as far in advance as we can, so contestants have a chance to try to get ready."

It's all I can do not to roll my eyes. If you don't do what I've done for the last several years, you can't understand what it takes to know a vast variety of songs and perform them well. It makes it a little harder on me to have to do a random song, but the challenge may wipe out some of my less experienced competition.

I grimace as I suggest, "How about we see how well I do in the early rounds of the competition before you change the rules for everybody? I might totally bomb out, and none of it would be necessary."

"I like that idea. If we change the script of the show, we have to re-block and change the lights."

Some administrative assistant who's been following Clover around knocks softly on the office door. "I'm sorry to disturb you, but I have the paperwork you requested, Ms. Branch."

"Oh good! Your revised contract is here," Clover says as she dismisses the office worker. "Are you ready to sign?"

I shrug and try to appear nonchalant. I don't want her to realize that this is probably the single most exciting day of my life. I take a moment to read the changes then I pick up a pen and sign on the proverbial dotted line. "I'm as ready as I'll ever be." With a few strokes of the pen, my life may never be the same.

"Very good. Do you have a song picked out?" Clover asks.

"I've narrowed it down to a couple. Do I need to

decide right now?" I ask.

"No, not at all," she replies. "The only person you need to talk to about songs is Lewis — he's the music coordinator. I just want to know because I'm randomly curious."

I grin. "You'll find out just like everybody else. I'll see you at nine o'clock tonight."

Clover rolls her eyes at me. "You are so lucky that I'm not on the judging panel this time."

I'm not sure if it's a punishment or reward, but I'm slotted to be last in the singing order. This could be disastrous since I'm sure the judges are tired. I'm pacing backstage, just waiting for my turn to finally arrive. After watching me for a while, Tara takes my hand and leads me to a cluster of chairs tucked away in a back corner.

She steps in front of me to help keep our conversation private and signs, "Aidan, please stop and take a deep breath. Trust me when I say, you've got this in the bag. I've been listening to people sing for three and a half hours. There are only about four good artists in the group, and none of them are as good as you."

"Are you saying that to make me feel better?" I ask as I rake my hand through my hair. I grimace as I touch my hair and find it caked with hair product. "Yuck! Why do I have to wear all this crap? It's a singing contest. I'm not trying out to be a Ford model."

Tara giggles and teases, "What? You don't like the makeup? I think it looks very fetching. It brings out the green in your eyes."

"Gracie, you are so not helping. Thanks for reminding me I look like a Cover Girl model. Rory will laugh his butt off when he sees me in mascara."

"It's all part of the game. Just look at it like it's part of your costume for the show. It's supposed to make you look better on TV, and that's the point, isn't it? You want to attract as many viewers as possible," she suggests.

"I guess …"

"You've helped me get ready for countless performances." Tara grins. "Now it's my turn to return the favor. So, buck up and put your big boy panties on. It's time to put on the show of your life."

"That's what has me worried. What if it's the show of my life, and I blow it?"

Tara shakes her head and pokes me in the chest to emphasize what she's saying, "First of all, you're too much of a professional to blow it. Secondly, even if you do, I'll always be your biggest fan."

I know Tara is only supposed to be the interpreter right now, but I quickly give her a hug and kiss the top of her head.

"Thanks Gracie, I needed that. Your faith in me means everything," I murmur against her hair.

A production assistant approaches and announces, "You're up, buddy. Knock 'em dead."

Tara squeezes my hand as I walk away. I take a deep breath and stroll onto the stage with confidence I'm not sure that I actually feel. There's something to be said, though, for the "fake it 'til you make it" school of thought.

Mary Crawford

As I sit at the piano, I seek out Tara's face in the crowd. She's sitting near the front with her hands in a prayer-like position. I have been struggling with my song choices all day, but as I consider my relationship with Tara, I settle on the perfect choice. As I begin to play Elton John's *Candle in the Wind*, I let go of all the stress of the week and focus only on Tara. In the blink of an eye, my song is over. It takes me a moment to come back to reality and look around. I must have done okay since the judges and audience are on their feet and clapping wildly. It's a surreal moment. My whole life I've wanted this hype, but the one person I want to impress the most seems frozen in her seat, with tears streaming down her face. Staying on stage is one of the hardest things I've ever done. I want to check on Tara, but I know that she would hate it if I blew this moment just to help her.

Just when I'm about to throw in the towel and check on her — despite the consequences, she raises her eyes to look at me. Her eyes are teary, but she has a smile on her face as she signs, "Beautifully perfect."

I feel as if all the oxygen has rushed back into the room, and I can breathe again. The judges are interviewing me about my performance. I hope I'm giving socially acceptable answers, but I'm in a daze. I have no clue what they're asking. When they've finished interviewing me and providing feedback, I gingerly walk backstage. My body is on adrenaline overload, and I'm as wobbly as a baby giraffe. I go to the backstage area I now consider 'ours.' I sit down and I'm guzzling a bottle of water when I see Tara enter the backstage area.

As soon as I stand up to welcome her, she runs at me in a dead sprint. To avoid a painful collision, if nothing else, I pick her up and swing her around in my arms. She drops her head back and laughs with joy. When I set her down on her feet, she exclaims, "Aidan, that's the best I've ever heard you play the piano, and your singing was amazing. You nailed it. I'm so proud of you!"

"Umm ... thanks," I stammer. "Whenever I hear that song, I think of you and how your talent was extinguished at far too young an age."

"I don't know, I think the song works for you too. You're the one who's hidden his talent far too long. If I could sing half as well as you do I would be advertising it on a sandwich board in the middle of Main Street. I don't think I'm as gifted as you."

"If it gets too bad, I can turn off my receivers," I jest.

"If you've ever heard me sing, you wouldn't call it an extreme precaution," she says. "But I need to talk to you about something else that's a little more critical than my singing skills."

CHAPTER FIFTEEN

TARA

WATCHING AIDAN SING MAKES me break out in goose bumps. His sense of musical timing and emotion are incredible. He doesn't belt out the song like a Broadway singer, but his voice is powerful in its own quiet way. After he finishes his song, I look around the audience and everyone seems as transfixed as I was. The judges absolutely love it.

I want to turn all fan-girl on him, but unfortunately it's time to step back into my professional role. I have to settle for a subdued hug.

"Aidan, they want all the contestants to wait in a special social media lounge. I don't know what the environment will be like in there. If I interpret for you, there won't be any disguising the fact that you're deaf," I explain, reflexively using sign language. Once I get into the groove of using sign language, I often forget to stop, even though I know Aidan has his receivers turned on.

A frown passes over his face as he considers the implications of what I've told him. He just shrugs. "I guess everyone will eventually find out anyway. Maybe it's better if everyone knows sooner rather than later."

"Aidan, there's one more thing. If it's the social media room, there are likely to be cameras and live feeds. Do you want to do all this on camera?" I ask with trepidation.

"Well, I hope nobody's a jerk about it, then." Aidan quips. "Because that would just be bad PR."

We walk into a large lounge with computer screens and couches strewn throughout. There is also a buffet of sorts. It's awkward. Aidan was the last to sing, so he's also the last contestant to reach the lounge. Some contestants have been sitting here for almost four hours and seem to have developed friendships. Before we walked in, I could hear conversation buzzing from out in the hall, but once Aidan steps into the room, it becomes eerily silent.

The atmosphere is immediately tense as another contestant calls out, "Hey! They said I couldn't bring my girlfriend. How come you can bring yours?"

"I'm his interpreter," I explain.

A young girl pipes up, "You mean he can't speak English?"

I shake my head. "No, I'm an interpreter for the deaf."

The first contestant smirks and looks directly at Aidan, "There isn't nobody here who's deaf. You all are scamming the system so she can be here."

I raise an eyebrow at Aidan silently asking him who should address the issue this time. He subtly points to himself.

"Actually, I am totally deaf. I use cochlear implants to help me." Aidan informs him. "Sometimes, in loud, unfamiliar environments, they don't function as well as I need them to. Tara is here to help me get acclimated to the environment. After I've been here for a while, I will know where it's easiest for me to hear."

The young girl looks completely fascinated as she asks, "So, how do you hear now? You're talking to us just fine."

"Thank you. I've worked hard on my speech. It wasn't always this clear. I can hear because I had a cochlear implant placed in my ear to simulate sound. It's not perfect, but it's better than not being able to communicate with anyone."

"Does it hurt?" The young girl asks.

"I was a little sore when they put them in, but now they don't bother me," Aidan replies, smiling at the girl's curiosity.

Another contestant says, "That's amazing. I've never heard of a deaf person singing."

The contestant who originally confronted Aidan argues bitterly, "I don't buy it. You're cheating somehow."

Aidan turns to the contestant beside him and asks him, "Do you mind if I borrow your guitar?"

"No, go right ahead. I trust you know what to do with it," he answers with a smile.

Aidan turns to the one naysayer in the group. "What would you like to hear?"

The young girl's eyes widen. "Just like that? You don't have to learn the song, first?"

Aidan laughs softly. "I guess it depends on what he requests."

The guy who challenged Aidan narrows his eyes. "I'm gonna make it tough on you and pick a song from before you were born."

Aidan grins. "Go ahead. I love a good challenge."

"Okay, I've decided," the other contestant says with a mischievous glint in his eye. "I want you to sing *Rocky Mountain High*."

Aidan grins. "Great choice. I love John Denver." He picks up the guitar and strums, tapping his foot with the rhythm. Softly, he starts to sing. The other contestants appear to be riveted.

When he finishes, the guy with the smart mouth counters, "I don't know, maybe he's from Colorado or something? I don't understand how he did that."

The young girl exclaims, "That's too cool! Do you know other songs too? Like modern stuff?"

Aidan shrugs nonchalantly as he retorts, "I know all sorts of songs. What would you like to hear?"

"I know, I know!" she exclaims. "I bet you don't know the *A-List*."

"Well, you'd lose that bet, if you were old enough to gamble. I happen to love Ed Sheeran," Aidan changes positions so he can play the guitar more easily.

I've heard Aidan sing and play guitar many times now, but just when I think he can't surprise me, he does. Watching him play, it's as if he feels the music the way I used to as a dancer. It appears the lyrics, even if they're not his words, come straight from his soul. Playing a mini concert for the other contestants, he's so lost in the magic of the song he doesn't seem to notice they're there. The song is tragically beautiful and haunting at the same time. He seems able to convey the emotion of the song without seeming cheesy.

When he finishes, he seems embarrassed when the other contestants give him a rousing round of applause. An older women contestant sitting in the corner mutters, "Geez, you're so good, I should probably save myself the trouble and drop out right now."

The young girl comments, "That was amaze-balls. Can I get an autographed copy of your CD when you win?"

Aidan chuckles, "Let's not jump the gun. Singing for you guys on the couch is totally different from singing on stage. I may not even make it through the first round."

The guy who challenged Aidan's deafness remarks, "Buddy, if you don't make it past the first round, you're not the only person with a hearing problem. The judges would be crazy not to send you through."

Aidan blushes. "Thank you, I appreciate the compliment. Have I satisfied all of you that this is not a gimmick? I've worked hard like all the rest of you. I want this to be a fair competition on an even playing field."

His challenger smirks. "With your talent, I doubt the playing field is very even. I think you're going to blow us all away."

"I don't think I'll walk away with it so easily," Aidan argues. "I've never sung in front of cameras or anything. Some of you guys have probably done that and will have a leg up on me."

Clover and her assistant come into the room and Clover announces, "All right guys. We have the results of the first round of eliminations. Please come back to the stage to get them."

I want so much to go to Aidan and hold his hand when he gets the news. Still, I know, to maintain credibility, I have to behave professionally.

Everyone shuffles up on stage. They have a bleacher section for the contestants to sit on. On the other side of the stage, there's a smaller section currently empty and roped off.

The host of the show arranges the contestants in lines with no explanation. After quite a bit of meaningless chatter and promotions, he tells the people standing in the other line to sit down and instructs Aidan's line to go sit in the new set of bleachers.

My heart rate speeds up because it looks like Aidan has made the cut. I knew he would. Yet seeing it unfold in front of me live is surreal. I suppose it's the way parents feel when their kids do well at a recital or sporting event. At this point, I'm not beyond telepathically wishing Aidan is in the winning group. I'm sitting on the edge of my seat when they finally announce the names.

Yes! Aidan is through to the next round! I am a bit dizzy. I don't know if it's the situation or the fact that I skipped breakfast. Aidan notices my paleness, I guess, and comes over to see if I'm okay. I assure him I'm fine, I just need some juice to drink. While he finds food for me, I formally introduce myself to the contestants.

I hear someone calling Aidan's name. I hurry to alert him because he hasn't noticed. I tap him on the shoulder and sign, "AJ, listen! They want to talk to you."

The voice paging him was none other than Clover Branch. Apparently, Aidan needs to attend the contestants meeting.

"Want me to interpret?" I offer.

"I've got this. Grab yourself a piece of cake and celebrate. I'll catch you later," he says as he leaves the room.

———◆•◆———

After the meeting, Aidan's jaw is set and his expression is mutinousness. "Come on, Tara we need to get back to the hotel. I have lots of work to do," he announces angrily in a staccato tone. He tersely waves goodbye to the other contestants on his way out.

"Don't you want to go celebrate with pizza and beer?" A friendly contestant asks.

Aidan shakes his head. "No thank you. I'm pretty tired. It's been a long week for me. I'll see you guys tomorrow."

When we get back to our hotel room, I ask him, "What happened in the meeting that has you breathing fire?"

Aidan takes a deep breath and explains, "I don't know if I just didn't understand the agreement before I came, or if they're changing things. When I first signed up, it was my understanding we would do about three days of filming and then we would need one more visit before the live competition starts."

"So what's the problem?" I ask, not understanding

what he's getting at.

Aidan grits his teeth. "If I was singing, it wouldn't be so bad; but they have me booked for two weeks solid on media junkets. It's crazy. Why can't we just play our guitars and sing? Why do we have to be a multi-media presence?"

I feel a knot forming in my stomach. "There's no way I can stay that long. I've got class and a huge project due."

"Yeah, I know. I think, as the number of contestants grows smaller, the noise will be less of a problem for me. I can do it by myself if I have to. Let's cross that bridge when we come to it."

"Aidan, I think we're on a threshold. I can't afford to lose my job. It's not much, but it helps me keep a roof over my head. I can't be here, but I don't want to abandon you."

Aidan walks up behind me and gently turns me around to face him. I look down because I don't want him to see the disappointment in my eyes. He strokes my cheek until I raise my eyes to meet his intense gaze. "Gracie, I would never think you abandoned me," he assures me. "This isn't your fault. Five Star is the one who decided to change the schedule. Of course, I would love to have you here every day — but, I know that's not how real life works."

I take a deep breath and decide it's my turn to open up a little. "Aidan, you have no idea how much I wish I could stay. These past few days have been remarkable. You've helped me fight the demons I had all but surrendered to and you've helped me rediscover who I am. You have made it possible for the two parts of my life to come together. Because of you, I'm starting to feel whole again."

I wait anxiously to see his response. It was incredibly difficult for me to admit everything I'm feeling. Feeling this attached to Aidan is terrifying. I can't help but think about how much my mom lost herself because of her undying love for my dad. Although, now that Aidan has come back into my life, I can better understand such all-encompassing love.

Aidan pulls me into a tight hug, picks me up and spins me around. For a non-dancer, his moves are pretty good.

"Tara, I'm thrilled I've brought happiness to your life," Adrian admits. "Sometimes, I'm afraid I push too much. All I've ever wanted you to be is happy. If being with me is what makes you happy, that's even better. Because, even though this is one of the most stressful periods in my life, I'm ecstatic to be here with you. I've gotten to the point where I can't imagine my life without you in it."

I give him a quick, sweet kiss as I pull away. "So, what does this mean for us?" I call over my shoulder as I go into the bathroom of the hotel room.

"Well, I suppose we'll do what busy couples do all the time. We juggle our schedules and try to be with each other as much as we can. I don't want you to sacrifice your dreams so I can reach mine," Aidan replies.

I feel my frustration level growing. "Aidan you're saying all the right things, but it's more complicated than you're making it out to be. What if your dreams are more important than mine right now?"

"Tara, that's ridiculous! My dreams might be different from yours, but they're not more important."

"You can't argue with the fact your dreams are more time sensitive than mine right now. Maybe that makes them more important. Besides, I'm so far behind in my degree what difference will a few more months make?" I counter.

"It makes a lot of difference to *me*," Aidan declares. "You've worked really hard to get where you are. I don't want to jeopardize that."

"I understand, but —" I start to argue but Aidan interrupts me.

"I don't want you to take this the wrong way because the help you've been giving me is invaluable and I probably wouldn't have gotten this far without your support. Truthfully, I've functioned just fine without an interpreter for almost a decade," Aidan says in a quiet somber voice.

"I know, but if I have the tools, I should help you."

"Gracie, I've waited many years for you to notice me and want to be my girlfriend. If push comes to shove, I'd rather have you as my girlfriend than my interpreter," Aidan insists.

"Why can't I be both?" I ask, almost petulantly.

"In a perfect world, you could be both. But, we've both got lives and careers to juggle and sort out between us. Things are complicated, for sure."

I feel my breath catch as I hear him use that word again. A wave of insecurity washes over me as I ask,

"Aidan, the last thing I want to be is a complication or distraction. You can be honest with me, is that how you see me?"

"For freaks sake, no!" Aidan exclaims, his voice heavy with emotion. "You are what makes me smile when I wake up and the memories I cherish when I go to sleep. I'd be lying if I said you weren't a distraction. Yet, I've never been more focused on making myself the best person possible so I can make your life better. You are a distraction in the best sense of the word. I think about you hundreds of times a day, but that's not a bad thing."

"You can't deny I'm a complication," I assert.

Aidan rejects my logic as he says, "Gracie, you are one of the most complicated people I know. Complicated isn't bad. My life is so much better now. I don't want to go back to simple."

My eyes tear up. "I don't want to go back to simple either. But, I don't want to lose myself in the identity of us like my mom did. My mom didn't know who she was without my dad and eventually it killed her. Sometimes, when I'm with you it's so easy to rely on your strength and humor I forget to fight my own battles. I don't ever want to be in the same position my mom was."

"I don't want you to ever be in that position either. That's why I don't want you to set aside your own aspirations just so I can reach mine. It's not fair of me to ask you to. I'm going to continue in this contest as long as my luck holds, but I want you to go back to school and kick some serious academic butt."

"What if you need an interpreter?" I ask.

"Well, then I'll do what I should've done in the

beginning. I'll ask for one to be provided for me," Aidan states.

"You don't think it'll be a disadvantage in the contest?" I inquire, curious about his changing stance on interpreters.

Aidan chuckles lightly. "We've already let the cat out of the bag on my deafness. I think everybody knows about it. If somebody has an issue with it, it's their problem not mine. Since Five Star is the one who changed the shooting schedule, they need to provide another interpreter since your schedule is now booked."

My shoulders sag in relief as I realize he is going to get the help he needs whether he gets it from me or not. "Okay, I'll go back to school. I want you to promise to pull in an interpreter, even if you think you don't need one. I'd hate for you to lose this contest because you misinterpret an instruction or something." I state firmly.

Aidan puts his fingers up in the Boy Scout salute as he pledges, "I promise."

Something about his gesture cracks me up. When I stop laughing, I chastise him a bit, "Aidan Jarith O'Brien, I happen to know you were too busy to be a Boy Scout. You and your brother spent hours and hours in the studio rehearsing. You probably couldn't even pick out a Boy Scout from a lineup if you saw one."

Aidan turns red and gets a sheepish expression on his face. "I may never have been an actual Boy Scout, but I did help Dolores lead the Cub Scouts one year. Does that count?" he teases.

"Well, it does earn you brownie points," I offer.

"That's better than nothing," Aidan quips. "Now that we've gotten all the serious stuff out of the way, can we get something to eat? I'm starving."

"Poor baby! I wouldn't want you to a faint from hunger," I tease. "Just let me change out of my 'uniform' and I'll be right with you."

I practically sprint to the bathroom, stopping only momentarily to grab a handful of clothes. I'm not even sure what I have to wear. Heather and Kiera were ruthless when they went through my wardrobe and got rid of all my slouchy clothes.

Aidan is hungry, so I don't bother to take a shower. I throw off all of my black interpreting clothes and pull on some blue jeans. I have two shirts to choose from. One is a perfectly boring long-sleeve T-shirt. The other is a lined lace camisole in emerald green. I know which one I would have chosen before Aidan came back into my life, but I don't want to play it safe now. With a little trepidation, I put on the camisole. I study myself critically in the mirror after I redo my makeup. I am surprised by my own reflection.

The color looks spectacular on me, and my shoulders are still toned and muscular despite being away from dance for years. I brush out my hair and leave it flowing over my back and shoulders because I know Aidan likes it down.

I marvel over the fact that I'm making wardrobe choices based on a guy's opinion. It shows how far I've come in a few weeks. I can't believe I'm purposefully dressing sexy. It's one of a thousand little changes I've made because of Aidan's influence and support.

So the Heart Can Dance

When I leave the bathroom, Aidan's back is turned. He's out on the balcony again with his guitar, playing a song I've never heard.

I sneak up behind him and place a soft kiss on his ear lobe. Initially, he startles and jumps at the intrusion. As soon as he sees me, a carnal expression crosses his face. "Gorgeous Gracie, you can interrupt me anytime."

The open desire on Aidan's face stuns me for a moment, but then I realize I probably have the same expression on my face whenever he is near me.

"Com'ere, Tara," he coaxes, standing and holding out his arms.

I walk into his arms as if I've been doing it my whole life. I lay my head on his shoulder for a moment before raising my face to his, inviting him to kiss me.

Aidan hungrily devours my lips in a passionate kiss.

For a moment, I'm tempted to allow my mind to go to dark places. But, Aidan's insistent presence and wonderfully sensual mouth reminds me this is an entirely different situation. Once again I decide to trust myself, as well as Aidan, and go with the flow.

I wind my fingers through the curls at the back of his neck and pull him even closer, standing on my tiptoes to get better access to his amazing mouth.

Eventually we have to break apart to get a breath, and Aidan murmurs, "Geez Louise, Tara. You give new meaning to the words 'welcome home'. We'd better go before I forget all my good intentions."

We're both breathing like we've run a marathon, and I seriously question whether I want him to honor those good intentions.

"Umm, I'll grab my coat," I stammer as I try to collect myself and calm my raging hormones. "Are we going to walk to someplace close or call the car service?"

"I think we should walk," Aidan suggests. "I'm suddenly in need of a little cold air before dinner."

I shoot him a coy smile as he helps put me on my jean jacket. "Sounds like a prudent plan," I wink.

———————◆•◆———————

We end up at an Irish pub where I'm introduced to a whole new menu of foods. It's actually quite delicious, and Aidan and I have a great time feeding each other bites from our plates. Just as our meal is concluding, a small cover band starts to play beside a dance floor that's about the size of a postage stamp.

Aidan gets up from his chair, walks over and stands in front of me. He holds his hand out gallantly. "Tara Isamu, may I have the honor of this dance?"

Before I can answer, Aidan pulls my hand towards his mouth and kisses the back of my hand.

I'm so charmed by the old-fashioned gesture I momentarily forget I no longer dance. I nod and whisper, "I'd love to."

It must be difficult for Aidan to hear in this environment, but he reads my lips clearly. He grins and leads me to the dance floor.

While we wait for the next song to begin, I get nervous as I remember how long it's been since I've danced.

Aidan notices the expression on my face, links his fingers with mine. "Tara, this is not a performance. It's just us. I've got you. Relax and enjoy."

I take a deep breath and follow his lead. He's right. The restaurant patrons are paying us no mind as the band plays. The first song is an upbeat song called *Better Together*.

Aidan smirks when he hears the music. "It's a good thing I stay in shape rock climbing, or you would totally wipe the floor with me. Jack Johnson might spell the end of my very short-lived dancing career."

I arch an eyebrow at him and tease, "Come now, this is only a medium tempo song. You're not afraid of a little sweat, are you?"

Aidan's eyes darken as he studies me. He draws his finger down across my bottom lip as he remarks in a sexy growl, "You wish. I'm the one who thinks a bit of sweat is sexy, remember?"

"As I recall, you think *everything* is sexy. I'm not sure I should be impressed," I quip as we settle into a foxtrot of sorts and move around the small dance floor as smoothly as we can. I have forgotten how much fun it is to dance with another person. Aidan has a huge grin on his face, and his eyes are bright and happy. It's the most relaxed I've seen him since we arrived in California. As the song ends, he gathers me in a hug and whispers, "Thank you, Tara. That was incredible."

I return the hug joyously and kiss him briefly. It's a huge step for me, but I'm very aware we're standing in the middle of the dance floor.

The band takes notice of our body language and

immediately launches into a slow song. I recognize this one because I have it on my playlist. The band is doing a decent job covering Ray LaMontagne's *You Are The Best Thing*. I'm impressed.

Aidan tucks me close to his chest and rests his chin on my head. I'm glad I decided not to wear heels, because I fit perfectly in his arms. We sway back and forth in what could be only loosely termed a waltz. Yet I've never felt so beautiful, even without fancy costumes and choreography.

The band segues into a new song. I can hear the smile in Aidan's voice as he says, "I wasn't expecting Hunter Hayes, but I love this song. The lyrics are great songwriting."

The lyrics are so touching, they almost make me cry. I realize I'm actually in a relationship like that. The person who I'm with wants me and cherishes me. It's something I always dreamed of having, but never thought would ever happen to me. I do indeed feel wanted for the first time in what seems like forever. I look up at Aidan, as I comment, "You're right, it is the perfect song because there's no doubt I feel "*Wanted*" when we're together."

When the song ends, Aidan pulls me into a tight embrace. Standing there, forehead to forehead, hearts pounding a million miles a minute, Aidan declares, "I could have written every word of that song, because it's exactly how I feel. I want you to know that I want you. Physically, intellectually and emotionally — I need you."

There's no holding back my tears now, and they stream down my face. "That's convenient, because I feel the same way about you." I say, attempting to smile, though tears are brimming and threatening to fall.

Aidan wipes my tears away with the pads of his thumbs. "Why the tears, Gracie?" he asks. "This is a happy day for celebration."

"I'm crying because this is better than I ever dreamed. These are tears of happiness."

"Okay. You had me scared there for a second. Because tears aren't the reaction I wanted to hear when I pledged my undying love."

My eyebrows shoot toward my hairline and my jaw goes slack with shock. "Is that what we're doing here?"

"Well, to borrow your phrase, we're on a threshold," Aidan replies with a slow grin.

CHAPTER SIXTEEN

AIDAN

As WE WALK BACK toward the hotel room, I'm mentally kicking myself for allowing my mouth to get ahead of my brain again. I didn't mean for the conversation to get so deep. Everything I said to Tara was absolutely true, but I'm not sure it was smart to share my feelings so soon. I might scare Tara off for good if I don't back off and give her more time.

Tara nudges me with her elbow. "Aidan, are you even listening?"

"Sorry, I was thinking." I interlace my fingers with hers.

"Should I be worried, or is this just part of your mysterious songwriting process?" Tara inquires, chewing on her lip.

"I didn't mean to scare you. Sometimes I get lost in my thoughts. I think it's an occupational hazard. I do have to work on my song tonight. So, what did you say that I missed?" I ask.

"Oh, it was nothing important," Tara says dismissively.

"Despite appearances to the contrary, what you say is important to me," I coax. "Please tell me again."

Tara flushes a pretty shade of pink. "Really, it's no big deal. I said I was really surprised how much fun I had dancing. I thought it would be a much bigger deal."

"That's great news! Hopefully the rest of your dance skills will come back just as easily."

"I hope so too," Tara replies wistfully. "I've missed dancing … maybe more than I realized."

"Let's work on it after this competition. I want you to dance like a puppy playing in a meadow."

Tara laughs lightly. "I'm not sure I was ever that carefree, even as a kid. You may be setting your sights a little too high."

"Still, it will be fun finding out what you can do. You were totally magnificent as a kid. I can't imagine what it will be like to see you dance ballet as an adult."

"Aidan, it's been years since I've danced. I'm sure I'm going to totally disappoint."

"You never know until you try. I'm sure you'll be beautiful and graceful — just like you always were."

<hr>

As I sit in hair and makeup waiting for my turn, Tara comes to my rescue with an extra large triple shot of espresso. I am so exhausted I can barely think. I seem to be vying for the worst boyfriend of the year. I started out with good intentions, but something went awry.

After dinner and dancing, Tara and I returned to our room. She mentioned she was sweaty from dancing. I offered to run her a bubble bath, but she just laughed and insisted she was a big girl and could run her own water. She took her cell phone and a book with her to the tub. When I teased her about it, she said she had worked all day and deserved a long "stay-cation" with her bubbles. Her effervescent laugh hit me in the core of my being. I haven't heard her laugh so freely since we were kids.

Since she was occupied, I decided to work on her song. Unlike the weather in Oregon, it's unseasonably warm in Southern California. I took my lyric book and guitar to the balcony and began writing. I've never written anything quite so personal and capturing my feelings for Tara in a song is a slow process. I want to show the changes in her life and how she's become my inspiration, muse and hero.

It's difficult to capture all facets of Tara in a simple song. She is the essence of complicated. Everything about her is a study in contrasts. She's the personification of grace and beauty, yet she perceives herself as awkward and gangly. She routinely kicks herself for not being stronger in the face of adversity, but *I* see only resilience. I see the child who practically raised herself and also pulled herself out of an emotional hell. I have no idea how she accomplished everything while alone in the world. I see a woman so beautiful, she takes my breath away. Still, when she looks in the mirror, that's not the woman she sees. I see a woman who feels she can trust no one, even herself. Yet I've seen her open herself up to me in ways I never thought possible. She claims she's not lovable, but I'm falling deeper in love with her each day.

I struggle to capture all my emotions — past and present — in a coherent song. Contest or not, this is the most important song I've ever written. I only intended to write until Tara got out of the bathtub. But the next time I glanced at the clock, I realized I'd been writing for over three hours. I quickly put my guitar down to check on Tara. She fell asleep on the couch with the throw blanket casually tossed over her body and it's nearly fallen on the ground. I picked it up, tucked it around her, and softly kissed her. When she didn't even stir, I let her sleep. I brushed my teeth and stripped off my clothes before collapsing into bed.

I woke up this morning with Tara curled around my body, with her head resting on my chest. I was astonished by her gift of trust. I was tempted to lie there and soak it all in — until I looked at the clock. I was so tired last night, I forgot to set the alarm. We had less than thirty minutes to get to the studio. I didn't want to wake her, but she would've been furious if I didn't allow her as much time as possible to get ready.

After we woke up, it was a mad dash to get showered and dressed. We literally ran out the door. This was not the romantic start to the day I had hoped for. Not only did I completely ignore her last night after dinner, I was anxious and short tempered as we got ready to go this morning.

I study Tara's body language as she hands me the espresso. She doesn't appear upset with me. If the shoe were on the other foot, I'm not sure I'd be as quick to let it all go.

I take a long drink of my coffee and scald virtually every taste bud on my tongue. Tara watches me with a look of vague amusement. "Next time should I bring a bunch of roasted coffee beans for you to munch on like sunflower seeds? If I had known you wanted to drink it all in one gulp, I would have put more cream and sugar in it."

Before I can formulate a suitable response, my name is called. Again, I have to make a tough call about which song I want to sing. I briefly consider singing a Sam Smith song with my guitar since I played piano in the last round. But I'm not as familiar with his song as I am with my other choices. It's a relatively new song and I haven't done it as many times. My brain is so sluggish from lack of sleep, I'm afraid I might massacre the lyrics.

So I walk over to the piano, lean into the mic, and announce to the audience, "This was a big hit for Billy Joel in the 1970s and it's one of my favorites. I've spent many years being a piano man, a guitar man, saxophone man... Well, you get the picture... I hope you enjoy it."

I've literally played this song a thousand times or more. It's a perennial favorite at wedding receptions, because it's a good sing-along song. I have developed my own signature embellishments of the introduction and chords. I can tell when the crowd realizes it's the classic *Piano Man*. The crowd erupts into thunderous applause and the audience sways in time with the music, or at least, what they think is in time with the music. I learned a long time ago not to follow the crowd's lead on the timing. As I sing about the loneliness of endless gigs on the road, I am more determined than ever to win this contest and put those days behind me. I finish the song with a flourish. I'm proud of the way I pulled it together and performed.

I scan the audience for Tara. She is sitting in the front row holding up a glow stick as if it's a candle. I mentally chuckle at her imitation of the quintessential groupie.

I go back stage to await the results in a scene eerily similar to yesterday's. It's almost like the movie *Groundhog's Day*. After a little polite, stilted conversation with my fellow contestants, they finally call us in to give us our results.

The judges give me a well-deserved jab for choosing a song so similar to the last round from the same era. It's a valid criticism. Overall they seem to like it, so I may have a decent chance of staying. I have to wait until all the other contestants have heard their critiques before I'll know if I'm brought back for another round. After a tense drawn-out segment where our names are drawn at random, my name was the last one called. I nearly pass out from relief when I hear my name. I swear I hear Tara shouting over the din of the crowd, "Way to go, Aidan!"

If Tara didn't have to go home this afternoon, I could celebrate my partial victory. As it is, my elation is tempered by a small thing called life. My morose attitude is quickly adjusted, though, when Tara strips off her interpreting jacket and lets down her hair, in a billow of rich dark satin, and launches herself at me. I have to catch her with both hands and brace myself against the couch behind me. Otherwise, she would have toppled us to the ground in her enthusiasm.

For the moment, she seems to have forgotten the halls back stage aren't exactly private as she rains down kisses on my face. "Oh my Gosh, Aidan! I don't think you could have done that song any better. It was perfection. I'm so proud of you!"

"Yeah, I was happy with the way it went," I respond modestly.

"Well, you should be proud. Everyone loved it!" she insists. "Come on, let's grab lunch before I have to go to the airport."

"Will you be okay on the flight back?" I ask. "I know flying is not your favorite thing."

"If I get nervous, I'll just remember what it was like to have you sit beside me holding my hand." Tara is saying all the right words, but I can see the tension in her body.

"I wish I could take you to the airport. Unfortunately, I have to tape a bunch of promotional spots for the show."

"Aidan, you pay attention to the contest and I'll manage everything else," she firmly instructs. "You can't afford to be distracted. I'll be fine, I promise."

Lunch was interesting. We were both trying to put a positive spin on less than ideal circumstances. It makes me think what life might be like if we both had to work all the time to make ends meet. It's a daunting thought. The facts are simple. I want Tara in my life, and if I have to juggle Tiki torches to make it happen, I will.

As lunch draws to a close, Tara says, "I need to catch the shuttle to the airport."

I gather her in a tight embrace and kiss her deeply. When I pull away, I kiss her on the forehead. "I have to hope I won't be home too soon, sad to say, or this would all be for naught. But keep the home fires burning for me either way, okay?"

"Always," Tara promises as she gives me a lingering kiss.

CHAPTER SEVENTEEN

TARA

LOOKING UP AT THE clock, I wonder if class will ever end. It's one of my required classes to graduate; yet I already covered this material in my AP English class in high school. Really, how many ways are there to interpret *The Scarlet Letter*? I usually enjoy this class, but today I can't stay focused. Apparently, both my brain and heart stayed behind in Los Angeles.

I haven't heard from Aidan all day. He sent me a text this morning to tell me he was on his way to the studio, but it wasn't the same without me. I should've stayed, because it isn't doing me any good to be here. I can't seem to think about anything except Aidan. It's disconcerting because I never wanted to be one of 'those girls' whose entire life revolves around a boyfriend.

My mom was an accomplished woman before she met my dad. They met in college where she was in school to become a speech therapist. After they got married, she gave up all that because my dad had to travel so much. Before I came along, she travelled with him. It must have been exciting to travel to all those exotic places my dad visited while serving as a translator. My arrival must have put a wedge between them. Still, I have greater sympathy for my mom. Now I almost understand why she felt her world had ended, when my dad died. Understanding why she did it doesn't erase all the pain. She owed something to me as well, didn't she? I don't know. I know I need to protect my heart from that kind of pain.

Hopefully, my next class will go by a little more quickly. I've almost finished all my sign language classes. I seem to have a natural talent for picking it up, and I wonder if it's something I inherited from my dad. As a translator he spoke several languages. I wish I could still speak the Japanese he taught me, but after so many years of disuse, most of it's gone.

It's hard for me to believe the difference between the two classes. When I'm signing, time flies by before I can blink. As I'm leaving the classroom, my professor stops me. Immediately my heart sinks because for the life of me I can't figure out why she needs to speak to me. I thought I was doing well in this class. When we get to her office, she closes the door. I'm on the verge of a panic attack.

"Ms. Isamu, I think you know I consider you one of my most talented students." Professor Solomon states with a smile.

"Thank you very much," I reply with a self-deprecating shrug. "I enjoy your class."

"Well, you're a joy to teach. That's actually what I wanted to talk to you about."

I stare at her for a moment, a quizzical expression

on my face. "Uh, okay."

"Relax, I'm not here to give you bad news. I pulled you aside to see if you'd be interested in helping me with an outside assignment."

"You want me to interpret for you?" I ask, thoroughly confused.

Professor Solomon grins. "In a manner of speaking, I do. I am helping out with a school camp for deaf and hard of hearing junior high school students, and I need some help. I can't interpret for everyone. You are such a natural born teacher, I thought you might enjoy the opportunity."

"Really? Do you think I'm ready?" I ask, trying to tamp down the excitement in my voice. "Shouldn't you ask one of the seniors?"

"If I thought any of them were as good as you, I would have," she replies pointedly. "Your interpreting style is more suited to this assignment. Do you think your skills are up to the task?"

"I'd like to think they are," I answer honestly. "But I haven't had a lot of experience working with kids. When is this?"

Professor Solomon nods as she answers, "I have a feeling you'll do just fine. The camp is the second weekend of next month."

"I'll ask for the time off, but I can't promise anything until I get my schedule," I answer cautiously.

"I understand," she says. "Just let me know."

I'm still watching the clock. This time, it's because Aidan is supposed to Skype me at 8:30. I can't wait to tell him my news. I try to distract myself with homework, but it's not working. I'm not sure I'll have any recall of what I just read, since my brain is so busy with other things.

Finally, at 8:25, my computer chirps to inform me Aidan is beeping me from Skype.

I honestly try to do the good girlfriend thing and ask him about his day before I share my news. But Aidan isn't having any part of it.

"Gracie, your eyes are dancing. What's up? Have you already found a new boyfriend?" he teases.

"Never," I insist. "You've ruined me for all other men."

"You have no idea how happy that makes me," Aidan answers with a big grin.

"It's true. You've spoiled me. It's my honor to spoil you. Still, I'm curious what's making you so happy."

"Well, I was offered a temporary job," I explain.

Aidan's eyes widen. "Another job? When on earth are you going to fit it into your schedule?"

"That's the really great thing! It's for school credit. My boss at the gas station allows us time off for school-related stuff, so I should be okay."

"I see. So, what's this new mystery job?"

"I get to use my sign language skills," I say, nearly bouncing out of my skin with excitement. "Out of everyone in the class, my professor chose me. She thought I would be a natural match for this environment."

Aiding gives me a wry smile as he says, "Gracie, I'm not surprised. You're one of the best sign language interpreters I've ever seen. Nobody would ever know you haven't graduated yet."

"Still, I haven't worked with kids. I'm afraid I will look like a buffoon."

"Gracie, stop stringing me along," he practically growls. "What in the heck is going on?"

"Oh, I can't believe I didn't tell you!" I say, chagrined. "My professor chose me to work at a camp for junior high school kids."

"Congratulations Tara," Aidan declares. "I've always wanted to do that."

"Thank you," I say bashfully. "I just hope I'll do a good job

"Hey, no shortchanging yourself," Aidan instructs firmly. "She wouldn't have chosen you if she didn't think you could do it."

"So how was your day?" I ask, eager to hear how he did.

"Weird. It was just weird," Aidan responds, stress written all over his face.

"What happened?"

"Well, the good news is, I made it through another round of competition. They threw a curve ball at us today. We had to sing outside of our usual genre. I sang some Garth Brooks. I think they were a little surprised I could pull off country."

"I'm sure it was amazing, I'm so proud of you. So what was the bad news?" I ask with trepidation.

"I think the producers sometimes forget I can hear with the cochlear implants. Right in front of me, they were asking all the other contestants how they feel about me being deaf. I noticed they were taping these interviews. Nobody was particularly mean, but a couple of them think my deafness gives me an unfair advantage."

"You're right, it's strange they would tape those interviews after they promised not to make it a central issue of the competition. I have a bad feeling about this."

Aidan nods his head. "So do I." He rests his head against the back of his chair and rubs his eyes. I can tell he has gotten little sleep. "Why would they go to all the trouble of making promises if they planned all along to renege?"

"Because people are scum-buckets?" I suggest, not so tongue-in-cheek.

Aidan sighs. "I hope my gut is wrong on this one. But you warned me not to do business with them." His usual upbeat demeanor is absent. He looks so destroyed I wish I could crawl through the computer screen and give him a hug.

"Aidan, you have no idea how much I hope, for once in my life, I'm wrong about something like this," I state emphatically.

"I hope you're wrong too," Aidan says. "Because, if this turns out the way I think it's going to, I'm toast."

My eyes fill with tears. "Aidan, remember, no matter what happens. I'm still your biggest fan."

The next morning, as I'm setting my DVR to record after hearing a teaser for the show, I shake my head in dismay. I thought I knew pretty much all there was to know about bullying, from my own experience. But, after hearing the promo, it's clear my bullying experience was strictly for amateurs. The producers had raised bullying to an art form.

At first, I'm in complete shock. Now I'm just angry. The producers are doing exactly what they said they wouldn't do.

I send Aidan a text message. "I'd advise you to stay away from any television sets today."

A few moments later, I receive his incoming message. "Too late. Rory sent me a link to it."

"What did you think of it?" I tentatively ask.

"Well, to be honest, I could have lived without hearing the opinion that I shouldn't even be competing against 'normal people', because that's what the Special Olympics are for."

I cringe when I read the message. I know this is the last thing he wanted. I wish I would have stayed there with him, because at least then I could accomplish something more than sitting at the counter, eating solo.

"That's awful! She should get kicked out of the competition for unsportsmanlike conduct."

"Eventually, she was. But, I think the damage is already done," Aidan states, shaking his head. "If they go through with this promotion, I'll be getting sympathy votes and I don't want to get those kind of votes."

I raise an eyebrow even though he can't see me. "Aidan, with all due respect. In this kind of show, a vote is still a vote. You have no control over whether your singing or your deafness gets you a vote," I argue.

"Still, it feels like cheating to me," he responds, his voice laden with frustration.

"Aidan, if I was on one of the shows, don't you think they would use every second of my tragic life story and play it to the hilt?"

"I suppose. This feels different. It's like they are trying to set me apart from all the other contestants. I want an honest competition."

"What are you planning to do?" I ask.

"I guess I'll see what happens tomorrow," the long delays between his answers showing his fatigue.

"I hope we're both wrong, and they don't exploit your life just for ratings."

"I'm praying you're right. I've discovered I like this winning stuff. It's cool to be recognized. I'd like to be known as something other than Rory's talentless little brother."

I smile. "You could never be thought of as talentless. After all, I have personal, intimate knowledge of how well you kiss. That's a very special talent, and you have plenty of it."

Aidan adds a funny emoticon of lips on the Skype screen. "I'll be sure to list that skill on my resume. People will be super impressed."

"I don't know, Aidan … with your movie star looks,

if you add spectacular kisser to your resume, you could be booked for the next decade," I tease.

"Look at you being all sassy," observes Aidan. "Why does it have to surface when I'm a thousand miles away?"

"Oh, I'm sure there will still be plenty of sass when you get home," I tease.

"Gracie, don't torture me!" Aidan exclaims. "I hate being alone."

"I never thought in a million years I would admit this, but I hate it too," I confess, as I run my thumb lightly over his profile picture after I send the text. It's surprisingly difficult to say good bye.

Chapter Eighteen

Aidan

I watch with morbid fascination as my life story is dissected in the latest promo piece produced by Five Star. It's exactly the type of promotion they assured me they wouldn't do. Heck, I've even got my own theme song now. Of course, the focus of the promo is not the years I've spent becoming a musician, the bands I've been with, or even my songwriting credentials. It's a quintessential pity-me campaign. A somber, overly dramatic narrator is telling the audience what a horrific childhood I had and how meningitis robbed me of my hearing. It goes into great detail about the allegedly gruesome surgery I had to "fix myself" so I wouldn't be a burden to those around me. Then, to add insult to injury, they had a few of my fellow competitors lament how unfair it is for me to compete against them, because I might have technology in my cochlear implant to enhance my singing.

My emotions are all over the map. I'm totally ticked that they felt I wasn't doing well enough in the competition to compete like a regular guy. I'm upset about the way they portrayed my family. Granted, we haven't always gotten along and I did feel abandoned when they followed Rory and left me behind. Still, staying with Dolores is one of the best things to ever happened to me. I can't really criticize my parents' choices, because they hadn't been in that situation before. I'm sure they thought they were doing the most logical thing.

What upsets me most is that this promo makes it appear I think deafness is a crippling defect. I have lots of very successful friends who are deaf and haven't elected to get implants. They'll be offended by the tone of this promo spot. In the deaf community, being deaf is not necessarily considered a disability or liability; it's a cultural identity. This promotion makes it seem as if I'm embarrassed to be part of the deaf culture. That's simply not true. I chose cochlear implants for two very practical reasons. First, the isolation was stifling after being able to hear for so many years. Secondly I felt, as a musician, a major tool had been taken away from me. It was important to hear what I was playing. However, they completely glossed over how difficult the decision was for me. It was extremely scary, knowing I could lose what little hearing I had left in a gamble cochlear implants would work for me.

My mind goes back to the insecure teenager I once was. I was a child stuck between two worlds, not fully belonging to either. That's one of the reasons I wanted to compete without any mention of my deafness so I would be evaluated solely on my skill. I wanted to identify with other musicians as just another musician. Now, I'm back to being the different one, the one who doesn't fit.

Waves of nausea wash over me as I consider the

So the Heart Can Dance

ramifications of Five Star's actions. I should've paid more attention to Tara's warnings. If Five Star is willing to break their word so easily, who's to say there's even going to be a prize at the end of this competition? We're supposed to get a record contract and a cash prize if we win. Now I wonder if any of this is real, or if it's all a charade. I wanted this to be real so badly that I blew right past the warning signs. I feel incredibly stupid. I can't stop hoping my doubts are overblown, and it's all a misunderstanding.

Suddenly, the throb at the back of my neck turns into a full-blown headache. I sink down on the bed, bury my head in my hands, and massage my temples. My phone rings and I reflexively answer it. I have no idea who's on the other end or if I'll be able to keep myself composed enough to have a coherent conversation. My brain is going in a million different directions.

"Hello? Aidan, are you there?" Tara asks. Our phone connection is so bad, she could be calling from Mars.

"Gracie, let me call you back. My phone is being strange —" I got cut off before I could tell Tara goodbye.

I immediately call her back, but adrenaline is making my hands shake so much, I can barely push the buttons. "Tara, I'm sorry. I didn't mean to hang up on you, but my phone lost its signal," I explain.

"I know," Tara responds with worry in her voice. "I really need to know if you're okay."

"Yes, I'm fine," I reply automatically. I'd really rather not tell Tara I've made a huge mistake. But as soon as I think the thought I realize how ridiculous it sounds.

I sigh as I revise my answer, "No, I lied. I'm not okay. I mean, physically I'm okay, but I feel like my life is falling apart."

I hear Tara's gasp through the phone. "I knew it. I just knew it. Something really bad happened, didn't it?"

Before I can censor myself, a groan slips out.

"Aidan, you're scaring me. What the heck is going on?" she demands, her voice breaking.

"Gracie, I'm fine," I insist. "I'm just upset. Maybe you were right all along. This whole gig may be nothing but an elaborate hoax. I should've listened to Dolores when she said, 'If it's too good to be true, it probably is.' I feel like the world's biggest idiot."

"Don't be too hard on yourself," Tara advises. "They had all the bells and whistles to make it look legitimate. Even I began to second-guess my instincts."

"That's a good question, how did you even know I needed your help and how did you know not to trust these guys?" I probe.

"Well, it's kind of hard to explain over the phone, but I'll try," Tara answers reluctantly. "How much do you believe in the paranormal?"

"Tara, I grew up with somebody from Louisiana who was a huge believer in folktales and ghost stories, so I'm pretty open. Are you going to tell me a ghost told you all this?" I tease.

Tara chuckles softly. "No, but my story is equally out there. You remember that my mom was part Native American, right?"

I can't fathom where she's going with this. "Uh huh,

I vaguely remember you telling me, years ago when you told me your middle name."

"My mom had the gift of 'knowing' bestowed upon her by one of the elders in her parents tribe. My mom could tell you what was going to happen in your life, with uncanny accuracy."

"That must've been fun as a kid," I quip.

Tara chokes back a laugh. "Let's just say, I had a healthy respect for honesty. Anyway, I seem to have inherited some of my mom's skills. I'm nowhere near as talented as she was, but I can often sense when something bad is imminent."

"That could be scary. Do your friends run when they see you coming?"

"I don't have a bunch of friends. Many people are totally creeped out by it. The women in the Girlfriend Posse are used to it now, so it doesn't bug them much anymore. My premonitions are not always bad. Heather calls me a human lie detector. She says having me around is a way to cut through all the BS of dating. I knew Jeff and Kiera would be together, even before they spoke."

"Does it get exhausting, being the keeper of all the knowledge?" I ask, suddenly curious about the toll such a gift would take on Tara.

"I often wish I could turn a blind eye to what I see coming. It's not fun when people think of you as their own personal dream-buster."

"I'll be brave. What does your gift say about us?" I ask with some trepidation.

Tara pauses on the other end of the phone. My

heart sinks. What if her intuition, premonition, or gift doesn't show us together? How would I overcome that? I'm persuasive, but I might not stand a chance against her mystical foreknowledge.

I hear Tara give a small sigh, and in my mind's eye I see her shrugging eloquently. "Unfortunately, my special powers don't apply to my own life. If they did, I could've avoided a lot of heartache."

"It must be frustrating, if you can't control what you see."

"Oh, you have no idea," she mutters. "I wouldn't worry too much about us. My plain old womanly instinct tells me we started out as friends and still like each other a lot. That bodes well for us."

I breathe a quiet sigh of relief. At least, the cosmos isn't against us. "But you could sense something was wrong before you even called. So does your gift extend to me?"

"The best answer I can give you is — sometimes. I have more insight into you than I typically do for anything in my personal life. But I don't see everything, or what I do see is difficult to interpret."

"Do you have a sense of what will happen with this competition?" Suddenly, it occurs to me maybe I don't want to know. I should make this decision independent of any special knowledge. "Wait, I'm not sure you should tell me. If you tell me, I would be gaming the system and it would give me an unfair advantage to know the outcome."

Tara gives a small sound of approval. "I knew you were a guy with a strong moral compass, but this confirms it. However, I've made my suggestions pretty clear all along. I don't know all of what happened today, but I can sense someone broke your trust. It would be hard for them to earn it back, especially in a competitive environment with a lot happening quickly."

"Well, Gracie, there's no reason I can't tell you what happened. Five Star put it out there for the world to see," I snarl. "It wasn't just my trust they broke, they ruined the competition for everyone else, too. The other contestants are never going to trust I wasn't behind this whole publicity deal."

"What does your gut tell you to do?" Tara asks quietly.

"My gut tells me to walk away. Honestly, I should probably even run," I admit. "Still … it's hard for me to give up my dream."

"AJ, you're not giving up on your dream! You're adjusting the itinerary."

I sigh and scrub my hand over my face. "So, how do you suggest I do this? I can't just ditch work. If you get a reputation for being late or absent, it follows you for years."

"If it were me, I would tell them in a place and time which requires them to take responsibility," Tara suggests.

I chuckle. "Tara Grace, I can't believe you're advising me to stick it to the man."

"Well, they deserve it don't they?" Tara asks pointedly.

"They really do," I concede. "This might be fun."

The nauseous feeling hasn't gone away; in fact it's worse, as I'm waiting backstage for my turn. When we all go on stage to be introduced, Clover Branch makes an announcement to all the contestants, "We've had some questions about the authenticity of our performers. So, for today's round, you will be singing a song randomly chosen by Twitter users."

The older gentleman, Derron Waxell, looks directly at me and mutters under his breath, "I knew you were trouble. Maybe you should've stayed with the Special Olympics."

White-hot rage flashes over me and I have to consciously release my grip on my guitar before I ruin the fret. "Pardon me, I don't think I heard you right," I reply, my voice shaking with anger.

"I think you heard me just fine," Derron answers. "The reason we have to do it this way is because no one believes you can sing. If it were not for you, we could use the songs we rehearsed."

He's right, of course, and it draws me up short. I sigh and shake my head apologetically. "That's true, I guess. I'm sorry. I don't like what they're doing any more than you do. It's a bad break all around."

If I was wavering in my decision, the conversation sealed the deal for me. I wish I could go rock climbing or jogging or something. I need to punch a few walls. I haven't been this angry since I was a teenager.

I'm the third singer to go up tonight. I have no idea what song the audience will choose for me. The other two contestants before me were given mainstream pop songs all of us are likely to know. I've had to do this for them already, so they know I'm familiar with lots of songs. If the producers paid attention to my resume, they should've known that before I even got here. If the audience wants to, they can take the opportunity to make this the challenge of my life.

Carrying my guitar, I walk to the center of the stage and await my fate. Having no control over song choice is absolutely terrifying. All the talent in the world won't save me if they pick a song I don't know or one out of my vocal range.

The overly peppy host, Glenn Smokes, shoots a cheesy smile at the camera before announcing, "Let's see what the audience chose for our next contestant, Aidan O'Brien." He turns and says, "Having bravely overcome so much in your life already, I'm sure you'll have no difficulty. Your courage is an inspiration to us all."

It was all I could do not to roll my eyes. Being called brave, courageous, or inspiring is one of my pet peeves. I'm just dealing with life. It's not like I have a whole lot of choice. Firefighters, paramedics, and police officers are heroes. I'm just a guy with a guitar, trying to make a living. I look at the camera with what I hope is a semblance of a smile, glance at the audience, and respond, "I've never been one to back down from a challenge. I only hope America chooses a song I've heard of."

Glenn gives an exaggerated laugh as if I've told the funniest joke ever. "Well, I think the audience has a great deal of faith in you. I hope you've heard of Big and

Rich," he declares, pausing dramatically before announcing, "America wants you to sing *Holy Water*."

I try to hide my shock. *Holy Water* is not a bubblegum pop song. It deals with domestic violence and sexual assault. There's no way I can sing this song without thinking of Tara in every single syllable. It will be a huge success or an epic failure; nothing in between. Sometimes I have a hard time keeping my pitch when I'm emotionally invested in a song. I decide to play the piano. It comes to me easier than guitar because I've been playing the piano far longer.

The walk from the stool to the piano seems endless. The audience is waiting in total silence for me to begin. As I play the first few notes, there is a smattering of applause. The song is emotionally wrenching, but I'm grateful, now, for my eclectic taste in music. The fact that I even know this song is a bit of a miracle. It's not wedding reception material, by a long shot. Once I start, the rest is kind of a blur. I can only give it my best. When I finish, you can hear a pin drop. For a moment, I panic, totally unsure what it means. Maybe the audience needs a moment to catch its breath after such a heavy song, or maybe I've bombed.

Finally, applause breaks out as I walk to the center of the stage. In this round, the producers have elected not to give us any feedback until the end. I just have to shake the host's hand and walk off stage.

After everyone has sung their random song, we're all called back on stage. My palms are sweating and I feel like I can't take a deep breath. I'm not sure when I became so invested in winning. It's really not my nature. That was more Rory and Tara's scene. I tend to be more laid-back. Yet, here I am waiting, with bated breath, to find out what total strangers think of my work. All this angst isn't even for the big finale yet. We are merely competing for Twitter and text votes to move to the next week. If you have the highest Social media score, you win the weekly bonus prize. Last week, one of the kids won a new car. It's too bad I came in second. My van has seen better days and I could use a new set of wheels. I wonder what the prize will be this week.

Gradually, they eliminate contestants until it's down to me and Tasha Keely. I'm not surprised. She's only thirteen, but Tasha has a real set of pipes. As we go to commercial, she takes my hand and whispers, "I know you're gonna get it. But if I have to lose to anybody, I'm glad it's you."

I smile at her optimism. "I'm not sure I would write off your chances so easily. Your version of *Royals* will make Lorde shake in her boots."

Tasha gives me a grateful grin. "Thanks, Aidan. Good luck."

The stage manager calls us to the middle of the stage. Tasha still has a death grip on my hand as the host announces the weekly prize, "The winning song tonight will be released as a single on iTunes." Tasha starts jumping up and down with excitement. I have to admit, I'm tempted to join her. It's a huge opportunity and potentially worth a lot of money. We are both holding our breath when the Head Judge announces I've won the most votes by a slim margin.

I'm still in shock when Tasha gives me a smug look

and murmurs, "I told you so. That was an amazing song. It almost felt like you were living it."

"Th-thanks," I stammer. Before I can say anything more, the stage manager announces that we've gone to commercial again.

I immediately search for Clover Branch. When I find her standing at the perimeter of the room, I jog over to talk to her.

When she sees me, she exclaims, "Aidan, we're not done with you. You need to go back on your mark and say something about your win."

"I know," I answer. "But I want to make sure I heard everything correctly. Did you say the prize package of releasing the song is mine — regardless of whether I win or lose the overall competition?"

Clover nods. "Yes, it doesn't matter what happens from here on out the song is being released as we speak."

I run back to my mark and hit it right before we come back from commercial. I have a couple of minutes to catch my breath because the producers have brought in an up-and-coming rap star to do a guest shot. Fortunately, I'm not live on camera right now. I steel my nerves for what's about to come. I hope Tara will be proud of me.

After his song ends, the host waves me over for my victory speech of sorts. I hate this part of the show. It feels like I'm rubbing my success in the face of the other contestants. Tasha especially doesn't deserve it. She is destined to be a star and I don't want to make her feel bad about her performance.

Glenn Smokes, the host with the toothpaste-commercial-worthy grin, asks me the same question he's asked for all the other rounds, "So, Aidan do you have anything to say about your win?"

I'm sure he's expecting the same sort of benign gratefulness I've expressed in earlier rounds. But instead I utter the scariest words I've ever said, "Glenn, I'm proud of my performances on this show, and I hope people draw strength from songs like I performed tonight. Unfortunately, out of fairness to the other competitors, I'm going to step aside."

A collective gasp goes up from the audience, the stage crew, and the other contestants. For the first time, Glenn is not smiling at me as he struggles to formulate a question. I watch his mouth open and close several times like a guppy. When he can finally formulate a question, he asks me, "Why in the world would you do that?"

"When I agreed to appear on the show, it was my understanding I would be treated like every other contestant. It's all I've ever wanted. Unfortunately, somewhere in the process, someone decided promoting my persona as a person with deafness became more important than maintaining an even playing field. I'm not ashamed of my deafness, but I don't want it to be used as a marketing tool. That was never my intent. To maintain my integrity, I'm withdrawing from the competition. It's the only fair thing to do."

Glenn looks incredulous. "Are you sure you want to do this? You won't be able to wake up tomorrow and change your mind."

I nod as I reply, "I'm sure. I've enjoyed my time on

the show more than you can imagine, but it's the only ethical thing I can do at this point."

The stage manager is frantically signaling for us to wrap up our interview.

Glenn takes note as he says, "Well, there you have it folks. We won't have an elimination this week because Aidan has withdrawn from the competition."

As soon as the cameras shut down, Clover Branch storms over and screams, "I can't believe you did that to us after all the money we invested in you. If it weren't for me, you wouldn't even have had a chance on the show. I stuck my neck out for you!"

"Look, Ms. Branch. I really appreciate the opportunity. If you value me so much, maybe you shouldn't have broken our agreement," I state emphatically.

"Well, to be honest, I figured you'd be grateful for the extra promotion. Who in their right mind wouldn't be? After we started running those promotions, votes for you went up eleven percent," she replies defensively.

"Don't you understand you made my argument for me?" I ask with exasperation. "If I have to rely on sympathy votes to get me through, then I don't deserve to be the winner. I warned you the one thing that was important to me was that everyone would be treated equally in this competition. You made a spectacle of my deafness and I'm totally not okay with your choice. I'll have to find another way to make it because I won't do it by cheating. I wish the show the best."

"I suppose you'll insist we follow through with the prize package you won tonight?" she asks wryly.

"Yes, ma'am I am. It's only fair since you changed the format of the show even though I asked you not to and you violated our agreement," I explain.

"Fine!" She hisses through clenched teeth. "But don't expect any other favors from Five Star. We were hoping to represent you after the competition was over, but consider the offer withdrawn." With that announcement, she turns on her heel and rushes off of the stage.

I grab my guitar from backstage and sink onto an old stool. I can't help but wonder if I've made the biggest mistake of my life. Why is standing up for what you know is right always the most painful choice?

CHAPTER NINETEEN

TARA

WHEN A CUSTOMER COMES through the door, I look up from the TV my boss has stashed beside the counter for bad weather alerts. It's just a little TV made for a camper, but my boss hooked it up to cable so he could watch the golfing channel. When it's slow, I watch my shows too. It's frustrating to watch because the little mobile television is smaller than a couple of index cards. I wish I could see better because I can't quite make out the expression on Aidan's face.

Geez, how long does it take this person to pick out a bag of potato chips and soda? This customer always gets the same thing when he comes in here anyway. I'm usually not this inpatient, but I don't want to miss Aidan's performance. After what seems like forever, the guy checks out and I can go back to watching television.

That's weird, when I talked to Aidan this morning, he was planning to do a song on his guitar. I don't understand why he's walking over to the piano. *Crap*, I wonder what I missed.

He starts to play a song outside his usual genre. As I listen, I realize the lyrics could have been written about me. I know he didn't write the song because I've heard it on the radio before when I rode in Tyler's truck. But it's a stunningly accurate portrayal of how I feel. It traces my steps from innocence to self-destructive behavior and from loneliness to love. I've done a lot of praying to make my past go away. I love that the song recognizes to become a survivor, it's important to have outside support. I understand now since I've begun to share my story with my friends, I should've done it much sooner. The song so precisely describes my journey listening to it inflicts an interesting mix of pain and catharsis.

Before I know it, the song is over and Aidan is walking off stage. It was without a doubt the best I've ever heard him sing. I watch the other two competitors sing. They are good, but not even close to Aidan. Of course, I freely admit I might be a touch biased. When they announce him as a finalist, I'm not at all shocked. It's so cute to see him interact with the younger contestant. It's clear they've become friends.

Wait … did I see what I think I just saw? I wish I was at home with my DVR so I could rewind it to make sure. Still, I'm pretty sure I saw Aidan flash me the sign for "I love you" together with my name sign. My name sign is unique. It's the sign for war paint and an acknowledgment of my long hair. It's hard to miss if you know what you're looking for. Wow. Just wow. I had a pretty good idea we were headed in this direction; I didn't realize he was planning to acknowledge it so publicly. Maybe I'm making too much of this, but I feel like one of those girls whose fiancé proposed in the middle of

Wrigley Stadium.

I study his body language when the camera pans to him during another group's performance. My heart pounds with anticipation. I think he's actually going to do it. I wish I could be there to support him. After the world's longest commercial, Aidan is front and center. The hyper host is interviewing him. Oh my gosh! He just quit the show. He must be heartbroken. Yet, I'm so proud of him. I know this was *not* an easy decision for him. It's a huge leap of faith. If I were in his shoes, I'm not sure if I would be brave enough to make the same choice.

My shift ends at eleven o'clock. At last! I hurry home and hop in the shower because no matter what I do, when I work at the gas station, I end up smelling like a walking gas pump. After the world's quickest shower, I log on my computer to see if he's available on Skype.

Aidan must've been waiting for me, because as soon as I log on to Skype, my computer beeps to signal he's calling. There must be a delay in the connection because after I say, "Hello," I hear him say, "Where are you, Gracie? I can hear your voice, but I can't see your face."

Twin boxes pop up on my computer with our video streams in them. "I'm right here," I tease.

"I've had the longest day ever. I'm afraid I just made a huge mistake."

"I don't think you made a mistake. I think it's going to be the smartest move you ever made," I assure him. "I like to think goodness and honesty always win out in the end."

"That's all well and good in theory. The reality is I'm unemployed. I cancelled all of my upcoming gigs for a while because I didn't know how long I would be on the show. At this moment, I'm a tank full of gas away from sleeping on my mom's couch."

"I'd rather have a guy with principles over a guy with the fancy job and car, any day of the week," I announce.

"Well, I'm glad to hear it. Because I don't have a fancy job or a fancy car."

An idea percolates in my head. I'm not even sure it's a good idea, but it sounds fun. "Do you want a temporary job?"

"What kind of job?" he asks cautiously.

"Your expression is too funny! It's a legitimate job, Aidan. I guess, more accurately, it's a bona fide volunteer position which could morph into a position which could lead to something more."

"I can't afford to be choosy. But you still didn't tell me what kind of job it is."

"I thought I told you about this," I muse. "Remember, I told you I get to work as an interpreter for a camp? They're still looking for volunteers. I thought it might be cool for the kids to see what you've accomplished."

"I'm not really sure I'm your guy. I don't feel like I've accomplished much, right now, other than maybe screwing up my life," Aidan laments.

"Aidan, I know it seems bleak right now. But Five Star isn't very trustworthy. Who knows how they would've hijacked your career and made it something you never wanted it to be?" I offer sympathetically.

I can see Aidan sigh deeply. "I guess, intellectually, I know that. Still leaving the show was one of the most frightening things I've ever done in my life."

"I understand. I really do. You have to believe something better is coming around. You're just too talented for it not to."

Aidan smiles a crooked smile. "You're required to say nice things because you're my girlfriend, but I don't know what the public will say. They may not be as supportive."

"I know it was a terribly scary gamble. I think it'll pay off."

"Are you being an enthusiastic cheerleader, or do you have a real sense of these things?"

I shrug. "I don't know. I suppose it's a bit of both."

"Are you ever wrong?" he asks, full of curiosity.

"If I am, I don't hear about it. People don't usually follow up with me unless they want more information."

"Your prediction is one of the few pieces of good news I've gotten today, so I'm going to roll with it."

"Aidan, I was watching at work, so I had a few interruptions. Did I hear them say *Holy Water* was released on iTunes?"

For the first time tonight, Aidan gives me a genuine smile which goes all the way to his eyes. "Yeah, that was pretty sweet. I wasn't expecting it at all. Hopefully it will do well, and I'll get something out of this whole experience."

"I thought I read in the contract that you get to keep a portion of the proceeds for any of your music they release to the public," I reply, trying to recall the contract language.

"You're right, I do get to keep about one cent per download. At that rate, I don't expect to get rich anytime soon," Aidan responds.

"Oh well, it's better than nothing," I reason. "The notoriety you get by withdrawing from the contest may get you further than those royalties."

"I hope so. Being broke royally sucks."

"I totally agree. Most days, I'd rather be a rich person," I commiserate.

"So, since your days are suddenly free … Are you interested in helping me host the camp for the junior high kids?"

Aidan shrugs. "Sure, it sounds like fun. It's not like I've got job offers stacking up at my front door."

"Okay, I'll let my supervisor know you want to help out. You'll have to fill out an application."

"That's not a problem. It's not like I don't have a bunch of free time right now," Aidan quips.

"Oh, come on it's gonna be fun," I cajole. "What could be more fun than a bunch of hormonal junior high school kids on a field trip?" I cross my eyes, mimicking Aidan's classic cheer-up-move.

"Sounds like a barrel of monkeys to me."

"Not to sound greedy or anything, but when are you coming home?" I ask.

"My flight leaves the first thing in the morning. I had to sweet talk the hotel manager because Five Star cut off funding for my room. It's a good thing they like me around here, or I would've been homeless in LA."

"Oh, that sucks!" I sympathize. "Can you come over later?"

"Just try to stop me…" Aidan declares.

"I'll be at home studying for tests. I have class for an hour and a half starting at two o'clock."

"Great, I'll see you later," I respond.

"Gorgeous Gracie, thanks for turning my day around," Aidan says as he clicks off the camera.

I send text messages to Heather and Kiera as fast as I can type.

"I need an emergency session of the Girlfriend Posse, can we meet for breakfast?"

Heather immediately texts me back. "I can do Panera's at 8:30. I have to go to the restaurant supply store."

As I'm reading Heather's text, one comes in from Kiera. "You know me, I don't need a good excuse for Panera's."

Heather dumps her purse on the chair next to the table as she does a quick inventory of me. "Wow, this is about as frazzled as I've ever seen you, so what's going on?"

"Can we grab something to eat and wait for Kiera?" I suggest. "I don't want to tell all this twice."

"That sounds good to me. I love their bagels here. I can make them, but it's such a pain," Heather responds.

At that moment, Kiera comes zipping in with Becca on her lap.

"Sorry I'm late. Somebody in Mindy's school drop off zone had a flat and I got stuck behind them. My dad had a doctor's appointment this morning, so he wasn't able to watch Becca," she explains.

"No problem," I assure her. "We just got here ourselves."

"Oh, Tara, are you getting any sleep?" Kiera asks with alarm in her voice. "I've never seen you not put together."

"It's a long story. I recommend you get food and drink for this."

Heather looks worried. "Is it really that bad? Now you have me scared."

"That's what you guys are here for. I need you to help me decide if I'm freaking out over nothing," I explain.

"Take a deep breath, Tara," advises Kiera. "We'll figure this out."

As we go back to our table, Heather asks, "So how are things with you and the hunky musician? I saw him the other day on television. You are one lucky chick. Not to poach your guy or anything, but he's pretty amazing to look at."

I give Heather a hard look. "Aren't you already stringing along an adorable hunk of your own? Get your eyes off my guy!"

"I hate to tell you this, Tar, there probably aren't too many women out there who don't take a few minutes to admire your man. You might as well get used to it," Heather teases.

I know Heather is teasing, but there's some truth to it. Even before he gained this notoriety, Aidan could attract people to him — all people. I have no doubt he'll quickly have his own set of groupies.

Kiera notices my expression and says to Heather, "Geez, Heather, way to freak her out even more. We're supposed to be her support system."

"It's all right, Kiera, I know my guy is a hot commodity. It's not a newsflash to me. Aidan is charismatic. I have to suck it up and accept it."

"You have a drop-dead gorgeous guy falling all over himself to make you happy. Can you tell me what the issue is here?" Heather asks. "Because I think it sounds like a recipe for success."

"I know you guys are going to think I'm crazy. But … I can't stop thinking all of this might be too good to be true. I'm afraid to trust it."

Kiera nods her head in agreement. "I totally get it. I felt that way when Jeff and I started dating. He was everything I always dreamed of in a guy. I spent a lot of time wondering what he saw in me and why his response to me was different from everyone else's."

"What did you do about it?" I ask.

"In a nutshell, I got over myself," she retorts with a self-deprecating chuckle. "I finally saw myself through his eyes and was amazed at his view of me. I decided I deserved happiness, even if it eluded me in the past."

"That sounds like what I need to do," I concede.

"But it's so scary. What if he changes his mind, or what if I've dreamed up this whole fantasy?"

"Honey chile'," Heather says with an exaggerated Southern accent, "I've seen the way that man looks at you. The chances of him changing his mind are slim to nothing."

"I know. He basically confessed he has loved me since he was about six." I watch Heather and Kiera getting a little misty-eyed.

Kiera looks at me with sympathy and asks, "How is this a problem? I think it's sweet."

"I don't know!" I reply in frustration. "It all seems too good to be true. How can he be in love with the person I was back then and still be in love with the person I am now? We're two different people! It doesn't make any sense."

"Oh sweetie, what that buzzard poop did to you … it didn't change who you are. It just changed how you react to things," Heather declares.

"Are you sure? I feel so different. I feel like he robbed me of the chance to be me."

"Warren Jones may have changed you. But if he did, he changed you in good ways too. You're tougher and stronger and more observant now."

"That's true. Do you think it's possible Aidan really does love both sides of me? You know, the way I was before and after."

"I think it's not only possible, but probable," Kiera assures me. "Your man, is a born protector. He would do everything in his power to keep you safe. I think it's safe to say he loves all of you, even the parts you don't like about yourself."

"Yeah, that pretty much sums it up," I say with a small smile. "But how can I trust myself to make the right decision?"

"Having been there, I don't know if anyone decides to be in love. Love is a state of being. You just are," Kiera says sagely.

"What if he hurts me?"

"You mean emotionally?" Heather clarifies.

"Yes," I answer. "I feel stuck. I don't want to go back to how it was before Aidan came back into my life. But I'm scared of what happens in the end."

"Why do you think it has to end badly?" Kiera asks with a confused expression on her face.

"Everyone in my life leaves, eventually." I answer bluntly.

Heather gasps. "Tara, that's not true. Kiera and I have been here for years and we have no intention of leaving. I don't know Aidan well, but from what I have seen, I don't think he plans to leave, either."

"Your friendships mean so much," I say as my eyes tear up. "I'm so grateful you guys are here. But I still feel like it wouldn't be fair to Aidan for him to end up with me. I'm one screwed up chick."

"I don't think you're all that screwed up. You're way too hard on yourself." Heather insists. "You've accomplished so much in your life."

"Okay, but what I know about romantic relationships you could fit on the head of a pin and still have room left over," I state with embarrassment.

"Oh, sweetie, do you think you're the only one who feels that way?" Heather asks.

"Heather has a point," Kiera agrees. "Before I met Jeff, I didn't even know what I was missing. I thought I had an idea, based on the love stories I could check out from the library. But I had no idea how to find or recognize the right person who could change my life. I was so young when my mom got sick and died, I never got to see my parents in love. I missed out on a lot. I bet the same thing is true for you. But just because we've never seen love work well doesn't mean it can't happen. I mean, look at William and Isabel. They've been married for decades and they still act like newlyweds."

"It's true!" Heather adds. "Both sets of my grandparents were in love forever. My parents are still together, too."

"Okay, I'll admit I may not have the healthiest perspective on interpersonal relationships, but what if Aidan would be better off without me? I don't want to hold him back. I love him too much."

Kiera gives me a soft smile. "Do you hear what you just said?"

"Of course I did!" I sputter. "I said Aidan might be better off without me."

Kiera's grin is even bigger. "You did say that. Far more importantly, you said you love him."

I sit in stunned silence for a moment. "I did, didn't I?"

Heather giggles. "You act surprised. Is this a

newsflash for you? Do you know how Aidan feels?"

I smile at Heather's reaction. "Yes, as a matter of fact, it does feel like a newsflash. For a long time, I lost any ability to love men. I was barely functioning. Yet somehow, Aidan has not given up on me. He's been able to show me I am capable of a full range of emotions. I always assumed I would be alone forever, but now I know I don't have to be."

"That's amazing, Tara," Kiera responds. "I'm so glad he's brought some normalcy into your life. I hope he loves you too."

I blush a little. "I think he truly does. Did you guys see last night's episode of America's Next Star?"

Heather and Kiera respond simultaneously. "Yes!"

"I taped it last night," Kiera says. "The ending was a big shock. But I thought I saw a message for you. He looked right into the camera and then flashed the sign for I love you. There was a sign after that, but I don't know what it was."

I blush even more. "That's *my* name sign."

"Oh my Gosh!" Heather exclaims. "Aidan announced his love for you on national TV. How cool. I want to find a guy who'll do something like that."

Kiera nods. "That's huge! Did you know it was coming?"

"No, not really," I reply. "Well, that's not exactly true. Aidan has never been bashful about expressing how he feels about anything — good or bad. He's been hinting his feelings for me run deep. I didn't expect him to say it publicly, with everything else that was going on."

"So you knew he was planning to leave the show?" Heather probes.

"I knew it was a possibility," I concede. "We talked through his options, but he was still conflicted about it the last time I talked to him."

"You know what this means, right?" Kiera asks me.

I look at her blankly, trying to figure out where she's going. Finally, I shrug to indicate my level of cluelessness.

"It means he trusts you to be involved in the most difficult decisions of his life," Kiera explains. "That's major. Guys can be weird when it comes to their careers. Trusting you enough to talk about it is a great sign."

"Do you really think so? I don't know. I'm worried we may have connected too quickly."

Kiera laughs out loud. "Listen, you might not want to gauge the proper relationship pace by me. I met someone, fell in love, and became a mom in about four months. Despite being unorthodox, it seems to work for us."

Heather pipes in with, "I don't profess to be any great expert, but I think love takes as long as it takes. At least, that's what I'm hoping. I want to be swept off my feet by someone and have it hit me like a flash of lightning."

Kiera smiles at Heather. "I hope it happens that way for you too, but there's no one right way to fall in love." She turns to me and states, "You and Aidan have been friends for decades. It's not like you're strangers to each other. In fact, who knows, if your lives hadn't gotten in the way, you might have been together years ago, and you'd have a few kids by now."

Her words paint such a bleak picture, it almost takes my breath away. What would've happened in my life if I had fallen for my best friend at twelve or thirteen instead of chasing after older guys? What kind of person would I be now? If I was that person, would Aidan still love me? The possibilities are mind-boggling.

Kiera notices I've turned pale and whispers, "Tara, I didn't mean to make you sad. You're always telling us, things tend to work out the way they're supposed to. I'm just sorry you have had so many crappy things happen to you."

"It's okay," I assure her. "My brain went to a dark place for a minute. It's not your fault."

Becca wakes from her nap and fusses in Kiera's lap.

Kiera takes her out of the front carrier and offers her to me, "Do you mind? I have to get things arranged here."

I shake my head and hold out my arms to take her. "I'm always happy to hold this little peanut."

"Hey, what about me?" Heather says, sticking her bottom lip out in an exaggerated pout. "When is it gonna be my turn?"

"You can hold her after she eats," I offer with a wink.

Heather snorts and exclaims, "Gee, thanks a lot! Give me the kid with the dirty diaper while you get her when she's nice and clean."

Kiera rolls her eyes at our little squabble. "Okay, children, that's enough," she teases. "It's not like you guys don't get to hang out with my kids all the time. Do you guys mind if we move to a back table? I need to nurse her and she can get kind of rambunctious. I don't want to be flashing the whole world."

After we move I hand Becca back to Kiera. It only takes a second before Becca is thoroughly settled.

"She looks content," I observe.

"We both are," Kiera says with a beaming maternal smile. "You'd never guess that I ever struggled to induce lactation. We're old pros at nursing now," Kiera says as she plays with one of Becca's curls.

"I remember how hard it was," I reply. "Were you ever scared out of your gourd? The changes came so fast in your life. How in the world did you ever cope?"

Kiera shrugs. "We didn't set out with any master plan. We just dealt with things as they came up, and the greater the challenge, the more we pulled together. If you had asked me last year if I would be married with two children in a matter of months, I would've thought you were crazy."

"That's good to hear. My relationship with Aidan seems to have lurched from one calamity to another. First, we were held at gunpoint by your crazy ex-father-in-law. Then I practically fainted. Soon after, I had a huge freak out in front of him that made me nearly catatonic. Let's not forget it was partially my input which convinced him to give up his dream of winning the competition. I can't figure out why he wants to be with me. I'm a walking disaster."

Kiera looks over at me with understanding eyes and murmurs, "I don't know how much clearer Aidan can be.

As near as I can tell, he's shown you love in every interaction you've had since you were kids. I think you can trust this one. It's okay to let your heart go." She looks down at Becca and smiles a tearful smile. "Trust me, it's worth the risk because you'll never know how far love can take you until you surrender to it."

The emotion of the moment was almost too much to bear as I realize I'm being stupid about Aidan. Kiera's right, we need to just feel what we feel.

"When should I tell him all this?" I ask, suddenly feeling panicked. "It's one thing to admit I love Aidan to myself; it's a whole other thing to tell him about it."

"I think the moment will present itself and you'll know it's the perfect time to say something," Heather suggests.

"You guys know me, I sort of suck at expressing feelings. I haven't had much practice because I've been alone for so long. What if I mess this up somehow?"

Kiera chuckles. "The way Aidan protected you at our wedding, I doubt there is anything you could do to dissuade him from loving you."

"Maybe so," I concede. "But I want to do this right."

Heather's sighs. "That's what we've been trying to tell you. There is no right way to love someone. Everybody figures out their own path."

Chapter Twenty

Aidan

I'M TRYING TO CRAM my feet into the cramped space under the seat in front of me. I see now what a great advantage it is to fly first class. In the grand scheme of things, I don't mind because I'll see Tara in a couple of hours. She took one of her exams early so she could pick me up at the airport. I don't know how she pulled that off, but I can't wait to see her. I didn't know it was possible to miss someone the way I miss her. Being around her settles my restlessness and makes me feel at peace with myself. I've had a hard time finding a soft place to land in my life. She gives me a sense of home.

I no longer need Tara's song for the competition, but I feel driven to finish it. I've never had to struggle this hard to write music. I hear it one way in my head, but when I play it, it doesn't seem to have the same magic. I've been doing tons of rewrites trying to get the song to match my vision. My worries are probably pointless. Tara won't be as critical as I am. She will love it because I've written it. I want it to be perfect. I'm not good at expressing emotion, when I'm not singing. I tend to joke and fool around a lot to cover up my feelings. I want this song to be one long love letter to Tara. The love letter she deserves.

I get my lyric book from my backpack and start to work. The ambient noise in the airplane is driving me crazy. It's a frequency my implants seem in tune with the endless drone of the engine. I'm tempted to turn off my implants to silence the chaos, but without Tara here, it's a dangerous thing to do. If there's an emergency, I might not hear what's happening. So, I clench my teeth and try to concentrate on what I'm doing.

Finally, the pilot announces we're approaching PDX, the biggest airport in Oregon. I'm getting antsy with anticipation. Getting antsy while you're strapped into a seat is not the best combination. It seems to take us forever to taxi to the gate. I only have one small suitcase with me which I stashed in the overhead compartment. I grab it and practically sprint toward the gate.

When I first notice Tara, she has her back toward me and she's looking out the window to find my plane. I take a moment to appreciate her beauty. Her hair is free today. Usually, she wears it up in a ponytail. She is beautiful always — but I particularly love her hair when she lets it down.

Tara freezes for a moment as if she can sense someone is watching her. Warily, she turns. However, once she determines it's me, her entire expression changes to one of pure joy. She grabs her purse which is sitting at her feet and comes charging toward me. Finally, we have the moment I envisioned when I first saw her at Kiera's wedding. It's almost as poetic as it's always portrayed in countless commercials and the movies. Or, it would've been, had a child not wondered in between us. Tara had to stop and direct the toddler back to his mother. She smiles at me shyly as she shrugs as if to say, "What are you going to do?"

I rush toward her and we collapse in each other's arms. I know I'm a songwriter and I'm prone to think cheesy thoughts, but, this is about as perfect as life gets.

Tara pulls away and holds my cheeks between her hands. She studies me like she's trying to memorize every detail of my face. She whispers, "I didn't know it was possible to miss someone as much as I've missed you. It almost feels like you were amputated from me and my soul had phantom pain."

She pulls my face toward hers and kisses me with more assertiveness than I've ever seen from her. We're in the public concourse of a busy international airport, but my body doesn't care. I get drawn further into the web of desire as Tara continues to plunder my mouth with a sensual kiss.

When she finally pulls away, I take a moment to catch my breath. "Tara, if that's the welcome back I'm going to get every time, I should leave regularly. But I can't. I've missed you so much, I can't even coherently quantify what I'm feeling."

Tara smiles coyly. "I don't know. It seems like you're doing a pretty good job to me."

She snuggles into my chest with her arms around my torso and kisses me again.

The little boy who she helped earlier is staring at us with surprising intensity. Nothing like having a child watching public displays of affection to pour ice water on your libido. I back up and look into Tara's eyes as I try to even out my breathing. "Tara, you and I could start a forest fire with the heat we generate, even though this environment is not conducive to romance. What do you say we go home?"

"It sounds like a good plan." Tara lays her head on my chest. You would think it would be easier for me to keep things under control since she's not kissing me. But everything about her is erotic, to me. Her hair smells absolutely phenomenal, and its gloriously long length tickles my arm as I place it around her waist. Who would've thought simple smells like ginger and coconut could be such powerful aphrodisiacs?

Tara took back the majority of my clothes when she went home, so we don't have to stop at the luggage carousel. As we're walking toward my car in long-term parking, Tara stops me and asks, "How are you really?"

"I can't actually say. It changes like quicksilver," I answer. "One minute, I'm calm, cool, and collected about it and I can rationally tell myself everything will work out the way it was meant to. The next moment, I'm completely consumed by rage. Sometimes, it's directed at Five Star. Other times, I turn the rage on myself because I was too gullible to see what was happening."

"Don't be so hard on yourself," Tara says, as she climbs in the van. "These people make a living out of conning people. They're professionals. They didn't want you to question what they were doing because it hurts their bottom line. It's as if we got relegated to the kid's table. We prided ourselves on playing the game smart. We didn't realize they were playing professional poker while we were stuck on Go Fish."

Tara's comparison cracks me up, but it's true. "Well, thank you for not being pissed off at my stupidity," I grimace.

"Are you not even listening to me?" Tara asks with frustration in her voice. "Why on God's green earth would I be mad at you? I'm not mad. I'm so proud of you, I can barely stop smiling. Do you know how hard it is to find a guy who stands up for what he believes in?"

I smirk a little. "Obviously, I don't know — but I'll take your word for it."

Tara rolls her eyes at my attempt at humor. "Funny. But you're missing my point. Jobs come and go, but if you don't have your integrity, you have nothing. You have more integrity in your hangnail then those people have in a whole corporation."

Her defense of me is incredible. I'm used to facing almost constant criticism of my choices. This is a refreshing change of pace.

I reach across the console and grab her hand. "Thank you for making a hard choice seem like the only choice. I'm already feeling better about it."

She squeezes my hand. "You know I'll always be your number one fan, right? It doesn't matter to me if you make it big or not. I like being with you, even if we have to live like impoverished college students. I'm already used to top ramen and macaroni and cheese."

I snicker. "Well, I don't think it will get that dire. But it might be tight for a while until I get my bookings back up," I explain. "On the upside, I don't have to save for a demo tape anymore. I've got two months worth of them. So, I'll have enough to live on for a while."

Tara winks at me. "Gee, that's too bad. I was kind of looking forward to being your sugar mama."

I hoot with laughter and I pretend to be stabbed in the heart. "Come on now, I'm not that much younger than you."

Terra sticks her tongue out at me playfully. "Well, the fact remains, you're still younger than me. So you'll have to ignore my cougar-like tendencies."

"Why would I want to ignore them? They sound intriguing," I answer with a wicked grin.

"I should've known you'd find a positive spin on it," she chuckles.

"Any time I spend with you is positive," I announce.

"Do you want wine with that cheese?" Tara asks sardonically.

I hold up my hands in a defensive posture, "Hey it's not my fault you don't take compliments well and I have to keep repeating myself."

"Well, you certainly know how to make a girl blush. All the flattery isn't necessary."

"I hope to be around for a long time, so get used to it. I sent you a special message last night in front of millions of people. Did you catch it?"

"Yes, luckily I did. I would have been crushed if I would've missed it"

"I'm glad you saw it and I'll be happy to tell you every day, if you let me."

"What do you mean when you say, 'If you let me?' Why wouldn't I be thrilled?" she asks incredulously. "Of course I'll let you stay, for as long as you want to."

"When I go back to washing dishes, I'm afraid you'll write me off." I look down at the floor in shame.

When I look back up, Tara's eyes are flashing with anger. "Do I look shallow to you?" she demands. "What part of our past gives you the idea I would think anything like that about you. You know what kind of house I was raised in. Do you think I have any room to judge what other people do for a living?"

I'm taken back by her vehemence. "Tara, I never meant to suggest that. I know you would never criticize me. But I feel like I need a more stable career than waiting tables if we're going to be in a serious relationship," I explain.

"You have a job!" Tara argues. "You are a singer-songwriter. You're not an amateur karaoke singer, you're a spectacular, professional musician who is popular enough to be booked months in advance."

"Sure, I can — three or four nights a week — but lining up a few gigs isn't the same as a career. It could dry-up tomorrow. What if I can't support you?" I respond, "You deserve so much better than what I can offer right now."

"Okay, I'm going to throw the BS flag. You've given me more in the past few months than anyone has in years. If I needed material things, I could buy my own," she states firmly.

"Well, you shouldn't have to work crazy hours at the gas station to be able to go to school. It's too dangerous if nothing else."

Tara scowls at me. "Aidan, don't be ridiculous. I have enough martial arts training to open a dojo. If someone tried something, they would find themselves in a world of hurt. Further, if my life was about money, I've already got plenty of my own, thank you."

Tara's statement has me totally stumped. "If you have plenty of money, why are you even bothering to work?"

Tara exhales as a myriad of emotions cross her face. "I'm going to tell you something virtually no one knows. The only people who know are the people involved in the case. My attacker was dumb enough to go around bragging about what he did. Several years ago, I won a civil judgment against Warren Jones. I have more money than I'll ever spend," she spits the words out as if they were abhorrent to her.

"Now I'm even more confused. If you have enough money to live on, why are you killing yourself to work all these side jobs?"

"Because that money is blood money. If I spend it, it makes me no better than a streetwalker," she answers, avoiding eye contact with me.

Of all the things I expected her to say, that was not one of them. I am completely befuddled by her logic. I try to conceal my shock "Not true," I insist. "Warren Jones got punished. That money is the fine for his actions, and not nearly enough at that, no matter what the amount. How you spend it is up to you. No one in their right mind would consider it payment for the savage sexual encounter."

"So, you're suggesting I should live it up on the half a million I got from Warren's trust fund?" she asks. "Wouldn't it be hypocritical? I don't want to benefit from what was done to me. Every time I spend a dollar of that money, I would feel as dirty as the night it happened."

"I can understand where you're coming from, but you're *wrong*. It's *not* payment for the so-called sex he had with you. Rape is not sex. That settlement is just compensation for the hell he put you through. You deserve every penny and more. If he ever gets out of jail, he should have to volunteer at a sewage treatment plant and roll around in other people's crap all day. You should blow it just to make sure he never has another dime to spend. If it involves pampering yourself, feel free to indulge. You've earned that right," I declare.

"You don't think it would be wrong for me to spend the money?"

"No!" I exclaim. "If you want to wipe your butt with one hundred dollar bills, it's nobody's business but yours. By denying yourself what's rightfully yours, you're giving him far more power than he deserves."

Tara looks contemplative. "Well, I've never looked at it like that. But you are right. The only person I'm hurting is myself. I'm still giving him power over my life, and that's not right."

"You're darn right, it's not. So what's on your wish list of things you've put off, because you told yourself you didn't have the money?"

"I've always wanted to pay my tuition and books

without scrambling around for scholarships," she admits.

"Oh, come on! You can do better than that," I cajole. "What's on your 'way out there' wish list? One of my first choices would be to restore your 72 Baja. But ... that's just me."

Tara smiles as she considers that option. "I've always wanted to fix it up to honor my parents. It's about the only thing left to remind me of the two of them."

"Well, consider it as good as done," I announce. "What else do you have on your wish list?"

Tara ponders her options. "Well, I've always wanted a new laptop. I guess this is as good a time as any."

"I think you have way too much common sense," I retort. "I want to hear your wildest fantasies."

"When I was a kid, before all of that crap happened, I wanted to own my own dance studio," she replies shyly.

"What's stopping you? You could build a phenomenal state-of-the-art dance studio and still have tons left over."

Tara arches an eyebrow. "Have you forgotten I don't dance anymore?"

"But that's where you're wrong," I argue. "I've personally seen you dance twice, since you told me you don't dance anymore. So I don't think you can say that about yourself anymore. You, my dear Gorgeous Gracie, are indeed a dancer."

Tara rolls her eyes at me. "Aidan, you know what I mean. I don't dance like I used to."

"So, maybe you're a little out of practice. I don't for

a minute believe you're incapable of dancing. Even the small amount we did on our date shows me you still have what it takes to be a great dancer."

In a small, tentative voice, she asks, "Do you really think so?"

"Tara, there isn't anybody who works harder than you do. I have no doubt if you decided to go back to dance, you could run the amazing studio of your dreams," I state emphatically.

"What about school and the interpreting program?"

"I don't think there are any time limits on your dreams. You can finish up your degree and plan the dance studio on the side. It's not as if you need to immediately make money," I tease.

Tara chuckles. "No, I guess I don't. I'm not sure when I'd have the time."

"I'm sure you'll figure it out. I'm really not trying to push you into one thing over the other. I just want you to know you have options."

"Okay, but all this is overwhelming right now. I need some time to think about it before I make any decisions. I'm not as spontaneous as you are."

"I understand. I don't want you to think I'm pushing you into anything. I hope you go back to dancing though. Your gift is so phenomenal, it would be great if you could teach other people what you know."

"I've often thought how fun it would be to teach Mindy how to dance. I think she may be a natural talent," Tara offers.

Mary Crawford

"There you go, then," I grin. "You already have the beginnings of a solid marketing plan."

Tara's cell phone rings, startling us both.

"Hello?" Tara answers.

"No, I haven't looked it up."

"You're kidding?"

"Yes, he's right here. I'll tell him."

"Okay, thanks for calling. I'll talk to you later."

After Tara hangs up the phone, I ask, "What was that all about?"

Tara turns to me with a grin so bright it could light a city. "That was Heather, letting me know your single released last night is already number ten on the country music charts. It's the third most popular downloaded music track on all of iTunes."

The news is so shocking, I almost forget I'm driving. "What?" I exclaim. "It must be some kind of mistake! There is no way an unknown artist like me would climb the charts that fast."

"Well, it's true. Heather was so excited, she double checked it. I think we can put to bed all your fears of not being a serious artist. You are now, officially, a singer-songwriter. Something tells me your table-waiting jobs are a thing of the past."

"Man, I hope so. I don't mind working with most of the customers, but the pay totally sucks."

"Congratulations, I am beyond proud of you. This is cause for a celebration; what do you want to do?"

"To be honest, I want to go home and take a

324

shower. I've got enough hair product in my hair to support a third world country. I want to get back to being plain, old Aidan O'Brien."

"Works for me. You should know, Heather made you some delicious chicken soup and homemade bread."

"I only met Heather at Jeff and Kiera's wedding. If she keeps feeding me like that though, I'll be her new best friend.

"Not so fast, Heather can get her own guy. In fact, I would venture to guess she already has one, even if she doesn't know it yet," Tara explains.

"If it's the guy I'm thinking of, I met him at the wedding. He's pretty determined to win her hand, I think."

Tara giggles. "Yes, I think that's what Ty is planning to do. He just has to figure out how to approach the 'hand winning' first."

"I remember watching them at the wedding reception. I don't think Tyler's going to have to worry about winning her affections. She seems to like him a lot already."

"I don't know precisely what is going on because we haven't talked about it, but you may be right. I think she is more interested in Tyler than she lets on."

"He seems like a good guy."

"I think he is, or I wouldn't trust him with Heather. She has to decide whether she likes him or hates him. She's been vacillating for a while," she elaborates.

"You know me, I'm always inspired by good, mushy love story. It makes for great songwriting."

Tara grins. "I bet. So, it seems like I might not be the only person whose financial situation just improved, and that means it's time for me to turn the tables on you. So what's your big dream?" Tara asks with a twinkle in her eye. "Oh my gosh, I still can't get over what this will mean for you. Do you know how many downloads it takes to get all the way to number ten? You'll have so much exposure you'll be booked out three or four years. You'll be so famous I'll have to make an appointment to see you. I'm so proud of you."

I take a moment to bask in her approval. It's so great to see her happy and excited. I'm grateful for this moment, if only to see her so happy. But she's right. I can't imagine what having a hit on the country charts is going to mean for my career.

In the meantime, it's fun to dream. "I don't know if we have time to share all of my dreams with you. In case you don't remember, I'm pretty much a full-time daydreamer."

"I remember that. You could make my bleakest day better by telling me your vision of your future. You were planning to become a famous concert pianist who went by the initials AOB. You used to paint me word pictures of how perfect your life was going to be when you made it big. You were going to buy the company that made Pokémon cards and go to McDonald's in a limousine every day for lunch. Do you remember that? I wonder how different your dreams are today."

I chuckle as I remember the pretentious little kid I was, back in the day. "Well, a lot of my dreams are scaled back a bit. A decade in the music business has made me a tad more realistic. Some of my dreams remain the same. First, I would like to make high-quality demo tapes with some of my original songs on them. Singing cover songs at wedding receptions is fun, but it's not where I want to be. I want to make my own music. If I don't get to sing it myself, I'd like to write for some big name stars. I'd like to create a program that donates guitars and wind instruments for kids who are in the hospital long term. I've never forgotten how lonely and isolated I felt in the hospital. If it hadn't been for Dolores encouraging me to become a songwriter, I don't know if I would've survived that environment."

Tara nods in approval. "I like your grown-up dreams. They sound amazing. I hope you —"

I interrupt her to say, "But wait, you haven't heard the most important part of my dreams."

Tara laughs. "You're funny. It's like you're an overgrown eight-year-old in an adult's body. Okay, I'll bite. What's more important than what you just told me?" she asks.

"Whenever I dreamed about what my life would look like when I grew up, I always envisioned you by my side," I confide. "The way I see it, you're my good luck charm. You were the best part of my life before I became deaf, and you're the best part of my life now."

Tara looks like she's about to cry. "I'm glad you think so. Because you're the best part of my life too."

CHAPTER TWENTY-ONE

TARA

THE LAST TWO WEEKS have been totally insane. Between my finals, work and being blindsided by a vicious head cold, I've barely had time to text Aidan, let alone see him. Even though Aidan thought he would be without work, he was booked for two weddings back-to-back right after he changed his Facebook status to reflect his availability.

The last time I saw him, it was incredible. We came back to my apartment. Only someone totally in love with me would like my grilled cheese sandwiches and tomato soup. Heather and Kiera have tried on many occasions to teach me how to cook. Unfortunately, I think I'm unteachable. I can't seem to get everything cooked evenly and on the plate at the same time. My lack of skill didn't seem to faze Aidan at all. He acted like it was the most high-class, gourmet meal he'd ever eaten. I know he shouldn't lie, but it's sweet he was willing to do so to save my feelings.

My dad would've liked Aidan. Even though I was young, my dad would tell me about the man I should marry. He told me the man who loved me should always be polite and respectful and, above all, he should think I hung the moon. I can check off all of those boxes with Aidan, and so much more.

After my sorry attempt at cooking dinner, Aidan suggested we watch a movie. We watched an old classic Eddie Murphy film. I couldn't even tell you which one because honestly, I wasn't paying attention. My apartment is so small the only place for us to watch TV was on my big king-size bed. So Aidan propped himself up against the headboard using all my pillows. He made a space between his legs and placed me there. I have to admit, with my head and back on his chest, he made a pretty good pillow. Aidan used his phenomenal hands to give me a neck and back massage. After that, we just sat quietly and watched the movie. Occasionally, he would give a small chuckle which would shake his whole chest. Eventually I noticed his breathing slowed and evened out. It appears I'm such exciting company, my presence encouraged him to completely sack out in my bed. Rather than fight it, I pulled up my comforter to cover both of us and soon after fell asleep. So much for my grand romantic plans, but I had one of the best nights' of sleep I've had in forever.

When I woke up, he brought me a tray of toasted English muffins and eggs. Now it was my turn to sample his cooking skills. Unlike his false praise of mine, I didn't have to embellish at all. His food was scrumptious. I invited him to join me on the bed for breakfast. It's amazing how sensual it is to feed someone else. Eventually we kissed. I was getting more confident of my ability to make out. It seems like such a quaint term, but it's exactly what we were doing. I was making up for lost time. I missed all these experiences in high school and college. When I was going through my self-destructive phase and sleeping with random guys, it was never this intimate. I'm totally amazed that something as benign as kissing can be so provocative.

Maybe it depends on who you're kissing. Aidan is so careful to walk the line of being respectful of my boundaries and pushing them at the same time.

Aidan got a call from the restaurant where he worked. Apparently, most of their service staff was out with the flu, and they needed Aidan to fill in immediately.

I had mixed emotions about this pesky development. Part of me wanted to get this momentous first step over with, so I could stop worrying about it. I was still afraid I'll freeze up and have a panic attack. I know Aidan will be patient and help me work through it, but I want to stop thinking about what I've lost and move on with my life.

He was so sweet about it though. He felt incredibly remorseful about leaving me in the lurch. I assured him it was not his fault, but he still sent me a bouquet of flowers, with two words written on the card: 'Rain check?' For some reason, I was incredibly amused. For a man who specializes in writing prose, he was remarkably succinct.

I sent him a text message that said, "Name the time and place." I even got brave and sent him a seductive selfie.

He immediately sent a text that said, "Next Friday night, 7:00 PM, my place."

Since my last class on Friday is over at five o'clock, I'll have plenty of time to get to Corvallis before seven.

Then he sent me a picture of himself cross-eyed, making a funny face. With the caption, "Woman, you must be trying to kill me. I might not make it that long."

I responded, "I didn't want you to forget what I look like. Friday is too far away for me too."

My phone beeped immediately, "Gorgeous Gracie, there is no danger of me forgetting what you look like. I have memorized you. I see you every day in my dreams."

I about melted on the spot. I still can't believe we are at this place. I've never been so happy.

———— ◆ ● ————

Heather, Kiera, and I are having an impromptu meeting of the Girlfriend Posse at Heather's food truck, because she's in the middle of a huge wedding cake. She's making endless rose petals out of sugar paste while we talk.

Kiera looks me over and nods her approval. "Is that what you're planning to wear tonight?"

I look down at my clothes with concern as I reply, "Yes, I was planning to. Is it okay?" I picked the linen jumpsuit with special care because it's a great color on me and makes me feel positively girly.

"You look ravishing," Heather responds. "Aidan's gonna love it, but there may be some access problems."

"Heather!" I exclaim, "Way to put it all out there."

She just laughs. "Well, that is the plan for tonight, am I right?"

I blush scarlet red and answer tentatively, "Umm, I

guess so — but it sounds so official, when I say it out loud. Do you all think I'm making a mistake?"

Kiera steps in as mediator, as she often does between Heather and I. "Well, I think you look stunning and, if it gets to that point, most guys like nothing better than a puzzle. Your choice of wardrobe will not stand in the way of a determined guy," she remarks with a large grin on her face.

"Why would you think you're making a mistake? I thought you were totally gone for this guy." Heather interjects. "By the way, did you ever tell him how you feel?"

"I did, in a roundabout way," I confess. "Aidan was telling me how much I mean to him and how much he wants this to last forever. I took the chicken way out and just agreed with him. I should've said it more directly. But I'm so bad at all this."

"I understand, sometimes it's hard to find the words. But you really need to try. He can't know what's going on in your head unless you tell him," Kiera advises. "Are you and Aidan on the same page now?"

I nod, "I'm pretty sure we want the same things. But I'm afraid of messing things up. I haven't done this in a really long time and I haven't had sex while sober since Warren. What if it doesn't go well?"

Heather puts down the flower she's working on and looks at me directly as she responds solemnly. "Tara, if he loves you like he says he does, there isn't anything you can do to mess it up. If you have a setback, Aidan will be there to help you through it. If he can't step up for you when you need him, you need to toss him to the curb."

Kiera pats me on the shoulder as she says; "I think you're putting way too much pressure on yourself. If it happens between you today, then great. If it doesn't, it's not the end of the world. Go over there and just have fun with Aidan. If a romantic moment presents itself, you'll know what to do. I think you may be psyching yourself out too much."

I sigh deeply as I concede, "You're probably right."

Heather grins at me as she teases, "Are you prepared?"

"Prepared?" I stare at her blankly.

She puts her flower down, strips her gloves off, walks over to her purse and hands me something. "Yes, prepared. Did you miss your personal health class?" Heather teases.

I almost drop the strip when I see that they are flavored. "Seriously? Who thinks of these things?" I stammer awkwardly.

"Guys!" Heather and Kiera say simultaneously.

"Hey, don't knock them until you've tried them." Kiera quips. "At least Heather saved you the embarrassment of getting your prophylactics from your dad. Jeff couldn't look my dad straight in the eye for days after he pulled that. It was too funny."

I chuckle at the memory of Kiera telling the story of when Denny left them a note condoning their relationship and announcing that he wasn't ready for any more grandkids. I suppose they're right, there are worse places to get sexual advice than from your best friends.

"Alrighty then, I'll just take these and be on my

way." I retort as I stuff them in my purse. "Wish me luck."

Heather smirks, "Oh, I don't think there's any luck involved — unless you count 'getting lucky.' Now go have some fun and stop stressing yourself out. I've heard sex is a good stress reliever."

"You guys are so bad. I'm going to get out of here before you embarrass me any more. I may or may not have a story to share the next time you see me."

"You better have stories because I live vicariously through you and Kiera," Heather calls out as I walk toward my car.

As the GPS on the phone tells me I've arrived at Aidan's house, my heart is pounding. I'm not sure if it's anticipation or terror making my pulse race. I don't know why I feel like tonight is a make it or break it event for me, but I do. I take a few deep breaths to calm down. I try to tell myself this is just Aidan and it's not a big deal. Yet, I feel like everything I've gone through since I was fourteen is converging today. If I can move beyond this hurdle, I think I can move past anything. Maybe that's the problem; what happens if I can't?

I rest my head against my steering wheel as I take a few moments to calm down and collect myself. Suddenly, I hear a knock at my car window. The sound is enough to almost send me flying through the roof of my car. I turn to ascertain the source of the sound. I breathe a sigh of relief when I see Aidan's smiling face. With one last deep breath, I open my car door. I hope Aidan doesn't notice my hands are shaking.

"Come on, Gracie, let's get you out of the rain; it's cold out here," Aidan says as he takes my hand, helps me out of the car, and brushes a kiss on my cheek. As we enter the house, I notice it's a quaint little log cabin with an inviting fireplace in the living room. I'm impressed. I don't know where I expected Aidan to live, but this wasn't it. But, on the other hand, it totally fits his love of the outdoors and rock climbing.

"Nice digs," I comment as I continue to look around. There are stunning nature photographs everywhere in the room. There's also a portable piano set up in the corner. Aidan's favorite guitar is propped up next to an old barstool.

"I'd like to take credit for it, but I'm house-sitting until my client's son gets back from a year-long sabbatical in Ethiopia. He's over there helping them build wells. If I ever get to build a place, it's going to look a lot like this," Aidan explains. He rubs his hands on the side of his jeans. He used to do that all the time before piano recitals when he was younger. Aidan might be as nervous as I am.

"Are you okay, AJ?" I ask as I watch him fumble with my coat while trying to hang it up.

"Yes, … I mean no." Aidan shrugs helplessly. "I don't think I've ever been this nervous, not even on a nationally televised TV show."

"Oh my gosh, I'm so glad it's not just me," I breathe.

"No, Gracie, it's not just you. I've been on pins and needles for days," Aidan admits. "I want you to have the perfect night."

"Well, don't worry about me. I have fun every time I'm around you. I'm sure tonight will be no different."

Aidan walks up to me and says, "I don't know why, but today does feel different."

"I'm trying not to think about that. I want to relax and have fun."

"Okay, I'll put fun on the agenda for sure," Aidan quips. "In the meantime, would you like dinner?"

"Of course. You know me, I'm always starving," I reply. "But first I'd like to start the fun part of the night." I'm wearing high heels, so I'm nearly as tall as Aidan. I thread my fingers through the hair on the back of his head and draw him close for a kiss. I kiss him deeply, enjoying the textures of him.

At first, Aidan is on board with my exploration, but then he pulls back and groans. "Tara, if we continue down this road, there won't be any dinner," he admits with a shaky voice as he exhales roughly. "I need to feed you before we get distracted."

"If you must," I pout. I can't keep a teasing grin off my face.

"Indeed, I must," Aidan retorts. "If you're going to faint, I want it to be from wanton desire, not because you forgot to eat."

"How did you know I skipped lunch today?" I ask.

"Well, I didn't know for sure you skipped lunch, but I figured you might've since your Friday's are busy," Aidan responds. "You need to take better care of yourself. We have to keep up with junior high school kids this weekend. You'll need all the strength you can muster.

Did you bring your bags? Please tell me you're going to spend the night, since we'll have to be up at the crack of dawn."

"I did bring my duffel bag." I state, laughing at the wistful expression on his face. "I left it in the car."

"What?" Aidan protests. "Do you have something against sexy slumber parties?"

"Not in principle. But, I've never actually been on one before."

"Well, I have a treat for you. I even have s'mores by candlelight planned. Just let me get your bags before we get distracted again."

As he turns to leave, he kicks over my purse that's sitting on the floor beside the couch. Much to my mortification, those brightly colored gifts from Heather fall out.

I gasp in horror and hurry to pick them up, but Aidan is faster than me and has longer arms. So, he reaches them first. He raises an eyebrow at me and carefully examines the contents before saying, "I see you got cherry and grape."

I blush bright red. "Oh, those were *not* my idea. Heather gave those to me as a gag gift."

"So, you're saying I shouldn't read anything into this?" Aidan teases. "Your best friend gave you lollipop flavored condoms for no reason at all?"

I bury my head in the cleft between his neck and shoulder and mumble, "Okay, so I may have over-shared. I told you I was nervous about tonight, and my friends thought they could help me calm down."

"I want friends like that!" Aidan exclaims. "They sound like a blast."

"Well, if you stick with me, they will be your friends. Kiera and her dad have a habit of taking you in and making you feel like family, while Heather likes pretty much everybody. She's so funny, she could be a standup comedian."

"I noticed she had the crowd rolling at the wedding. She has a gift for saying the outrageous — but I don't think she was far off base with her present. I think we're definitely headed in that direction. Don't you?"

Of all the scenarios I had played out in my head, this was not even remotely close to what I thought might happen. It was shortsighted of me, given Aidan's propensity to push boundaries and his overwhelming curiosity. I had hoped maybe we could slowly ease our way into lovemaking without having to talk about it first. This approach is probably better; I just have to summon up the nerve to be honest.

I take the plunge and answer his question. "Yes, we are definitely headed there. I can't make any promises, but that's where I'd like us to go," I admit. I am proud of myself for being able to admit it out loud. I've spent a lifetime isolated and keeping to myself. To admit I need or want someone is a big deal.

True to form, Aidan wants more information as he pushes, "But why now? I don't want you to feel like you need to do something you're not prepared for, just because I'd like to go further. I love you enough to wait, however long it takes for you to be comfortable."

Oh wow! It's clear I'm going to have to lay all my

cards on the table for Aidan to understand how far I've come. Kiera's advice about him not being able to read my mind unless I tell him what's really going on rings loud in my head.

"Aidan, I don't think you understand," I begin to explain. "I want to be here with you more than anything I've ever wanted. I love you enough to let you into my closed off cocooned world. You once told me you wanted to break me out of my cocoon one strand at a time. I'm here tonight because you've successfully set me free. I'm not the same person I was a few months ago."

An expression of awe crosses Aidan's face as he processes what I've said. "I don't want to make any assumptions," he murmurs as he crushes me into a hug. "Are you saying what I think you're saying?"

Tears well in the corner of my eyes and I can't seem to control them as I reply. "Yes, you heard correctly. Aidan Jarith O'Brien, I am in love with you."

Aidan pulls away so he can study my face. "Gracie, why are you crying? This is the happiest news I've gotten in years. Why does it make you sad?"

"Aidan, these are happy tears. I'm not sad. In fact, I'm beside myself with happiness and relief," I explain.

Aidan being Aidan, he caught the one odd word. "Relief? Why do you feel relieved?" he asks in a puzzled voice. He cups the side of my face with his hand and wipes my tears away.

I draw in a shuddering breath. "For so many years, I didn't dare dream I would ever be happy again. I was so lonely. I had to focus all my energy on keeping my abject fear at bay and pretending to feel normal. It was exhausting."

"Tara, I am so sorry," Aidan murmurs. "If I could go back in time and stay part of your life, I would in a heartbeat."

"I know you would," I assure him. "That's where the relief comes in. Being with you reminds me what real life is supposed to be like. Loving you has given me freedom. Freedom to live and to dream. I'm dreaming of a future and for once, it doesn't terrify me."

"Gracie, I dream of our future every day," Aidan says with a gentle smile. "You've given me freedom too. Because you love me, I have the freedom to stand up for what I believe in, even if it costs me my dream. It doesn't matter if the whole world sees me as a failure, because you'll always be on my side."

"Of course I will. There's nowhere I'd rather be. Someday we'll be in a retirement home, and I'll be teaching everyone to dance while you serenade them with all the oldies," I tease.

Much to my surprise, Aidan doesn't dissolve into laughter at my silly vision of the future. Instead, he leans in to give me an excruciatingly tender kiss. "That will be beautiful. I will have the most stunning wife in the whole place."

"Oh, you don't know that," I protest. "I could be as wrinkled as a raisin and as deaf as you."

Aidan chuckles. "Well, luckily for us, we both know sign language. It doesn't matter what you look like on the outside, you'll always be beautiful. I think traveling around in a big Airstream trailer and seeing all the sites will be more our speed. I can see you racing down the beach while I ogle your shapely bum. Of course, I'll be bald with a paunch by then, and I'll never be able to keep up with you."

I giggle as I joke, "Oh, I'll wait for you, slowpoke. After all, if we've been running all these years, I'll be totally used to it."

Aidan grins at me. "I should put your smart mouth to better use. Let me feed you as promised. Would you like steak or a salmon fillet?"

"You actually know how to cook? I'm impressed."

Aidan shrugs nonchalantly. "Don't be too impressed, I'm just throwing them on the grill."

I roll my eyes at him. "I should've warned you what a truly terrible cook I am before you fell in love with me."

"Don't sweat it, Tara. I can live on Top Ramen if I need to. In fact, sometimes I do just for economic reasons."

"I don't think you understand how kitchen challenged I am. I routinely burn Top Ramen."

The look of astonishment on Aidan's face is hysterical. But he quickly pulls himself together and says, "Wow! That takes some special kind of talent. I didn't think it was possible to burn it."

"Trust me, I have smoke damage on the ceiling to prove it."

"Well, I guess when we're divvying up household chores, I'll be the one in charge of cooking. Unfortunately, that might mean you're relegated to scrubbing toilets." Aidan says with a smug smile.

I stick my tongue out at him. "Interesting plan, but

you might want to rethink your strategy. It might be to your benefit to reward me for not cooking."

"Point taken. I'll see what I can do about teaching you to cook so we can share duties. For now, though, do you think you can handle tossing salad while I do the grilling?"

"I don't know ... are there knives involved?" I retort smartly.

"No, there don't have to be. You can tear the lettuce apart with your hands. In fact, that makes for a crispier salad," he informs me.

"Why would it make a difference?" I'm sure I look very confused.

"Because the knife can bruise the lettuce," he explains. "Stick with me and eventually you'll be a master in the kitchen."

With that boast, he takes me by the hand and leads me to the kitchen.

After a delicious dinner, we go into the living room and sit in front of the fireplace to play Scrabble. Aidan plays Scrabble differently from anyone I've ever seen. He makes up all sorts of random rules like all the words have to rhyme or you can only use nouns or verbs. It takes forever to play the round when he decides we can only use words which name body parts. By the time we are done, my side aches from laughing so hard.

All of a sudden, a pillow hits me in the shoulder. "Aidan, did you throw a pillow at me?" I ask through a fit of giggles.

"Yes ma'am, I did. I have pretty good aim, too," he

brags.

"I'm not sure I want to know, but why did you throw a pillow at me?" I pick it up off the floor and toss it back at him.

"Now you're getting into the spirit of things," Aidan answers. "It can't be a proper slumber party without a pillow fight."

"I'm new to the world of slumber parties, but I think we're both supposed to have pillows for this to work," I reply, still baffled.

Aidan lobs the pillow back to me with a gentle toss. Then, from behind his back, he pulls out another pillow. "Now we're evenly armed," he announces.

The smug look on his face brings out my competitive juices. There's something hard-wired in me that makes me unable to turn down even the silliest of challenges. That tendency got me into a lot of trouble at the martial arts studio. However, I think I'm safe here.

"You should come here and kiss me to prove there are no hard feelings."

Aidan's face lights up at the prospect of kissing me, so he drops his pillow and walks over to comply with my request. He's so focused on my mouth, he fails to notice that instead of dropping the pillow, I put it behind my back. As he kisses me lightly on the lips, I pull the pillow from behind my back and bop him on the top of the head. "Gotcha!" I exclaim, then spin around and start to run.

Aidan backs up to retrieve the pillow he dropped. "I've got to hand it to you, Gracie. I didn't think you were capable of cheating."

"Cheating? Who me? I thought all was fair in love and war," I tease.

"Oh, are we going to play by those rules?" Aidan asks ominously. "You better prepare yourself Gracie."

"I think you forgot I've been your friend for years and I know your weaknesses," I threaten as I stick my tongue out at him. However, I'm not taking any chances, so I take off at a dead sprint around the kitchen island. Unfortunately, I forgot I took off my shoes when we were playing Scrabble. So, when the long pants legs of my jumpsuit hit the wood floor, I go sprawling at frightening speed.

"Uh-huh, who is at a disadvantage now?" Aidan jokes as he catches me in his arms before I hit the floor.

"Please don't torture me!" I plead as I try to catch my breath. "I'm so sorry I cheated." I try not to giggle.

Aidan spins me around in his arms and states, "I think I can put your body to better use."

"Really? Because I was kind of having fun," I remark with a wink.

"I think what I have planned might be more fun," Aidan suggests as he slowly peruses my body with his eyes.

"I don't know about that. I guess it depends on your plan," I tease.

"How about this?" He leans his head down to kiss me.

When I pull away, I reply, "I could be on board with this plan."

I no sooner say the words than Aidan scoops me up in his arms and carries me to his bedroom and sets me in the middle of his bed. I am surprised to see books on nearly every surface. Old books, new books, fiction, and nonfiction. They all seem to be bookmarked and dog-eared. At my look of curiosity, Aidan merely shrugs and explains, "I said school wasn't my thing; I never said I didn't like to learn."

"You always acted like you hated it when we were kids," I reply, needing to fill the electric atmosphere with chatter.

"I was embarrassed because you were so much better than I was," he clarifies. "So, I played school off as a joke so you wouldn't know how much I struggled."

I strive to understand. "Why did you always know the answer if the teacher asked a question?"

"Once I learn something, I pretty much remember it indefinitely."

"Wow, that's cool. That skill must help with songwriting."

"Mm-hmm," he responds noncommittally. "Can we talk about something else like how beautiful you are?"

I smile shyly as I confide, "I don't know if I'll ever get used to you talking about it."

"Well, you should just get used to it because I plan to tell you every day, forever so your heart can dance."

I feel my eyes misting over. "Aidan, you've summed up our relationship perfectly. You have brought joy back into my life so that my heart can dance. You always did that for me even when we were kids. I've fallen in love with you and I can't imagine life without you," I admit with a tearful smile.

Aidan runs his hand down my side as he leans in for a kiss. I yelp in surprise. "I don't remember being so ticklish," I confess shyly.

Aidan grins at me. "You already know I'm over-the-top ticklish. I'll be nice to you if you're nice to me. Deal?"

Wide-eyed, I mutely nod my agreement.

"I was hoping you'd say that," Aidan whispers as he kisses me thoroughly. "How am I doing?"

I'm confused by his question. "What do you mean?"

"I promised to be nice to you. Did you think that was 'nice'?"

I blush because I missed his implication the first time. "Yes! It was very nice," I stammer. "I enjoyed it very much."

"I'm glad," Aidan murmurs as he kisses me again. "Because, I'm having fun. Sometimes it pays to be the nice guy," he jokes as he captures my lips and gently nibbles on my bottom lip.

I capture his mouth for a kiss. Pulling away, I reply, "See, I can be 'nice' too." I wink.

Aidan groans harshly and lets out a ragged breath in my neck. I freeze as the blood in my face drains out so quickly that I feel faint. I can't even breathe. My body starts to shake so violently that my teeth rattle.

Aidan's expression turns to a concerned frown as he pulls me into a sitting position and links his index finger with mine. He snags a bottle of red liquid from the dorm-fridge beside the bed. I wrinkle my nose when I see it. "Is that your crappy so-called-healthy-Kool-Aid?" I ask with disgust.

He raises an eyebrow at me as he patiently answers, "I might not be all heroic like Jeff, but I recognize the symptoms of shock. It may not be your favorite, but you need to drink this PowerAde."

I try to affect a pouty face, but it's not very effective since my teeth are chattering like some demented dime store toy.

"Drink," Aidan commands, holding the bottle up to my lips.

"Fine," I answer, trying to sound sarcastic; instead I sound breathless. "Since when did you become Mr. Bossy-Pants?" I take a few sips and I'm surprised to find that it tastes much better cold.

"If it involves your well being, I'll be as tough as I need to be," Aidan responds without hesitation. "I love you and it's my job to help keep you safe. Now, do you want to tell me what happened a second ago?"

I bury my head in my hands as I mumble, "I'd rather not; it's stupid and embarrassing. It's not at all how I wanted today to go. I had a whole different day planned. Honestly, I don't know what happened. I was having a really good time making out with you." I breathe faster and tears start running out of the corners of my eyes. I am shaking like a drenched Chihuahua puppy.

Aidan gently pulls my hands away from my face and weaves his fingers through mine. He holds my hands loosely between us on the bed as he massages my wrists with his thumbs. We're sitting cross-legged facing each other. "Tara, look at me and do what I do," he instructs softly with his deep, soothing voice.

Immediately, my eyes shoot to his gaze as if I'm being hypnotized by a master magician. When he takes a breath in through his nose and blows it out from his mouth, I do the same. Then, he slowly repeats his actions again for a third and then a fourth and then a fifth time. Pretty soon, I notice my breathing has slowed down significantly and I can catch a breath on my own without having to mimic Aidan and my shoulders don't feel as heavy. I can finally meet his gaze steadily.

"Aidan, I'm so sorry. I love you and I don't know why it all went off the rails. Maybe I was never meant to fall in love. Maybe I'm supposed to be alone for my whole life. I suppose this is my punishment for secretly being mad at my mom for all the hell she put me through when I was little or maybe it's because I acted like a whore after my life was destroyed," I respond dejectedly. Nothing that Aidan could ever say to me was worse than I was feeling about myself.

Aidan visibly flinches at my words. "Gracie, you have to stop," he growls, his eyes tearing up. "I love you too much to allow you to treat yourself that way. Would you say any of that stuff to any of the women you met in your support group?"

"Of course not!" I exclaim in outrage. "Who would do that? I'm not barbaric."

"Well, apparently you would," he answers somberly as he looks me directly in the eyes. "Because that's exactly what you've been doing to yourself. Are you different from the other rape survivors in your group? Do you use different survival techniques than countless other rape survivors do, every minute of every day across the world?" Aidan asks softly.

"No," I whisper roughly. "I should have been stronger. I was an elite athlete."

"You were a fourteen-year-old girl going through something no one of any age should have to go through — let alone a girl with no father and a mother who was as good as gone," he argues. "You were dealt the worst of all unfair hands. The surprise isn't that you made a few missteps, it's that your life doesn't look like a pinball machine chock full of them. Tara, you have no idea how remarkable it is that you've risen above what happened to you."

"But I ruined our time together, yet again," I insist.

Aidan sighs as he kisses the backs of my hands and murmurs, "Gracie, I consider it a miracle we found each other again. Every moment we spend together is precious to me. Maybe you don't remember, but you've seen me through some pretty hairy times, too. There were times my mouth got ahead of my ability to defend myself and you were the one to patch me up. You never complained about it. I often tricked you into reading things out loud for me because it was easier for me to process the information. You did it willingly, even though you had your own studying to do. That's what friends do for each other. When someone is having a rough time, the other friend steps up. Whatever this turns out to be, we were friends first. I'm never going to judge you. The jerk who did this to you? Oh, heck yes! But *you*? Never in a million years. No matter how much blame you pile on yourself, this was never your fault."

"I could have done things differently —" I sputter in one last attempt to shoulder the blame. I don't know why I'm trying so hard to show him I'm not the sweet little girl he once knew. I thought I had worked through most of this in counseling. But it's rearing its ugly head anyway. Maybe I'm trying to prove to him I'm not worth his generosity and grace. Perhaps I'm setting up a test he can't pass. During my counseling, I learned this can be a common reaction among survivors.

A brief scowl passes over Aidan's face. "There isn't a single decision we make in any given day, from the way we put on our socks, to the breakfast cereal we choose to have, to the way we order our coffee, we couldn't do differently. I hate to deflate your argument, Gracie, but that's not going to hold enough air to blow up a balloon. So, do you mind telling me why you're trying to piss me off?"

"I don't know," I confess. "I wonder if I'm worth your time, I guess. Maybe I'm just too screwed up for you to even bother with. Maybe you're just too good for me. You deserve better. You're on the edge of this great music career and you don't need to be held back by an emotional cripple like me." I didn't even realize I was crying, but now I feel big fat tears splashing down on my forearms.

Aidan's body turns rigid as his eyes flash brightly. "I must not be communicating clearly here," he snaps. "You still don't get it! None of this means anything if I don't have you in my life. I'd just as soon be making French fries in the back of the house twelve hours a day, if I don't get to keep you. The top of the Billboard charts means nothing if I lose you." He drags his fingers through his hair, nearly tearing it out of his scalp. "I thought you knew that," he whispers with a defeated sigh. His shoulders are slumped and he's randomly tracing the stitching on the quilt with his fingers as if it could play a melody.

Instinctively, I launch myself at his chest and loop my arms around his neck. I plant a soft kiss on his lips and murmur, "Of course I know, AJ! I've always known. I'm just so scared. What if this is all there ever is, between us? What if I can't get better? What if I always nearly hit the ceiling when you come up quietly behind me? What if you get frustrated because you have desires I can't meet?" I ask, not wanting to know the answer.

Aidan gathers me in a warm hug and gently returns my kiss before carefully returning us to our previous positions and linking the index fingers on our left hands. It's an unconscious gesture of comfort for him. He strokes my cheek with his right hand as he confesses softly, "Tara, do you think you're the only one who's terrified? I've been afraid since the moment we met again. I'm petrified you'll discover I need you way more than you'll ever need me, and behind all my smiles and jokes I'm pretty much a shy, geeky guy with hardly any true friends but you. One day I'm afraid you'll decide you want someone more accomplished and educated, or someone who isn't spinning his wheels chasing some far-away dream. You're going to want somebody who doesn't think Tom and Jerry cartoons are hysterically funny and Cap'n Crunch is a perfect breakfast. The honest truth is, I may never be that guy. Knock-Knock jokes still crack me up and probably will 'til the day I die. I'm just built that way. I'm the one wondering if I'm good enough for a classy, exquisite woman like you," Aidan explains with a quirky smile.

I answer his smile with a sloppy, crooked smile of my own. "It seems we've come to a few mutual misunderstandings. Your quirkiness and over the top sense of humor are some of the things I like best about you. They balance my tendency to be far too serious and focused. You give me permission to laugh at myself and the world around me. If you hadn't done that for me when I was little, I would have been crushed under the weight of my sadness, fears, and responsibilities. Even now, you've given me the ability to look at my circumstances in a whole new light and remember what it's like to be strong."

Aidan lets out a low wolf whistle as he jests, "Wow! You make me sound like I was doing something valuable with my life instead of just being the class clown."

"AJ, that's exactly what I'm trying to say. So stop trying to brush it off as a joke. I'm being serious. You were a very big part of why I went to class every single day, even if I stayed up all night taking care of my mom. Without you, I don't even know if I could've made it. I was so sad about my dad dying that some days, seeing your face was the only reason I got out of bed for weeks on end. I was in love with you for a very long time before I even knew it."

"So, when did you know?" Aidan probes.

"The first time? Or now?" I blush positively crimson when I realize how much emotional underbelly

I've exposed.

Aidan's jaw drops so dramatically, he looks like a Looney Tunes cartoon. I expect multicolored question marks to float from his skull at any second.

I can't help myself. I giggle and snort as I contemplate his expression.

"Oh come now, Aidan," I admonish. "It can't be that big of a surprise. You never even tried to hide your feelings from me. I was bound to notice and reciprocate at some point."

Aidan looks completely flummoxed as he scratches the side of his head and stammers, "Well, yes but —"

"I think I felt the first flutters the day you bought me bandages and fixed my feet instead of buying collectible toys with your money. But I wasn't sure I wasn't hallucinating about my feelings," I reveal in a rush of words.

Aidan chuckles as he confirms, "No Gracie, it was very real — frighteningly real. Rory teased me about it for months."

I grin as I imagine that scenario. I suppose Rory was a tad envious of our close relationship. Even as handsome as Rory always was, he never had the easy charm Aidan had. I think he was always jealous of that, even if he would never admit it.

"But when did you know for sure?" Aidan pushes.

"I didn't know until it was too late," I answer somberly. "I had come back from a grueling dance camp and I was ready to start the new school year. I was excited to show you all the new skills I learned from a famous choreographer I'd worked with. For the first time since I was six, you were not there to greet me. I remember opening my locker really carefully, to see what you had hidden there. I was sure you were around the corner waiting for me to find whatever creepy crawly thing you had hidden. I even spent time during the summer practicing a dramatic pratfall so I could pretend to have a wicked case of the vapors like the vaudeville act we'd played the spring before. But there was nothing spooky in my locker, and you were nowhere to be found. Every teacher I asked just shook their head sadly and said, 'Oh you poor dear, didn't your mother tell you?'"

"I left the school in hysterics. I roamed the streets for two days looking for you. I finally decided you must be like everyone else — since I loved you, of course, you left me. I went back to school and summoned the courage to ask one of the janitors. Remember the one with arthritis so bad, he would never use a dustpan because he couldn't bend down? Well, I asked him if you have left me and he answered, 'Shur 'nuff chile' he done gone to live with them gators.' I didn't know exactly what that meant. But I knew it wasn't anywhere around where I was. Once again, because I loved someone, they were gone. I vowed to never love anyone ever again."

Adrian turns a little green like he was going to be sick. "You mean to tell me, my parents never said anything to you about me being sick?" he demands.

"No, not really. After several months, after I had heard rumors at school, your mother told me you had chosen to go a different direction in your life and were choosing to stay with some friends so you didn't have to be around the performing arts. No one ever gave me any hint you might need me. In fact, I thought they were telling me you didn't want to be around me. I let the matter drop. Shortly after that, as you know, my life fell apart and I had other things to deal with.

Adrian shakes his head and drags his hand down his face like he's trying to clear a bad image on an Etch-a-Sketch. "I would expect this kind of behavior from my dad, but I'm shocked it came from my mom. She knew all along that I've been in love with you since I was about six. I told her I was going to grow up and marry you. I know she thought I was joking, but I would think my behavior over the years would've convinced her otherwise. Like you said, people three states over could probably tell I was in love with you. I followed you around like a starving bloodhound. Even the substitute bus drivers knew," he says, frustration dripping from every word.

"I don't know. Your parents were pretty invested in keeping the partnership between Rory and me together because we had been dancing together so long. Maybe they were afraid, if they told me the truth, I would no longer dance with Rory. Their fears were probably well-founded; if I'd known how they treated you, I wouldn't have stayed. They must have known me well enough to figure it out. You know how vested they were in success in those days."

"Yeah, with me out of commission, they had all their eggs in one basket," he hisses sarcastically. "They tossed me aside like a bag of over-ripened peaches. They totally messed with my self-esteem. It took me a long time to believe in myself again. Thank heavens Dolores was patient with me, otherwise it could have been a total mess."

"Don't get me wrong, I'm not condoning anything they did. They made atrocious decisions. In a way I can't help but be grateful. We're here, so the strange and winding paths we both took seem suddenly worth it. I can't be sorry for that." I kiss Aidan tenderly on the lips.

I feel the tension drain from his body as he starts to relax into the kiss and kiss me back with excruciating slowness. "Well, if you put it like that, maybe I can't be angry at my parents. Their actions led us to right here, right now. This is as close to perfect as it gets. On that note, do you sleep on the left side of the bed or the right, because I'm beat and we have to get up early to collect a bunch of junior high kids. We should get as much sleep as possible. I have a feeling I'm going to experience a whole new level of tiredness I've never experienced, even when I worked as a hotel manager."

I groan when I hear that. "Does this mean I have to participate in some elaborate hazing ritual?" I ask in a resigned voice.

"I'm not exactly sure. I've heard some wild stories about school camps. I'm pretty sure most are urban legends, but you never know. So I'll ask again, what side of the bed do you want?"

"I'm not picky," I say with a lift of my shoulder. "You pick and I'll take leftovers." I grab a pair of yoga pants and t-shirt and head to the bathroom.

As I look at my red eyes and nose in the mirror, I wonder what the heck I'm doing. I've settled nothing. In fact, I've lost ground. The only thing I know for sure is we love each other, and we have for a long time. Is that enough to sustain our relationship for a lifetime? I hope so. I don't want to let him go. I'd like to think my daddy sent Aidan to me to love me, because he couldn't anymore.

Chapter Twenty-Two

Aidan

While I wait for Tara to come out of the bathroom, I try to concentrate on a biography of Steve Jobs so I don't look like a creepy stalker. In reality, I'm listening to see if she needs me. It hurts that she still questions whether she is worthy of my love. If she only knew how much simple joy I derive from making her happy, it would astonish her. I know it's the clichéd stuff of pop and country songs, but in my life, the sun really does rise and set on her shoulders.

My heart skips a beat when Tara appears. She's wearing an oversize t-shirt which says, '**Live as if you were to die tomorrow. Learn as if you were to live forever. —Mahatma Gandhi**' and sleek black yoga pants. She reminds me of the dancer she used to be. All she needs to complete the look is a couple of pencils haphazardly sticking through her hair for taking notes on a choreographer's feedback.

Her dramatic makeup is gone. In its place are gracefully arched brows and delicately pink lips. Her hair is now in a messy ponytail. But she looks just as beautiful to me. It's a different kind of beautiful, but gorgeous just the same. She looks younger and more delicate, but still amazing. I lecture my body to tamp down its involuntary reaction. I don't want to scare her away again. I try to remind myself to stay in the friend zone for now.

She notices my scrutiny. "What? You're looking at me funny."

"I am not. I was just noticing we look like a couple of veteran slumber partiers. I feel like I should be braiding your hair and painting your toenails, or something."

She smirks at me. "Do I really seem like the type to you? Being a girly girl really isn't my thing."

"I don't know, you seem to cross genres pretty well, to me. You looked like a fashion model when you showed up at my door, but I like this too," I tell her.

Tara giggles. "To use one of Heather's expressions, 'Well, aren't you just the sweetest little thing?'"

I arch an eyebrow at her. "Does she really get away with stuff like that in Oregon?"

She nods. "All the time. People eat it up; they think Heather's straight out of *Steel Magnolias* or something. It's weird."

I chuckle. "I need to start hanging out with those friends of yours; they sound like a great crowd."

"They really are cool," she declares as she stifles a yawn.

I prop myself up on the padded headboard and pat the bed beside me. "Would you like me to sing you to sleep?"

Nodding eagerly, Tara hops up in bed beside me and hands me my acoustic guitar. Somehow, I manage to tuck her in next to me and balance the guitar on my thigh. I know she's a huge fan of Elton John, so I start to play *Your Song*. I've barely made the transition into *Tiny Dancer* before Tara's breathing evens out, and she melts into my side. I set the guitar down on my side of the bed, careful not to jar any of the strings. I slither down in the bed, resting her head on my chest while I cover us with the antique quilt. Silently I offer a prayer that this is the picture of domesticity we can maintain for years to come. I reach over to set my cell phone alarm for four-thirty in the morning and cringe when I realize we have less than six hours to sleep. I shut my eyes and savor this dream for as long as it lasts.

I wake up to Tara looking at me in horror. At first, I thought I had done something inappropriate like acting out my vivid, erotic dreams. Apparently not, since Tara seems fully dressed and shows no signs of being thoroughly kissed. I look around the room in total confusion and search Tara's face for clarification.

"Oh my gosh!" she exclaims burying her face in her hands and turning slightly pink, "I totally drooled all over you. Why didn't you say something?"

"Well, it could be because a.) I didn't notice, or b.) I don't care, or c.) all of the above.

"Aidan, that's so disgusting! Are all guys this way? I missed so much not having my dad around. I would know this stuff if he was alive. Do you really not care, or are you just being nice?"

"No, Gracie, I really don't care. I can take a shower like a big boy or you can help supervise," I tease.

Intriguingly, her eyes flash with interest, but she also quivers visibly. "Um, I don't think I'm ready for that quite yet. Still, it sounds … interesting. I guess I better go get started. We don't want to be late for the bus. That would make us look bad as chaperones."

I take her embarrassment and confusion as a hopeful sign. Clearly, she still feels the chemistry between us. I'm just gonna have to take it excruciatingly slowly and carefully. I can't wipe the grin off my face the whole time I'm taking an admittedly cold shower.

My shower was quicker than Tara's, so I scramble up eggs and fix some toaster waffles and cut up some strawberries and peaches.

When Tara walks in the kitchen, she sighs with pleasure as she says, "Man, that smells good. I didn't realize how hungry I am, until now. I was too nervous to eat much last night. I still don't understand how you seem to remember everything I like, from the way I like my steak to my preferences in eggs. It's kind of freaky. I haven't seen you in more than a decade. Maybe you've been stalking me!" she accuses with a grin.

I shrug nonchalantly. "No, but it would be a gross understatement if I said I paid close attention to you in those days." I'm cursing my Irish complexion because it hides nothing when I blush. "If we were in school these days, I might be called a stalker." I laugh wryly.

"Don't get me wrong. I'm flattered. It's just really unusual. I don't think my own mom knew so much about me, and I doubt my best friends today understand me as well as you do. It's a bit unnerving."

"Well Gracie, we'd better eat up. We have twelve minutes to be out the door or we're going to be late." I prompt. I stretch and pop my back. "Why did we think this was such a good idea again?"

Tara groans as she blows on her coffee, "I can't quite remember; it's a little fuzzy right now, but I think my professor said something about being a good person and Karma. There may have been vague references to extra credit and career opportunities—but right now, my eyelids feel like they have weights attached to them, and I'd just as soon be curled up in your nice comfortable bed with your chest as a pillow."

My coffee about burns a hole down my windpipe as she makes her blunt admission. I do my best to cover my reaction, but I'm not quick enough.

She looks at me with a startled expression on her face and asks innocently, "Something wrong AJ?"

"No," I fib a little, "I'm fine. I swallowed wrong. Maybe I should slow down just a little." I take a deliberate bite of my waffle and chew slowly to illustrate my point.

Much to my surprise, she seems fascinated with my mouth and Adam's apple when I swallow. I'm not sure I even want to ask. I think I'll leave this one to my imagination.

Tara looks at her cell phone and asks if I have a travel mug. Her question nudges me out of my thought bubble, and I rush to grab one from the cupboard and pour her coffee into it. I chose a second travel mug for myself and put in about twice as much sugar.

Tara looks like a quintessential Oregonian this morning with her thermal t-shirt and plaid flannel over-shirt, Levi's, and boots. She also looks adorably tired. I urge her to take a fluffy oversized feather pillow with her, since we have about a forty-five minute drive to meet the buses. On the way out the door, I grab a fluffy blanket. While she was drinking her coffee, I put our bags in the back of my van.

When she climbs into her seat, I carefully buckle her in the seat and tuck the blanket around her. She gives me an amused look and raises an eyebrow in question.

I grin. "Remember what I said about your personal safety? I reserve the right to be Mr. Bossy Pants. Feel free to recline the seat and continue to sleep like it's not the crack of dawn. Don't I make an exemplary boyfriend?"

"Actually, you really do. You had fresh coffee and breakfast this morning, you gave me the big bathroom, and you don't really care how I look. I can't ask for much more. So, yes, you get big boyfriend points. I'm gonna take you up on your offer for a nap. I'm still exhausted. I'm used to sleeping in on Saturdays. This is ridiculous!"

"Okay, I'll try not to sing too loudly to the radio," I tease.

Tara cuts her gaze sharply at me as she chides, "Don't you dare keep quiet on my account. I don't want to miss one of your concerts for any reason. Feel free to serenade me any place, any time."

"Okay then, your wish is my command," I respond as I start an *a cappella* version of Kenny Rogers *You Decorated My Life*.

Tara sniffs delicately. "Aidan Jarith O'Brien, I can't

sleep if I'm crying. Songs like that will get you so many boyfriend points you won't know what to do with them."

I puff out my chest as I respond, "What can I say? I try. But I'll try not to make you cry next time." With that, I transition into *Happy* by Pharrell Williams.

Tara giggles. "You're a silly man! How am I supposed to sleep when I want to get up and dance?"

I file that little piece of information away for later use and answer, "I'll try for more middle-of-the-road elevator music. The kind of stuff I play at corporate events. Now shut your eyes and go to sleep," I instruct as I hum *Brahms Lullaby*.

With a small smile on her face, Tara complies. I don't turn the radio on during the whole trip. I sing a whole repertoire of songs old and new which have a message for Tara. She looks so still, curled up against the window. I have no idea if she's even hearing anything I'm trying to tell her through the lyrics, but I'd like to think somehow her subconscious mind is hearing my intent.

We pull up at the drop-off point just a few moments before a convoy of buses. I smile to myself as a bunch of junior high school kids arrive, looking very much like kindergartners with their noses pressed up against the bus windows. I know they wouldn't like the comparison very much because I remember junior high school politics clearly. The yearning desire to look cool and sophisticated amongst all of your friends, and especially your enemies.

Tara and I have been officially designated as people of authority, with shiny new lanyards hanging around our necks. Truth be told, I'm as anxious as all those twelve to fourteen-year-olds. I expect to break out with a fresh case of acne at any second. I haven't been using my American Sign Language much in the last decade and I worry I won't remember enough of it to be a proficient communicator. What if I'm not an impressive enough role model for these kids? After all, my only "real career" a counselor could recommend if they're worth their credentials is waitstaff. It's not very impressive. I don't even have a college education.

Tara notices my panicked expression and signs, "Aidan, what's wrong?"

I sign back, "Feeling a little in over my head. Are you sure I'm supposed to be here?"

Tara laughs at me as she signs, "Yes! You're a goofball. They're more excited about having you here than me."

Just then, the students start filing off the bus and we have to start interpreting instructions and lining the students up appropriately. The barrage of questions is overwhelming. Tara handles it like a champ. She seems to thrive on the chaos. The more giggling kids surround her, the happier she seems. After the initial rush is over and we sort the kids into groups and add some dropped off by parents, we regroup. We board the buses and settle in for the last leg of the trip to Champoeg State Heritage Area.

Tara and I end up in the middle of the bus, on opposite sides of the aisle. There's a group of chatty kids around us with hands flying a million miles an hour. Much to my relief, my signing skills are rapidly coming back and I'm able to keep up. One girl with purple and blue hair nails me with a shrewd look and asks; "You know this is an arts camp, right? Why are you here?"

Internally, I breathe a sigh of relief as I realize my credentials might actually be perfect. "Well, all told, I play about thirteen instruments, I write songs, some people think I'm a pretty decent singer, and I've been deaf since I was a kid," I respond dryly.

Another girl with dreadlocks looks at me with wide eyes and signs excitedly, "OMG you're *Aidan O'Brien!*" She even used my name sign. "Did you really leave because they were going to make fun of your deafness, or did you demand more money like they said in the tabloids?"

I chuckle and sign back, "Yes, it really is me, and I actually did leave because they were going to make it a pity party over my deafness and try to make my family look like evil monsters. They were going to make the whole story about my hearing loss and none of it about my singing ability."

A boy with spiky blond hair signs, "That bites, man! I saw you, and you sounded tight."

"Do you have CI's too?" I ask, pulling my hair back so he can see mine.

He nods as he turns his head so I can see his. He has hysterical covers on his that look like alien eyeballs. "I've had mine since I was eighteen months old," he voices and signs.

"Cool customization. I didn't get mine until I was almost seventeen," I sign while I vocalize.

"That's weird, you don't sound too deaf," he

observes.

"I was hearing until I was eleven when I got meningitis. That might have something to do with it."

Another dark-haired girl with dark brown eyes points to Tara and signs, "Is she in your band?"

"No, she's not in my band. In fact, I don't even know if she likes to sing. I know she's a phenomenal painter, but I'll let her tell you what she thinks her artistic talents are."

If looks could kill, I'd be dead on the spot. Tara shoots me a laser death-stare as she smiles at the kids and answers, "Actually, I do like to sing, but I'm nowhere near Aidan's league, so I keep it to myself. I do paint. Airbrushing is my favorite. If we have a chance this weekend, I might do a little face-painting. I brought my supplies with me." Tara stops and takes a deep shuddering breath before going on. After collecting herself, she signs with slightly trembling hands, "A long time ago, I used to dance professionally with Aidan's brother. I had stuff come up in my personal life and I stopped for a while. But I've recently started dancing again."

The girl with dark curly hair ducks her head for a moment before shyly signing, "I think I've seen your videos on YouTube. Did you dance with a guy named Rory? He doesn't look very much like Aidan though. He has dark hair."

Tara grins affectionately at the shy young lady. "I can't believe those videos are still out there! I was an awkward young thing compared to all of his handsomeness, wasn't I?"

"No! I don't think so at all," the teenager protests. "I think you're amazing. I want to be just like you. You dance with your heart. I swear, even your fingertips dance. My ballet teacher was completely impressed by you when I showed her the videos. She's not even going to believe me when I tell her I've met you in person. After she saw the videos, she kept telling me to point my toes just like you. She said you have perfect form."

It's fun to see Tara get the hero worship she should have been getting all along. She is at once completely embarrassed and totally flattered.

"Well, it's been a long time since I've trained hard," Tara demurs with self-deprecation. "You wouldn't even recognize my dancing now."

I make a dramatic motion of stage whispering to the kids as I sign, "She's still as awesome as she ever was."

Tara's light laughter travels through the bus like raindrops on a tin roof as she jokes, "You do know I'm an interpreter, and I can understand every word you're saying?"

The teenagers laugh at our good-natured banter. One of them pipes up, "I bet they dance wicked good together."

Tara raises an eyebrow at me and observes, "Well, it *is* true that he's made progress since he was a kindergartner."

The girl with purple and blue hair signs excitedly, "That's rad you guys have known each other so long. Do you think you guys will get married?"

The look of surprise on Tara's face is priceless. She

thought we could play it cool and not let on we're a couple. I told her we probably couldn't carry off the ruse, because teenagers are incredibly insightful and would eventually bust us. I didn't expect them to do it so quickly. Still, I think it's pretty funny. She told me to let her handle any questions about us. So I'm waiting to see how she handles it.

Tara blushes clear to the roots of her hair as she tries to school her expression into a neutral façade. "Aidan and I have been friends for a really long time and we just started dating, so we really haven't had time to talk about that," she signs.

The shy girl who wants to be a dancer regards her carefully and signs, "I don't know if I believe it. You guys act like my oldest sister who's been engaged since she was seventeen. She's a sophomore in college now, and she is getting married this summer. I kind of thought you guys were already married."

"Totally!" chimes in the guy with the dreadlocks. "You guys are dead ringers for my parents, and they've been married for twenty years. I figured you had a couple babies at home."

I wink at the kids and sign, "Maybe someday. But Tara is finishing up her college degree and I've got plans for my music career before I get too old."

I glance over at Tara and she looks ready to swallow her tongue or kill me, I'm not sure which. She signs quickly, "I'm not sure they need to know that level of personal detail."

"Oh relax," I answer. "It's not like they can't tell by the way I look at you. I worship the ground you walk on.

Besides, we're going to make adorable kids someday."

A collective sigh goes up from all the girls sitting around us. Tara just rolls her eyes and signs, "You're incorrigible." Laughter travels through the crowd around us.

"I admit that," I sign with a wide grin. "You're stuck with me, because I'm yours."

"Oh for Pete's sake, don't encourage him," she cautions. "He'll just get worse. We won't be able to live with him by the end of the weekend. He'll think he's so funny, he'll start telling himself jokes." Now the laughter gets even louder.

The head teacher on our bus takes notice of our ever-growing audience and announces, "Since Aidan is so popular, perhaps he would like to come to the front of the bus and lead the icebreaker exercises."

I shrug and sign while voicing, "Sure, I've got no problem with that. It sounds fun. I'll send Tara to the back of the bus, so she can interpret from there, and everybody can see the instructions." I've been to multiple music and band camps, so I've got countless camp games under my belt. I can do them in my sleep. First up is a series of games intended to help with memorization of names. The tricky part is to adjust them to an environment where we don't have name tags and pens. Some of them will be tricky to adapt to sign language. But I improvise, and they turn out to be fun. Next, I focus on games which help the teens find other kids with similar interests and personalities. This is not only loud and riotous, but also extremely entertaining. In the end, the kids are laughing and having a great time. Nearly everyone is signing and talking to someone else on the bus. Tara and I figure we've done our jobs for now and sat back down in our seats.

The kid with spiky blond hair — who I've learned by now is Zach, turns to Tara and signs, "This is going to be totally cool. Usually, they assign us chaperones who know next to nothing about sign language and even less about the arts. You two are experts in both, and you're not old as dirt."

I smirk as I sign and voice, "Don't be too sure of that, I'm older than I look."

"Really? How old are you?" he signs quickly.

"Old enough to know not to spill the beans, and old enough to tell you I wish I had taken the time to invest in college and not played the usual free spirited dude with the rebellious heart," I sign.

"Why didn't you?" Zach asks, a curious expression on his face.

"Because I was too busy being pissed off at the world to pay attention to the long-term plan, and I thought I was too smart and talented to need an education," I answer candidly.

"You seem to be doing okay, I saw you on TV," he argues, signing emphatically.

"Okay is a relative term," I reply. "The TV thing was a brand-new gig and it didn't work out so well. I've essentially been a wedding singer for over a decade. One time, some of my former band mates took my whole catalog of songs because I didn't know anything about copywriting my own material. It was decades of work. If

I'd gone to college and taken some basic business courses, I could've protected myself. Ignorance got in the way of my career. The school of hard knocks is a good teacher, but getting a higher education is a shortcut around stuff. I was also offered a shot at auditioning for Juilliard, but I was too proud to take it. You don't know how much I wish I could go back and remake that decision."

Zach's eyes widen as he processes what I said. "Dude! You turned down an invitation to audition for Juilliard? Freakin' Juilliard! People train their whole lives to have a chance to go to Juilliard. That's straight up crazy talk there. Were you doing drugs or something?" he asks with astonishment.

I laugh at his response. I can't help myself. He's not wrong. "You're absolutely right, Zach. The answer is no. I don't even have the excuse of being on drugs. I was just feeling sorry for myself. I thought maybe they were only giving me the chance to audition because I was deaf, and not because of the way I played the piano. In those days, I was still having difficulty adjusting to my cochlear implants. I was throwing a major tantrum against the whole world, and I hadn't adjusted well enough to know how good or bad my playing might be. Several years later, after one of my concerts, I met a couple of faculty members who served on the admissions committee. They spent some time talking to me. Of course, I felt like a complete idiot when they told me they didn't even know I was deaf when they saw my demo tape and decided to invite me to audition. The moral of the story is, I blew a perfectly legit opportunity which could've changed my life, over a figment of my imagination."

Zach whistles softly under his breath. "Harsh."

I nod. "Epically. If you see an adult who appears to have all their stuff together, don't assume they had a smooth path to get there. They may have a story similar to mine. They might've taken a completely different path, if they could go back and do it again. It never hurts to ask. Sometimes people have really good advice to give and are willing to share their war stories."

"Cool!" Zach signs. "I know my dad played in a band in high school. I think he's afraid to tell me about it because he thinks I won't go to college if I pursue music. But I want to go to the Berkeley School of Music in California. I want to study composing. I think my parents believe I can't be a musician because of my deafness. That's why I was so excited to see you on TV so I could show them it's possible to be deaf and a successful musician at the same time."

My heart squeezes a little. I wonder if I made the wrong decision in leaving the show. I guess I didn't realize so many people were counting on me to succeed. "Zach, I shouldn't give you the wrong impression. I didn't need the television show to be successful. I've been fully booked almost every night of the week for several years now. If I wanted to play bigger venues, I probably could. I like to play weddings, birthday parties, renaissance fairs, and bat mitzvahs because I like to see people's reaction to what I'm doing. The reason I still do things like wait tables and be a bouncer is because I'm saving to cut a professional quality demo tape. If I wasn't, I would still be able to comfortably pay my bills. I also like to travel around to go rock climbing in some pretty exotic places and that costs some bank."

Zack smirks at me. "Plus you got a banging hot girlfriend. My brother says high maintenance girls cost some cheddar."

I have to disguise my disgust at his language and attitude as I quickly sign, "Check your attitude and have some respect buddy. You should never talk about women that way. Not that it's any of your business, but Tara's totally the opposite of high maintenance. But even if she was, it would be my pleasure to make her happy. Watch your language. I don't ever want to hear you talk about women or girls as 'banging hot.' Are we clear?"

Zach blushes and tucks his chin to his chest as he responds, "Crystal clear. No disrespect" He fidgets a little before he asks. "Still, don't you think it's unfair guys have to pay for everything?"

"It's a sign of respect and a tradition," I explain. "It makes girls feel honored and valued. I've found most women don't feel comfortable with guys paying for everything over the long-term and will offer to split the check or alternate paying for dates. Anyway, nobody makes you. It's a choice."

A look of relief passes over Zach's face as he signs, "My dad just got laid off and they cut my allowance way back. It takes me forever to save up for a date."

"What instrument do you play, Zach?" I ask. If I had to guess by looking at his hands, I'd say a string instrument, probably guitar because his fingers are heavily calloused.

Zach sits up a little straighter and replies, "I can shred the electric guitar better than people twice my age."

"I used to give music lessons when I was a kid. It

was a great way to pick up extra money. I had an unhealthy addiction to video games and collectibles. My parents refused to fund my hobbies, so I had to figure it out on my own. So I gave lessons to all of my friends and their friends. I was making some serious money. After I became deaf, I switched over to teaching songwriting."

Zach's eyes light up as he excitedly signs, "Do you really think I could do that?"

"If it doesn't interfere with your school work and you have your parents permission, I don't see any reason why not. I'd be happy to go over and talk to your parents about it, if you'd like me to," I offer.

Zach's jaw drops open as he whispers, "Are you serious?"

"Totally. Just let me know when and where," I promise.

"I'll pay you for your time," Zach insists.

I shake my head as I decline, "That's not necessary, Zach. I have two weddings coming up, but we can schedule a time around those."

"Thanks, man, you don't know how much this means," Zach signs, looking close to tears.

"Actually, I have some idea," I answer, feeling equally emotional. "At one point in my life a perfect stranger came along and it made all the difference in the world."

The buses pull into a rest stop and the students eagerly pile off. Tara and I bring up the rear of the line. The teacher standing outside the bus says, "Would you two mind monitoring the outside of the bathroom doors for a moment to make sure we don't have any stragglers?"

"Sure, we'd be happy to," Tara answers immediately, signing and voicing simultaneously.

For the first time in hours, we find ourselves alone on a bench a few feet from the bathroom doors. Tara turns to me and whispers in my ear, "I can't tell you how much I love you right now. You are a phenomenal human being. You are a rock star on so many levels. What you're doing for Zach is possibly going to mend his relationship with his parents and allow him to pursue his lifelong dream. It's one of the most selfless things I've ever seen anyone do. It's worth a ton of boyfriend points."

I have to work hard to remember there are about seventy-five impressionable young teenagers around us as a warm tingling sensation roars through my body like a forest fire.

"Ah, Tara … are you trying to kill me here?" I ask with an anguished moan.

Tara laughs lightly as she looks at me. "No, not intentionally."

A student comes bounding up to Tara and signs rapidly, "I asked Ms. Hamilton and she said were having a dance tomorrow night. Will you perform for us, Tara?"

A second student immediately chimes in, "Yes! Please, please, please, please?"

Tara looks thoughtful. "I guess I could put together a short piece, but only if I have a dance troupe to back me up. Do you know of anybody who might be interested in learning a few dance moves? I can hold a dance class tomorrow, if you'll round up a few students."

One of the male students crowded around our bench raises his hand and shyly asks, "Is this class only for girls?"

Tara answers his signed question by signing, "Of course not, some of the best dancers in the world are men."

The head teacher comes to take our place so we can use the restroom. As she walks us toward the restroom doors, she comments to Tara, "I'm so thrilled you decided to step up and teach a class. This is what we were hoping for all along. Don't get me wrong, we know you have exceptional skills as an interpreter, but you are renowned in the arts community as well. We were hoping you would bring a bit of both to our camp. The fact you have a nationally famous boyfriend is a happy coincidence too."

Tara looks stunned. "Wow! I'm surprised anybody remembers anything about my career as a dancer, it's been so long ago. It's rare anyone says anything about it. I'm almost never recognized."

The matronly teacher looks at Tara quizzically "Honey, don't you ever Google yourself?"

Tara appears befuddled., "No, why would I? I don't really dance these days. I'm not famous for anything now."

I know the answer to this because I Googled her after I found her at Kiera's wedding. "Tara, there are several fan pages dedicated to you and forums that are aimed at asking you to come back to the dance world," I respond carefully.

"AJ, why didn't you tell me?" She looks dismayed.

"I didn't tell you, because I didn't want to freak you out. You seemed dead set against dancing again, and I didn't know how you would react. I didn't want to add any more stress to your life."

"You're right. I would've gotten the heebie-jeebies," she concedes. "I've got them now. Don't you think it's a little weird that perfect strangers are so invested in what I do?"

"If you were an average, everyday dancer, maybe," I agree. "Tara, your talent is so extraordinary people didn't want to see it lost to the world. Your gift is amazing, and it touches a person's soul in a way they don't want to forget, once they've seen it. Remember what you said to me this morning about wanting to hear me sing anytime and any place? That's the way people feel about your dancing. Even if it's in a snippet in a commercial, they'll pause what they're doing to stop and watch because you're so captivating."

"Really?" she asks uncertainly.

"Really!" I insist. The little crowd around us echoes my sentiment.

"I always thought people came to see us because of Rory. I was just his arm ornament."

One of the other female teachers scoffs and mutters, "More like the other way around, you were the one with real talent. He was okay, but you were the star."

"Wow, this is mind blowing. This puts my entire childhood in a completely different light."

"Huh, it seems like I know somebody who tried to tell you how great you were all along," I tease.

"Yeah, I know," Tara concedes, "but how was I supposed to know back then? You were Rory's little brother who used to give me candy and hide spiders in my locker."

The matronly teacher comments, "That's just so precious. He was in love with her back then too."

Tara rolls her eyes. "Does everyone on the planet know you love me?"

The other teacher chimes in, "Sweetie, its as obvious as the freckles on his face. I don't think he could hide it if he wanted to. You may as well put the man out of his misery and marry him."

"Hold your horses, people!" Tara exclaims. "We just started dating!"

The matronly teacher just nods sagely. "That may technically be true, but you've been in love with him almost as long as he's been in love with you."

Tara looks accusingly at me. "Aidan O'Brien, did you tell them our whole life story?"

I shake my head. "Gracie, I've been with you all day. I haven't even had a chance to talk to these ladies, let alone tell them our very complicated saga. We kind of defy explanation."

"Then how do they know our whole story?" Tara pushes.

"Well, have you ever heard the eyes are the window to the soul?" I ask.

Tara nods, her eyes full of doubt.

"I believe our love story is written in our hearts and souls, and every time someone looks at us, they can see a little bit of our love story with every beat of our hearts."

"Oh my gosh, that's so beautiful!" gushes the younger teacher. "If you decide you don't want him, can I have him?"

"I'm sorry, ma'am," I respond. "My heart has belonged to Tara since I was six and I don't see that changing 'til the day I die."

Tara's eyes mist over. "I'm sure you can see why I was only a little bit older when he captured my heart too."

Both teachers simultaneously ask, "Then what are you waiting for?"

"Tara and I recently reconnected after being apart for many years," I answer diplomatically. "We're still making sure our love is as strong as we remember it."

The younger teacher comments, "Well, best of luck to the two of you. We'd better let you go, because the buses are going to take off, soon. You guys give me hope that someday I'll find the perfect man for me too."

"It was nice to meet you both," Tara responds warmly. "We'll see you back on the bus."

Before we part ways to go to the restroom, Tara frowns and signs, "So much for keeping our relationship status under wraps."

Smothering a grin, I remind her with a shrug, "I told you keeping it a secret would be a lost cause."

Chapter Twenty-Three

Tara

Getting a yurt full of girls to sleep is a bigger challenge than I imagined. This is especially true when they can communicate clandestinely. Finally, at around eleven o'clock, everyone seems to be asleep.

I just get my head on the pillow when my cell phone vibrates. I reach beside my pillow to pick it up. It's a picture of a teddy bear from Aidan with the caption, "Is all quiet on the home front?"

I quickly respond, "Yes, finally. Thank goodness :)."

"Nice job! I wanted I love you! to be the last thing you saw tonight."

My heart melts. Aidan's thoughtfulness knows no bounds. I immediately reply, "I <3 you too. Good night."

Morning comes far too early. After everyone piles into the main cabin for breakfast, there are a series of breakout sessions. During a brief staff meeting last night, The camp directors determined I would hold a painting class first thing in the morning when the light is better.

So, we take a bunch of easels out into the meadow and I hold a seminar on using light and shading for perspective. It was actually more exhilarating than I anticipated. These students are bright, perceptive and eager to learn advanced techniques. They're so talented, I wish I had twice as much time to work with them. Unfortunately, they have to get cleaned up for another session.

I notice Aidan was holding a class on songwriting technique. I wonder how his group went. My next class is an introduction to airbrushing. Sadly, I don't have enough equipment for everyone, so this one will be primarily a demonstration class. I'm going to draw on my days on the carnival circuit for this one and do caricatures of each student. Because of the way I'll have to teach the class, I asked for a cap on the number of students, and I was shocked to hear, even though this is my first year at the camp, they had to turn kids away. I feel weird about that; it breaks my heart a little because I wish I could take on every student who's interested in art. I don't know what I would've done without drawing and painting in my life.

As students file into a decommissioned cabin we're using for a classroom, I notice the group of students include several of the teens who have been hanging around us, including Jasmine, the girl with purple and blue hair. She is simply stunning, notwithstanding her hair. She'll be a great caricature study. I think I'll start with her.

I greet the class with some introductory remarks, and I set up my cell phone to play on the flat screen TV. "An airbrush is an incredibly powerful tool. You can paint something as small as cookies or as large as an entire wall.

I would recommend using two different paint guns for each, though." As I'm signing and speaking, I point to the TV, which shows cookies and a cake I recently helped Heather complete, and then the fairy forest I painted on Mindy's bedroom walls. I'm exceptionally proud of the work I did in her room. I also show a portrait of Mindy and her sister Becca, and then a stunning night sky. When the slide appears on the screen, a collective gasp goes up from the audience. Another slide features a series of caricatures I did for the Boys and Girls Club. "As you can see, you can use an airbrush to do something serious or something very funny. It's one of the most versatile tools an artist can have."

The noise level in the room rises as the students talk back and forth. Many people are under the impression that sign language is completely silent. During animated conversation, it really isn't. Gestures are often punctuated by various noises, and deaf kids rarely realize how loud they are. I interrupt the class by asking Jasmine to come forward. "Jasmine, do you feel comfortable modeling for the class?"

"Really, you want to paint me?" she asks pointing to herself.

"Yes, really," I tease. "Somebody has to be first. I'll try to get to all of you."

Jasmine walks to the front of our makeshift classroom and sits on a tall stool. Fortunately, the former art teacher left behind a big pad of high-quality watercolor paper. I place it on an easel and open it. I already tested my airbrush gun, so it's ready to go. In no time at all, I have her caricature finished. After all of my years traveling with the carnival, I can do these with lightning speed. When you're trying to make money at this, volume is the name of the game. I look at the rest of the class. "I forgot I don't have a Sharpie, does anyone have one in their art supplies?"

Jerome, the guy with dreadlocks, steps forward with a fine-tipped black one and signs, "Will this work?"

"It's perfect," I respond with a wide smile. I autograph and date Jasmine's picture with a flourish and hand it to her. "Jasmine, you should lay your picture over on the back table to dry."

Jasmine studies her picture for a minute before signing, "How did you know my eyes are my favorite feature? Most people would have played up my hair. It's the most obvious thing about me."

I shrug and reply, "I don't know, maybe it's the artist in me, but the first thing I noticed about you were your beautiful eyes."

"This is so cool! I'm going to get this framed. Thank you so much."

I feel myself getting hot with embarrassment. "It's no big deal, I'm just glad you like it."

I pick a shy kid from the back row to go next. On and on it goes until I have done twenty-five caricatures. Everyone seems absolutely thrilled with their little masterpiece. We have about 20 minutes left in class so I have everyone put their name in a basket and I draw three. Those three students get to come up and play around on a blank sheet of paper so they can get a feel for what it is like to hold a paint gun in their hands. It is pretty amazing for everyone. There is definitely a learning curve involved in handling a paint gun and one student accidentally sprayed the front of my shirt. She instantly crumbles and a look of horror passes over her face as she crosses her arms in front of her defensively. I wink at her as I show her my paint splotched denim shirt. "Why thank you," I sign while I vocalize. "This is my favorite painting shirt and it needed a little something. Your addition gave it just the pizzazz it needs."

For a moment, the student looks frozen in her spot. Finally, she breaks her silence "Does this mean you're not mad at me?" she asks tentatively.

I smile at her as I interpret my answer for the rest of the class, "Of course I'm not mad at you. Look at my shirt. Obviously, I've done this to myself many times. Painting can be a messy endeavor so make sure you cover things around your workspace that you don't want to be a different color." I point to the clear painters tarps I've hung from the ceiling with removable poster hanging gum.

The student sags with relief and gives me a shaky smile as she asks, "Can I try again?"

I nod encouragingly. "Knock yourself out, the canvas is yours."

As it turns out, this student has a deft hand at airbrushing once she gets the hang of controlling the brush. She makes a few neat spheres.

The next student has been paying attention to the lessons learned and is quickly able to blend three colors to make a remarkable seascape. When I praise him, he nonchalantly shrugs and signs, "I do something similar with watercolors all the time."

"Whatever medium you used to develop your skills, your work is amazing. If this is the first time you've ever used an airbrush, it is even more impressive. Excellent work!"

The last student to draw a number looks more like she should be in the accounting club rather than arts camp. I examine her pressed khaki pants and white oxford shirt and yellow cardigan sweater. I'm curious about what she'll paint. She picks up the airbrush with confidence. Clearly, she's done this before. Much to my shock, she starts to paint in a mural style reminiscent of the best street art. She paints the camp name and caricatures of the quaint log cabins and yurts. I watch her in total awe. I look down at my watch and there's only six minutes of class left before we have to break for lunch. I'm worried she may not have time to finish. It's a shame, too, because her piece has the makings of a masterpiece. I glance out at the rest of the class and they're completely mesmerized by her work as she's adding trees and forest animals. I don't blame them. I'm enamored myself. It's captivating to see another talented artist at work. I shouldn't have worried about time, because about a minute before class is due to be over, she sets down the airbrush and steps away.

I mentally chastise myself. If my life has taught me anything, it should be not to judge a book by its cover. I grab the Sharpie pen and hand it to her as I sign, "Please put your autograph on your work. It's extraordinary. Trust me when I tell you, if you stay on this path, someday somebody's going to pay you a lot of money for artwork like that."

"Tell that to my dad," she signs angrily. "He says I

can't paint anymore because I have to get a 'real' job. I only got to come because I got a 4.0 and I chose this as my reward."

"I'm sorry," I answer empathetically. "Sometimes, parents don't understand the soul of an artist." I put my arm around her shoulder and squeeze it lightly as a sign of support.

As she signs and dates her painting, I instruct the rest of the class, "It's probably best to let your paintings dry until after lunch. I'll take a break from my afternoon session at three o'clock to let everyone back in here to get your pictures. It's been great fun showing you how to work an airbrush today."

The student who painted the mural sticks around to talk to me. She introduces herself as Sadie and asks me how she can prove to her dad that artists make money. I encourage her to contact several art schools and ask them if they've done a survey of alumni students. Many times, alumni associations like to brag about their success stories.

Sadie smiles her first genuine smile I've seen since she's been here. She extends her hand for me to shake, then changes her mind and gives me an enthusiastic hug. "Thank you so much for all of your help. This class was a blast!" With that, she literally skips off to lunch.

I am so focused on Sadie I didn't see Aidan standing on the fringes of the room until he peeks around the plastic tarp. "She seems happy."

"She should be," I answer with a happy gleam in my eyes. "She painted this without any help from me."

Aidan comes closer to examine the painting and

whistles softly between his teeth. "Wow! She is good! I mean art gallery good."

"I think so too, but apparently, her parents disagree. I had a conversation eerily similar to the one you had yesterday. You were right, it does feel empowering to help them."

"Well, my super-heroine, I came to take you to lunch. Don't even think about skipping it because you're busy," he warns, knowing my tendencies all too well. "I have a feeling our afternoon will be a workout like we've never seen before."

"Ugh, don't remind me. I started the day tired, and I've been playing catch-up all day — but I have to admit this is the most fun I've had in a long time. What about you?"

"Many of them have already written songs that blow my early stuff out of the water. I wish I was half as talented as some of them. Come on, we'd better go before all the good stuff is gone. Don't you remember how everybody hoards the cookies?"

"Hold your horses, I have to put this on the table to dry. I don't think you will starve to death in thirty seconds."

He walks up to me and spins me around so I'm in his arms. Suddenly, he gives me a deep passionate kiss. It takes my breath away in more ways than one. When he pulls away, I exclaim, "Aidan Jarith O'Brien! We could've been caught. This place is crawling with students."

Aidan looks down at the floor and says, "I'm sorry, Gracie. You're right. I got carried away. I haven't seen you all day. I said I was starving and I wasn't kidding. Besides, when have you ever known me to do the safe thing?"

I lift his chin and look into his deep green eyes as I give him a soft smile. "Almost never," I concede, "but let's not get fired from our first gig as chaperones. Let's go feed your other hunger. Maybe it will distract you."

Aidan smirks at me. "It would have to be a mighty powerful lunch to do that."

I dramatically place my hand over my chest, bat my eyelashes and proclaim, "I do declare Mr. O'Brien, you say the sweetest things."

"Well … it's true!" Aidan protests with an exaggerated shrug.

<hr />

After lunch, the cleaning crew breaks down the entire great room in the main cabin. The polished wood floors will be great for dancing. The teens are back from their short nature walk. I am astonished to find out I have forty-two students in my dance seminar. That's well over half of all of the students who are attending the camp. A whopping sixteen of them are male. That's a percentage almost unheard of in dance classes. The dance teacher comes in and the PE teacher accompanies her. I've gathered that the dance teacher is hearing, but the PE teacher is entirely deaf. The PE teacher, Melinda Norse, signs, "We heard this was the hot hangout spot and figured you might need help with crowd control."

"Thank you," I sign gratefully. "Honestly, I was expecting about fifteen."

I turn to the class and ask them to line up in rows. I show them a series of stretches they can do with a partner. Of course, being junior high school kids, they laugh when some of the positions get awkward. I chuckle and tell them, "Just wait until you get advanced enough to do lifts. Your partner will be more familiar with the intimate parts of your body than you are. You have to get over being embarrassed about it. It comes down to a matter of safety as well as art."

One of the older boys in the back immediately raises his hand and asks, "Will we be doing this today?" as he eyes another student I assume is his girlfriend.

"I don't know yet," I answer. "I'll have to assess everyone's skills before I can decide. Does anyone here like retro music?"

To my relief, a bunch of hands shoot up. "Well, I'm glad to see you love it because, we're going to do our take on the classic Michael Jackson song *Thriller.*"

An excited murmur goes through the crowd as Jasmine asks, "Are you going to paint our faces?"

Another student adds, "Yeah, can we dress up?"

I grin at their enthusiasm. "Well, I guess it will depend on how quickly you guys can learn the choreography. I'll need those of you who have dance experience to help out with the people who don't. This is a big group of people. I'll try to get to everybody as best I can. I might not be able to help you immediately. If you understand a dance move well and you see someone who doesn't, I'd appreciate it if you step up and give them a hand." The other teachers space themselves evenly throughout the room. I notice even the principal has snuck in the back door and is hanging around the back of the room.

I start out by handing out earplugs to the hearing individuals in the room because the best way for those who are deaf to interpret music is to feel vibrations through the floor, and it can be painfully loud for those of us with average hearing. Before I turn on the music, I start out by explaining the basic eight count and how I use it to teach choreography. I explain the earplugs and instruct people to put them in and those with hearing aids or cochlear implants to turn them down or off. I turn the speakers on and lay them down so they are facedown on the wooden floor. Even through the earplugs, it sounds a bit like a rock concert. I survey the teenagers and see they're grinning as they feel the vibrations through their feet. I have a closed-circuit TV aimed at me and projected on a big-screen TV behind me. I'm so lucky this facility is used for business conferences and has the technology available. Now, all the students in the room can see not only my dance moves but also my hands as I'm signing.

For the next hour or so, I go through the choreography one small chunk at a time. I'm pleasantly surprised, in a group this size, how many quality dancers there are. There are probably five extraordinary dancers, another ten very good ones, fifteen passable, and the rest are just here for fun. Those are better odds than I expected.

I spend most of my time with the just for fun group. After another half an hour of individual focus, almost everyone is doing pretty well. So I have a run through from the top. Amazingly, it goes better than I could've ever expected. We take our three o'clock break and I go back to the cabin to distribute paintings.

After we return to the main cabin, I do one more

run through. This time, I add my own solo. I put a contemporary dance twist on it. It feels so freeing to be in full on dance mode around other dancers again, even if they are a bunch of teenage students. I'm so lost in the world I'm creating, I'm a little startled to hear cheering and calls for an encore. I give a deep dancer's curtsy and recoil my hair bun which came loose during the dance. "Thanks, everyone. You'll see a different piece tonight because I improvised that. Who knows what I'll come up with tonight?"

Jasmine looks at me with astonishment. "You just made that up on the spot?"

I nod as I catch my breath.

"That's epic!" she exclaims.

"Thanks. Okay, you guys were totally focused and on point, so we have some extra time. You have an extra hour and a half to get showered and make costumes. Remember, they can't be too elaborate and you have to be able to move in them. You can't put anything on them that will fly off and injure your neighbor. Girls, make sure you don't put any moisturizer or foundation on, because the face paint won't stick to it. You can go back to your cabins and put eyeliner and mascara on after I'm done with your face. You don't have to copy the original *Thriller* video, because we're doing our own spin on it. So be creative."

"Who's going to do your face, Ms. Tara?" pipes up a student from the back row.

I search out the crowd and find Sadie. "Well, I was really impressed today by Sadie's skills. I was kind of hoping she might do me the honor of painting my face,"

I reply.

Sadie blushes a deep shade of crimson "If you're sure you trust me, I'd be happy to."

"Okay everybody, I'll be in Cabin Mount Rainier starting at four o'clock. Face painting will be done on a first-come first-serve basis. Remember, dinner is only served until six o'clock."

———— • ————

Fortunately for me, I have a costume of sorts already figured out. It doesn't take me any time at all to change into a dark green leotard and a skirt with chiffon ruffles which look like thousands of small leaves. I braid my hair in dozens of small braids that will make my hair look curly once they dry and I undo them. So, I hurry over to the cabin where I first taught class this morning to set up my face painting station. I like to heat up my face paints slightly because I find that people jump less if the face paints are warmed.

To my surprise, Sadie is there waiting for me. Not only that, she is dressed in a very similar costume except hers is in fall colors and she actually has fall leaves attached to hers. When we compare outfits, we both laugh. "I'm here to paint your face before the crowds come," she offers.

I show her how to load the face paint into my face-painting gun and place the hairdressing gown over my clothes. I look in the mirror and use bobby pins to make sure my hair is out of my face. Then, I place a shower cap over my hair. I sit on the chair and instruct, "I'm going for a mother nature fairy-type look here with maybe a couple of flowers and butterflies and some lady bugs. But I'll leave the precise details up to you."

"Cool beans!" She applies a base coat to my face and neck. "Is it okay if we pull the cape down for a minute so I can paint down to the top of your leotard and your hands?"

I smile at her creativity. "Sure, go for it." She quickly paints the front and back of my hands and my neck and shoulders. I'm trying hard not to peek because I want to be totally surprised by the finished product, but I'm so tempted. She effortlessly changes the bowls out to change colors. She is swift and efficient but not rushed. In no time at all, she sets the brush down and asks me if I've got a way to paint fine lines. I point to a case of eyeliner pencils in nearly every shade.

"Awesome. This is exactly what I need," she responds. After a couple of minutes, she puts the pencil back and announces, "I am finished. Would you like to check it out to see if you like it?"

"Sure, but I'm positive I'm going to love it." I walk over to the full-length mirror and gasp with pleasure as I see the effect she's accomplished. She has given me a green complexion with silver sheen. It makes me look positively ethereal. She added butterflies, flowers, and ladybugs as I requested, but she gave them a 3-D effect so they literally look like they're coming to life out of my skin. "Sadie! I couldn't have done this better myself and I've been doing this for years. I can't even find the proper adjectives to describe how wonderful I think you are."

Sadie shuffles her feet and signs, "Really? You're not just saying that?"

"Of course not," I confirm. "I'd like to help you find scholarships to go to art school when you're ready."

I tap the seat I just vacated and ask her what she wants on her face. She signs that she would like a classic autumn scene with pumpkins and acorns with some spider webs and cute field mice. She emphasizes that she wants the field mice to be cute and cuddly, not creepy. I immediately get an idea, so I place non-latex gloves over the work she's done on my hands and get started on hers. After applying a base coat all over her hands, neck and face, I start with acorns and cranberries on her hands. On the right side of her face, I paint a cornucopia over her right ear and jawline. I add two field mice chasing the pumpkin.

I think it's cute. I hope it's not too juvenile for her. I help her take off the cape and shower cap. She walks over to the mirror and laughs out loud. She turns and signs, "I love it! It's exactly what I wanted. It looks like the decorations my favorite teacher used to put up in our classroom." Her expression turned serious for a moment as she signs, "Is it okay if I stay here for a while to see if anyone wants me to paint their face? It was so much fun I'd love to do some more. Do you think anyone will choose me?"

"Of course they will," I state. I stand next to her so she can see me in the mirror. I turn toward her so she can read my signs. "Take a close look. Give your honest opinion. You won't hurt my feelings, because I already know the answer. If you were looking at these paint jobs in a magazine, and you didn't know who did which face, which would be your favorite? Honestly, who did the better detail work?"

Sadie looks in the mirror and concentrates on our images. A look of amazement crosses her face. She turns to me and signs, "You weren't kidding. The one I painted is more detailed, my strokes are a little bit more even and my blending is slightly better. How can that be?"

"It's probably a combination of things. Not everyone is born equally talented and I'm completely self-taught. I've never really had an art class. I had already graduated from high school before I did anything artistic like this. The whole focus of my childhood was exclusively dedicated to dance, so I didn't explore anything else until after I left home," I explain.

"How old were you?" asks a wide-eyed Sadie.

"Not old enough. Both of my parents were dead, so I ran away and joined the circus. Trust me, it's not all it's cracked up to be in books. That's why I'm just now finishing my college degree at my age. Whatever you do, don't choose my path in life. It's a good way to destroy yourself."

"Wait!" Sadie interrupts. "I thought you and Aidan are really happy together?"

"Oh, we are," I insist. "Aidan is my only constant happy."

"People are talking about you guys around camp," Sadie advises shyly. "They say Aidan fell in love with you when he was six, but you hated him. Is that true?"

"No," I correct. "We were best friends and I just waited too long to tell him my feelings had changed. He got sick and moved away before I could tell him. I was about your age when it happened."

"That's tragic," Sadie signs. "But you found each other again."

"We did, and I'm grateful every day," I confide.

"So your choices weren't bad, just difficult and unusual," Sadie signs.

"When did you get so smart?" I tease.

"I was just born that way, I guess," she signs with a small smile and a shy shrug.

Chapter Twenty-Four

Aidan

I'M PUMPED ABOUT HOW tonight is going to go. I now have eight band members for tonight's dance. The large band and I have rehearsed three numbers and a surprise for Tara. A smaller group made up of just Zach, Darius, and I worked on a few more, after the others peeled off to go on a whitewater adventure.

I'm surprised to see Tara at dinner. She sent me a text earlier to tell me she would probably miss it because she had to do face painting on several students to prepare for tonight's dance.

Mindful of our earlier conversation, I fight the urge to kiss her in front of a mess hall full of curious teenagers. Yet, only two words come to mind when I see her — sex goddess. I move up beside her and murmur in her ear, "Good evening, gorgeous Gracie. Would you like dinner? I made you a plate because I was planning to take it to you."

With a teasing smile she asks, "What are you trying to do? Break the record for the most 'best boyfriend points' on the planet?"

I wink. "Nah, just taking care of my woman, since you have a tendency to put yourself last. How did you get done so early, anyway?"

"You know the mural I showed you this morning? The one Sadie did? Sadie volunteered to paint my face and hands. When students saw what a great job she did with me, they wanted her to do their faces too, so we ended up splitting the workload pretty evenly tonight and got it done in half the time. Most of the more grisly looking zombies and other monsters are her work. She's also a master of Hispanic art and anything to do with the Day of the Dead."

I glance around the room and notice more than half of the students and faculty have paint jobs. "You must have allowed people outside your class to join in on the face painting fun." Tara chuckles. "No, would you believe I had forty-five students in my class, plus four teachers and administrators?"

"That's wild. I guess that explains why the other seminars were virtually empty. I heard they actually had to go recruiting to get enough people for the whitewater rafting trip. I'm told it's usually so full, they have a waiting list a mile long."

As Tara finishes her hamburger and potato chips, I invite her to help me decorate the main cabin for the dance. She shrugs. "Sure, that sounds like fun. I never got to do those kind of things when I was in school. I always wanted to be one of the popular kids and be on the pep squad, but it never happened. I'll go put on the last touches of my costume while they're tearing down the dinner setup."

"If you had been a cheerleader, I would've done my darndest to be a star jock in any sport, even if it was underwater basketball," I tease.

Tara smirks. "I believe the proper name for that is water polo, isn't it? Did you play any sports?"

"No, I was too busy being an angry, disaffected teenager. I was pretty good at basketball, when I played with Dolores' boys, but I didn't care enough about it to compete. I regret some of those decisions now. If I had more friends around me, I might have adjusted better."

Tara sighs as she nods her head and signs, "Me too. I might not have gone so far off the deep end, if I would've had more sane voices around to help me."

I lace my fingers through hers as I muse, "I don't know, we seem like a pretty good fit for each other — despite our pasts or maybe because of them." I squeeze her hand. "I'll see you at the dance tonight. I'll be the one with gel in my hair, and I'll have my dancing boots on."

"What a coincidence. I'll also have copious amounts of hair gel. I may or may not wear silver lipstick, but I most definitely will be wearing my dancing shoes."

———————◆———————

If I thought Tara looked stunning before, she took it up a notch or two. She has sparkly stuff on her eyelids and long, false eyelashes. She took her hair out of the braids, and it's falling in waves down her back. She even has sparkly glitter spray mixed with the promised hair gel. Her lips are accented with bright silver lipstick. She's wearing tights which look like wood grain. She looks like a forest nymph, in the best meaning of the word. It seems as if she could perform magic at the wave of a wand.

I walk over to Tara and kiss her hair, so I don't mess up her face paint. I step back and gently grasp her forearms as I face her. "You are, by far, the most beautiful date I've ever had."

Tara's eyes light up with mirth. "Really, AJ? Ladybugs and silver lipstick turn you on?"

"Everything about you turns me on, if you're covered in paint or not," I answer sincerely. It still baffles me that she has no idea how beautiful she is.

Tara rakes her eyes over me and stops to study my admittedly over the top rock 'n roll star outfit. "You're not looking so bad yourself, Aidan." I blush. I'm not used to this much flash. I let some of the teenagers help accessorize my outfit to make me more hip and modern. Even my cochlear implant is decked out. The students were amazed to find that one of my ears was pierced. I had them pierced a long time ago as an act of rebellion against my dad. He was focused on his family looking so perfect, even when we were crumbling from the inside out. It was my way of making a protest statement. I long ago stopped wearing earrings, so I'm surprised the hole was still open. Tonight, in a tribute to Tara's outfit, I have a sterling silver leaf in my ear and a black leather band around my wrist, with a small dream catcher attached. I'm also wearing a black fedora adorned with a single jade arrowhead.

The art teacher and the two teachers who teased us about our love story are absolute pros when it comes to decorating large spaces, and they're essentially done by the time we arrive to help. Tara sets up finishing touches on a few roundtables around the outskirts of the dance floor with small LED lights intended to look like candles and large shiny doodads that look like miniature party hats and glitter. When everyone is satisfied it looks festive enough, I sit down at the piano and perform a mini concert for Tara. She warns me, "Aidan O'Brien, don't you dare make me cry. My face paint is not completely waterproof. Keep your tearjerker songs to yourself for now."

"Don't look at me!" I protest. "I can't help it if you find every single thing I sing sentimental."

As a joke, I launch into the Sesame Street classic, *C is for Cookie*. Much to my amazement, Tara mists up with tears. I watch her with alarm as I sign, "Gracie, I meant it as a joke. Honestly, I didn't mean to make you cry."

Tara frantically signs back, "No! Don't stop! It reminds me of my dad. We used to watch *Sesame Street* and *The Electric Company* together because they were great for grammar skills. Those were some of the happiest times in my life. I just remembered how much I miss him. Please, go on."

I nod my understanding, but I'm still concerned. "Is it going to hurt you more if I sing my favorite Sesame Street song?" I inquire.

"It may sting a little, but the joy of those memories will make up for it," she answers with a watery smile.

I finish out *C is for Cookie* and transition into one of my all-time favorites, *Rainbow Connection*. I don't know if Tara remembers this, but one of my childhood dreams was to become a Jim Henson puppeteer. I was so sad when I grew up enough to understand the legend had passed away and I wouldn't be able to learn from him. I still tried extremely hard to learn every voice of all the characters in the Muppet universe.

The matronly teacher who I've since learned is named a very sensible Mildred Brown pulls a Kleenex from her pocket and surreptitiously hands it to Tara as I get to the chorus. I watch with concern as Tara dabs delicately at her eyes. I mentally kick myself, because I knew I should've moved on to a different genre, but Tara gives me a tumultuous smile and signs, "Thank you. I love you so much."

I breathe a huge sigh of relief. When I finish the song, I sign, "I love you too," which in sign language translates roughly to 'I love you the same'. There is no truer statement. For as long as I can remember, Tara has been the other half of my heart and soul.

I play *Walking on Sunshine*. At the moment, I can't remember who the original artist is. I just know I play this song a lot at class reunions.

Tara grins as she signs, "Nice! I feel like I need to put on some neon-colored leg warmers and scrunchies."

"Feel free to break out some breakdancing moves over there. No one is stopping you," I say, as I play the piano solo.

"Thanks, but for once I'm going to pass up a challenge. I've got bigger things to do tonight," she remarks.

"That's too bad, because I'll bet you do a mean wave."

I notice a large cluster of students coming in the door, so I quickly wrap up my impromptu concert and greet them. I lose sight of Tara as she puts on her social hat as well and is swallowed up by a crowd of students.

For the first half hour, the dance is typical of every bat mitzvah and mixed gender birthday party I've ever played. The boys are lined up on one side of the cabin and the girls on the other. A few brave faculty members are awkwardly trying to dance to music they're unfamiliar with to get the ball rolling, but no one is willing to make the first critical move to crack the ice.

Suddenly, I hear the sound system abruptly squawk as Tara strolls onto the stage, turns on the presentation system, and jacks up the speakers. She has a bowl of earplugs she passes out to the audience as she simultaneously speaks and signs instructions. "If you can hear normally and would like it to stay that way, I recommend using these. If you have a cochlear implant or hearing aids, I recommend turning those down or off. It's about to get obscenely loud in here. We're about to get this party officially started, so get ready for the 'No Beats and Slow Feet Dancers.' When you see them dance, you'll see they have a very wicked sense of humor, because nothing could be further from the truth."

Tara glances over at me and signs instructions, "When you see me give you a signal through the curtain, please play track one on the playlist."

I have no problem doing this for her. It's a familiar routine. Her mom rarely pulled herself together enough to attend her performances, and often it was a performer's responsibility to get a friend or family member to cue their music for a competition. In turn, she was often my page-turner for music recitals, because my parents were out of town auditioning with Rory.

I give her a thumbs up and sign, "No problem, I've got you covered." I walk over to the presentation controls and watch the curtain for her signal. When I see her hand, I press play and jump off the stage to sit in the audience. I'm grateful she gave us the warning to turn down our cochlear implants. I can feel the opening beats of *Thriller* come up through the soles of my feet. It's an organic experience. The crowd cheers when they see their classmates all decked out in costume and full-face paint.

The dancers line up with military precision. I have no way of knowing which faces she painted and which were done by the student, Sadie. They all look Hollywood worthy. It's an eclectic group of costumes, from bubblegum cute to almost graphically gross. One guy looks like he has an earthworm crawling out of his eye. It's very realistic. The students work their way through some very complex choreography. I don't personally do a lot of dancing, but I've hung out enough with Tara and my brother to know the difference between watered-down choreography and the tough stuff. I can tell Tara didn't take it easy on these guys, even though they had little time to learn it.

One student is clearly having trouble staying up with the rest of the group. Tara quietly works her way back through the rows of students to stand beside him and help get him back on track. Her encouragement is very subtle, and most folks probably don't even notice, but it's obvious to me, since I'm familiar with Tara's ability to have discreet side conversations in sign language.

Suddenly she stops and moves her way to the center of the group. The music changes to an instrumental version of *Thriller,* with a heavy emphasis on piano and drums. The students peel away from Tara to form a semi-circle around her. In effect, it places her in her own spotlight. Tara does a unique cross between jazz and contemporary dance. It pays homage to Michael Jackson's dancing without being an exact copy. You can see nods to the moonwalk and the sharp almost B-Boy krumping moves, as well as the complex footwork Michael Jackson was famous for. Despite the complexity, Tara never loses her grace and style; at heart, she'll always be a ballet dancer.

Tara fades back into the group of dancers and another group emerges. These must be the dancers who intend to pursue dancing as a career. They are more advanced than the rest of the group and are performing more complex moves. Tara and the dance teacher are spotting them as they're performing a series of difficult lifts. One student performs some seriously impressive slow motion animation. For the finale, the total group comes together and performs intricate, synchronized moves.

When they finish, the entire audience is on their feet wildly waving their hands in the air, in the deaf culture's version of clapping. Row by row, all the dancers take a deep theater style bow. At the end of the bow, students push Tara to the front and present her with a bouquet of yellow roses. Once again, everyone in the room stomps their feet and waves their hands in appreciation.

Tara turns and acknowledges all the other dancers. When she faces the audience again, she signs, "Thank you so much, but I couldn't have pulled it off without the help of these very talented dancers." She turns and motions the dancers off the stage. As she does so, she signs discreetly, "Play track two." I wait for the last person to clear the stage before pressing play.

To my delight, it's *Everybody Wants to Rule the World* by Tears for Fears. Tara, the administration, faculty, and all the students who performed go over to the students standing on the sidelines and pull them into the middle of the dance floor to dance. I walk over to a couple of girls and invite them to dance with me. After copious amounts of giggling, they both consent and we proceed to the dance floor. It's hard to see under the disco light, but I'm pretty sure they're making fun of my ancient dancing style. I will be the first to admit I'm not up to date on modern dancing techniques. I should've had Tara give me a brush-up session. As I look around the room, though, almost everyone seems to be having a great time. I spot Tara with her head tossed back in full-on laughter. It makes me smile. Just before the song ends, Tara goes over to her cell phone and adjusts the settings so that her playlist will play automatically. The next few choices are much more modern and include artists like Lorde, Rihanna, Beyoncé, Miley Cyrus, Ed Sheeran and Usher.

Finally I have to leave the dance floor to get ready for my set. It's been so long since I've danced I've forgotten how exhausting it is.

Jumping onstage, I sit on the stool and grab my guitar. The rest of the band sees me and hops on stage. It's a little strange to have someone else back me on piano, but Doug is a superb keyboardist. I let the guys in the band choose songs, for the most part. They've chosen an eclectic mix. We start with *Wanted* by Hunter Hayes, move on to *Lego House* by Ed Sheeran, and finish with *Home* by Philip Phillips.

The crowd again goes wild. The boys are eating up their newly attained status as rock stars in the making. As planned, the boys and I leave the stage and evenly space ourselves across the dance floor after I make a quick stop at the presentation station to replace Tara's phone with mine. I punch up a song on my playlist and press start, then run back to take my place in line. Much to my amusement, the guys have come up with fedoras of their own. I decided to surprise Tara with a little choreography of my own, so we somewhat haphazardly invented our own line dance to Jesse McCarthey's *Beautiful Soul* by watching YouTube videos. It's not terrible, if I say so myself. I hope Tara is paying attention to the lyrics, because that's why I chose this particular song.

The guys don't know this, but the dance is not the biggest surprise I have in store for her. I hope my actions don't make her cry or throw her into a panic attack, but she seems more relaxed here than I've seen her in any other environment. I'm wearing a wireless mic which feeds into the speakers, so when the lyrics start, I step out of the line and sing directly to Tara. As I watch her expression, I can tell she's paying attention to the lyrics. They are so true. I'm not with her just because she's a pretty face. I love her beautiful soul, and I would chase her forever if it takes that long to win her love. By the time I finish the song, she is standing in the front row, which is perfect for what I plan to do next.

I motion her closer to me. When she's standing directly in front of me, I link her left index finger with mine and stick my right hand in my vest pocket. I kneel on one knee as nearly everyone in the room gasps, including Tara. Tears gather in her eyes and her hand starts to shake.

I'm so glad I turned my cochlear implant back up so I can hear her whisper, "Aidan Jarith O'Brien, you are so lucky I love you so much, because otherwise I might kill you. As it is, I'm ready to faint."

I smile crookedly as I sign and vocalize, even if my voice is rough with emotion, "Tara Grace Windsong Isamu, you have been my best friend for as long as I have memories. I cannot imagine my life without you. Will you please walk by my side and be my beautiful soul partner for as long as we live?"

I wait the longest seconds of my life. I thought the wait for my cochlear implant to be turned on seemed infinite, but it was nothing compared to this. I can hear every resounding beat of my heart. The whole room is an echo chamber. I swear I can hear the entire audience hold their collective breath.

Finally, Tara looks up at me with tears streaming down her face. She signs yes with her left hand as she voices the word in a husky, barely there tone. She flattens her hand out to allow me to put a small teardrop shaped diamond ring on her finger. She draws in a deep breath when she sees it. "Aidan, it's beautiful. It's perfect for me. When did you pick it out?"

I flush a little as I admit, "That morning after breakfast, when I ran into you on the beach after Jeff and

Kiera's wedding."

Tara places her hand over her heart in shock. "Geez, AJ, I thought this was quick. The tryouts and taping of the TV show took months. Kiera and Jeff have been married almost a year now. How could you have possibly known the day after you found me again?" she asks with a confused expression on her face.

"Tara, you were my best friend for so many years," I explain. "That never changed in the time we were apart. When I found you again, it was like finding my other half. I knew we'd have things to work out, but I never doubted we would be together, forever."

Tara sways a little. "Wow! That's a lot to process. I want to marry you, but I'm not sure I'm ready — at least, not right away. I only have a couple terms of school to finish. I bounced around so much in my life, I'd like to finish something just once."

I gather her into a close embrace and murmur in her ear, "Timing is just a detail. I'll wait for you."

She collapses against me for a second before collecting herself and straightening her spine. "How do I look?" she asks, a bit frantic.

"Perfect as always, Gracie," I assure her, as I gently pat her face with a tissue.

"Aidan O'Brien!" she chastises, "can't you be serious for a single second?"

"I am perfectly serious," I insist. "Aside from a little glow at your temples from non-stop dancing, you've come through this whole ordeal unscathed. We established a long time ago I don't give a rat's patootie about a little sweat. So it's all good."

"Not funny, AJ!" she huffs as she grabs the Kleenex from my hand and dabs at her hairline.

"I wasn't trying to be funny," I explain. "Gracie, there isn't a time I don't find you stunning. No joke. I have to go finish my set with the boys. Go have a cold strawberry lemonade and some chocolate chip cookies. If you wouldn't mind, would you please bring your fiancé a lemonade?"

"Sure," she stammers as she studies her ring. "This is so surreal. I still can't believe it! Oh my gosh! I'm engaged!"

As if on cue, it seems like the whole audience signs, "Kiss, kiss, kiss!" They stomp their feet and wave their hands for emphasis. Tara and I probably look shell-shocked. That moment was so intensely personal, I think we both lost track of the fact they were even there.

I shrug and look at Tara as I say, "Well, it was drilled into us for years — you always have to do your best to please an audience. What do you say?"

She elegantly lifts a shoulder and an eyebrow as only she can do. She bites her bottom lip in indecision for a second, then announces, "I would hate to let them down. It would be a pity since everyone has worked so hard."

I figure that's as close to a hand-engraved invitation as I'm going to get, so I place one hand behind her back and the other at her waist, then draw her close for a kiss. In deference to the age of our audience, I don't give her the type of kiss I'd really like to, but for dramatic flair I drape her over my arm in a Hollywood type kiss. When I do, several of the students start to whistle and stomp their feet. Many of them are high-fiving each other.

When I pull Tara upright and we back apart, she signs to me and voices for the audience, "Wow, Aidan! You sure know how to make a woman weak in the knees. It's a good thing I've taken you off the market."

Titters of laughter travel through the audience and grow louder as I respond, "The feeling is mutual, gorgeous Gracie, believe me."

One of the students pipes up from the audience and says, "They should have a couples' dance like at the prom."

Another girl agrees and adds, "I have the perfect song on my playlist," she runs to the front of the cabin and attaches her phone to the presentation system.

I turn my cochlear implants back off as John Legend's *All of Me* blasts through the speakers. I pull Tara closer to me in a rather PG-rated rendition of a Rumba. She is like a wish, a dream, and an answer to my prayers, all wrapped up in a fantasy. This is actually not the first time we've done this dance. I don't know if she even remembers, but Rory went through a flaky stage where he was always late to practice, and I often stepped in as her practice dummy. She always thought it was amusing because I took great care to disguise my true feelings under the guise of class clown. Secretly, I always rooted for Rory to be as late as possible to class. I never overtly sabotaged him, but I didn't exactly encourage him to get there early.

So the Heart Can Dance

It's odd to be performing such a personal dance in front of nearly a hundred very curious sets of eyes, but we make the best of the sweet, sentimental moment. I'm having the same kind of epiphany Tara had a few moments ago. My best friend just agreed to be my wife, and the weight of the world is lifted off my shoulders.

413

Chapter Twenty-Five

Tara

I DIDN'T THINK IT was possible to be completely mortified while being as happy as you've ever been in your whole life. Yet that's how I'm feeling, along with a million other things. Happy as I am, I have doubts, and I'm not sure I have any of the right people to talk to about it. My parents are dead, so are my grandparents, and I have no siblings or anyone else. I didn't expect such happy news to hurt quite as much. Suddenly, I'm feeling very alone in the world.

Maybe I'm just being irrational and stupid, I don't know. After watching what a few years of marriage did to my mom, I am more than a little scared to become so dependent on someone else. My logical side kicks in and realizes one reason I've never been able to fall in love with anyone is because I never fell out of love with Aidan. Even when he was gone, I measured every guy I met against Aidan and they all fell short. They never stood a chance.

My fears must be written pretty clearly on my face

because Mrs. Brown comes to me after the dance and offers me one of the administrators cabins with the sage advice to "Ignore the fear in your head and listen to the hope in your heart." When I look surprised and confused, she confesses that at an earlier time in her life she was once at a crossroads and she didn't take the time to work it out and she's regretted the decision every day of her life. She wants to trade places in the cabins so Aidan and I would have a private place to connect and talk and do whatever we need to do to work through our problems. With that parting line, she winks at me and told me to "Give love a chance."

I am so embarrassed. I don't even know how to formulate a socially acceptable reply other than, "Thank you so much, I appreciate it."

She pats me on the shoulder. "For what it's worth, I think you two have more than a fighting chance. You guys seem to love each other. Fight for the real thing; it really is worth it."

Aidan walks up behind me, It's evident he must have heard nearly the whole conversation because he replies, "Thank you ma'am, I appreciate the sacrifice you're making, it means the world to us. I will fight for Tara. Now that I've found her again, I won't let her go easily. There is no need to worry."

"Yes, thank you very much. We appreciate your generosity." I give Mrs. Brown a quick hug.

Aidan steers me toward her cabin. I stop him dead in his tracks as I ask, "What about all of our stuff?"

"I've taken care of it. The PE teacher packed up all of your belongings while the girls were at the campfire tonight. She left a note explaining that you would be back tomorrow for your classes."

I sag gratefully. "Thank you for saving me from an awkward discussion."

"I'm not sure you should give me credit for purely altruistic motives. If you went back to your dorm room, you would be bombarded with countless questions. This way, I have you all to myself," Aidan reveals with a lecherous grin.

"If I didn't know better, I might think you had nefarious plans for tonight," I tease.

Aidan grins at me. "I can't say the thought hasn't crossed my mind, but I think we have stuff to talk about first."

I frown a little as our cheerful banter grows serious. "Yes, I suppose we do. That was quite a surprise you pulled tonight. Talk about coming out of left field. Don't get me wrong, the ring is beautiful — but don't you think it's a little soon?" I ask, admiring my ring once again. I've been staring at it every two minutes. I wonder how he could know exactly what to get me. I've never even mentioned what kind of rings I like to wear. I hardly ever wear any jewelry unless it's a special occasion. "Come to think of it, how did you know what kind of ring to get me?"

Aidan pats the rustic log bed as he puts pillows up against the headboard. He cuddles me against his side as he signs, "Do you mind if I sign? My voice is shot. I got a little carried away showing off for the kids at rehearsal."

"No, of course not," I sign. "Do whatever makes you feel comfortable. That's the nice thing about being bilingual."

"Don't think for a moment I take it for granted," He rubs his temples in exhaustion. "First and foremost, I chose that ring because I knew it would look fantastic on your long graceful fingers. I know you are not a fan of over the top and ostentatious. Sequins, for instance. Hate is too mild a word."

I smile against Aidan's shoulder as I interpret his signs. Ostentatious is a hard word to finger spell. But he's right; I always complained mightily if I had to wear anything with sequins, which were almost always present on my dance costumes. "I can't believe you remember how much I hate sequins."

Aidan smiles fondly at the memory. "Yeah you did, but not as much as you hated fluorescent colored feathers."

I smirk as I add, "Remember that stupid costume with the headpiece so heavy, I could barely hold my head up?"

Aidan grins, but I watch as his expression grows serious again. "Tara, I want you to know there's another reason I chose that ring. I know how proud you are of your heritage. I remember you telling me about the strong women in your ancestry who stood up to the Trail of Tears. I thought the teardrop shape of the diamond might be a nice way to honor them."

The depth of Aidan's understanding of my many layers, long hidden from the world, is beyond my comprehension. The story he's referring to is one I shared with him when we were working on a family heritage project somewhere around the fourth or fifth grade. He was working hard to find a nugget of happiness relating to my family because I was grieving the loss of my father. He distracted me by talking about generations far removed from my recent pain. First, he shared legends about his Irish ancestors nursing others through the Great Potato Famine. Of course, I fell right into Aidan's trap. He knew I was so competitive, there was no way I could leave a story like that without a counterpart from my own heritage. I uncharacteristically opened up about my Native American ancestors who traveled the Trail of Tears. It felt good to share something from my mom's side of the family I was proud of because, during that time, there was so little to celebrate about my mom. She stayed in bed all the time and cried all day. She rarely talked to me. If she did, it was to tell me to stay away from men, because all they ever did was leave. This was confusing as a ten or eleven-year-old because I knew it wasn't my dad's fault he was killed by the Chinese government for doing his job.

One of the lasting lessons of my childhood was to trust no one, because everyone leaves. My mature, clear thinking brain knows it can't possibly be true, or at least, it's not that simple, but the scared orphan in me wonders if Mom might have been right all along. My fears around this topic will be front and center of my discussions with Aidan tonight, even if they're partly a distraction from my other problem, the big one. PTSD. Tonight is the night I must decide if I'll rule my fears, or they'll rule me. It's time to put up or shut up. If this weekend has shown me anything, it's shown me Aidan can roll with the punches and come out of the other side smiling. He can easily adapt to any situation with his humor and joy intact.

I threw him into a completely unfamiliar situation and he was, literally, a rock star.

Sure, he sprang a surprise wedding proposal on me in public, but Aidan has never made any secret that forever after is his plan for us. Even when we were little, he always put my needs above his own. After he found me again, he has always made it clear he isn't leaving unless I order him to. I have only myself to blame if I was taken by surprise tonight.

Aidan taps me on the knee. "Did I lose you, Gracie? Did you fall asleep?"

"No, I didn't fall asleep! I was just thinking, you always seem to know me better than I know myself. You know things about me I've never even shared with the Girlfriend Posse. I haven't known them enough years to tell them everything you know about me. It's a bit daunting. I doubt I know you that well, even if I should."

"Sure you do," Aidan assures me. "What kind of pet did I want growing up?"

"That's an easy one," I answer without thought. "You wanted a black and white Great Dane you planned to name Cruella."

"Okay, here's a harder one. Who did I write a fan letter to after he was dead?" he challenges.

"I don't know this for sure, but if I were to guess I would say Jim Henson, because you cried for about two weeks after you found out he was dead," I answer carefully.

"See, you know more than you think you do, because I've never told another soul about my letter. You know me well enough to put it all together. I cried because Jim Henson's passing felt like it was the death of my first dream. I had to reinvent myself after that and determine a whole new direction for my life. But even then you were part of my new dreams. There was never a time when I saw life without you. Many times I wondered whether I would be good enough for you, especially right after I got sick. I figured you would never accept the new damaged me."

"Isn't it weird? We were both convinced that we loved each other, yet unsure of our own ability to be loved," I observe. "What happened between my parents, her losing him, me losing them both, you disappearing — it made me skittish about love. The rape was a final blow to any dream love could actually happen for me, or if it did, if it could last. Here I am staring down at one of the most beautiful engagement rings I've ever seen in my life. It fits me perfectly, physically and spiritually, and it was given to me by my best friend. My head spins when I think about all the things that happened to bring us here."

Aidan brushes my hair out of my face so he can see my expression. "So, where do we go from here?" he signs.

"I think it's time to let you clip those silken strands of fear. Let's get rid of the cocoon that's surrounded me all these years, so my heart can dance," I sign with a shaky smile. My pulse is beating as fast as hummingbird wings as I wait for a response from him.

It doesn't take him long to process what I've said. He smiles tenderly and signs, "Are you saying what I think you're saying?"

"Yes, I want to marry you, more than anything in

the world. I'd like to finish school first so I'm not distracted by all the wedding preparation. I know how insane it got with Kiera's wedding. It's not something you can do with part-time focus. So, rather than split my focus, I'd rather wait until I graduate before I plunge into the world of weddings."

"That sounds reasonable to me. I have some goals I'd like to pursue before taking on the role of husband, too. I'd like to be able to work full time as a musician, rather than bouncing back and forth between temp jobs. After my experience with Five Star, I should look into some business management or business law courses to help with the business side of being a musician."

"That sounds really perfect, Aidan. This weekend has been an eye-opener for me too. I'm trying to think of ways to combine my two passions. I had so much fun teaching this weekend. I'm thinking of opening a creative arts center for people with disabilities or disadvantaged backgrounds, where I could teach both dance and art and still use my interpreting skills. It would be cool to have a dance troupe built from a mix of able-bodied and differently-abled students," I explain.

"That sounds like a great idea!" Aidan's signs are animated. "The guy I'm house-sitting for recently closed down his boxing gym because the tenants stopped paying rent. He'd probably let you hold classes there in exchange for making it look lived in to deter squatters and criminals."

"That would be amazing. Is it in Corvallis?" I ask, excitement lighting my eyes.

"It's on the outskirts toward Monmouth. It's my

Mary Crawford

understanding this guy inherited the place from his family, so it's no skin off his nose if he doesn't make a ton of money in rent. He just wants to have honest business people in there," Aidan answers.

"Well, it would be great if that's true. But you know how I feel about things which seem too good to be true."

Aidan chuckles. "I totally understand. I felt the same way when he offered me such a phenomenal place to house sit and offered to pay me to do it. He's a genuinely nice guy."

"Whatever you say," I respond skeptically. "I'll believe it when I see it. Life has taught me differently."

Aidan sighs. "I guess if anybody has the right to be a glass empty kind of gal, it's you. I wish I had the power to go back and make life treat you better. The only thing I can do is take your breath away every day from here on out. Anyway, you can afford to pay him rent."

In one smooth motion, Aidan turns his body, slides his arms under my legs and around my back, and pulls me up on his lap. He takes his time as he thoroughly kisses me. I've been craving this kind of kiss all week. It tugs at all my previously inhibited desires. Instinctively, I dig my fingers into the strong muscles on Aidan's shoulders trying to get even closer. I press my chest against his. My thin leotard hides nothing. When we come up for air, Aidan breathes harshly and signs, "Every time I touch you, you redefine beautiful for me."

I smile at him and sign, "Thank you, but right now I think we both are rather strange examples of beauty." I reach up and drag my thumb over his bottom lip. He sucks in a sharp breath at the unexpected contact. I grin as I show him the layer of silver lipstick and glitter on my thumb. "Is this the look you were going for?" I tease.

Aidan looks sheepish as he admits, "It's not my *most* manly look, so I'll say no. I bet you're getting itchy by now, too. Hang tight. I'll be right back."

Aidan carefully sets me back against the pillows. He grabs two large ice buckets and heads toward the restroom. I'm curious what he's doing, but with Aidan, it's hard to tell. He could be planning anything from giving me a manicure to setting off bottle rockets. There's just no telling. Whatever his plan might have been, I didn't count on falling asleep as I waited for him to return.

The next thing I know, Aidan is gently washing off my face paint with a warm, soapy washrag and rinsing with warm water. I haven't had someone else wash my face in years; it feels amazing. I think if I won the lottery, I would hire someone to give me facials regularly because I find them so relaxing. Aidan is exceedingly careful not to get makeup in my eyes as he wipes every trace of face paint away. The slightly rough texture of the washcloth is sensual on my over-sensitized skin. My breath comes in short pants.

Aidan seems composed enough, but his hands are trembling slightly as he takes my hand and diligently cleans each finger, pausing to kiss my engagement ring before briefly taking it off to clean under it. This time, as he slides it back on, he gives me a deep searing kiss that makes me want to curl my toes. After he finishes with both sides of my hands and wrists, he places a feather light kiss on the inside of each elbow. My body shudders with anticipation.

Aidan rolls me onto my side and lifts my hair off the nape of my neck. He gently removes the paint, being careful not to pull the small hairs on the tender part of my scalp. After rinsing my hair, he kisses the vertebrae from the nape of my neck to the top of my leotard. This has me gasping and moaning involuntarily.

"Easy Tara, we'll get there. Relax and enjoy the journey," Aidan murmurs.

Truthfully, I just don't want him to stop touching me.

Aidan takes in my flushed face and closed eyes. He laughs out loud and teases, "So it's like that, is it?"

I fervently kiss him. "You have no idea."

"I'll bet I do," Aidan counters. "Every time I've so much as thought of you in more than a dozen years, I've needed a fire extinguisher."

Oh, well now, maybe I don't want him to stop talking after all, I think to myself as I sigh contentedly and melt in his arms.

EPILOGUE

AIDAN

SITTING IN THIS CHAIR and watching the pain in Tara's eyes is the hardest thing I've ever done. It's even more nerve-racking than singing on an awards show a few weeks ago, when I was nominated as Best New Artist of the Year for my cover of Holy Water. I know all the stars joke about it being an honor just to be nominated, but in my case it's true. Cover songs are rarely ever chosen, especially when an artist has little other work out there.

Tara gave me permission to release the single I wrote for her, *So the Heart Can Dance*. Even though the song is incredibly personal, Tara thought the message was important enough she wanted to share it. To my surprise, it's quickly traveling up the charts.

Today, dressed in a conservative suit, Tara is doing one of the bravest things I've ever seen her do. She is staring down her own personal nightmare eye to eye. That scum-ball had the nerve to ask for a parole hearing based on his assertion he's good with kids in the prison ministry program. He's representing to the board that he wants to start a ministry program for at-risk youth upon his release. Tara decided the best way to prevent this from happening was to tell her story in person. We drove to Portland so she could appear in court to tell her story under oath and face down this evil monster.

My muscles are cramping from the effort it takes to hold myself back from lurching out of this chair and seriously messing up the smug creep. Yet, I know Tara would be extremely upset with me, if I stoop to his level.

Right now, the lawyer for Warren Jones is suggesting Tara consented to the sexual activity. It's all I can do not to spring out of my chair and slap the dude across the face. If he only knew what devastation his client caused in Tara's life, he wouldn't be trying to defend the asshat.

At first, Tara looks stunned by the lawyers tactic. She gathers herself and answers in a strong, clear voice, "No, sir. I did *not* consent to any kind of sexual activity. I was fourteen years old. I'd never even been kissed. I did not consent to having Mr. Jone's knee placed in the middle of my back and my arms constrained behind me with a leather belt while he repeatedly violated me with his penis, fingers, and a beer bottle. The only thing I consented to that night was to go see a PG-13 rated movie with Mr. Jones and two of his friends. It was supposed to be a group date, not the worst day of my life that would have repercussions for the rest of my life."

The colleague of the attorney doing the questioning shoots to his feet and yells, "Objection, non-responsive."

The person leading the parole board hearing merely

glances over at the attorney and tells him to sit down. "This isn't *Court TV*. You can't object to your own question, just because you don't like the answer. Perhaps you'll pick your battles more carefully next time."

The attorney sputters, "But that's not what he told me happened —" The audience titters with laughter as the panel calls a recess to deliberate.

Tara steps off the stand and sits next to me. "Boy, he's not nearly as sexy with cracked veneers, receding hairline, and middle age paunch, is he? It appears prison life has been a little tough on him. He's looking a little pasty. He's missing his bronze 'I'm-a-sex-god glow,'" she signs with a smirk. "Win or lose, I've won. I have everything I've ever dreamed of, and he looks like a deranged mole."

I squeeze her hand as the parole panel files back in the room and we all stand. The court official directs us to sit as we await the verdict.

"Warren Jones, although we applaud your volunteer work within the prison system, it is not enough to show you have changed your behavior. You're not attending mandatory counseling sessions as you've been ordered to do, and you're causing disciplinary problems in the prison system. According to the testimony of three witnesses, you are somehow finding a way around the security measures and allowing other prisoners access to the computer even when their computer privileges have been revoked."

I can see Tara's knuckles turn white as she grasps the edges of her chair in anticipation.

"Therefore, in light of your irresponsible behavior

in violation of our rules, Warren Jones, your parole is denied and any personal belongings you've purchased in the prison commissary will be confiscated until your release."

Just then, Warren stands up from where he's been sitting, turns around, and faces Tara. "You're a dead woman walking. I hope you know."

The room erupts in chaos, but my eyes are on Tara as she turns several shades whiter and sways in her chair. Eventually, order is restored to the room. One panelist on the parole board addresses Tara and asks her if she's okay. "Yes ma'am. I'm fine. Last time I was not prepared for a monster like Warren Jones. This time, if he decides to come after me, he'd better be worried about his personal safety because I know a thing or two about defending myself now, and none of them would be pleasant for him," she answers confidently as she stares directly at Warren Jones.

The person who handed down the decision turns to Warren Jones. "That was an incredibly stupid thing to do. But I'd venture to guess you didn't get here by making smart decisions in your life. Instead of trying to pretend you've made progress, you should put your energy into actually making some progress. Take responsibility for what you did. If there is help and counseling offered to you, take it. Let this young lady move on with her life. You need to focus on improving your own for a change."

With that pronouncement, he bangs the gavel on the table beside him and says, "The parole hearing of Warren Jones is now concluded. Parole is denied."

The atmosphere today is completely different. What a difference two days can make. Tara is flitting around my house like a hummingbird, in a stunning green dress and frighteningly high heels. She's trying to put in the earrings Rory gave her for Christmas.

I don't even try to hide my desire as I stand in the doorway and watch the intricate process. When Tara finally looks up, I remark, "Gracie, I don't think I've ever seen you look more beautiful."

Tara touches her earrings. "Aren't these stunning? I'm totally surprised how easily Rory has accepted me back in his life. His wife, Renée, is so sweet. Can you believe she's going to have the girls sign up at my dance school? She says Rory has a tendency to let cuss words slip out, so she won't let him teach your nieces to dance. I feel bad for Rory. Renée's choice had to sting a little."

"Actually, I meant that *you* look absolutely gorgeous, but your earrings look fine too. I don't think Rory will complain about you teaching his girls to dance. He's a great dad to the girls, but being in a room with several shrieking kids isn't really his thing,"

Tara studies my outfit for a moment and returns the compliment. "Thank you, Aidan. You clean up pretty nicely yourself." Abruptly Tara turns to leave the room, brushing a kiss across my lips as she flits past me. In a few moments, she comes stomping back in the room with her graduation cap in her hands. "Can you help me pin in this thing? My hair is so slippery, it won't stay in," she practically growls in frustration.

I shrug. "I can try. But just so you know, I'm no Jeff. I can't work wonders with hair."

Tara perks up immediately and remarks, "Oh, you're right! He can fix it if it gets wonky. Go ahead and give it your best shot. I don't want to bother Jeff unless I have to."

I give her a teasing grin. "I'm not an expert at this or anything, but don't you want to get into your gown first?"

Tara looks down at herself in surprise as she exclaims, "Oh crap! I knew I was forgetting something."

I walk over to the door where she steamed the gown earlier. I help her step into it. She is so graceful. You would never guess she has five-inch heels on. I place the cap on her head, careful to center it as I gingerly pin it in place. I kiss her softly and say, "I'm so proud of you, Tara Grace. I'll bet your parents are dancing today. In a round-about-way you became an interpreter like your dad, you just speak a different language — my language. In my book, it doesn't get more perfect." As she's doing last minute touch ups— like putting on her tassel, I pull out my camera and take several candid shots. "I still mentally pinch myself every morning when I realize the dream I had when I was six is coming true. We have been through so much in the last two and a half years. But most of all, we've survived, thrived, and found the love and music that ties us both together. Now that our hearts can dance, there is so much more to come."

Suddenly she looks at me with a surprised expression on her face as her lips curl up in a slow, contented smile. "Aidan, you're right as usual. I was so busy falling in love with you, I forgot to notice the moment I found perfect again."

The End (for now.)

Aidan and Tara's story continues in Joy and Tiers available now.

NOTE FROM THE AUTHOR

Dear Reader:

Thank you so much for reading *So the Heart Can Dance*.

The story continues in *Joy and Tiers*.

Tyler Colton is obnoxious.

If he is so offensive, why does Heather LaBianca find this army officer turned Sheriff completely irresistible?

They fight like cats and dogs. The only things they have in common are their best friends.

Yet, when a family tragedy strikes, Tyler is there for Heather.

Is it possible Tyler is the hero Heather has searched for her entire life?

You'll love this humorous look at unlikely friends to lovers.

Get *Joy and Tiers* in paperback, e-book, or read for free with Kindle Unlimited now.

Thank you,

~Mary

Because love matters, differences don't.

RESOURCES

If you need help immediately, call 911.

National Sexual Assault Hotline:
1-800-656-HOPE (4673)

National Domestic Violence Hotline:
800-799-SAFE (7233) or 800-787-3224 (TDD)

Domestic Shelters.org— A tool that enables you to find a domestic violence shelter in your area by ZIP Code or address. You can search by the specific service you need. There are also informative articles about how to help someone who may be a victim of domestic violence or sexual abuse.

RAINN (Rape, Abuse, Incest National Network) — The nation's largest anti-sexual assault organization. RAINN operates the National Sexual Assault Hotline at 1.800.656.HOPE and the National Sexual Assault Online Hotline at rainn.org, and publicizes the hotline's free, confidential services; educates the public about sexual assault; and leads national efforts to prevent sexual assault, improve services to victims and ensure that rapists are brought to justice.

Take Back The Night—Media links, literature and other information about surviving and preventing date rape. Many of these resources are beneficial for helping survivors as well as their family and friends through the healing process.

When Georgia Smiled—A Foundation created by Robin McGraw to create and advance programs that help victims of domestic violence and sexual assault live healthy, safe and joy-filled lives. Initiatives include a phone app that helps create a safety plan for use in domestic violence date rape situations, education initiatives for use in high school and college settings and support programs for women.

Loveisrespect.org— Our mission is to engage, educate and empower young people to prevent and end abusive relationships. Highly-trained peer advocates offer support, information and advocacy to young people who have questions or concerns about their dating relationships. We also provide information and support to concerned friends and family members, teachers, counselors, service providers and members of law enforcement. Free and confidential phone, live chat and texting services are available 24/7/365.

Band Back Together —A comprehensive community page with a variety of resources.

ACKNOWLEDGEMENTS

Although at its core, So the Heart Can Dance is a love story, like so many of us, the characters deal with, and overcome pain and obstacles. As in real life, not every day is a perfect journey forward. Yet, they find strength in each other.

One of the reasons that I became a writer is that it gives me the opportunity to talk about things I really care about. Preventing sexual assault, domestic violence and child abuse are among many causes that I hold close to my heart. I can't thank you, my readers, enough, for sharing my vision and supporting me by purchasing this book, leaving a review, and telling others about it.

For my friends and family members who shared their own personal, painful stories with me, I am profoundly grateful for your courage. I'm sorry for your pain, and I hope stories like this can help begin a conversation so that it won't be quite so hard for others to listen and really hear what you're saying. We may not say it often enough, but we see your strength and admire it.

If you are in a dangerous situation, there are people willing to help. I've included a resource list for survivors and their families.

On a personal note, I would be remiss if I didn't acknowledge some of the people that helped me put this book together.

Lori Castle, we share far more than just a birthdate. We're more like twins separated at birth, even though you live far away in New York. It has been wonderful working with you as my creative sounding board.

Bobby Treat, your help as beta reader and emergency editor have been a lifesaver. You're going to whip me into a writer yet. I found your personal reactions to the novel even more helpful. Thank you for sharing.

Erin McDade, thank you for getting me unstuck when I have writer's block.

To my fellow writers that I keep in touch with via the Internet and occasional phone call or over Skype, thank you so much for your time. I know your time is limited and valuable. Your friendships mean the world to me.

~Mary

Because love matters, differences don't.

ABOUT THE AUTHOR

I have been lucky enough to live my own version of a romance novel. I married the guy who kissed me at summer camp. He told me on the night we met that he was going to marry me and be the father of my children.

Eventually, I stopped giggling when he said it, and we've been married for more than thirty years. We have two children. The oldest is a Doctor of Osteopathy. He is across the United States completing his residency, but when he's done, he is going to come back to Oregon and practice Family Medicine. Our youngest son is now tackling high school where he is an honor student. He is interested in becoming an EMT.

I write full time now. I have published more than thirty books and have several more underway. I volunteer my time to a variety of causes. I have worked as a Civil Rights Attorney and diversity advocate. I spent several years working for various social service agencies before becoming an attorney.

In my spare time, I love to cook, decorate cakes and of course, I obsessively, compulsively read.

I would be honored if you would take a few moments out of your busy day to check out my website,

MaryCrawfordAuthor.com. While you're there, you can sign up for my newsletter and get a free book. I will be announcing my upcoming books and giving sneak peeks as well as sponsoring giveaways and giving you information about other interesting events.

If you have questions or comments, please E-mail me at Mary@MaryCrawfordAuthor.com or find me on the following social networks:

Facebook: www.facebook.com/authormarycrawford

Website: MaryCrawfordAuthor.com

Twitter: www.twitter.com/MaryCrawfordAut

Made in the USA
Columbia, SC
16 June 2023